AMBUSH

"A nail-biter with some wicked twists . . . Fast paced and nonstop . . . Sydney is fleshed out, flawed, gritty, and kick-ass and you can't help but root for her. Nickless leaves you satisfied and smiling—something that doesn't happen too often in this genre!"

—*Bookish Biker*

"*Ambush* has plenty of action and intrigue. There are shoot-outs and kidnappings. There are cover-ups and conspiracies. At the center of it all is a flawed heroine who will do whatever it takes to set things right."

—BVS Reviews

"*Ambush* takes off on page one like a Marine F/A-18 Super Hornet under full military power from the flight deck . . . and never lets the reader down."

—*Mysterious Book Report*

"*Ambush* truly kicks butt and takes names, crackling with tension from page one with a plot as sharp as broken glass. Barbara Nickless is a superb writer."

—Steve Berry, #1 internationally bestselling author

"*Ambush* is modern mystery with its foot on the gas. Barbara Nickless's writing—at turns blazing, aching, stark, and gorgeous—propels this story at a breathless pace until its sublime conclusion. In Sydney Parnell, Nickless has masterfully crafted a heroine who, with all her internal and external scars, compels the reader to simultaneously root for and forgive her. A truly standout novel."

—Carter Wilson, *USA Today* bestselling author of *Mister Tender's Girl*

"Exceptional . . . Nickless raises the stakes and expands the canvas of a blisteringly original series. A wholly satisfying roller coaster of a thriller that features one of the genre's most truly original heroes."

—Jon Land, *USA Today* bestselling author

"*Ambush* . . . makes you laugh and cry as the pages fly by."

—Tim Tigner, internationally bestselling author

DEAD STOP

"The twists and turns . . . are first rate. Barbara Nickless has brought forth a worthy heroine in Sydney Parnell."

—BVS Reviews

"Nothing less than epic . . . A fast-paced, action-packed, thriller-diller of a novel featuring two of the most endearing and toughest ex-jarheads you'll ever meet."

—*Mysterious Book Report*

"A story with the pace of a runaway train."

—Bruce W. Most, award-winning author of *Murder on the Tracks*

"Want a great read, here you go!"

—Books Minority

"Nickless is on my favorite-writers list now."

—Writing.com

"Riveting suspense. Nickless writes with the soul of a poet. *Dead Stop* is a dark and memorable book."

—Gayle Lynds, *New York Times* bestselling author of *The Assassins*

PRAISE FOR BARBARA NICKLESS

THE DROWNING GAME

"An intensely engaging and original murder mystery leading to a climactic resolution, and highly recommended."

—Midwest Book Review

"*The Drowning Game* is filled with rich scenes of Singapore life, from the haunts of the super-rich to Singapore's teeming back alleys. Nickless's research is impeccable, and her twisty thriller is a chilling story of international intrigue and deception."

—*Denver Post*

"One of the author's formidable strengths is her ability to craft a believable, flawed, female lead that people can relate to on a variety of levels."

—*Rocky Mountain Reader*

PLAY OF SHADOWS

"A brisk and clever whodunit with chills and verve."

—*Kirkus Reviews*

"Barbara Nickless hits the ball out of the park on this one . . . This is the third in the series but can be easily read as a stand-alone."

—Midwest Book Review

"*Play of Shadows* is an artful mystery, heavily researched . . . and one that combines a contemporary serial killer with a complex of ancient myths and symbols."

—*Denver Post*

"An intense thriller that resonates with dark myth, *Play of Shadows* is another fascinating case for Dr. Evan Wilding, one of the most interesting and original protagonists in mystery fiction. I want more!"

—J. F. Penn, *New York Times* and *USA Today* bestselling author

"*Play of Shadows* is a work of mythic proportions! Once again Barbara Nickless demonstrates her masterful storytelling, and her outstanding character development. We get to see a more nuanced side of Dr. Evan Wilding (already my favorite literary character), his archaeologist brother, River, his assistant, Diana, and detectives Addie Bisset and Patrick McBrady of the Chicago police department as they delve deeply into mythology (the Minotaur of Crete) to solve this grisly crime and stop the killer's deranged game. Nickless skillfully plays with the idea of Shadow, as we see the darker side of humanity. Barbara Nickless's research is staggering, her grasp of mythology is impressive, and the story is riveting. Once I got started, I could not put it down. This is Barbara Nickless's finest work to date."

—Francesca Ferrentelli, PhD, LPC, mythologist and psychotherapist

"Featuring a truly sinister monster and one of the best chase sequences put to page, *Play of Shadows* is equal parts harrowing and intriguing. Fans of the series will be familiar with the multilayered tensions between Dr. Evan Wilding and Chicago detective Addie Bisset, but this time out Evan's brother River adds a feisty, action-oriented element to the mix. The puzzle they face is a doozy, the clues are manifold, and the trail they follow is littered with traps. *Play of Shadows* is as smart as it is captivating, right down to the last page."

—Mark Stevens, author of *The Fireballer* and the Allison Coil
Mystery series

DARK OF NIGHT

"Nickless's character-driven mystery unfolds on a panoramic scale . . . Engrossing bits of scholarship tucked into a nifty procedural with amiable sleuths."

—*Kirkus Reviews*

"Evan and his immediate circle fascinate . . . Fans of religious thrillers will have fun."

—*Publishers Weekly*

"Captivating, compelling, and completely intriguing! Sherlock Holmes meets *The Da Vinci Code* in this brilliantly written and seamlessly researched adventure, where clues from the ancient past propel contemporary global intrigue. This is an immersive and atmospheric thriller, with an unforgettable main character, and I could not put it down."

—Hank Phillippi Ryan, *USA Today* bestselling author of
Her Perfect Life

"Readers rejoice: Dr. Evan Wilding is back, and *Dark of Night* is another great vehicle for his wry brilliance. The novel is fascinating and twisty with unforgettable characters and writing that took my breath away. You'll want to clear your calendar for this one."
—Jess Lourey, Amazon Charts bestselling author

"*Dark of Night* had me at Moses papyri. Stolen antiquities, dark forces, cobra bites. What a wonderful read. What an adventure to sink into. What beautiful writing. I loved it."
—Tracy Clark, author of the Cass Raines series, winner of the 2020 and 2022 Sue Grafton Memorial Award

"Dr. Evan Wilding is absolutely my new favorite fictional human. His witty charm, his intellect—matched only by his wry humor—along with his goshawk sidekick make him exactly the kind of character who captures an audience within a few lines. Add in the talented and tough detective Addie Bisset, a death by cobra, and a collection of sketchy people all seeking the same priceless artifact, and *Dark of Night* will have you flipping pages well into the night. Barbara Nickless is a phenomenal talent, and she just gets better with every book. *Dark of Night* is her best yet. Bravo!"
—Danielle Girard, *USA Today* bestselling author of *The Ex*

"Missing artifacts? The dark underbelly of the antiquities world? Murder by . . . cobra? Count me in. *Dark of Night* is a top-notch thriller with an unforgettable lead in Dr. Evan Wilding. It's no surprise that Barbara Nickless has fast become one of my favorite authors. I tore through this novel at breakneck speed and can't wait for the next adventure."
—Hannah Mary McKinnon, internationally bestselling author of *Never Coming Home*

"*Dark of Night* is a superb novel . . . After reading the first book in the series, I was hopeful that a second book would be as good or better. I wasn't disappointed. With the new book, Barbara Nickless has solidified a great new mystery series."

—BVS Reviews

AT FIRST LIGHT

An Amazon Best Book of the Month: Mystery, Thriller & Suspense

"Well researched."

—*Kirkus Reviews*

"[In] this intense psychological thriller . . . Evan and Addie race to prevent more bloodshed. Hints of a romantic relationship between the pair enliven the story, and references to *Beowulf* and Viking history add depth. Readers will hope to see more of Addie and Evan."

—*Publishers Weekly*

"Brilliant Evan Wilding, with his goshawk and unusual friendships, will fascinate those who read for character."

—*Library Journal*

"*At First Light* is a winner."

—*Denver Post*

"A high-intensity thriller that will take your breath away . . . Barbara Nickless is an awesome talent."

—*Mysterious Book Report*

"The moment I finished this intelligent and pulse-pounding psychological thriller, I was ready for Book Two . . . Dr. Evan Wilding is one of the most interesting fictional characters I've met in some time . . . Author Nickless's prose is crisp and, at times, poetic. Her descriptions are vivid but balanced. I became immediately attached to her engaging and well-drawn characters. In some respects, *At First Light* is reminiscent of Dan Brown's *The Da Vinci Code*. I highly recommend this book to fans of fast-paced thrillers that include riddles, ancient languages, and literature."

—Claudia N. Oltean, for the *Jacksonville Florida Times-Union*

"*At First Light* is a stunner of a tale. Barbara Nickless has fashioned a deep exploration into moral depravity and the dark depths of the human soul in a fashion not seen since the brilliant David Fincher film *SE7EN*. This wholly realized tale is reminiscent of Lisa Gardner, Karin Slaughter, and Lisa Scottoline at their level best."

—Jon Land, *USA Today* bestselling author

"Barbara Nickless has crafted a dark, twisty thrill ride with a bad guy to give you nightmares, and a pair of protagonists you will want to come back to again and again. Lock your doors and curl up with this book!"

—Tami Hoag, #1 *New York Times* bestselling author of *The Boy*

"*At First Light* by Barbara Nickless is one of the best books I've read in a long, long while. With unique and unforgettable characters who match wits with a devious, sophisticated, and ritualistic serial killer, this complex and compelling story is as powerful as a Norse god and just as terrifying. I can't wait for the next book in the series featuring Detective Addie Bisset and Dr. Evan Wilding! Bravo!"

—Lisa Jackson, #1 *New York Times* bestselling author

"A deliciously twisted plot that winds through the dark corners of the past into the present, where nothing—and nobody—is as they seem. *Dead Stop* is a first-rate, can't-put-down mystery with a momentum that never slows. I am eager to see what Barbara Nickless comes up with next—she is definitely a mystery writer to watch."

—Margaret Coel, *New York Times* bestselling author of the Wind River Mystery series

BLOOD ON THE TRACKS

A *Suspense Magazine* Best of 2016 Books Selection: Debut

"A stunner of a thriller. From the first page to the last, *Blood on the Tracks* weaves a spell that only a natural storyteller can master. And a guarantee: You'll fall in love with one of the best characters to come along in modern thriller fiction, Sydney Rose Parnell."

—Jeffery Deaver, internationally bestselling author

"Beautifully written and heartbreakingly intense, this terrific and original debut is unforgettable. Please do not miss *Blood on the Tracks*. It fearlessly explores our darkest and most vulnerable places—and is devastatingly good. Barbara Nickless is a star."

—Hank Phillippi Ryan, Anthony, Agatha, and Mary Higgins Clark Award–winning author of *Say No More*

"Both evocative and self-assured, Barbara Nickless's debut novel is an outstanding, hard-hitting story so gritty and real, you feel it in your teeth. Do yourself a favor and give this bright talent a read."

—John Hart, multiple Edgar Award winner and *New York Times* bestselling author of *Redemption Road*

"Fast paced and intense, *Blood on the Tracks* is an absorbing thriller that is both beautifully written and absolutely unique in character and setting. Barbara Nickless has written a twisting, tortured novel that speaks with brutal honesty of the lingering traumas of war, including and especially those wounds we cannot see. I fell hard for Parnell and her four-legged partner and can't wait to read more."
—Vicki Pettersson, *New York Times* and *USA Today* bestselling author of *Swerve*

"The aptly titled *Blood on the Tracks* offers a fresh and starkly original take on the mystery genre. Barbara Nickless has fashioned a beautifully drawn hero in take-charge, take-no-prisoners Sydney Parnell, former marine and now a railway cop battling a deadly gang as she investigates their purported connection to a recent murder. Nickless proves a master of both form and function in establishing herself every bit the equal of Nevada Barr and Linda Fairstein. A major debut that is not to be missed."

—Jon Land, *USA Today* bestselling author

"*Blood on the Tracks* is a bullet train of action. It's one part mystery and two parts thriller with a compelling protagonist leading the charge toward a knockout finish. The internal demons of one Sydney Rose Parnell are as gripping as the external monster she's chasing around Colorado. You will long remember this spectacular debut novel."
—Mark Stevens, author of the award-winning Allison Coil Mystery series

"Nickless captures you from the first sentence. Her series features Sydney Rose Parnell, a young woman haunted by the ghosts of her past. In *Blood on the Tracks*, she doggedly pursues a killer, seeking truth even in the face of her own destruction—the true mark of a heroine. Skilled in evoking emotion from the reader, Nickless is a master of the craft, a writer to keep your eyes on."

—Chris Goff, author of *Dark Waters*

"Barbara Nickless's *Blood on the Tracks* is raw and authentic, plunging readers into the fascinating world of tough railroad cop Special Agent Sydney Rose Parnell and her Malinois sidekick, Clyde. Haunted by her military service in Iraq, Sydney Rose is brought in by the Denver Major Crimes unit to help solve a particularly brutal murder, leading her into a snake pit of hate and betrayal. Meticulously plotted and intelligently written, *Blood on the Tracks* is a superb debut novel."

—M. L. Rowland, author of the Search and Rescue Mystery novels

"*Blood on the Tracks* is a must-read debut. A suspenseful crime thriller with propulsive action, masterful writing, and a tough-as-nails cop, Sydney Rose Parnell. Readers will want more."

—Robert K. Tanenbaum, *New York Times* bestselling author of the Butch Karp and Marlene Ciampi legal thrillers

"Nickless's writing admirably captures the fallout from a war where even survivors are trapped, forever reliving their trauma."

—*Kirkus Reviews*

"Part mystery, part antiwar story, Nickless's engrossing first novel, a series launch, introduces Sydney Rose Parnell . . . Nickless skillfully explores the dehumanizing effects resulting from the unspeakable cruelties of wartime as well as the part played by the loyalty soldiers owe to family and each other under stressful circumstances."

—*Publishers Weekly*

"An interesting tale . . . The fast pace will leave you finished in no time. Nickless seamlessly ties everything together with a shocking ending."

—RT Book Reviews

"If you enjoy suspense and thrillers, then you will [want] *Blood on the Tracks* for your library. Full of the suspense that holds you on the edge of your seat, it's also replete with acts of bravery, moments of hope, and a host of feelings that keep the story's intensity level high. This would be a great work for a book club or reading group with a great deal of information that would create robust dialogue and debate."

—Blogcritics

"In *Blood on the Tracks*, Barbara Nickless delivers a thriller with the force of a speeding locomotive and the subtlety of a surgeon's knife. Sydney and Clyde are both great characters with flaws and virtues to see them through a plot thick with menace. One for contemporary thriller lovers everywhere."

—Authorlink

"*Blood on the Tracks* is a superb story that rises above the genre of mystery . . . It is a first-class read."

—*Denver Post*

A VOICE
IN THE
DARK

Also by Barbara Nickless

Sydney Rose Parnell Series

Blood on the Tracks

Dead Stop

Ambush

Gone to Darkness

Evan Wilding Series

At First Light

Dark of Night

Play of Shadows

Stand-Alone

The Drowning Game

A VOICE IN THE DARK

BARBARA NICKLESS

Published by Thomas & Mercer, Seattle

www.apub.com

Amazon, the Amazon logo, and Thomas & Mercer are trademarks of Amazon.com, Inc., or its affiliates.

EU product safety contact:
Amazon Media EU S. à r.l.
38, avenue John F. Kennedy, L-1855 Luxembourg
amazonpublishing-gpsr@amazon.com

ISBN-13: 9781662533723 (paperback)
ISBN-13: 9781662533730 (digital)

Cover design by Zoe Norvell
Cover image: © Stephen Shepherd / plainpicture;
© Olena Zaskochenko / Shutterstock

Printed in the United States of America

To Michael J. Coumatos
He taught us all how to be in the world

Where is evil then, and whence, and how crept it in hither?
What is its root, and what its seed?

—*Saint Augustine*

1

Sometimes Katelynn hates her twin brother as much as she loves him.

Jason says he doesn't believe in anything, not anymore, and she should leave him alone with his darkwave music and sadistic shooter video games, the shades pulled so his room is as black as a tomb. But Katelynn fears something sinister has sidled into Jason like a virus, like the fungal infection from *The Last of Us*.

She's terrified of what he might do.

This afternoon, Jason was supposed to drive her home from school after cheerleading practice, but he told her he had to take care of something and to call Mom. *What "something"?* she'd asked, but the only answer she got was dead air. Now her mind is on Jason, not her stunt work. They're working on their pyramid, and she needs to focus. She's the flier. The top girl. The floater. After she slams into the mat not once, not twice, but three times, Coach calls a halt.

"Your body wants to quit," Coach tells the squad. He's looking at her. "Not your mind. Who's the boss?"

"Our minds," the team shouts back.

Katelynn, though, is pretty sure it's her mind that wants to quit.

Twenty minutes later, she climbs into her mom's Defender SUV.

"How was practice?" Mom asks. She's already pulling away from the curb. Andrea Heath—famous ad executive—is *always* in a hurry.

"It was okay," Katelynn says.

Her mom gives her a sideways glance. "Just okay? Your hamstring hurting again?"

"No. It's good." Katelynn takes a deep breath. "Look, before we get home. Can I tell you something and you won't tell Dad?"

The hands-free Bluetooth chimes in. "Phone call from Luke. Answer or ignore?"

Luke is Mom's partner at the ad agency.

Mom says, "Katie-did, this call is important. Big client, last-minute panic. Just hold that thought for two seconds, okay?"

Katelynn feels as if she's scrabbling at the edge of a cliff as the ground gives way. She's tried a bunch of times to talk to her mom about Jace, but her mom keeps ghosting her, as if her bougie job is more important than her son. Maybe money and prestige are fungal infections as ruthless as whatever's taking root in Jace's brain.

"Whatev," she says.

Mom takes the call. "Luke, what's up?"

Katelynn half listens as Luke launches into a terrified scree about the CEO of Three Peaks Aviation. The man is threatening to take his business elsewhere if they don't deliver the ad copy before midnight. Mom tells Luke the work is almost finished, and she'll send it to Three Peaks well before the deadline. "Just leave me alone for the next few hours so I can focus. Okay?"

By the time Mom has soothed Luke and disconnected, they're almost home. Mom peels around the corner.

"Mom! You're gonna take out a kid one of these days."

"Sorry, Katie-did." She taps the brakes. "Now what were you saying?"

Katelynn pulls herself out of her sulk. "Something's wrong with Jace. He's all . . . I don't know. Gloomy." Something in Katelynn wants to laugh. Gloomy like the apocalypse. "He says we're all NPCs."

Mom powers up their driveway and pulls into the garage. She shuts off the engine and sighs. "You know, if you look up *sullen, moody,* and *angry* in the dictionary, all the entries cross-reference your brother.

Katelynn nearly jumps out of her skin when a man enters the kitchen. It's like a mountain manifested between the stove and the island: shoulders wide as the doorway, head square like a box. His thick beard reaches the snap on his jeans. She bites back a scream. Through the window, she sees her mom walking down the long drive toward the mailbox.

"Rick," the man says. "Sorry if I startled you." He fishes a business card out of his shirt pocket. "Your dad called. Wi-Fi is acting up. Probably just need a new router. But I might as well check out the entire system. I'm almost done." He smiles and winks. "Enjoy your soda."

He leaves as suddenly as he came, disappearing through the opposite door into the living room.

She looks down at the card. RICK'S REPAIR—ALL TECH, it reads. There's a phone number and a website.

Her phone chirps.

Elise:

You there?

Katelynn types:

just met Hagrid

some IT dude fr w beard + wizrd hair

my dad rly knows how to pick 'em 💀 💀

Elise:

LMAO

maybe ur a wizard

Katelynn:

Nah

jace is the wizard

i'm just a dumb muggle

ttyl 😎

Katelynn grabs the soda and chips. She peeks into the living room—no sign of Rick—and heads toward the stairs.

She's halfway up when she notices how quiet it is.

Not regular house quiet. Dead quiet.

Whatever Rick the Repairman is doing, he makes zero noise. No video game explosions or gunfire bleed through Jason's door. No squawk of the violin from Eric's room. No Dad yelling into his phone.

She glances back down the stairs. Mom is taking a long time. Probably talking to Mrs. Swanson, who always wants to chat with whoever grabs the mail.

Katelynn glances up to where the stairs disappear into gloom. *Don't weird out,* she scolds herself. She keeps climbing.

Near the top, she pauses again, one foot hovering above the last step.

"Jace?" she calls.

No answer.

She glances toward his door. Closed. It's always closed. As if the rest of them are zombies he's got to keep out of his sanctuary.

Closer by, Eric's door is also closed.

The hall feels colder than it should, like a window's open somewhere. The overhead light is on, but it's feeble in the falling gloom. She sniffs. Something smells bad. Like oil and . . . sewage.

She opens her mouth to call out again but changes her mind.

Leave him alone, she tells herself. *Go to your room. Close the door. Put in your earbuds and binge Blackpink.*

But something's not right.

So instead of crashing out, she sets the soda and chips on the floor and walks to Jason's door. She raises her hand to knock, but when there's no sound from the other side, she puts her hand on the knob and turns it.

She peers in.

The stench hits her, strong here. The room is dark, save for a shaft of light spilling from the closet door, which is ajar. Jason stands in the middle of the room, his back to her, the closet light illuminating a razor-thin slice of his skinny frame. He wears black jeans, a black tee   his usual clothes—and he grips something in his right hand. It looks like a game controller, and she wonders what her brother is doing standing stock-still in the middle of the room, clutching his GameSir. The computer screen is blank.

Plus, it really, really stinks.

She looks more closely at the controller. *Oh God.* "Jace? Is that Dad's gun? Oh, dude, you're in so much trouble."

Jason spins in place, startled. He's pale and wide-eyed, shaking, staring at nothing. Katelynn feels a strange internal snick in her mind, like the pieces of a puzzle clicking into place all at once. She suddenly gets it: Jason is considering suicide. Probably he's been thinking about it for a long time, and she's been too stupid to see. He told her once to get lost, and so she did, flouncing off in a huff and leaving him alone with his pain. Her few stabs at reconnecting have been pathetic. *Dad's such a total loser sometimes,* she'd say. Or *Dinner sucked, didn't it?*

Each time, Jace glided right on by as if she were a passing breeze. An NPC.

Now she knows: She didn't just leave Jace alone; she abandoned him. And now he's going to kill himself.

Her stomach heaves. It wasn't just her, or their mother who wouldn't engage, or their father building a wall out of his anger. It was all of them.

"Oh my God, Jace. Put it down." Just like that, she's crying. "What are you thinking? Please put it down."

He hardly seems to see her. Hardly seems to know she's in the room. There's something dark spattered on his cheek, and he's standing over a huddled lump on the floor. Clothes? She takes a step closer with the harebrained idea of grabbing the gun. Then she looks again at the ground.

It's not a *what* on the floor. It's a *who*. Eric.

"Oh my God!" Her voice rises from a hollow cavity in her chest.

The shaft of light widens as the closet door swings open.

For a second the old Jason is back. There's a spark in his eyes. "Run, Katelynn," he rasps. "Run!"

She spins toward the hallway, tripping over her own normally graceful feet, almost falling, missing the doorway and smacking into the jamb. She stumbles into the hall, trying to find her voice. Trying to scream. *Mom! Dad! Eric . . . Eric's . . .*

But the words won't come.

She's almost to the stairs when something hits her from behind. The floor rises to greet her, slamming into the bones of her face.

Stars, she thinks as pain pulls her under. *There are stars.*

2

"Keep your gloves up," I snap.

The skinny teenager scowls but complies, her gloved hands rising until she's blocked my jab toward her face.

"That's good." I circle, pivoting forward, then back, as I come at her with a series of cross feints. Wisps from my ponytail stick to the sweat on my face. "Weight on your back foot for the slip. Elbows tucked. Stay on the balls of your feet. Keep it light, Livvie. Light. You're a cloud. A moonbeam. Not a tree sloth."

This earns me another scowl. I swipe sweat from my chin to hide a smile.

At five foot three, her arms inked with the kind of tats a friend gives you in her bedroom, sixteen-year-old Olivia Diaz weighs ninety-seven pounds soaking wet. She appeared at the Glove Pit a couple of months ago, wanting to know how to fight. The first time she walked in, she hesitated just inside the door. I'd been skipping rope, but I stopped and watched this scrap of a girl take in the cracked weight bags and scuffed rings, the exposed overhead pipes and the pendulous speed bags—all the grittiness of a small-time boxing gym. She'd inhaled the rank odors of sweat baked into canvas, fresher sweat on teen bodies, the sour tang of liniment. A trace of bleach lingered under it all, not enough to mask the funk but enough to say we tried.

She could have turned on her heel, but instead she'd smiled like she'd found home.

I decided then and there to take her under my wing. The gym is for at-risk teens, and all of them have a story. So do most of us coaches. I wanted to hear this girl's.

Livvie doesn't look like much. But I learned fast that she's got a mean left hook. That hook will take her a good distance once she gets some oomph behind it. Her focus now is trying to pack on the pounds and bring her footwork up to the level of her hook. That last part is my job.

"Move around, Livvie. Distribute your weight. All the power comes from your feet."

She shuffles. Bounces. "Yeah, boss."

She took to calling me "boss" after watching *Million Dollar Baby* and trying to turn me into a female version of Clint Eastwood. In her eyes, at my creaky age of thirty-two, I look the part. Next thing, no doubt, I'll be spouting nose hair and wearing reading glasses.

"Left foot on the silver," I say, pointing to the line of duct tape. "Toes at one o'clock."

I learned boxing from my uncle. Not because he thought girls belong in the ring, but because—as a private investigator—he'd seen what girls had to put up with. He wanted me to be able to take a punch from an assailant and bounce right back up, swinging.

He taught my brother as well. Kevin was a rising champ until someone offered him fentanyl and all his troubles evaporated in a puff of blue powder. Addiction runs in the family. Our parents and grandparents loved the bottle—gin, rye, vodka. But a stronger demon has sunk its hooks into Kevin.

Livvie needs to learn her own skills. She's a looker, with waist-length brown waves and immense green eyes. With her petite size, she screams *target*. By the time she showed up at the Glove Pit, she'd been sexually assaulted twice. She refused to press charges.

Half an hour later, I call a halt. We're both sweating, gasping for breath like landed fish. I check the clock on the wall. I have an hour until I need to be in my office at the FBI's resident agency in Boulder. I'm a member of the FBI's Colorado VCAC team—Violent Crimes Against Children—and our field office's coordinator with the Behavioral Analysis Unit in Quantico, Virginia.

Plus, Livvie is flagging.

"You been eating protein like I said?" I ask.

She rips the tape off her gloves. "You mean that mystery mush at school they call lunch?"

"I brought you some powder. What happened to that?"

Her gaze slides away. "My stepdad says it's a stupid fad. He tossed it."

The bastard. "It's okay. We'll get more and keep it in your locker here." I glance at my watch. "Hit the showers, then we'll stop at First Watch for eggs and bacon."

Pleasure lights her eyes before she retreats into the seeming indifference she's built out of life's first lesson: If you don't care, they can't hurt you.

She says, "That'd be okay, I guess. Can I get pancakes?"

"Protein first. Then sugar. And not much of that."

She shows her small teeth. "Blueberry."

My phone buzzes with a text. I glance down.

Hey, Agent Belle. Helen. It's Clif Burgess. You remember Derrick Tremblay?

We were right. He had help.

A fuse ignites in my gut, sparking through my veins like electricity. Derrick Tremblay. Damn.

I turn to hide my reaction from Livvie, but she dances around me as if we're still in the ring. Our eyes lock, and I know she sees shock in mine. She's aware of my job with the FBI, and her own eyes light up.

"Serial killer," she whispers.

I push her toward the showers, and she grins and darts away.

Clif is Detective Clifton Burgess with the Denver Major Crimes Division. We haven't spoken more than a handful of times in the last five years. We met when I was an expert witness and he the homicide detective on the Derrick Tremblay case. Back when I was a rising star in the field of criminal humanities and hadn't considered the FBI as a career path. Back before the Tremblay trial shattered both my personal and professional plans.

We were right. He had help.

The help Clif's talking about is the Midnight Man. Our mysterious ghoul who might or might not exist. The whisperer in the night. The ghost in the machine. The voice of my nightmares.

Clif's next text consists of two words:

He's back.

3

You don't get used to murder. You just find a way to live with the constant heartbreak of man's inhumanity to man.

After a shower and a quick breakfast with Livvie—McDonald's instead of a place with real flatware—I make the drive from my off-site Boulder office to Denver in under forty minutes. Traffic's bad on US-36, but not a nightmare. Maybe the traffic gods heard my pleas.

Now I sit at a conference table as Clif enters the room. We're downtown, on the fourth floor of Denver PD's headquarters on Cherokee Street. Cold morning sun slants through the half-open blinds, striping the walls with pale light. A built-in corkboard dominates one end of the room; mug shots paper the remaining walls. Steam rises from the coffee Clif sets in front of me. I nod my thanks.

"You look like life is treating you well," he says as he sits across from me.

"It doesn't suck. But I wouldn't pay for a front-row seat."

He laughs, a rasp like a wire brush on steel, and we spend a few minutes catching up: his promotion to Detective Five, my current stint with the feds. He still fishes during his off time. Walleye and perch, mostly. I still run three to six miles daily and spend my free hours coaching teens or curled up with a book. If I'm really going all out, I'll make popcorn and watch a crime show. Neither of our lives is anything to brag about: He's a widower and I a defiant single, and we're both obsessed with the criminal mind.

Clif adds sugar to his coffee. He shuffles some papers. "Traffic bad?"

"Not too."

Once handsome and robust in the way of a middle-aged Morgan Freeman, Clif, at sixty-two, seems like a man with one foot wedged in the grave. He's the kind of thin where you have to run around in the shower to get wet. His complexion has grayed from ebony to something closer to ash, and he's bruised around his startling hazel eyes. Deep lines carve canals into the hollows of his cheeks. He looked bad five years ago, when he was first diagnosed with stage IV melanoma, and now he's another ten pounds lighter. But he's beating the odds. Maybe it's that "save the world" rechargeable battery Clif and I share. It keeps us plowing forward—cancer, career changes, and life's vicissitudes be damned.

Now our easy camaraderie makes it feel like we've never been apart. I should have called him more often. Checked in to see how he was doing.

Clif finishes messing with the papers. "I'm really glad you're here, Helen," he says. Then he clears his throat and dives in.

"Twenty-four hours ago—Tuesday morning at 0730—police received a request for a welfare check at a residence in Platt Park owned by Michael and Andrea Heath. The call came from an employee at Andrea Heath's ad agency, who was unable to reach his boss by phone. Officers arrived and approached the house. The place was locked up tight—no sign of forced entry—and there was no response when they rang the bell and pounded on both front and back doors. After locating a key under a flowerpot and obtaining approval from their sergeant, they made entry. They found the body of Andrea Heath at the bottom of the home's main staircase and called for backup. She'd been shot through the head.

"As they continued their search of the home, one of the officers detected the smell of propane. They were exiting the home when an explosion occurred, starting an inferno. Investigators are working on determining the trigger. The officers escaped without injury, but by the time the fire department arrived, there was significant damage to the home. And, of course, to the bodies of what turned out to be three victims, all shot. Denver PD's Major Crimes got the call at that point."

I look at the photo Clif slides across the table: the ruins of the kind of Spanish-style home popular in Colorado, backed by thickly branched blue spruces. I note the remnants of stucco walls and a red tile roof. What might have been a fountain in a front courtyard and the blackened spikes of a wrought iron gate.

Clif says, "The Fire Investigations Unit is looking into the cause of the explosion. Based on preliminary findings, including the presence of two propane canisters in the kitchen, they suspect arson."

"Was anything caught on camera before the explosion?" I ask.

"Security cameras at the Heath residence and those of their neighbors were disabled. The last videos to be uploaded from the Heath cameras show thirteen-year-old Eric Heath returning home from school Monday afternoon at three thirty, seventeen-year-old Jason Heath half an hour later at four, arriving in one of the vehicles registered to the family, a Volvo XC90. Then Andrea with Jason's twin, Katelynn, at six. Neighbors say the dad worked from home. Cameras went offline immediately after mom and daughter entered the garage." For a second, his entire face sags—a rare moment of emotion—before his cop face snaps back. "If you recall, local cameras were also disabled during the Tremblay murders."

I sip the coffee. It's been on the burner awhile. "I remember."

"You won't like this next bit." He pulls another photograph from a file folder and places it in front of me with blunt-tipped fingers: It's a crime scene shot of the body of an adult female. Her clothing has burned away, and her skin is blackened and blistered. What's left of her hair clings in tufts, like scorched grass on a battlefield. Her nose is gone, and her eyes are charred holes.

I hold up a finger and grab a bottle from my bag. I down two acetaminophen caplets with a gulp of cooling coffee.

"You good?" he asks.

"You bet," I say.

Next to the photo of the woman, Clif places two more photos. These show an adult male and a second male barely into his teens. These pictures are as grisly as the first, the victims' clothing gone, lipless mouths grinning, their arms and legs bent and hands curled into fists from the extreme heat—the pugilist pose.

As I study the photos, the familiar headache stabs, followed by a sucker punch of nausea.

I swallow.

"You need the trash can?" Clif asks. He has a gleam in his eyes, the bastard. Cops find humor where they can, and Clif knows my weakness.

"I'm fine."

He toes a plastic trash can in my direction. "You barf in my conference room, I'll work this by myself."

I glare. "Tossing your cookies is just weakness leaving the body."

He laughs. "Should I start bringing you cookies?"

Most FBI agents and analysts are good at compartmentalization when it comes to the gruesome cases. Lucky me, I'm the exception. I've got two years of regular law enforcement under my belt, and I've spent my three years with the FBI studying hard and working harder. I now have knowledge of interrogation, profiling, forensic psychology and pathology, case management, risk assessment, the works. I can load a fifteen-round Glock cartridge in twelve seconds, run a mile in six minutes, and wrestle 250 pounds of angry male to the ground and slap on handcuffs before he knows what's happened. I'm a PhD criminal humanities specialist who can kick ass in a bar fight.

But five years into witnessing the worst humanity can do, I still get ill viewing the wreckage. A therapist told me my headaches come from repressed trauma. She said I'd seen something terrible when I was a kid, and the headaches mean there's a war going on between my desire to remember and my need to repress. It's true that my parents died in what police labeled a murder-suicide. But Kevin and I'd been sent to visit family in another state a week before they died. It was our summer vacation. We didn't see their bodies until they'd been cleaned up for the funeral.

And this morning my queasiness also comes from the fact that I've seen nearly identical photos before. On the Derrick Tremblay case.

He's back.

Clif raps his knuckles on the table, yanking me into the present. "We're waiting for confirmation from the medical examiner, but it's likely the victims are Andrea and Michael Heath and their thirteen-year-old son, Eric. We have the video footage prior to six p.m., and a neighbor spoke with Andrea Heath at the mailbox after Andrea and Katelynn arrived home. The neighbor described Andrea as in a rush—standard operating procedure, apparently—but not upset." Above the sharply knotted tie, his Adam's apple looks like it needs room to breathe. But his expression resembles that of a funeral director's—somber, compassionate, a trace detached. Clif's a good cop. "Putting aside your stabbing headaches," he says, "I'd like to know what jumps out at you in these photos."

Artificial cream curdles in my stomach as I lean in.

"Despite the damage to the bodies from the fire," I say, "we can see that the victims were shot prior to being exposed to the flames. Execution style, a single bullet between the eyes from what I'd guess was a nine-millimeter pistol. The man was shot and likely killed while sitting at what looks like"—I squint—"maybe a desk. You said the dad worked from home. The woman, as you noted earlier, is at the bottom of a staircase. It's hard to tell with the fire damage, but I see no indication the bodies were moved. Although it looks as if maybe their blood was smeared before the fire baked it." I look up. "Was it?"

"We'll get to that."

"Okay," I say. "Maybe the man was shot first, and the woman was killed trying to flee. Probably they are the parents of the third victim, the boy, who is in what's likely a bedroom—there's what appears to be a bed's metal side rail. I'd guess the fire started in a part of the house away from the victims, perhaps the kitchen—you mentioned propane canisters. A room on the lower floor, anyway. The flames came through the walls and up through the floor here"—I point—"and were put out by firefighters with what was likely class A foam—you can see the residue—before the bodies were partially consumed. The man's body sustained the most damage, suggesting he was closest to the source of the fire, which is another reason to consider the kitchen. Maybe a study on the main floor."

I look up and cock an eyebrow.

"Spot on, junior." Clif gives me a soft smile of acknowledgment. "I'm waiting on ballistics, DNA, additional fingerprints, autopsies, the works. The only thing we have so far is a pistol that was stashed behind and partially protected from the fire by a washing machine located near the kitchen on the first floor. It's a Springfield nine millimeter registered to Michael Heath. The lab lifted Jason's prints from the grip—they had them on file from NCIP, the National Child Identification Program. No other prints were found on the gun. We don't know where the kid is. Or his sister. They vanished before police and fire arrived. Amber Alert's gone out, and the media is pushing for information. There's already a lot of interest in the family. The case has gone national."

"We can use that," I say. "We'll get eyes looking for those kids."

"CARD is working it."

CARD—the FBI's Child Abduction Rapid Deployment unit. If I'd made it into the office this morning before Clif's call, I'd be working it, too.

Reflexively, I check the time on my phone, pushing against the gaping maw of despair that wants to swallow me whole every time a kid goes missing. "They've been gone more than twenty-four hours. Assuming they're not the perpetrators . . . it's bad."

Clif nods. He knows as well as I do that a child's risk for harm is greatest in the first hours after he or she is taken, putting Jason and Katelynn well into the danger zone. One study found that 89 percent of murdered child victims are dead within twenty-four hours of their disappearance. Forty-eight hours, and the chance for a rescue drops faster than a piano out a window.

Some experts put it at nearly zero.

Clif notices my frown. "Your Denver CARD team is one of the best in the nation," he points out. "Others will be joining in as need be. I just want to know, before we go any further, if you see what I do: an alarming resemblance to the Tremblay murders."

I'm already leaning toward agreement. But I close my eyes and think. It's important not to rush or be swayed by someone else's conviction. Suggesting a link between the Tremblays and the Heaths will be equivalent to slamming a hornet's nest with a bat, then hanging around to see what happens.

Six years ago, in 2020, on a warm August night, sixteen-year-old Derrick Tremblay shot his parents and brother, killing them instantly. He had written a suicide note and—after the murders—started a fire that mostly destroyed the family home. When firefighters and police arrived, he stood outside the burning home, injured by an apparent suicide attempt but still alive despite the note in his pocket. The gun he held was splashed with his parents' blood—likely from backspatter due to the close-range shots. Traces of gunshot residue were found on his hands, although he'd washed them. Home security cameras had been disabled—it was later determined that Derrick had deactivated them. He neither confessed nor denied his guilt. In fact, after murmuring words about "transformation" and the "Midnight Man" and "none of this is real" to the first officer on scene, he went completely mute. When his case went to trial, where he was tried as an adult, he remained mute, making it damn hard for his attorneys to defend him. He's been mute in the years since, based on what little I've heard.

Five and a half years ago, when I was a recently hired faculty member at Colorado College and new at providing expert testimony, Derrick got under my skin in ways that surprised me. I'd expected to find him repellent. After all, he'd committed the worst kind of sin: the cold-hearted murder of his entire family.

But seeing him day after day, mute, forlorn, and broken, stirred in me a strange sympathy. The picture the prosecution built—that of a mentally sane but inexplicably evil teen—didn't sit right. Maybe because I don't believe in evil as a malevolent force. I believe in trauma, pathology, broken brains. We don't need the devil when we've got ourselves.

Now, under Clif's watch, I return to the destroyed bodies in the photos. Adrenaline drills a drumbeat in my blood. The victims and the cause and manner of their deaths, the teenage suspect, the type of home and the neighborhood, the fire—they're all tragically familiar. Which means we could have a copycat.

Or—I raise a hand to where my pulse throbs in my neck—my former mentor, Dr. Benedict Hoffman, and I were right. Derrick didn't plan the deaths of his family alone. The Midnight Man is out there, hiding behind a digital mask and driving unhappy, alienated teens into murder.

I open my eyes and take a mental step back. It's way too early to be making these kinds of suppositions. I need to be neutral.

"There are some similarities," I say.

"Similarities." He leans back, looking pleased with himself. "You think I'm getting ahead of myself. But I saved the crown jewels." He pushes a blueprint of the house across the table. "Starting with this. The room belonging to the older son, Jason Heath, here"—he taps a penciled *X* on the paper—"was over the garage, which was built with fire-resistant drywall and had limited upward fuel, so the room wasn't completely engulfed. That's where Eric's body was. We found remnants of a poster—*The Scream* by artist Edvard Munch."

"Okay," I say. That's something. Derrick Tremblay was a fan of Munch's painting. But I keep tapping the brakes. "We can't read too much into that. *The Scream* is world-famous. It appears everywhere in pop culture: TV shows, music videos, advertising. Both Jason and Derrick likely saw it multiple times. Probably been lectured about it in high school art class. It's basically *the* image for teenage angst."

Clif places a fifth photo on the table, spins it to face me. The man must be great at poker, turning over his cards one by one. "This is from a partially surviving wall in the parents' room in the home's north wing. Crime scene detectives ran a Kastle–Meyer test. We need confirmation from the lab, but it appears Jason—we've lifted his prints—drew the image in blood. The blood is likely that of his parents, based on forensic evidence. We'll know after DNA tests."

I hold off looking at the photo. "The smears in the parents' blood."

Steady green-brown eyes stare back. "Right. Meaning Jason drew the picture before the fire occurred. When the blood was fresh."

I try to imagine a boy dipping his hand into his parents' blood. But it's a mental cog that keeps slipping. The picture won't stick.

I pick up the photo.

The image on the wall above Andrea and Michael's bed is a crude outline of a man with his mouth agape, his hands pressed to the sides of his head. On the soot-covered plaster, the figure seems to rise shrieking out of a black void.

There's a rush in my ears like a subway train arriving.

A single crime scene contains hundreds to thousands of data points. There are the forensic elements, things that come from the crime itself: blood spatter, fingerprints, DNA, fiber and hair samples, bullet casings, evidence of arson or other patterns. Then there are the clues left because of the killer's psychology and his mental state—the idea of a disorganized or organized killer—and his MO: method of operation. Ted Bundy beheaded his victims. Dahmer dismembered and partially ate his.

Sometimes, and especially in cases of serial murder, there are deliberately arranged signs.

Ramirez—the Night Stalker—left satanic symbols.

The Zodiac created his own cipher.

Jason Heath left the image of someone screaming. Just like Derrick. It's Edvard Munch's *The Scream*.

4

Wednesday, 9:15 a.m. MST

Clif watches me. My mind races through possibilities.

After Benedict Hoffman and I were hired by the defense as expert witnesses—criminal humanists who could speak about online influencers—one of the first things we learned about Derrick was he'd been obsessed with the painting. He'd had posters of Edvard Munch's work in his room along with a tattoo on his right biceps.

During and after the trial, the painting—with its portrayal of a man's isolation and anguish—haunted my dreams. Hell, I'd been a fan of *The Scream* during my own miserable teens. In the week between leaving Colorado College and taking a job with the Grand Junction police, I visited Oslo's National Museum in Norway. I stood before Munch's work and contemplated the visuals of a man overwhelmed by the horror of searching for meaning in a meaningless world.

His agony is how I imagine the despair of bewildered teenagers everywhere, sucked into the vicious maelstrom of social media, where clicks and likes define your self-worth and spit back a constant message: *You aren't enough.*

For adults, this message is painful. For a kid trying to figure out his place in the world, it can be devastating.

The jury ruled that Derrick Tremblay committed a crime that was incomprehensible in its horror. But Benedict, Clif, and I agreed: He didn't do it alone.

I stack the photos and slide them back to Clif, but he shakes his head. "Those are yours."

"Thanks." I place the photo of the house on top. "Did you find computers? Laptops? Any phones?"

"The excavation of the house is ongoing, but so far nothing."

It was the same way with the Tremblay deaths: All digital devices had been removed from the property. They were never found and never again used to connect to the internet. Derrick either couldn't or wouldn't explain what happened to them.

"I spent last night writing up an affidavit for the entirety of the Heaths' digital records," Clif says. "I invoked exigent circumstances, but not all companies will comply. Thus the warrant."

No wonder he looks tired. The affidavit Clif submitted would have to be highly specific both in terms of summarizing the crime to justify the request and in listing the desired information to avoid violating Fourth Amendment requirements around unreasonable searches. This is true even with a murdered family. Truer, given any evidence recovered while exercising the warrant will have to hold up in court if the case goes to trial.

Clif says, "I requested phone records, emails, messages, chat logs, GPS data, online activity, cloud storage, and banking history going back four weeks. I asked for an accelerated response from the companies involved, but once the judge issues the warrant, it's still going to take days. Weeks, maybe, depending on the companies involved. I would have asked for a longer time span, but that would have slowed things down."

"Four weeks should be long enough to learn if Midnight Man influenced either of the Heath teens. And to establish his patterns."

"Unless that information is buried on the dark web, which— well, we might as well call it the unsearchable web. Then things get complicated." Clif shuffles through papers in a second file folder. Little more than twenty-four hours since he's been on the case, and it's already thick. He hands across a single sheet. "This is a photocopy of Jason's alleged suicide note. The original survived because it was in the back-yard, held down by rocks and well away from the house."

I read the note. It's in Times New Roman: typed, not handwritten. A thin line halfway down marks where Jason folded the original. There are photocopied splotches on the bottom half.

I read the note silently.

My family understands now. Their blindfolds are gone, and they are real players. They are free and will move into the real world, all together.

But I, I am in blood. I am steeped in it. For me, there is no hope.

"Steeped in it," I echo.

"'I am in blood,'" Clif intones in his gruff baritone. "'Stepped in so far that, should I wade no more, Returning were as tedious as go o'er.'"

"Shakespeare's *Macbeth*." I'm nodding. "The same reference Derrick Tremblay used in his suicide note." A chill slides along the nape of my neck, as if the ghosts of Derrick Tremblay's family have walked into the conference room. "Meaning that Jason believes he has committed such terrible acts that it is equally impossible to move forward or back. So maybe he decides to disappear?" I press my fingertips to the tender spot between my eyes. "What are these smears on the paper?"

"Blood. Again, based on a Kastle–Meyer test. We're waiting on the lab to confirm."

"We know Derrick studied *Macbeth* in his high school English class. We'll have to find out about Jason." I bring it up even though the coincidence of two teens six years apart homing in on that particular line from a seventeenth-century play seems remote; it's another indica-tion of a link between them.

"It's on our list of questions for when we meet with Jason's teach-ers," Clif says.

I rub the chill away as the detective passes over another paper.

"A copy of Derrick's suicide note, in case you need a refresher."

I don't, but I pick up the sheet anyway.

They are free! They were shadows. Echoes. Scripted loops in a world of lies. But I've freed them. They are Players now. They've entered the real world. I've done this for them. But I am ruined. How did it come to this? I am in blood. I am steeped in it.

"Both boys talk about who is a true human and who isn't," I say. "The teens are human, but their families aren't. Not until they die. Somehow death humanizes them, as if it's a kind of rebirth. A revelation. Sort of like having Neo's red pill from *The Matrix* shoved down your throat." I cross my legs and swivel gently, pushing back and forth on the ball of my foot. "You could have started our conversation with Jason's note."

Again that gleam. "I like laying the groundwork."

"You like messing with me."

"That, too."

He grins at me, and I roll my eyes.

I say, "Both boys misquote *Macbeth*. Did you pick up on that?"

"*Steeped* instead of *stepped*."

"It suggests they're using the same source. Something other than the original play."

"Or they just misquoted. *Steeped* makes more sense than *stepped* to the modern ear."

"Maybe. Derrick's suicide note is included in the trial transcripts, which weren't sealed." I bring the chair to a halt. "But if Jason asked for copies, the court would refuse him—a seventeen-year-old doesn't have a legit reason. Assuming he didn't get a copy from someone else . . ." Agitated, I resume my swiveling.

Clif finishes my thought: "Then how did he mimic it?"

"Exactly." I reread both notes. Although Derrick never explained himself, Benedict, Clif, and I had taken his suicide note to mean that Derrick thought he was saving his family by, paradoxically, murdering them. He believed that, through death, they would become real players—that is, fully aware and having free will. In psychological parlance, murders like those committed by Derrick are referred to as perverted mercy killings. Merciful because he thought he was saving them. Perverted because death was the result.

Cases of shared delusion or online manipulation—like the Slender Man stabbings—are rare. Somewhere in the 1 percent to 2 percent range. When they do happen, they're particularly horrific: The murders are nasty and brutish. Unfathomable. And the numbers are going up: With the rise of online influence and artificial intelligence, it isn't as hard as it used to be for a charismatic manipulator to sway emotionally vulnerable kids. In Derrick's case, he told police—in the moments before he went mute—that someone he called the Midnight Man had shown him the need for human transformation. But detectives and cyber experts found no evidence of any coach or groomer in either the real world or the virtual one. There was no Midnight Man, according to the prosecution. Only Derrick, trying to shift blame.

The jury had ruled for the prosecution: Derrick had acted alone. It was a case of perverted *justice*, not *mercy*. Case closed.

When I raise my head, Clif's patient eyes are weighing me.

"There's a five-year age difference," I say. "But their homes were only a few miles apart. Did these kids cross paths?"

"We've found no evidence they ever connected. The age difference, as you mention. And the kids in each family went to different high schools. Plus, the Tremblays had been in Denver only three months before their deaths. They hadn't had time to do much in the way of community building."

He drums his fingers on one of the folders. I spot a small sore just under the cuff of his long-sleeved shirt.

I hate cancer.

Clif's phone chirps. He glances down, frowns, and excuses himself. In the few minutes he's gone, I commit Jason's suicide note to memory.

When Clif returns, the shadows under his eyes have become trenches. "A hunter found a body," he says. "It's been identified as that of Jason Heath. Jason's driver's permit was in his pocket. Sheriff's department used fingerprints to confirm."

My heart slides sideways. "And Katelynn?"

"No sign."

The small hope I'd held that the twins might be found alive vanishes like snow on a sunny Colorado day. A lot of the time, hope is what we deal in at VCAC. It keeps us showing up at the office every day. But we also swim neck-deep in the flip side of hope, which amounts to soul-crushing disappointment. Most of the time, I feel good about serving in VCAC: I can help kids in ways I wished someone had helped my brother and me—before and after we lost our parents.

But on other days, it backfires.

I push to my feet, already picking up the photocopies from Clif and sliding them into my bag. "Where'd they find him?"

"Sandusky County." He's also packing up.

"Any family in that area we know about?"

"No. There's an aunt, Beatrice Harper, and two cousins in Salisbury, England. This place is in the middle of fucking nowhere, Ohio, thirteen hundred miles from where his family was killed. Allowing a few breaks, that's roughly twenty-three, maybe twenty-four hours by car. Meaning he and—presumably—Katelynn took off right after the murders on Monday night and arrived last night around the time I was brushing my pearly whites and heading to bed. The mystery is, why didn't he take either of the family cars? And, so far, we haven't traced him or Katelynn to any public transit or a ridesharing app. No car rental. With the neighbors' security cameras knocked out, we're reduced to checking traffic cams and running every vehicle. Detectives and patrol are continuing a door-to-door as we speak. A damn long process."

I'm pulling on my coat. "We've got something the kids didn't."

"What's that?"

"Airplanes. The FBI's travel office will get us seats on one of the government-contracted airlines. United, probably, since we're in Denver." I'm mentally running through what's in my go bag in the back of my vehicle. "Even if it means bumping a couple of passengers, we'll get to Sandusky while there's still daylight."

5

Wednesday, 3:15 p.m. EST

It's a three-hour flight from Denver to Cleveland Hopkins International Airport.

We lose two hours with the time change, and Clif and I and our go bags land midafternoon, local time. The cold hits as soon as we step outside, gnawing at exposed flesh. We're met at the curb by FBI agent Kirk Feldster, who was called in by the county sheriff when his office connected Jason to the missing teens from Denver. Feldster bounces out of the vehicle as soon as he spots us, badge already out, his breath misting in the cold. I peg him as forty, forty-one. He's athletic, well groomed, with the sharp-eyed friendliness of a savvy golden retriever.

The first thing I ask is whether there's any word on Katelynn.

"I wish I had good news, but we've got nothing." Feldster's grip is firm as we shake. "Glad to meet you both. I'll be driving you to the site. Here, give me your bags." He opens the SUV's liftgate, and our go bags vanish. "Detective Burgess, it's a small world. My dad knew you. He told me about your work on the Likanski case in Alamosa—those homegrown terrorists you tracked down. The way you put the financial pieces together? He said it was some of the best detective work he's seen."

I've never heard of the Likanski case. I cock my head toward Clif, waiting for an explanation. But Clif waves it off, and that's when I notice a faint tremor in his hands. Fighting cancer can be a full-time job, and Friendly Feldster is going to exhaust him. In just five minutes the agent has shown more energy than my lifetime cumulative total. Too bad I can't siphon off some of that bounce and give it to Clif.

"Hey, Clif," I say. "You mind if I ride shotgun? I get carsick."

I'm lying. I don't know if he picks up on my plan to give him a break—maybe even a shot at a nap during the hour-and-a-half drive. But he digs up a smile. "Should've brought some of those airsick bags."

At that, Feldster looks alarmed. I can see why when we get in his vehicle. It smells of leather and saddle soap, with a faint zing of lemon. There's not a crumb or a stain. I'm a neat freak, so it's my kind of place. I give him a reassuring smile.

"I'll be fine," I say.

Once we're seated and buckled in, Feldster hands me a sealed envelope before pulling away from the curb.

"That's the initial incident report and prelim from the coroner—hard copies. I've uploaded the full digital case file, such as it is, to our secure system."

I break the seal and shake the contents into my lap. Corners flutter in the roar from the heater. There's a scene summary with the date and time of discovery, the presence of Jason's fingerprints on the weapon—a ghost gun, nearly impossible to trace. No other prints on the grip. There are details on the location—GPS coordinates, landowner name, type of terrain, weather conditions. The responding deputies and times logged. And the name of the reporting party—Samuel Schreier. I skim each document and pass the entire lot back to Clif.

Feldster exits the airport, following the signs to OH-237 North toward I-480/I-71.

"Tell us about the reporting party," I say.

"Schreier's a hunter. The Sandusky County Sheriff's Office spent two hours interviewing him. A gunshot residue test was negative." Feldster steers onto an on-ramp and merges with the traffic hurtling along I-480 West. "Schreier was hunting rabbit, which is legal

November through February and which he does there on the regular. But he hadn't fired his rifle this morning. He and the gun both have their permits, and he's got a standing agreement with the owner of the property. Anything's possible, but it's the opinion of the sheriff's department that Schreier's clean. The property owner is also out of the mix—he's vacationing with his family in Florida."

I scan the coroner's prelim. Likely cause of death is a single gunshot wound to the head from a 9mm handgun. Bullet entered below the chin and exited through the top of the skull. Estimated time of death, Tuesday between 10:00 p.m. and midnight. Gunshot residue—GSR— was found on Jason's hands. That, along with the fingerprints, suggests a self-inflicted injury.

"No indication Katelynn was there?" I ask.

Feldster honks as a pickup truck tries to squeeze into a space meant for a MINI Cooper. "Not yet. We're beating the hell out of the sur- rounds, looking for any trace of her."

A light snow swirls along the asphalt. Clif's voice comes from the back seat. "What can you tell us about the locale?"

"The field where Jason was found is part of the Lake Erie Marsh Zone. The marsh zone is a remnant of the Great Black Swamp—it's a diverse area with federal, state, and private land ownership. A lot of marshes, a lot of forest. Some high bluffs. The sheriff has called in ground search, dogs, and drones to run tight search grids. They've already combed the structures on the property—there's a house, a barn, and three sheds. All negative. FYI, they obtained the owner's permis- sion, although with one teen dead and another missing, that was just going the extra mile."

I cling to what slim hope this search offers. I'm picturing how the hunt for Katelynn is unspooling between Denver and Ohio, driven mainly by the FBI's CARD unit. In addition to the Amber Alert, there are K9 and helicopter searches, interviews with relevant parties, and notifications to bus, train, taxicab, and rideshare companies. Local law enforcement is beating the bushes along I-70 and I-80. And as soon as we have the files, digital forensics examiners will scour every bit and byte of data. The media is already plastering the kids' images onto every available screen.

"The family dog is also missing," Clif tells Feldster and me. "An Australian shepherd named Daisy. I got confirmation right after we landed that none of the local vets has her. We'd assumed she died in the fire, but we haven't found so much as a tooth or a bone near the family home."

Feldster pops a stick of gum. "Missing teens, missing dog, dead family. A ghost gun. Like my kids would say—creepypasta."

He isn't using the term in the usual way. But I get what he means. *Creepypasta* about sums it up.

———

The field where Jason Heath died is a wind-bitten expanse of dead grass and frozen mud clotted with leafless trees, their branches limned with snow. Save for a wedge-shaped stand of woods to the northeast, the land rolls out like worn carpet, revealing distant fencing, fallen branches, hollows where snow lingers.

The empty space where a boy died under a lonely sky.

It's 5:35 p.m., bitterly cold. The sun is a pale circle hanging above the horizon, a bulb about to switch off. Long shadows thicken as a light snow becomes steady, collecting in the grass.

A lone deputy guards the road in; the investigative team has packed up and gone home. You've got to move fast when you're working outdoor scenes, especially in inclement weather.

We exit the vehicle. I huddle into my coat next to Clif and Feldster, hands in my pockets, hat pulled to my eyebrows. I scan the horizon, wishing I could prize Jason's last thoughts from the iron-cold soil.

"Hell of a place for a kid to die," says Clif.

The horizon swallows the sun and dusk clamps down, a lid on a pot, broken only by a flurry of crows whipping past and the black streak of telephone lines. Feldster gestures us forward. Crime scene tape flutters. Red flags mark the location of already-removed evidence. The hiss of spitting snow fills the void.

"Why here?" I say out loud.

"It's private," Feldster offers. His face is tanned even in winter, his laugh lines prominent. He's probably the life of the party at FBI functions. More power to him. "Smack in the middle of cornfields. No cameras. And there's easy access off the I-80 and I-70 corridors. Jason could have found this field on Google Maps."

I glance back over the ground we traversed. It's crisscrossed with footprints and tire tracks from the police and EMTs and the K9 search teams, but the tracks are now rapidly disappearing under the snow. "There were no tire imprints when police first arrived?"

"Just those belonging to the hunter's truck. But we found three sets of footprints. The boy's, where he walked into the field, and a set of size eleven boots—Cabela's insulated hunting boots. Those were Schreier's."

"And the third set?" Clif asks.

"Those are the interesting ones." Feldster pulls out his tablet and shields it from the snowfall to show us a video of two sets of tracks in deep snow among the trees. "Deputies took the video and casts before more snow hit. These tracks came from the northeast, through the woods, and stopped at the edge of the clearing, ten yards from where Jason's body was found. There's some overlap between the two sets. Same wind scoring on the edges. If these weren't made at the same time, it was within minutes. One set was Jason's, meaning he didn't come alone. This second set—based on the depth of the prints—suggests someone in the 250-to-280-pound range."

"He's got a long stride," Clif says, watching the video again.

"Right. I'd put him at six three, maybe six four. Big guy. His prints tracked back east on a slightly different route. Lucky for us, we had a bit of a melt yesterday afternoon, followed by a refreeze in the evening, which gave us a good hardpack to catch the prints. They vanish at the road, where we figure the driver got back into his vehicle."

"May I?" I ask, reaching for the tablet. Feldster passes it over. I squint at the screen, rewinding the deputy's shaky phone video before hitting play. "There." I pause the video. "You see how one set is clean and purposeful—consistent stride, deep heel strike. But the second set—look here—the gait's irregular. The right foot keeps dragging, barely clearing the snow. As if Jason is being hauled along through the trees."

I zoom in.

"And here—the footprints crowd each other. Way too tight for two people walking side by side. And it's not because of the trees. They're not bunched. This suggests forced movement. The second person's off balance, maybe being pushed. And the snow's kicked up along the edges. Like they were stumbling. Or resisting."

Feldster taps his temple. "Like minds. I told the sheriff the same thing. Jason didn't come willingly."

I hand back the tablet. "Tell us about the prints themselves."

"Men's Blundstone Chelsea boots, size fourteen. Score one for SICAR, which the sheriff used." He means the Shoeprint Image Capture and Retrieval database. "I cross-referenced and confirmed with our Footwear and Tire Tread Files database."

Clif speaks from behind his scarf. "We assume the person got into a vehicle. But you said there was only one set of tire prints."

"Right. It's a narrow road—fence on either side, as you saw. The hunter followed the same path as whoever was in the vehicle. His truck wiped out earlier tracks."

"Damn," I say softly.

The field shifts as twilight deepens. Shadows blend into the general gloom; shapes lose form. The wind whips the snow into trembling figures and rips them apart again, like brief hauntings. I stare at the woods where the video was taken.

Katelynn! I want to cry out. To make my voice pierce the darkness. But these woods and fields have been searched. If she was ever here, she's long gone.

By the end of the Tremblay trial, I'd begun to have quiet doubts about Benedict's theories and my own. Maybe the Midnight Man was nothing but a figment of our overheated, pop-culture-obsessed thinking. A digital echo of Benedict's idea that evil is real and solid and walks among us. Now here is tangible proof: two sets of footprints in the snow. Our first indication of Midnight Man's physical existence. Psychopath or Satan, this is proof enough for me that he exists.

I'm both jubilant and horrified. Benedict and I were right. But another family has died because we couldn't convince anyone of the truth.

My mind sketches an image of an immense man standing among the trees, watching a teenager die, perhaps ordering him to do so. A painful chill ripples across my shoulders, as if the Midnight Man is still there, lurking in the woods, watching us. His spectral presence slithers between the oaks and hickories, ungraspable as a cold breath.

My eyes meet Clif's over his red wool scarf, and I'm sure he's thinking the same thing.

I curl my fingers into fists. "You said the deputies took casts?"

Feldster's lips quirk. "When I asked that question, I was informed that detectives here are from Ohio, not Siberia."

It isn't that FBI agents doubt the ability of our peers in law enforcement. At least, not usually. It's that we believe we should trust but verify.

"Aren't Chelsea boots for urban use?" Clif says. "Winter sidewalks?"

"Funny you mention that. I asked around. The younger agents tell me that Chelseas are for sophisticated men who've got life figured out. That's a direct quote."

I snort. "Shoes can say so much about a person?" And as if any of us has life figured out.

He holds out upraised palms in a "who knows" gesture. "That's what I'm told. We're working on a list of online retailers and brick-and-mortars. But the rubber tread is worn, meaning the shoes are older, or he bought them used. I don't expect to pull anything."

Clif had turned to stare into the woods, but now he pivots. "Check online places like Grailed and Poshmark," he says. "We caught a guy that way. He was trying to do the whole *GQ* thing, and Grailed was the only way he could afford it. Maybe our unsub likes nice things."

Unsub—unknown subject. The unidentified perpetrator of a crime.

"Great idea," Feldster says. "We'll jump on that."

I shift my line of thinking. Feldster's age suggests he has a decade's worth of experience on me, and I want his opinion. "What are your thoughts on exactly what went down here? Aside from the obvious, I mean."

He fists his hands together, tips them in my direction. "It's possible someone came on the scene shortly after Jason's death and didn't report it. Didn't want to get involved. But the tracks—as you noted and as forensics agrees—suggest the two people came together. And of all the fields in Ohio . . ." He rubs his forehead under his FBI stocking cap. "I'd place money that someone brought Jason here and watched that kid shoot himself. Could be another teenager. Maybe even his sister, egging him on. 'C'mon, you coward. Don't chicken out.' That kind of thing. I've seen it too damn many times on forums used by the mentally deranged."

"A teenager with size fourteen shoes?" I ask.

"My fifteen-year-old wears size thirteen. Kid has twelve-inch paws. We call him Bigfoot." A twitch of his lips. "He doesn't take kindly to it."

"Assuming it's not Katelynn, who would this other kid be? Someone who came with him from Colorado?"

"Maybe. Or someone he met online. Like a member of the 764 network."

My face is half frozen in the cold, but I manage a scowl. The 764 is an online faction made up of what we call nihilistic violent extremists. Their goal is to bring about the destruction of society by sowing chaos. With this in mind, they use online platforms to befriend other teens and entice them to violence. Exactly like the Midnight Man. Except 764 didn't exist when Derrick murdered his family.

I hunch farther inside my coat. The wind has lifted, and it's got serious teeth. "You've checked the forums?"

"First thing. So far no one from 764 is crowing about Jason's death. Same for TCC—the true crime community. We've had people on it since the sheriff called."

"It's the same story on our end," Clif says. "No chatter."

I swap glances with Clif. Denver PD investigated TCC back when Derrick committed his crimes. The true crime community is made up in part by fans of mass murderers. Many of them are dedicated "Columbiners," worshipping at the altar of school shooters Eric Harris and Dylan Klebold, who killed thirteen students and a teacher back in 1999 and kicked off the school shooting epidemic. These members of TCC aren't the kind of true crime followers who love to weigh in and help solve a case. They're seventy thousand enthusiasts worldwide—and growing—who romanticize killers and believe that violence is a logical response to life's problems. Embedded in the TCC is a lot of ugly, including the fact that teens who murder their families often go on to shoot up kids and teachers at their schools while their TCC peers cheer.

Before committing murder, these teens usually crow about their plans. Their braggadocio and need for acknowledgment are a gift to FBI agents like yours truly who work in VCAC and keep an ear to this underworld. Often, thanks to due diligence, these kids get shut down before doing something we'll all regret.

Derrick was different. No online bragging. No threats against his classmates. His only target, apparently, was his family, and he was weirdly quiet about it. Jason's likely to fall into the same outlier category.

Unless there's a chat room in a hidden corner of the dark web—a fortress in an impenetrable forest.

Feldster's words break into my thoughts. "I want to point out that girls wear Chelsea boots, too. But I'm guessing Katelynn isn't another Bigfoot."

"Size seven," Clif says.

I go back to staring into the woods. Did a teenager from Denver find this lonely place all by himself? But if Midnight Man brought Jason here, why drive twenty-plus hours straight through to bring him so far from Colorado?

Because there's a link. There's something about Ohio that calls him here.

I look south, in the direction of Route 42. Distant headlights trundle past as the night thickens. Not far away, an owl hoots, and a moment later something small screams. The sounds send a primal shudder tramping down my spine.

Let us all sing praise for electricity and dead bolts.

"It's a straight shot on I-70 from Denver to here," I say. "Same with I-80 farther north. Maybe someone saw the twins at a gas station or in a public restroom and noticed what car they got in or out of."

"Whoever has them wouldn't risk stopping in a public place," Clif says. "Those kids were squatting in fields and eating whatever crap he gave them."

"They'd need gas."

"He could have extra cans."

I know he's right, and I hate it. Anyway, people are already searching. But the fact that Katelynn's not here could mean she and Daisy are alive.

Clif fists his hands under his armpits. "Agent Feldster, can you see what you can pull up on the property? Details on the current owner and any prior ones. Parcel size and zoning classification. Police reports connected to this property."

"Call me Kirk. And I've been working on it. Current owner's a guy named Hitchens, a local developer. He bought the land in a probate sale about nine years ago. But the title chain is weird. Before that, it was held in trust, and before that—nothing. It doesn't look like anything was digitized. And Hitchens doesn't have any information."

Clif's sigh is audible even through the wool scarf. "You've filed a request with probate court?"

"Yup. Clerk says there's a sealed juvenile record attached to the property—likely means the last heir was a minor. I'm pushing for timely access, but I'm not sure these people have heard of 'ASAP.' What are you looking for?"

A harsh cough bends Clif at the waist, so I jump in for him. "Something that connects Jason or his family to this location. Or a lead on who might have brought him here, assuming *they* have a connection."

Feldster switches on a flashlight. Shadows leap; the trees lean in. His face tightens in thought. "This field wasn't a random choice, is what you're thinking. I can say this—the Heaths don't have family here. And there's no record of them staying at hotels or rental homes or campgrounds anywhere in Sandusky or nearby counties, not in the last two years. We're still searching, and it doesn't mean there's not a connection. But if someone *did* drag those kids here, then Katelynn Heath had no part in killing her family. And that means she's in a world of hurt."

I'm not much into praying. If prayers worked, Kevin and I wouldn't have been sent to live with our aunt. We wouldn't have been trapped in her filthy home, pinned by her nasty tongue, her cruelty, and her daily drunkenness. Answered prayers would have meant my brother never swallowed that first blue pill.

But I find my lips moving silently anyway.

Be alive, Katelynn. Please. Be alive.

6

Unknown

Katelynn stands with her squad on the football field. The stadium lights are blazing, the bleachers full, her parents and brothers watching. *Everyone* is watching: the Ravens and the Spartans.

She is strong, calm, prepared. They've been practicing their pyramid for months, and they're ready. More than ready. She breathes deeply, and her lungs fill with the promise of this moment. She's here on the field at the start of the game, but her mind races ahead to the winning plays, to the postgame party unspooling through the night, to her and Daisy falling into exhausted sleep in her childhood canopy bed as dawn approaches.

She's also thinking of future fields and other games—wherever a scholarship will take her. Ivy League. New York City. A career as a well-regarded novelist.

She smiles as her squad calls counts—"five-six-seven-eight!"—and Katelynn feels it in her muscles and bones: that snap of timing, that perfect rush of air before the toss.

The two bases—strong guys with steady hands—lock their grips around her sneakers. The back spot counts them off, steady and clear. Her heart syncs to the rhythm. Her body knows what to do.

She vaults upward in a basket toss, legs tucked, arms tight to her sides, and then unfolds midair into a toe-touch so high the crowd gasps.

Her form is perfect. She feels it: the smack of her hands hitting her feet at the apex. Then she falls straight down, and they catch her like they always do.

No one drops Katelynn Heath.

From the toss, the pyramid forms around her—squad members stack on one another's shoulders, legs locked, backs straight, and she climbs fast, using hands, knees, muscle memory. One step, then another. She's the flier; the risk of catastrophe is hers. So is the glory.

At the top, she lifts her arms high and hits the final pose, standing on one leg, the other bent tight, perfect balance. Her fists punch skyward. The stadium lights burn hot on her face.

She's a star. *The* star.

Then the hands holding her begin to shake. She wobbles. The ground is suddenly very far away—so far that she can't see the field. The pyramid trembles and sways. The stadium lights flicker. Someone is breathing hard, and her flesh crawls.

"Hold it, Katelynn!" a voice shouts.

But it's the wrong voice. Not Coach. Not anyone on her squad. It's a man's voice. Low. Amused. Abruptly, she's on her back; a rough blanket rubs raw spots on her skin. The hands holding her ankles squeeze too tight, fingers like clamps. She cries out in pain, but the wind snatches her voice away.

Then even the wind is gone. The air is close, stinking of sweat and grease. She squeezes her eyes shut, trying to return to the stadium. For an instant she succeeds. She raises her arms again.

Then someone climbs through the stack of high schoolers, knocking them aside like Jenga blocks. Cheerleaders scream as they plummet earthward.

"Jason fell," the man tells her. "Totally fragged."

Jason.

The memory hits her like a fist from the dark. He'd been weeping. Apologizing. Clinging to her before he was torn away and taken out into the night.

Briefly, she's back in the stadium, high on the pyramid. She sobs with relief.

From nowhere, Daisy barks.

Then she, too, is falling.

7

Wednesday, 10:00 p.m. MST

Benedict Hoffman has been trying to save the world on and off for five years—at least that corner inhabited by teens searching for answers and finding only disappointment and, sometimes, tragedy.

Ever since the digital entity calling itself Midnight Man raised its sinister head at Derrick Tremblay's trial, Benedict has been working—without success—to find the individual he thinks of as his archenemy. Maybe it will turn out that Midnight Man is nothing more than a ghost in the servers, a sparking whisper of ones and zeros. But even if there is no flesh-and-blood human behind the digital mask, there's *something* scuttling around the dark web, luring children. Something evil.

Indeed, there are many somethings scurrying around the cesspools of the dark web. Benedict is hunting them down, one by one—tricky, given that sites are accessible only via IP and not searchable domain names. Obscurity is the name of the game. He combs hidden forums, scraping invite-only chat logs, and chasing fragmentary code through onion-layered servers where predators hide behind avatars and encryption. When he finds a malicious actor, he sends an anonymous tip to a white hat hacker group. Or he speaks with someone he trusts at one of the watchdog groups like Thorn. When he suspects terrorist activities, he reaches out to Tech Against Terrorism via a Cyber Threat Intelligence Network.

He has helped shut down thirty-seven bad actors.

But Midnight Man remains elusive. Benedict sometimes feels as if it's Lucifer himself he's chasing through Dante's nine circles of hell. He might have abandoned his seminary studies while in his twenties. But—he has learned—although you can take the boy out of the church, you can't take the church out of the boy.

Tonight, shortly after nine, he clips on Maggie's leash, locks the front door, and heads out from Colorado Springs' Old North End to walk the mile to a downtown coffee shop. The temperature hovers ten degrees below freezing; the cold burns his nostrils. There are no stars—cloud cover is dense and low, a pale pearl reflecting the city's lights.

He lets the Irish setter dictate their pace, waiting as Maggie sniffs out trees and bushes, leaving her mark wherever she sees fit. Until recently he found these late-evening walks invigorating. Once an early riser, he's become more of an owl than a lark. For that, he blames his time working alongside Father Antonio, assisting with exorcisms. Back when he believed the priesthood was his destiny, before more intellectual pursuits pulled him away. Now, long after he and his plans for the priesthood have parted ways, he remembers the guttural voices shrieking in unknown tongues, the vomit and blasphemy, the strange contortions—these haunted him, leaving him wide awake at 2:00 a.m., staring into the abyss.

Years later, he still wakes up at 2:00 a.m. Some nights, the abyss stares back.

Maggie shakes the leash; her tags jingle, pulling him back to the present.

"Sorry, girl."

A fortnight ago, his evening walks changed. The very air seemed to shift. Maggie took to pausing during their walks to give her soft, warning *whoof* at something only she could sense.

"What is it, Maggie?" he asks each time. And each time she gives a second warning *whoof* before moving on.

If he has a stalker, whoever it is has never approached. Never spoken nor left a sign. No anonymous phone calls or sinister emails. His days are as soothingly uneventful as most nights. Still, he has taken to carrying a six-inch utility knife in his coat pocket.

Tonight Maggie halts near the corner of Cascade and Dale. They've walked through most of the Colorado College campus. His office is behind them. Nearby is the numismatic museum with its treasure of coins. To the right and down a slope, the Fine Arts Center hunches against the gloom. This part of the campus is deserted.

He glances in the direction where Maggie stares. His human eyes detect only bare-leafed trees looming over an expanse of dead lawn. There's a sign for the Fine Arts Center and a statue of a North American Indian with a drum. Farther back is the museum itself, single story and straightforward. Nothing stirs. The only sound is traffic two blocks over.

He twitches her leash. "Let's go, girl."

She whines but obeys.

As they cross Dale, Benedict glances back. Shadows glide and shift among the tree trunks. He narrows his eyes. Paranoia can be a sign of mental disorder—he deals with this regularly in his weekend clients. But according to the famous Swiss psychiatrist Carl Jung, paranoia can also spring from a secret parallel knowledge. A form of dreaming while awake.

In other words, just because you're paranoid doesn't mean they're not out to get you.

"You think you can transform into a rottweiler?" he asks Maggie.

But she's lost all concern. She smells food and the rising energy of downtown Colorado Springs and tugs on her leash.

Ten minutes later, they push through the doors of Rocco's Coffee Shop, open 24-7. The place is alive with light and movement and the soft hum of chatter. College students come here to drink, to talk, to tackle their homework. A few, like Benedict, come for the public Wi-Fi. He walks in with the casual posture of a man running errands, not subverting federal guidelines. He orders coffee and speaks briefly with a few students. His students know he's waging some sort of cyberwar. After all, his specialty is the *criminal* humanities, a sweet spot at the crossroads of literature, pop culture, and sin. He studies the narratives people build around crime—how culture shapes the criminal, and how the criminal, in turn, reshapes culture. His lectures range from Greek tragedy to graphic novels, from medieval confessions to true crime podcasts. He teaches his students to read a killer's manifesto the way they might read a novel: for theme, structure, voice, and the mysterious human impulse beneath the act.

His classes are popular.

As he waits for his Americano with an extra shot of espresso, Benedict's gaze lands on a poster advertising an upcoming series of lectures at Colorado College on the biology of belief. Benedict himself is giving the third lecture, "The Shadow of Adulthood: Exploring Adolescent Morality," a title he's been saddled with, and which is sure to drive away potential attendees. But for the first time he notices that psychiatrist Dr. Scott Poole is kicking off the series with "The Myth of Evil: Understanding the Disordered Mind."

"I'll be damned," he says to Maggie.

After Benedict accepted that his inquisitive mind would be happier in academia than the church, he turned to the intersection of culture and crime to complete his PhD. He briefly shadowed Poole at the San Carlos Children's Treatment Center in Texas. There Benedict observed troubled children and teens, interviewing them to determine the impact of popular culture on their mental and emotional well-being. The degree to which these troubled young people were influenced by online information horrified him. When your role models are nineteen-year-old armchair psychologists on TikTok and antiheroes like Loki and Catwoman, how bad can things get?

Pretty bad, it turns out.

He supposes he should reach out to his former mentor, offer to take him to lunch for old time's sake. The idea doesn't give him pleasure. Things didn't end well between them after Benedict highlighted the adverse effects caused by Poole's video game therapy. And then there'd been the Tremblay trial.

Water under the bridge, right? They're both professionals. He'll give Poole a call.

At a table in the back, he sets down his highly customized, liquid-cooled laptop driven by the fastest graphic cards available and crammed with RAM. It sucks batteries dry like a kid with a juice box, but it's got the raw power his work demands. With permission he received months ago, he plugs directly into an ethernet jack, then routes through a multihop VPN and a privacy-hardened browser, burying his signal under layers of digital noise as he digs his way into the void.

People who don't know better think of the dark web as a single entity—a vast digital sea through which glide the zero-and-one equivalents of nuclear submarines and great white sharks.

The reality is more diffuse. And more dangerous. Each submarine, each shark, hides a portal to something darker and deeper. You can go forever and never touch bottom.

Tonight, as on many nights, Benedict slips on headphones and logs on to play the open-world game of *Eidolon*. He launches the gaming client on his laptop, which connects to a hidden dot-onion site he found months ago after an exhaustive hunt using a TOR browser. Posing as a sixteen-year-old boy with anger-management issues, he's been granted limited access. The gateway to what he really wants remains sealed, invisible to all but those chosen by the gatekeeper: *Underland*.

Benedict suspects the gatekeeper of *Underland* is Midnight Man.

After he'd successfully found, downloaded, and installed the gaming client, he'd had to upgrade his laptop to meet the power and speed requirements to play it. Then wait until another player let him into the lobby with the right access URL. This was followed by a waiting game—weeks of chatting with the other players as they passed through the lobby—until he was finally invited into the game itself. But he knows he's circling the perimeter of something colder, hungrier. *Underland* isn't hidden per se. Yet access to the full scope of the game remains encrypted in a player's behavior. Only the right kind of player can find the door.

And he isn't that player. Not yet.

Someone once told him in a private chat that the key to entering *Underland* is Animus. But he doesn't know who or what Animus is. And all his efforts to find out through casual mentions in the chat, by parsing the game's cut scenes, by actual play, have offered nothing beyond a few private messages telling him that summoning Animus is never a good idea. The comments are always followed by laugh emojis. Maybe the kids are pranking him.

He steps into the game. The imagined air inside *Eidolon* always feels fresh—Benedict fancies it as cool and moss scented. He stands on a cobblestone path that curves through a birchwood glen. Overhead, pale trees arch like cathedral vaults, branches bare but dotted with buds that shimmer faintly, out of sync with the summer season. A fox trails him at a distance, watching. Nearby, bells ring clear and sonorous.

He kneels beside a glowing herb cluster and gathers it—duskbloom, the system tells him. He'll use it to calm wayward spirits in the next village. The game's worldbuilding is graceful, lovely—astonishing, even. Tasks are small but satisfying. Kindness is rewarded with tokens or small artifacts: a luminous gemstone, a cup carved from shell, the sweet notes of a song he can call back later. Most adults would be surprised at how appealing teens find games like *Stardew Valley* and *Animal Crossing*, how much they love an escape from real-world pressures through low-stress gaming environments.

He spends a few minutes on the chat with another player named Nocturne2Blue—a girl he makes small talk with on the regular. She's furious with her parents, but never seems inclined toward violence. She spends a lot of time in the apple orchard.

An hour later, he logs off with nothing to show for his time. No change in the interface. No cryptic invitation. No veiled messages from the game master. He's completed three small quests, made offerings at two shrines, and exchanged riddles with an NPC who disappeared when

Benedict asked about *Underland*. He's played nice and occasionally not nice with the others. But whatever test he's taking, he's failed again.

He shuts the laptop and leans back. Maggie, resting beneath the table, twitches an ear at the scrape of his chair.

Benedict is not usually a patient man. But tracking malevolent actors has taught him that his greatest skills are patience and persistence. He'll be back. Tomorrow night and the night after. He'll keep moving through *Eidolon*'s dreamlike corridors and cobbled paths, gathering roots and feeding temple spirits.

He doesn't want to contemplate the idea that all this is for nothing. That Midnight Man is veiled behind impenetrable layers of the dark web, forever hidden. Sooner or later, Benedict will find his enemy. All he needs to do for now is make sure his identity remains secret. In *Eidolon*, he's a narcissistic teen, filled with hurt and rage.

Exactly the kind of boy Midnight Man likes.

8

Wednesday, 9:00 p.m. EST

It's Katelynn I'm thinking about as we board the 9:00 p.m. flight back to Denver.

I've caught up on her history, or at least the public version. Cocaptain on the varsity cheerleading team. Four-point-three weighted GPA. National Merit semifinalist and editor of the school's literary magazine. Awarded the school's "Rising Leader" prize in her junior year. Committed to regular volunteer work at a senior center and an animal shelter. A busy social circle. A dog named Daisy, which she rescued as a pup.

Our family dog had been a bad-tempered cur named Jaws. I can't resist someone who names a dog Daisy any more than I can turn away an abused teen like Livvie. For those of us who didn't get the shiny childhood we were promised, there are obligations.

Clif and I trudge down the aisle along with other passengers. Images flash through my brain, an unwanted slideshow. Katelynn and Daisy prisoners in a damp, dark basement. The two of them tied up and terrified in the back of a van.

In the worst slides, they're already dead.

The FBI travel office came through again, and Clif and I wedge into our seats over the wing. The flight is busy but not packed. I tuck my go bag under the seat in front of me and my parka in the overhead compartment. As the plane levels off and we're allowed to move around the cabin, people immerse themselves in books or napping or watching videos on their phones.

When the flight attendant comes by, we ask for coffee. I shift from the window to the empty middle seat so Clif and I can hash over what we've learned in low whispers, safe in the humming cocoon of the Boeing 737's engines.

Clif spent our brief time at the airport on his phone, catching up with the Denver side of things, and now he fills me in. "We're scheduled to interview students at Jason and Katelynn's high school on Friday. Here's the username and password to access last year's yearbook."

I snap a photo of his screen. "Why not tomorrow?"

"It's an off-site teacher workday," Clif says. "*And* Katelynn's cheer-leading team is in Greeley for a two-day competitive camp. They'll be home tomorrow night. Life goes on. Denver PD has been granted access to two social media sites. Jason's parents and brother, along with Katelynn, posted what you'd expect: pictures of school events, friends, family vacations. The dog. But Jason was silent. Or, like Derrick, he managed to erase most of his online footprint. It's going to take additional time to pull those pieces together."

I nod. It isn't possible for someone to totally erase their social media presence once they've created accounts. But a determined individual can significantly reduce their footprint. Jason could have deleted his accounts, removed his own posts along with any posts and photos he was tagged in, and utilized a privacy tool, which will monitor your online presence, delete any mentions of you, and deny third parties access to your information.

Outside of social media, there's a lot of slick software that can help you pull a digital Houdini. All that remains of your online presence is scattered bits of scrambled data. And—weirdly—a record of your mortgage, if you have one.

Still, if Jason had any social media presence at all, we ought to be able to find data archived in backups, search engine caches, and IP tracking logs. The FBI has tools and expertise that make us smarter than the average bear.

I say, "We might be able to find evidence of him in any chat rooms or gaming sites where he couldn't erase his presence because he didn't have admin capabilities. Unless our potential Midnight Man is the developer or a high-level site administrator—then *he* could erase evidence of his teenage targets once he's done with them."

"Like you and Benedict figured with Derrick." He palms his chin. "I'd bet half my pension that son of a bitch is out there and managed to get his hooks in Jason."

"Only half?"

The corner of his mouth crooks up. "Half's not nothing." He shifts to face me full on. "I'm not saying I'm narrowing the investigation. I won't force fit what we learn to match our theory. But those tracks in the woods . . ." He touches his hands briefly to his eyes, then lowers them. His eyes are dark hollows. "Here's what's on my mind: The Midnight Man beat us at the Tremblay trial. The son of a bitch was laughing all the way back to his cyber hidey-hole. But not this time, Helen. This time we find him. He helped murder that boy's family; then he dragged the kid to his death. So we locate his trail online *and* we run him along the ground before he pushes another teen into murder. We find Katelynn and Daisy, and we arrest this creep and put him away forever."

"Amen," I say.

"If we're wrong . . . then worst case, we divert a few resources. Not from Katelynn. Or Daisy. Nothing changes in our search for them. CARD's on top of that. But if we *are* right, then Midnight Man won't stop unless we make him stop. This could turn out to be my last case. I want him in prison before . . ." He looks away. "Before."

Before the cancer kills him, is what he means. I rest my hand briefly on his.

I've heard from men and women who've been with the FBI going on ten, twenty years who say there are some cases you never get over.

Cases so brutal or weird or horrifying that they lodge under your skin like botflies, and—when you're least prepared—they burst out and drive you to your knees.

That's what this is for Clif. Probably for me, as well. This will be one of the investigations that years down the road still wakes me up at night.

The flight attendant, an older woman with a gentle expression that makes you want to ask for a hug, deposits our coffee on our trays, slips us some cookies, and moves on.

I peel back the wrapper and take a bite. Sugar bliss.

"Tomorrow I'll reach out to our Behavioral Analysis Unit in Quantico," I say after I swallow. "Until we know exactly what we're dealing with, we'll want input from four of the five units—child victims, targeted violence, violent crimes against adults, and cyber. We don't need the research unit at this point. BAU will pull a team together to assist CARD and Denver PD. I'll serve as point, coordinating their efforts with ours in Denver."

"You willing to attend the autopsies? They're scheduled for two p.m. tomorrow, and I'd like your eyes."

"What if I throw up?"

"You won't be the first."

I look for that gleam in his eye, but he's serious. I nod. "I'll be there."

Clif looks like he wants to hug me. Must be something in the air. "You'll create victimologies of Katelynn and Jason? That's more your skill set and BAU's. Cops are good at the facts but not always the subtleties."

I hear what he's saying: There aren't many PhDs in the criminal humanities affiliated with the country's police departments. We're a resource that rarely gets utilized within boots-on-the-ground communities. My job will be to assist BAU in developing what are essentially profiles of the Heath twins. Victimologies are the study of a person's life, routines, relationships, vulnerabilities. Who they were, what choices they made, what circles they moved in. We build victimologies to answer two questions: Why this victim, and why now? Sometimes the answers lie in the victim's habits. Sometimes in the killer's fantasies. Either way, the victimology gets us closer to the person who held the knife, or the gun, or the keyboard.

"You got it," I say.

"And I'm guessing you'll want to talk to Benedict. He's back at the college. I don't know if he's still in the profiling business, but he'll want to know about this. Maybe he'll be willing to help."

Miserable heat spreads across my chest. I haven't spoken with Benedict since he walked away from Colorado College and out of my life two weeks after the trial ended, heading into a years-long sabbatical. When he told me he was leaving, that he *had* to go, my fear of abandonment washed over me like a rogue wave. For a short time, rage submerged love. I hurled a bunch of lies at him. That I was bored with him and our relationship. That I'd been having an affair. That I didn't even like his *dog*—sweet Maggie, who loved everyone.

All the things you say to wound and only mean in the heat of the moment. Maybe Benedict believed me. Maybe he didn't. But our relationship was over.

Clif, of course, doesn't know any of this. And I'm a consummate professional. Nothing to see here. I smile and nod. "Of course. If Benedict is still under contract with the FBI, I'll speak with him."

"Appreciate it," Clif says. "Now, if you don't mind, I'm gonna catch a little shut-eye."

He crosses his arms and leans back. Within seconds his mouth gapes open and he's snoring.

I might have tried a turn at sleeping, but the mention of Benedict has poked the bear. I angle toward the window and peer out into a darkness broken only by the plane's wing navigation lights. My shadowy reflection gazes back at me.

Before his abrupt departure, I'd adored Benedict. I'd placed him on a pedestal because of his groundbreaking work, been honored to see our names appear together in scholarly journals. As a PhD candidate, I'd worked my ass off for him.

Worse, I'd believed myself in love with him and he with me. Our physical relationship began after I'd finished my degree, when a partnership was no longer forbidden. Over long dinners, long walks, and postcoital snuggles, we'd planned marriage and kids.

And then he'd left.

His sudden departure wasn't the first time I'd been abandoned by someone I loved, starting with my parents. Over the years I've toughened up. But with Benedict I'd so wrapped my future up in his that the idea of going on without him was like being shoved off a cliff. Thus, not long after he vanished into parts unknown, I left Colorado College as well, taking my college degrees with me to a job in Grand Junction's PD. Eighteen months in patrol, then work as a detective in training. After two years on the job, I joined the FBI.

The flight attendant comes by to take our trash. I close the shade and then my eyes. Scattered conversations fall away as people nod off.

I push away the memories. My feelings toward Benedict can't influence my approach to this case. The search for Katelynn and the risk of more deaths mean all personal feeling must be siloed. If Benedict can help, we'll bring him in. With luck he's still under contract with the FBI, which will make adding him to the team an easy process.

I want whatever is in his brain regarding this case.

At the Tremblay trial, Benedict provided a profile of the person he believed was behind the facade of the Midnight Man. The perpetrator would be male. A software and coding genius who believes himself above societal norms and who sees the concept of family as either hypocritical or repressive. Probably not long out of his own teenage years, he would understand teen psychology and have an ability to lure teens in by appealing to their longing to be seen and considered special. He would have a ruse—perhaps operating as an AI companion murmuring promises in their ears or maybe creating a game that would—over time—convince the teens that the world of the game was the one true world, and real-world humans were "non-player characters." Characters without will or agency. Certainly Derrick's suicide note implied as much. "This individual," Benedict wrote in his assessment, "the so-called Midnight Man, likely perceives himself as a misunderstood genius. He develops a game or crafts a narrative in which he's the master and his victims are expendable pawns."

I sit up and snag my go bag. I dry swallow two acetaminophen caplets, then take out the copies of the photos from the crime scene. I'm looking for anything that points toward or away from Midnight Man. But I'm also testing myself. I can't call myself tough if I keep throwing up over crime scenes.

Or at autopsies.

But right on schedule, as I examine the photos of the burned bodies of Andrea, Michael, and Eric Heath, the familiar headache blooms. My stomach twists.

I squeeze past Clif and barely make it to the bathroom before I hurl my literal cookies into the toilet. I flush, take some deep breaths, then wash my hands and face at the sink.

My reflection stares back at me: a somber woman whose face men find attractive and women reassuring. I appear calm, cool, collected—a magic trick I learned years ago.

But while we can manage our expressions, our bodies aren't machines amenable to our control. I take a paper towel and dab at the sweat that has formed between my breasts and under my arms.

Before I met with the therapist, I blamed my squeamishness on having spent my teens idolizing Jane Austen. I entered college as a liberal arts major focusing on literature of the Georgian and Romantic periods—Austen's refined world was as far as I could get from the squalor and violence of my childhood.

I had never intended to abandon the tranquil world of Jane's Hampshire villages.

But in my sophomore year, I found myself inexplicably drawn to Dostoevsky and Tolstoy. To criminology. Repressed trauma? Maybe.

All I know is that if you want to see God laugh, tell her your plans.

9

It's nearly midnight when I walk into my apartment in Boulder, but I'm too amped to sleep. Sitting cross-legged on my sofa, I force myself to again go through the Heath crime scene photos, looking for anything new. Michael Heath dead at the ruins of his desk. Andrea Heath lying at the bottom of what was once a staircase leading to the second level. Eric slain in his brother's bedroom.

A headache pulses behind my eyes. My stomach protests.

Get over it, I tell myself.

In some respects, murder scenes are much alike. The blood and the body. The wounds. The chaos. The loss of dignity in death and the imagined indignity of the victim at having their body displayed in front of law enforcement officials, the medical examiner, and sometimes the public. If the murder occurred at home, investigators see rooms where the owner didn't have time to clean up before company arrived. Dirty dishes, strewn clothes, water spots on the bathroom mirror.

Sharing in this loss of privacy feels like kicking a corpse.

I set the photos aside and log on to my work laptop. I spend a few moments gazing at Katelynn smiling in her online yearbook photo. She's a beautiful girl with clear skin, perfect teeth, long blond curls, and wide blue eyes. Her purple-and-white Ravens cheerleading shirt announces to the world that she loves her school and her role there.

She and Livvie are almost the same age, but their lives couldn't be more different. I can only hope that Katelynn has at least some of Livvie's toughness.

I set the laptop on the coffee table, wait out the headache and nausea, and then scrounge through the refrigerator. I give a small yip of victory when I find a two-day-old container of Chinese takeout. I scrape it onto a plate, nuke it.

At a sound from the corridor, I pause. There's a shuffling and then silence. I shrug. A lot of my neighbors are night owls. I carry the take-out to the couch, angle the coffee table closer, and read through the list of household items that have so far been inventoried by crime scene techs. There isn't much—pottery, porcelain, and metal are the things that survive a house fire.

I turn to the task of creating a list of questions for the people Clif and I will be interviewing as we build our victimologies of Katelynn and Jason. Using the online yearbook, I add a few names to the list of students, teachers, and cheerleaders the school will make available, along with the cheer coach. I study the reports Clif sent of Denver PD's neighborhood interviews. Everyone agrees: The kids were polite, especially Katelynn, who was frequently seen walking Daisy. When they were younger, the kids shoveled driveways or raked leaves for a few dollars. They had the occasional lemonade stand. Once they hit high school, they mostly disappeared inside. Too busy—the neighbors guessed—to interact.

The police reports are thorough and cover a decent geographic area. Nothing stands out.

I make a few notes for Clif's side of the investigation: Look for anyone the kids might have babysat for; check to see if there's a church they attended or a youth group, a volunteer organization, any after-school clubs. There are the senior center and the animal shelter where Katelynn volunteered. Officers should talk to folks there.

I finish the sweet-and-sour chicken and create a digital file so I can draft the victimology report.

In broad strokes, Clif and I will focus on seven areas during interviews: social isolation, depression and anxiety, the desire for connection, intense episodes of rage, confusion about identity, a high engagement with technology, and risk-taking behavior like driving too fast or drinking and using drugs. Once I can flesh out Jason's personality, I'll look for comparisons with Derrick. These comparisons may show commonalities that reveal how the kids were dragged to the dark side.

When I finish, I shut the laptop and stand. I carry my plate into the kitchen, wash it, and towel it dry. I wipe a smear of orange sauce from the counter, wipe down the rest of the counters for good measure, rinse the sponge. Sweep the floor. Only then do I pour myself a club soda and lean against the counter, glancing with a clean freak's satisfaction around the room.

I grew up in the chaos of my aunt and uncle's home, although my uncle moved out two years after Kevin and I moved in. The house was filthy, with weeks of newspapers and mail piled on tables, clothes dumped on chairs, the floor serving as overflow for empty bottles, paperwork, TV remotes, broken electronics. As an adult, being surrounded by neatness soothes me. My motto: a place for everything and everything in its place. I read somewhere that chaotic minds require external order to function. Which sounds true to me—my thoughts ping from one idea to another with the rapidity of a gambler dropping coins into the slot. My friends tease me about being anal retentive, but I prefer "organized." Every man I've dated must pass the organization test: Any underwear on the floor, a dirty plate left overnight in the sink, wadded-up napkins on the table, and the guy is out. I don't offer three strikes. I don't mind picking up after myself. I won't clean up after another functioning adult.

Maybe my rigidity is why I'm still alone.

It's 2:00 a.m. I'm tired but I know I won't sleep. I hesitate, then open the fridge and eyeball the bottle of wine left by a friend.

I owe it to Katelynn to be on my game by getting enough shut-eye. A slug or two of sauv blanc would help me sleep.

Instead, I shut the door and lean my head against it.

I got hooked on sleeping pills in college, and sometimes it's still a battle to sleep without them. But I will not be my parents—raging alcoholics, according to my aunt, who poured her own drinks with a generous hand. Nor will I be like my brother, with his pills. Our genes and upbringing suggest who we'll become. But it's not fate. If we're self-aware and stubborn, there's some wiggle room.

It's not that I don't drink. I'm just careful that it's not much and only for pleasure and always with company. I've made rules for myself. Lines I won't cross.

I push away from the fridge. Time to spend a few hours staring at the ceiling.

I'm heading to the bedroom when I again hear sounds in the corridor. More shuffling and what sounds like low weeping. With thoughts of the Midnight Man in mind, I pick up my service pistol and approach the door. I peer through the peephole, but no one is visible.

Leaving the chain on, I unlock and open the door.

Slumped on the floor across from my door sits a badly beaten Livvie.

10

After stashing my Glock, I open the door and lift Livvie up and into my arms.

"Why didn't you knock?" I ask as she clings to me.

"I thought you'd be mad."

"I am mad. You followed me, right?" My voice is brisk. A coach's voice. "You broke the rules. But you're here now." I peel her off so I can take a good look at her.

"Damn," I say.

"Yeah."

She's done with crying—I know the look. I lead her inside the apartment and to the bathroom. I gesture for her to sit on the counter next to the sink. Before I tackle her injuries, I have her down extra-strength acetaminophen from my stash. Then I grab a soft washcloth and antibiotic gel and gently begin to clean the blood, tears, and snot from her face. She has a split lip, a cut on her right cheek that fortunately won't need stitches, and the promising beginnings of a black eye. My years as a boxing coach have given me a good eye for what injuries require a doctor and which ones I can handle myself. Livvie will heal on her own, but she's going to feel a lot of hurt in the process.

As I work, I start with the most important questions from a security standpoint. "When did you follow me home?" The addresses of FBI agents aren't public information.

She flinches as I clean the cut. "A long time ago. I called a rideshare and tailed you from the gym. I just wanted to know where hotshot FBI agents live."

If Livvie thought she'd be impressed, she must be sorely disappointed.

"And tonight?"

"I took the last bus I could get. Then I walked." She pulls away enough to shoot me a look of pride. "I read in a spy book about running SDRs. No one followed me."

I hide my smile at her reference to running a surveillance detection route. The girl's got chops. But tonight the temps are in the twenties, and she's not wearing much of a coat. Hella tough, as she'd say.

"So no chance someone followed you here?"

An eye roll, then a wince. "I told you. SDR."

Okay. We'll have to make do with that.

I move on to the next topic of importance. "Who did this, Livvie? Your stepdad?"

"It was just a guy."

"A guy."

"A friend of Connor's. He wanted to get handsy."

Connor is Livvie's worthless older brother. "What's his name?"

"Roadie. That's what everyone calls him. I don't know more than that."

"Where was Connor while his friend was busy crossing boundaries?"

"Connor doesn't care." For a second she looks like she might not be finished with the tears. When you're sixteen, you want the world to love you. Especially the part that's related by blood. But she shrugs it off. "Anyway, they're gone. Connor's found a place in Loveland to crash. I came here because I just . . ." A hitch and suddenly she *is* crying. "I just needed someone. You know?"

I do know. I do. Seeing Livvie's injuries carries me back to my childhood, to the cruelty of my aunt, to how Kevin and I tried to protect each other. A maelstrom of pain rises in me, and for a minute, while Livvie shudders, I hold her again in the hug she should be getting from her parents. I don't make any false promises, like telling her it will all be okay. She knows better.

I finish patching her up, leave her to take a shower, then open the sleeper sofa. I get sheets and towels and make the bed. When she emerges wearing one of my oversize tees, I hand her an ice pack with instructions to apply it to her split lip for ten minutes on, ten minutes off, until she falls asleep.

"You can spend what's left of the night here," I tell her. "I'll drive you to school in the morning. If that friend of Connor's comes sniffing around again, call the police. I mean it. Then call me. If I can, I'll come get you." I'm thinking about the investigation and how little time I'll have. But I can't turn my back on her. I wonder how Kevin's life would be different if we'd had a caring relative or a mentor, someone besides an aunt and uncle with weak parenting skills and a love of the bottle.

After Livvie falls asleep, I pull on a coat, retrieve my phone and my Glock, then head outside, locking the door behind me. I can't rest until I'm sure no one is watching the apartment, maybe waiting for the lights to go out.

The night is clear and filled with stars, the wind plunging the temperature below the posted twenty-eight degrees. Wind batters the evergreen trees in front of the building; somewhere, a gate rattles against its latch.

My apartment is in a cluster of similar buildings, many of them inhabited by students who can't afford to live closer to the CU campus. It's often noisy and not terribly private, but I enjoy being around young people; their energy and optimism remind me of me, five years back. Plus, they don't ask a lot of questions.

Students are often out at all hours, but tonight the weather has driven everyone inside. Traffic is light, and even the dogs are quiet.

I make a loop around the buildings, checking alcoves, then return to the front of the complex and stand in the gloom of a large blue spruce. Across the street are single-family homes. No one appears to be lurking in the shadows. I'm about to return to my building when a glint of light catches my eye.

I wedge myself deeper into the concealment of the tree's branches and duck down so that I can see below the thick limbs.

At first my eyes don't pick out anything. Cones of light from the streetlamps illuminate sections of the sidewalk. In between, the darkness is total. I see nothing. But goose bumps rise that have little to do with the cold. Maybe I'm paranoid, but just because you're paranoid—

There! One of the shadows on the other side of the road shifts and briefly takes the form of a man before melting back into the darkness.

I scoot out from beneath the tree. If the man is Connor's friend and he followed Livvie, then a direct approach is best. It will likely scare him off. If it doesn't, well, that's why I brought my phone and a gun.

"Excuse me," I call across the street. I'm polite. After all, the guy could be just a man out for a stroll. Unlikely, but Coloradans are tough. Maybe there's a dog on a leash I can't spot.

A small, bright flash of light glints on and off. Phone? Smartwatch? Flashlight? I approach the sidewalk. The figure doesn't move; I can't tell whether he's facing toward or away from me. "Can I help you? Roadie, is that you?"

The wind gusts, blowing grit into my eyes from the sand laid down by plows on the road. In another day, if the snow holds off, the sweepers will come through. But right now, sand swirls in the air.

"Hello?"

I'm braced for anything. But the man-shaped shadow turns and slips down the street, mostly avoiding the pockets of light. He's almost out of sight when his passing triggers a motion-detector light. For a second he's illuminated. A tall figure in a parka, with long legs and narrow shoulders. He doesn't look back, and a second later he's vanished.

11

The next morning, after quizzing Livvie about Roadie's build—he ain't much of anything, she tells me, a shrimp with fists—I make her a quick breakfast, loan her one of my coats, and drop her off at school with a packed lunch and a reminder to call the police if Roadie returns.

I'm thinking about the man outside my apartment building. And those size 14 footprints in the snow in Ohio. Feldster had estimated those prints were made by someone weighing as much as three hundred pounds. If he's in good shape, he'll be broad shouldered and thick through the chest and thighs.

The man I spotted last night was more in the 180-pound range and just over six feet. Too tall to be Roadie. And none of my other current cases would lead to a stalker. Benedict said Midnight Man would rarely leave his lair. Ergo, it was nothing—just someone out for a stroll.

Half comatose from lack of sleep, I drive south with the largest coffee available to mankind sitting in the console next to me. It's gone in ten minutes, followed by an energy drink. By the time I hit metro Denver, I'm sparking like a lit match on gasoline.

Before going to the field office, I crawl along I-25 with a zillion other commuters until I reach southwest Denver and pop onto an off-ramp, a cork flying out of a champagne bottle.

The Heath home sits in the one hundred block of the Platt Park neighborhood. Realtors describe the neighborhood as quaint and charming, and as I drive into the area, I can't disagree. Abutting Washington Park's 155 acres of well-groomed grounds, Platt Park boasts its own green space, boutique shopping, and a decent number of coffee shops. I drive up one street and down another, getting a feel for the place. Homes are a mix of historic Victorians, Craftsman bungalows, and modern renovations.

The Heath home was one of the renos.

I park behind a mobile crime scene van and a patrol car and step out. The air is as thin and clear as glass, the wrought iron fence around the property sparkling with frost. My nostrils flare at the stench of burned wood and plastic hanging in the air. Bouquets wrapped in plastic are stacked in heaps in front of the lawn, along with sagging balloons and stuffed animals. A soggy cardboard sign reads, COME HOME, KATELYNN AND JASON!

Jason's death has been all over the media, but no one has removed the sign. It's only been a day, I remind myself.

Across the street, a single media van idles, puffing exhaust. Two people in the front seat sip coffee in cups from Stella's Coffee Haus. One of them gives me a wave, but neither makes a move toward the door. Probably figure I'm just another tech who will tell them, "No comment."

The "no comment" part is spot on.

I close and lock the SUV's door and yank my stocking cap down against the bite of the Colorado winter. I duck beneath crime scene tape, sign in with the lone patrol officer, and trudge up the snow-clogged driveway. From behind a screen of trees, the ruins of the house come into view.

Clay roof tiles lie shattered across the snow and ash, some driven deep into an icy runoff that's frozen into charcoal-gray streaks down the driveway. The remaining eaves are blackened and brittle, beams above the windows heavily charred or fallen. Jagged glass clings to the empty frames where the front windows blew out. The garage door hangs partially detached, its tracks warped and twisted from the heat. Shrubs along the front walkway are flattened—some burned down to stubs, others sealed under a crust of fire-extinguisher residue.

Police records show that firefighters arrived eight minutes, fourteen seconds, after patrol reported the explosion. They managed to save part of the home's north wing and garage. That's how we know about the blood-painted image of *The Scream*.

From the driveway, I note where each family member died—the walls are mostly gone and the locations are mapped by yellow flags. Michael Heath in the study, shot point-blank. Andrea Heath at the bottom of the staircase, also shot point-blank—the stairs are gone, but portions of the wrought iron railings remain. Eric, found in Jason's bedroom on what was the second floor, endured the same fate. I sense their surprise and terror all the way down in my bones. Imagine their voices.

Jason, what—? Jason, why are you—? Put down that gun!

And Katelynn. What did she see and hear? Did she go willingly with her brother? Or was she marched out at gunpoint?

And why take the dog?

I walk around to the back, where a rectangular yard stretches past blackened rosebushes and ends in a cluster of fir trees. The remains of a deck have crashed to the ground, the supports burned to nothing.

Two techs in Tyvek, face masks, and beanies are sifting through the rubble. Screened debris lies in piles on a flattened area on the lot's north side. Red flags pockmark the ground, indicating where items have been retrieved. I pick my way across the yard, stirring up drifts of snow and ash, and introduce myself.

One of the techs lowers her mask. "We've found only one personal item so far this morning." She's Black, petite, looks fresh out of college. She walks me over to a folding table that holds half a dozen pottery shards, two warped sauté pans, broken dishes with Christmas themes, an ammo can, and a photograph in a plastic bag; clipped to the bag is a paper identifying where the item was found.

The photo is curled at the corners, blistered along one edge where the emulsion has bubbled and peeled. Smoke has dulled the surface to a soft sheen.

"It was inside this military surplus ammo can," the tech says, pointing. "We found the can in the remains of the room over the garage—Jason Heath's bedroom."

"Anything else recovered from there today?"

"Just this."

I lean in.

The picture looks like a yearbook shot. It shows a pretty girl of eleven or twelve with black hair combed neatly and tucked behind her ears. She wears a ruffly purple blouse and a pleasant smile.

Her startling violet eyes, though, show an eerie watchfulness unsettling to see in a child. Psychopaths have the same look—observant but not emotionally engaged.

It's a predator's stare.

The same disconnected gaze showed up briefly in photos of Derrick taken months before he murdered his family. By the time of his trial, that look had been shattered.

I turn the photo over. On the back, blackened and barely visible, someone has penned the following:

DO a Macbeth!! Transform the shit out of the NPCs!!

GlitchDoll + Breaker + E = FREEDOM!!

See you in the RW!!

The message is encrypted, but I can make a few educated guesses. *NPCs* are likely non-player characters—scripted characters in a video game. If so, then *GlitchDoll* and *Breaker* and *E* could be gamertags or usernames. *RW* might stand for "real world." And *Macbeth* is almost certainly the ambitious Shakespearean Scottish nobleman, stepped in blood.

Both Jason and Derrick had mentioned turning their families into real players—people who recognize the game and participate in it.

DO a Macbeth!! Transform the shit out of the NPCs!!

My nerves shoot pinpricks over my scalp, down my neck, and across my shoulders; it feels like insects scurrying over my flesh.

Someone sent Jason this photo. And that means he wasn't alone. There are others out there.

Waiting to be stepped in blood.

———

Half an hour later, I arrive at the Denver field office on Eighty-Sixth Street, grab a breakfast burrito at the cafeteria before my stomach devours my esophagus, and then dump my coat and briefcase in the fourth-floor law library, where visiting agents often sit. While I'm eating, I make a quick call to Human Resources to confirm that Dr. Benedict Hoffman is still under contract as an expert witness with the FBI. Next I reach out to BAU Supervisory Special Agent Zane Samir, fill him in on the case, and inform him that Denver PD wants BAU's involvement. We schedule a meeting for tomorrow at 6:00 a.m. MST. It's the earliest Zane can pull the team together—he mentions Sara Seward and Jim Wokowski—and it leaves the rest of tomorrow open for the high school interviews. I know that by the time the team meets, every member will be up to speed on the investigation and will have already started their own contributions.

These days, there's no need for me to fly to Virginia. We'll use a secure computer and connect online via Microsoft Teams.

Once the meeting is set, I take the stairs to the third floor to talk to the CARD squad's special supervisory agent in charge, Mackenzie

McConnell. I find her down the hall from her office in a conference room. Four agents and analysts operate landlines and monitor ongoing events on computers. The mood is that of a beehive: everyone busy on their own task, but all coordinated by the queen. The queen is Mac McConnell, who is leaning over the shoulder of one of the agents and pointing to something on the screen.

This room is ground zero in the hunt for Katelynn.

I knock on the open door.

Mac looks up. "Helen!" she says. She finishes speaking to the agent, then joins me at the door. She clasps my hand briefly. "A pleasure to see you." Her smile is warm, if strained. I know every second that ticks by without any word on Katelynn adds to the weight she carries.

Mac and I have worked one case together—a girl kidnapped by her abusive father. By following the not-too-bright dad's trail of credit card purchases, we found the girl unharmed at a ranch house in Wyoming in under six hours. That easy case aside, Mac—now in her early fifties—has worked some tough ones. Her bright-blue eyes hold a faint haunting I recognize; it's a by-product of dealing with abused children. Despite what she's seen, though, I'd bet my badge she's never thrown up in the airplane toilet.

"I expected to see twice as many people working a case like this," I say.

She closes her eyes briefly. "A lot of people have been reassigned. We don't have the resources we used to."

It's a lament I've heard in other departments.

"Anything on the hotline?" I ask.

"Only the usual crackpots. No substantial leads."

The crackpots are those who crawl out from wherever they hide between each murder and rape and kidnapping. Most of them are desperate to help. All swear they witnessed something having to do with the case. All of them take time away from the real work. Part of Mac's job is to coordinate with the media—to use them to help in the search for a missing child. But the more press the case gets, the more crackpots emerge.

"Let's go to my office," she says.

Once there, she gestures toward a chair. We both sit.

"I'm bringing in BAU," I tell her. "Video call tomorrow morning at oh six hundred."

"Good. We need them." Mac swivels to face her computer monitor. She taps the keyboard and opens a file. "We've searched Platt Park and nearby neighborhoods with drones, K9s, and door-to-door. Now we're expanding the search and reaching out to people who know the family to see if they've heard anything. We have yet to talk to the kids' friends and classmates—I saw a note that you're handling the school interviews?"

"I am. With Detective Burgess."

"Excellent. As you're probably aware," she continues, "our Toledo office and the Sandusky County Sheriff's Office are handling searches in Sandusky County. Other law enforcement is searching the I-70 and I-80 corridors. We're sitting at sixty-plus hours since Katelynn disappeared. Jason's death makes things even more urgent."

I scoot my chair forward, eyes skimming down the file on the oversize screen.

Mac says, "I've issued an alert to our offices and other law enforcement agencies across the country. I'll continue to coordinate with the Cleveland office. I remember the Tremblay case even though I wasn't involved. Didn't Clif Burgess work it?"

"He did."

"Does he believe there's an online actor behind these new murders?"

"He thinks there's a good chance. So do I."

"The jury found differently five years ago." It's not an accusation but rather an invitation. Mac wants to know what I think.

I relax a little; I always appreciate the chance to talk to someone who's open-minded.

"It's true we didn't find proof of Midnight Man's existence," I say. "But all of Dr. Hoffman's research—and mine—points out that these days, kids are more influenced by online factors than by their peers. Derrick was a lonely, unhappy teen who spent a lot of hours online, which left him ripe for exploitation. In most ways, though, he was normal. No psychosis, no psychopathy. No head injuries or brain tumors. Nothing in the family's past suggested that Derrick had been abused. It's hard to imagine him coming up with the idea to murder his entire family without encouragement and a reason that made sense to him. I'm guessing we'll find the same is true of Jason."

"And Katelynn? Do you think she helped her brother?"

"Girls aren't usually impacted by online influences in the same way boys are, but there are exceptions. It's just too soon to know. I'm operating from the idea that both Jason and Katelynn are victims, but probably not in the same way."

"You think someone is holding her?"

"Hopefully, I'll know more after I talk to her friends and teachers." I pull out my phone and show her a snapshot of the photo with its cryptic message. "Techs found this in an ammo can in Jason's room."

She picks up a pair of readers, then takes my phone and zooms in, studying the girl and the message. "Interesting symbology."

"The ammo can? I agree."

"Macbeth showed up in Jason's suicide note. And the rest of these words—they sound like gamer terms."

"I've emailed these photos to BAU. Their cyber people will drill down."

She meets my gaze. "This message suggests there are others out there. Maybe connected through an internet game."

"I agree."

She returns my phone. "Send the photos to me as well, please. And thanks for the new information. We'll add online gaming communities to our on-the-ground searches."

She makes a few adjustments to the file; then together we review CARD's action plan. Satisfied that the search for Katelynn is in good hands, I return to the library, where I scarf down the second half of my burrito and start typing up Katelynn's and Jason's victimologies with the little I have so far.

An hour into it, an alarm buzzes on my phone.

One thirty p.m. It's time to head to the Denver Office of the Medical Examiner.

Already I'm regretting that burrito.

12

Thursday, 1:50 p.m. MST

The afternoon is blustery and grim, the western sky an ominous billow-
ing of clouds over Mount Blue Sky and Longs Peak. I park across the
street from the Denver Office of the Medical Examiner—a long, low
gray building topped with a bright-blue roof. I zip my coat and step
into the wind, waiting for a truck to rumble past in a fog of diesel fumes
before I cross the street.

Inside, I sign in and pick up a badge, then follow the hallway to
the autopsy suite. A glance through the windows shows Clif is already
here with the ME, Dr. Ella Torres. I recognize another man as Dan
Miller from Denver's crime lab. He's just pulling a face mask up over
his mouth and nose.

Before entering, I slip on a disposable paper mask from a shelf. A
wave of cool air, acrid with chemicals, washes over me as I step inside
the suite.

Clif waves me toward where he, Dan, and Ella stand near a gurney
slotted to the workstation in one of the bays. I bump fists with Dan and
nod to Ella, who is arranging items on a steel tray. We all know each
other from past cases.

A tech arrives and introduces himself simply as Boyd. He raises a
camera and gestures to Ella that he's ready. He snaps photos while Ella
unclips the red seal on the body bag, which is used to show that the

body has not been disturbed since being placed inside. She pulls down the zipper.

The smell of burned flesh is dulled by refrigeration and the fans—but it still hits hard. My stomach flips, and I take a step back, pretending to adjust my mask.

No one notices—all eyes are on what's left of Andrea Heath as Ella begins her external examination, speaking softly into a mic. She confirms the known facts—age and sex—and estimates others, like Andrea's height and weight before the fire. She mentions that the only bits of clothing left are the zipper on the pants and the underwires on the bra. She describes Andrea's injuries: the burn pattern and distribution, which is primarily to the face and upper torso. She notes charring and blistering as well as heat fractures to exposed bone.

I let Ella's calm recitation carry me along while the tech twists and bends as he snaps photos. I force myself not to just look at the body, but to study it, working to separate the once-living woman from the wreckage of her corpse. This was a mother. A wife. The owner of a company. A good neighbor, according to the elderly Mrs. Swanson. A woman who thought her kids should have a dog. These facts are more important than anything else. But right now, we're focused on what she can teach us through her death.

Ella pauses. She points Boyd toward something I can't see. She takes measurements. "Left lower quadrant shows a deep contusion, roughly ten centimeters in diameter—oval shaped, with associated muscle bruising."

"Could that have happened after her death?" I ask. "Falling debris?"

"No. EMTs found her dead before the explosion, and we have clear subcutaneous hemorrhaging. She was alive when this happened. Maybe only by minutes."

"Any speculation on the cause?" Dan asks.

"It suggests someone struck her. Or she ran into something." Ella continues her patient probing. "The angle of force looks downward and lateral."

"She was on her back, and someone struck her from above?" Clif says. "But why strike her instead of just—" He stops himself. "Could this bruise be from someone leaning into her? Maybe holding her down?"

"Pinning her with an elbow or knee." Ella's eyes meet Clif's over their masks. "It's possible. It's hard to estimate gunshot range without skin or clothing present. But we have a clean entry into the skull. I'll let you know more soon."

Ella continues her work. The only sounds are the fans, the shutter on Boyd's camera, and our own shuffles and soft coughs. As Ella finishes the external examination and starts the Y incision, my stomach remains settled. And again, through the high-pitched squeal of the industrial saw biting into Andrea's skull.

This isn't Andrea. This is a corpse.

An hour in, Ella says, "There's no stippling around the cranial gunshot wound in the surviving subcutaneous soft tissues. And no soot or scorching in the wound channel or on the cranial bone. This is consistent with a shot fired from at least two feet away. No additional cranial damage. Of course, any contusions or abrasions were lost to the fire. Your next step will be to check with the firearms guys in the lab. I assume they'll be running simulations." She straightens. "I need to take a short break."

Clif, Dan, and I confer in the hallway.

"That bruise *could* mean that someone other than the shooter was holding Andrea down," Dan says.

"Or," says Clif, "he pushed her down, held her there—maybe while reloading—then stepped up and away before firing. There's only one set of prints on the pistol, and those belong to Jason."

"Could be the second shooter wore gloves," Dan says.

Questions beget questions. It is always this way.

Dan's phone rings, and he excuses himself. I check the time. "Clif, I have to bail on you. I'm heading down to the Springs tonight to talk to Benedict. I'm already going to hit traffic."

He tells me to drive safe.

"You did well in there," he says as I walk away.

I give him a thumbs-up over my shoulder.

———

By the time I head out, the clouds have settled in, a lid on a casket, and a few flurries whip around me as I hurry to my car.

I've checked the weather report between Denver and Colorado Springs. Snow, likely heavy at times, with accumulations up to three inches. More like four or five inches on Monument Hill. Typical for January in Colorado. But the worst is scheduled to come in after midnight, and it's unlikely state patrol will close the interstate. Earlier, I called the college's English Department to make sure Benedict Hoffman is in town. With that confirmation, I've decided to risk the drive. I don't phone; I know from experience that asking for his help in person will be more effective.

Plus, the idea of ambushing him gives me pleasure. Which is why I phoned the college and not the man himself.

I pick up a latte—pumpkin spice, sue me—and tune the radio to a soothing and nondistracting medley of piano and trumpet jazz duets. I merge onto the gridlock of I-70, then into rush hour traffic heading south on I-25. Once I'm out of Denver and have cleared the worst of the traffic, I think about my upcoming meeting with Benedict.

Like me and Clif Burgess, Benedict is fascinated by the criminal mind, although we approach our work from completely different perspectives. He's a Jungian-based criminal psychologist whose work explores the intersection of crime, popular culture, and the humanities; that is, how art, literature, philosophy, religion, symbolism, movies, television, music, and history both reflect society's crimes and engender them. Given the popularity of true crime podcasts and shows—along with the need to attract students—it wasn't hard for Benedict to convince the trustees at Colorado College to create a cross-discipline graduate degree called the criminal humanities, which is parked somewhat awkwardly in the English Department. Benedict's particular focus is serial killing.

Benedict consulted on multiple cases where the intersection of crime and culture offered a twist to the more obvious interpretations of a crime. In one, he advised on a double homicide in Santa Fe. An art gallery owner and his female assistant were discovered naked, entwined, and stabbed to death beneath an erotic canvas vandalized with splotches of red paint. Detectives suspected the assistant's boyfriend. The young man had been overheard threatening the gallery owner to "keep his fucking paws" off his girlfriend. And his only alibi was that he could recount the plot of *Unfaithful*, which he'd watched alone the night of the murders. To top it off, the boyfriend's DNA was found on the assistant's body. But Benedict identified symbolic elements within the graffiti that echoed the controversial style of a disgraced artist who'd had a public feud with the gallery owner. Guided by Benedict's analysis, investigators questioned the artist, ultimately uncovering a meticulously planned revenge against the owner. The assistant was an unfortunate bystander. After the artist's DNA was found on the canvas, the man confessed.

While working on my undergraduate degrees in English literature and criminology, I caught one of Benedict's lectures on YouTube—"Just *watch* him," a friend had told me. "He's brilliant. And he's hot." Both were true. But I cared more about his intellect. Benedict's ideas on how specialists in the humanities can help law enforcement by offering new perspectives convinced me I'd found a way to unite my interests. When it was time to consider a PhD, I applied for Benedict's criminal humanities program at Colorado College. We became research partners. After I'd earned the PhD and was hired into the department, we became colleagues—then, in short order, lovers. Despite my worries for my brother and my still-churning anger with my aunt and uncle, life was pretty damn good.

Our final case together was *The People of the State of Colorado v. Derrick Tremblay*. Our attempt to apportion blame to a mysterious cyber agent made national headlines at a time when people had yet to appreciate the full risk of the toxic mix of social media, online extremist groups, and AI. Our failure also made headlines; we were dismissed as paranoid technophobes who'd spent too many hours watching films like *Ex Machina* and *Demon Seed*.

The radio pulls me back to the present, serenading me with tunes from *Together Again in the Studio*—a collaboration featuring Wynton Marsalis on trumpet and Marcus Roberts on piano.

As my headlights pick out the tumble of snow from a gray-black sky, I mull over my approach to Benedict. Will my former lover be intrigued? Or will he slam the door in my face?

More importantly, can the FBI find the Midnight Man without Benedict's help?

And there's this: How will I feel, facing him? What if, in some grim, haunted corner of my battered heart, I find I still love him?

That will, to borrow words from Livvie, straight up suck.

13

Thursday, 8:00 p.m. MST

By eight that evening, I'm standing outside McMillan's Chophouse, a bar and restaurant in downtown Colorado Springs. The air smells of wet asphalt and minerals, and it's cold enough that my gloved fingers have gone numb. Frost glitters like mica on the parking meters and windshields, and sounds from inside the restaurant are so faint, they might be from another planet.

I'd have as much fun hanging around in a meat locker. And yet I linger.

Undetected, I followed Benedict here from his office at the college a few blocks north. If he's kept his routines, he'll be sitting at the bar with a tumbler of bourbon and ice, weighing the hearts of various people as if he's the Egyptian god Anubis. He'll be ruminating over whatever cases he's working and pondering the wicked acts of men, particularly those committed by psychopaths.

Benedict accepts that brain abnormalities, especially in the paralimbic system of the brain, account for the poor emotional functioning of psychopaths. But he also believes in evil. Point him to the fMRI brain scan of a psychopath, and he'll tell you that our fate isn't predetermined. There are plenty of malformed brains; their owners don't generally torture and kill other humans for pleasure.

We used to argue constantly about the human brain, like two cows chewing over their cuds. *Take just one thing,* he'd say. *Scientists can't explain consciousness. Neuroscientists might have identified the brain activities that correlate with conscious experience. They might know where in the brain different emotions emerge. But they still don't understand the mechanics of complex emotions like aesthetic awe, existential dread, or moral disgust. And they can't explain self-awareness. How does neural firing give rise to awareness?*

Our brains consist of matter, I'd retort. *And physical matter must obey physical laws. It's just a matter of time before we determine how consciousness arose.*

Quantum mechanics? he would scoff. *And how do you explain God? How do* you?

Our discussions after making love were always my favorite, our disagreements traveling a worn and comfortable path. Our argumentative words held tenderness while our bodies pressed together in sheer animal satisfaction. He'd pontificate on Saint Augustine while his fingers slipped through the tangles of my hair, his eyes on mine.

I glance up when a car drives past on Tejon Street, wheels whispering through new snow. The night has grown colder as the hours march toward midnight. Across the street, a homeless man pushes an overloaded shopping cart, the wheels squealing in the gloom. I hope he's got a warm hidey-hole somewhere.

Go on in, a voice tells me. It's the voice of the man who mentored me in my earliest days at the FBI, Special Agent Woodford. Woodford acts like a drill sergeant, but underneath the starched shirts, he's a softy. Whenever he saw me shrinking from a task instead of leaning in, he'd bend down from his six-four elevation and offer some version of *Fake it till you make it, Belle.* Or *Never let them see you sweat. The guys here are just waiting for you to clutch your pearls.*

He'd laugh at the idea that it's his voice I hear when my own isn't enough.

I go down a short flight of steps, yank open the door, and step into a gloom that's barely distinguishable from outside. But it's warm, and the hostess gives me a bright smile, her face illuminated by a small light clipped to her lectern.

"I'm just here for a drink," I said.

"Sit wherever you like. And enjoy."

The small space is mostly empty of people. A few low conversations, the clink of cutlery, an aroma of buttery noodles and seared salmon. Benedict sits at the far end of the bar, his back to me, brooding over the liquid amber in his glass.

The mirrors above the glass capture his pale face in cool light. He's hardly aged. He still bears that distinctive, unconventional appearance: high cheekbones, a long face, wide-set eyes, and a slightly prominent nose. His height, aloof demeanor, and even his unruly black hair—now tinged with gray—give him an aristocratic aura. I once described him as Byronic to a friend: irresistibly dark and mysterious. Emily Brontë's Heathcliff without the rage and thirst for vengeance.

For the briefest of moments I imagine being back in his arms, knotting my fingers in his thick hair, tugging on his lower lip with my teeth, feeling his mouth on my breasts. Once again waking each day at dawn to pull him next to and then inside me.

Stop it, Belle, I scold myself.

The bartender is clearly smitten. She pauses to talk with him every time she walks the length of the bar; her smile is inviting, although he barely glances at her.

I lift my chin, cross the room, and take a stool two down from his. I loop my briefcase strap over the hook beneath the bar and cross my legs.

"Dr. Hoffman, I presume."

"I'm not in the mood for company," he says without looking up.

"Is that Four Roses Single Barrel? Or have you had to downgrade your top shelf since you stopped publishing?"

Sarcasm is always my first retreat. I'm working on that. But what I've said is true. In my quick perusal of works by Benedict Hoffman, there's a paltry list of four papers published over the last five years. A shocking dearth for a scholar. I'm surprised the college lets him get away with it.

He swivels his head slowly in my direction, catching my reflection in the mirror. I don't know whether it's my words or that he's finally recognized my voice. His smile emerges like the sun on a winter's day: bright but cold.

"Dr. Helen Belle," he says, his deep baritone laden with sarcasm. "I wish I could say it's a delight. What wretched *Felis catus* has dragged you to my doorstep?"

Benedict is fond of sprinkling his conversation with foreign words and phrases. I used to think it was an affectation, until I realized it's just how his brain works, flitting in and out of languages without conscious thought. There's a full set of encyclopedias between those two ears, written in more than one language. It was one of many reasons I fell in love with him. A walking cultural and literary data bank? Sign me up.

I order club soda with lime and tell the bartender to put the drink on his tab. She glances a question at him, and he waves a magnanimous hand. "Whatever the lady wants. As long as she's quick about it."

I expected this coldness. He has good reason. The things I said before he left. The times since when he's reached out and I've snubbed him. I own it.

It still hurts.

His voice is as I remember: deep, cultured, purely American yet carrying strands of Stratford-upon-Avon. Benedict's ancestors are French and Anglo-Saxon; maybe genetic memories twine through the timbre of our voices.

The bartender sets my soda in front of me, then goes to check on a couple sitting at the other end of the bar. I shrug out of my coat and remove my wool beanie, smoothing my hair with my fingers. I was heedless of my appearance in grad school, more interested in attracting attention for my ideas than my looks. These days I spend money on a professional haircut and a decent wardrobe.

I wonder how Benedict views me now.

I wait. His curiosity will get the better of him.

"So," he says after a few minutes of silence. "Did a twist of fate bring you here? Or did you seek me out?"

I hide my smile—curiosity killed the *Felis catus*. "The Midnight Man is back."

His face shows nothing.

I slide over to the barstool next to his. A slender man, he somehow takes up most of the room. He smells the same—of pipe smoke and cashmere. I draw in a breath and then must force away the memories. Being this close to him is almost physically painful.

"Do you want to know?" I ask.

He waves a nonchalant hand. "It's why you're here, isn't it?"

I lower my voice. "Seventy-two hours ago, the Heath family was shot and killed in Denver's Washington Park. Mother, father, youngest son. The home was set on fire and mostly destroyed. The seventeen-year-old son, Jason Heath—whose fingerprints were found on the likely murder weapon—and his twin sister, Katelynn, vanished the same night, along with the family dog. Cameras in the house and on adjoining properties were disabled prior to those events. Yesterday morning, the boy's body was found in a field in Ohio. The girl and the dog are still missing."

Benedict says nothing. I press on.

"Jason's death looks like a suicide. Except he wasn't alone. Prints in the snow suggest he was forced into the field where he took his life. His companion was a big man, six foot three or four. Between 250 and 280 pounds. Jason's suicide note is remarkably like Derrick's. And, like Derrick, he left a painting of *The Scream* in blood. It's the Midnight Man, Benedict. He's back. He forced Jason to kill his family, then strong-armed the teen into killing himself. We have proof now. Midnight Man is real."

Benedict closes his eyes. His face still reveals nothing. But his left hand drops to his thigh, and his fingers tap as if he's playing the bass line of a song. He's a pianist, and this imaginary keyboard is how he processes. I sip my club soda and wait.

After a moment, he opens his eyes and says, "I'm familiar with the Heath case. Hard not to be, given it's all over the news. I agree that the painting and the suicide notes are interesting. You could have a copycat. But it's not the Midnight Man. Even if he left his miserable lair and walked out into the world, he wouldn't take the sister. Or the dog."

"But he'd take the boy? To Ohio?"

"Possibly. He has no interest in being an actor in the real world. His power comes from the dark web. If he were to emerge, it would only be to ensure his operative isn't left alive—he's probably still in a rage about Derrick's failure to kill himself. Thus, if Jason Heath also refused to cross the final line, the Midnight Man might have allowed him to escape. But only because it would be safer to track him down and kill the boy elsewhere."

"Why Ohio? We're not even sure how Jason got there. He disappeared from his home and showed up some forty hours later in that field. Dead."

Benedict returns his hand to his glass. His fingers are long and graceful, nails clipped close. "Traffic cameras?"

"Police are looking."

"What kind of dog?"

"An Australian shepherd."

"Male or female?"

"Daisy. A female."

He sips his bourbon, sets the glass down. "Tell them it will likely be a panel van with dark front windows and an obscured license plate. If he did take Jason, that's how he'd hide the boy and keep him quiet."

"That's it?" I'm disappointed. "A van with tinted windows is pretty low-hanging fruit, Benedict. Used by killers and kidnappers the world over."

He glides right past my frustration. "But it's not him. He wouldn't take the girl and the dog. He's uncomfortable in the everyday world, and another teenager would be dangerous, the dog a risk—forty-five pounds of muscle with teeth and likely a strong attachment to one or both kids. Unnecessary distractions. Ergo, not our guy."

"What if he's ready to step out of the virtual world? Expand his horizons?"

"I doubt if the Midnight Man leaves his lair even to buy groceries. Only an emergency would force him out, and he wouldn't extend his time in the real world any more than he had to. Plus, what use would he have for a girl and a dog?"

"What use does any pervert have for a young woman?"

Benedict's eyes meet mine in the mirror. In the blue light, we look as pale and drained as a vampire's victims. Only our eyes are alive.

"Nothing you've said goes conclusively to the Midnight Man," he says.

"That should intrigue you." I open the camera roll on my phone and show him the photo the techs found in Jason's bedroom. I thumb to the next photo with its cryptic message. "The message was on the back of the photo. Does it mean anything to you? Do you recognize the girl?"

He thumbs back and forth between the two photos. His expression changes, shifting subtly to one I can't read. Detached to guarded, if I had to guess.

I wait. After a time he pushes back his stool and stands. "Shall we move to a booth?"

———

We order two baskets of sweet potato fries along with a beef-and-Brie appetizer and a second round of drinks. This time, I ask for a nonalcoholic Negroni. I glance at the weather forecast on my phone. Snowfall in Monument and Castle Rock. I'd enjoy something stronger, but the drive home is going to be hellacious.

Benedict eats while I bring him up to speed on the rest of what we know. I show him the crime scene photos and the handful of reports

Clif has so far pulled together. I manage to do this without looking at the photos. I did well during the autopsy, but why test myself? I want to enjoy the beef and Brie.

He goes through everything quickly, then once again more slowly while I sip my virgin Negroni.

"You did a walk-through of what's left of the Heath residence?" he asks.

I tell him what I saw. A once-nice home in an upscale neighborhood. A medium-size yard, but heavily treed—enough to shield the home from neighbors' eyes. A few intact walls, but mostly rubble and ash. "Tentative findings say the fire started in the kitchen, where there were two propane tanks. Now"—I push aside my plate—"what can you tell me about the girl in that photo? And the message?"

Benedict is silent for a long time after I stop speaking. He works his way methodically through the rest of his fries—something for his stomach, not his mouth. Finally, he tosses down his second bourbon, rattles the ice cubes, and leans back in his seat. Our eyes meet.

"I'm sorry you came all this way for nothing," he says.

I'm startled. "What do you mean? Surely you have some thoughts."

"I rarely consult these days, and only on certain kinds of cases. Your Heath family isn't one of them."

"Brutal crimes used to be your bread and butter."

"Not anymore."

"You've changed." I want to call him a coward.

"As people do."

"The girl in that photo. Do you recognize her?"

"No."

"And the message?"

"Gaming jargon would be my guess. It doesn't mean it's tied to the crime."

"With the *Macbeth* reference? Come on. You're bullshitting me."

"I'm only pointing out that not all coincidences carry meaning."

I push. "The FBI will want you for this case. And Clif Burgess specifically asked for you."

A softness plays momentarily on his face. "How's Clif doing?"

"He's fighting melanoma. Still." I toss out my pride. "We need you, Benedict. Please reconsider."

He closes his eyes again; when he reopens them, the softness is gone. "These days, once I complete my classes for the day, I consult on one-off cases, not serial killers. And I work with people who suspect their troubles are due to paranormal occurrences—ghosts, poltergeists, demons. I can help, in some cases, by showing them the line between the movie they watched when they were six, the nightmares that followed, a recent television show, and their current belief that Satan is lurking in their closet. My clients are happy, but taking on these pseudoscientific cases means my reputation has taken a hit. Skeptics accuse me of abandoning clinical rigor for metaphysical indulgence—of choosing demonology over diagnosis, and of allowing my childhood trauma to shape a professional theology of evil. Even if the Midnight Man is back, do you really believe I would be an asset to your case?"

"What childhood trauma are you talking about?" A memory loops into place like a reel of film. "Your vision of what you thought was a demon when you were six? *That* trauma?"

He looks down at the ice cubes melting in his glass. He looks almost embarrassed. "It was real."

"I never—"

He lifts a hand, palm out. "Regardless, if you're here for either my opinion or my help, the answer is no."

I work to keep my mouth from falling open. It's the last thing I expected from him. I figured he would leap at the chance to capture the Midnight Man.

Then a light flickers on. "You're afraid of losing again."

"The girl is almost certainly dead," Benedict grinds on. "Same for the dog. There's nothing to be done for them. And, as I'm sure you recall, our theory about some evil mastermind lurking on the dark web was thoroughly trounced by the good and honest prosecutors of Colorado and a jury of Derrick's peers. Maybe they were right. Maybe Midnight Man was our fantasy."

A stew of anger and disgust stirs in my gut. "You don't believe that."

"It doesn't matter what I believe. As I see in my clients every day, belief doesn't always reflect reality. Maybe you and I, because Derrick was once a normal kid and was never a psychopath, maybe we conjured the Midnight Man out of wishful thinking and the ether to explain what we couldn't. We might as well have accused him of being possessed. Maybe that would have been closer to the mark."

Our old argument. Evil or a broken paralimbic system? Satan or erratic neural synapses? But the raising of old ghosts doesn't bring me the intellectual pleasure it once did. I take a swallow of the Negroni and count to ten. "I'm not sure I like this new Benedict Hoffman."

"You aren't meant to. But I'm glad to see you've recovered so well."

"As if you'd know." Spoken like a true adult. I've moved on from sarcastic woman to pouty child.

But that softness appears in his eyes again, this time tinged—if I turn my head the right way—with regret. "You look good, Helen. The FBI agrees with you. You must be a hell of an agent."

"I like the work. But I also miss academia." And I do. I miss being locked away in the world of research, guiding and teaching eager students, sharing chats with my intellectually curious peers, safe from the politics and ambitions of the world outside the collegiate cloister.

I also miss working with Benedict. At least the old version. I'm not sure who he is now.

He drains the watery dregs of his melting ice. "Yes, well, you aren't missing much these days. It's all 'publish or perish' and be damned about the students and their education."

"You haven't published."

"You've paid attention. Even as you've shut down all my attempts to reach you."

"I was hurt."

"So was I."

"I still think of you as my mentor."

"Only that?"

"I—" I'm flustered. What is he looking for? "I *need* your help on this case."

"That's where you're wrong, Helen. You don't need my help at all. And that's a good thing."

The toxic brew continues to churn. My emotions are often scrambled when it comes to this man, but right now they're quite clear: I want to belt him. "Six years ago, three people died and Derrick went to prison. Now four more have died under almost identical circumstances. It's probably not a copycat, and it's definitely not a coincidence. Midnight Man has been grooming other teens. Jason is the latest, but there will be others. In five years. In five months. Tomorrow. We can't abandon them."

"We can't save them, either." He tips back, stretching his long legs beneath the table and laying an arm across the back of the booth. "I'll tell you a secret. I spent a year hunting for our killer. But Midnight Man, if he's out there, is too clever for us. We'll never find him. We'll never even be able to prove he exists. He knows all the ins and outs of the web's underbelly. The hidden highways, the tangled paths, the secret castles and haunted byways. He knows how to blaze a trail, build a virtual village, and then burn it down when he's done. I've landed a few other fish and turned them over to the authorities. But hunting the Midnight Man is a wild-goose chase with a wily, invisible, and—I will now concede—possibly nonexistent goose."

"I never thought I'd hear you admit someone might be cleverer than you."

For the third time—maybe it's a record—there's that softening of his expression, a look, almost, of sorrow. "I don't believe you ever understood me very well, Helen, even if you imagined yourself in love with me. I'm not quite the arrogant villain of your memories. At least, I hope I'm not. Anyway, I won't waste my time or yours." He gives his ice cubes a final swirl and sets his glass on the table. He stands and shrugs into his woolen coat and wraps a scarf around his neck.

Then he leans down. "Even so, I wish you the best of luck."

If I *did* give him a swift uppercut to the jaw, would the bartender call the cops?

Benedict straightens, turns up the collar of his wool coat, and then spins on his heel and strides away. I watch him push through the door and mount the stairs before he disappears into the dark.

14

Benedict sails away from the restaurant in long strides, wrapping the scarf tightly as night enfolds him. To his disgust, it's not thoughts of Midnight Man that carry in his mind, although that's what he *should* care about. And the missing girl, Katelynn. And her dog.

Dear God, how could you not love a girl who names her dog Daisy?

But what lingers in the moment is Helen.

The truth is, he's already spent too damn many waking hours on the ghostly demon that is Midnight Man. Sometimes, when he's calm, he thinks he's getting close—a mere few lines of code from exposing the beast to the world. On bad nights, he's Ahab hunting the white whale: destructively obsessed and thirsting for revenge.

And now Helen has dumped a missing teen in his lap. What can he do for Katelynn except wish things were otherwise and continue with the work he's already doing? For although he doesn't know the girl in the photo—he was truthful about that—and he's never heard of GlitchDoll, he suspects the *E* in the message stands for *Eidolon*. And he's seen Breaker's avatar in the birchwood. Which means finding the real Breaker might be a way into *Underland* and thus—he hopes, he believes—locating the entity calling itself Midnight Man.

Unless, of course, Breaker was Jason.

He stops walking and considers returning to the restaurant and sharing what he knows with Helen. About the game and where on the dark web it's located and why he's been strolling the soothing woods of *Eidolon* for so long in pursuit of his adversary. But doing so won't help the FBI find Katelynn. Indeed, the opposite is likely. It's why he refused her request. The feds could rough shoulder their way into *Eidolon* with crappy avatars and weak covers, and Midnight Man would nose them out like a bloodhound. He'd fold up shop faster than an eel blinking back into its hole and depart for another more remote, more secure corner of the dark web.

This time Benedict might never find him.

He continues walking, and his mind returns to Helen. Like searching for scar tissue and finding an open wound.

She's a reminder of a simpler time, when he was sure of himself and his place in the world. On the most basic level, he'd forgotten how beautiful she is. The elegant planes of her face, her aquiline nose, her thick auburn hair that settles on her shoulders in smooth waves. Her posture—straight spine, relaxed shoulders—that curiously suggests both a willingness to engage if you're interesting—and a holding back if you're not.

More than her physicality, though, Benedict has spent the last hour dealing with the fact that Helen's mind is as enchanting as he found it to be from the moment she appeared in his office doorway and told him she wanted to be a criminal humanist. At the time, a Monday afternoon a month before the start of fall semester, he'd been engrossed in a book about how evil in modern society has cloaked itself in righteous cultural wars. He'd glanced up, amused at the enthusiasm in this stranger's voice, then stopped, intrigued by the vibrancy of her presence. He stood and waved her in, offered her a seat. Twenty minutes into their conversation, he'd agreed to serve as her adviser. Four years and one PhD degree later, with an all clear from the department, he'd declared his love for her on bended knee, Lord Darcy to her Elizabeth. He'd even said, "'You must allow me to tell you how ardently I admire and love you.'"

And though he was ten years her senior, and though he believed many things she did not, she'd said yes.

Then came the Tremblay trial—and with it, an unraveling he couldn't begin to explain, not even to the woman he loved. The case had fractured his faith in meaning itself. He left Helen not because he stopped loving her, but because he no longer trusted the ground they stood on. If Derrick had acted alone, if there was no Midnight Man whispering poison into his ear, then evil wasn't orchestrated. The world was shaped not by forces of good and darkness, but by randomness, entropy, and human frailty.

After walking away from Helen, he returned to Mexico, to the small village where he'd once assisted Father Antonio. There, instead of miracles, he'd found mundanity. Great faith, yes. But also small minds trapped in the all-consuming concerns of grinding poverty. The only devil in the village was a member of the Cártel de Jalisco Nueva Generación. David Silvano was an obese thirtysomething smuggler with a penchant for beautiful women half his age. His crimes were petty when stacked against the evils of the cartels. He drank coffee he never paid for, pursued young women with cruel—if empty—threats of rape, and roughed up the locals when the mood struck. Silvano's cruelties were woven so deeply into the fabric of the village that no one protested. Evil was as cheap as fifteen pesos for a *café* and as banal as the wind.

So Benedict kept running. He'd hiked into the mountains of Jalisco to camp and meditate. Alone in the forest, cross-legged in the damp hush of pines, his mind returned to the *thing* he'd seen in his mother's garden. A presence, crouched among the roses like a panther. The air had soured around it, the grass turned brittle and brown, and the petals blackened where it passed. It hissed at him—not like an animal, but like steam escaping from an underground fissure. He'd screamed for his mother, and the thing vanished. But it had left a darkness behind, thick and listening. A darkness that remained with him as he grew older.

After three months, he packed up his few belongings and hitch-hiked around Mexico and South America before returning to Colorado.

Helen was long gone and refused to take his calls. Another door shuttered. Another loss.

These days he keeps his head down. He still has his faith, still attends mass, although not with the frequency he once did. He enjoys his students and teaching. Walking Maggie. Counseling the occasional client. He can't say he takes pleasure in his work unmasking bad actors who prey on teens. But it's satisfying.

And he still, apparently, has feelings for Helen. A woman who feels nothing in return.

"Bad luck, old fellow," he says aloud in his best Darcy accent.

A cat mews from the darkness as he passes in front of the Colorado Springs Municipal Court building, the site of the Tremblay trial. Benedict pauses, glancing down the length of the paved courtyard, searching for the source of the wail. A human figure unwinds itself from the shadows and approaches, footsteps trudging through the new-fallen snow. Local streetlamps cast a blue glaze.

"Spare some change?" the man asks. "My car broke down and—"

"Stop," he says. "Save your story."

He takes in the hunched figure clad in a thin layer of filthy clothes, the man's breath frosting in the bitter temps, his entire body shivering with cold. The man—a kid, really—can't be more than twenty. Another soul trapped by the ravages of fentanyl or benzos or Tranq. Whatever poison has dug its claws into his brain and now holds it prisoner.

"You should get off the drugs," he says. There is no shaming in his voice. Only sorrow.

"I know, man. I will." The man stares at him.

The cat mews again. It's a kitten tucked into the pocket of the man's threadbare jacket. Two lost souls on a winter's night.

Benedict reaches into an inside pocket of his own warm coat and retrieves a gift card for a nearby all-night diner, Mary's. He keeps a supply on hand for occasions like this, a holdover from the days when he believed every soul could be saved. A belief he still wants to carry. He presses the card into the man's hand as Helen's words flash—apropos of nothing—in his mind: *The girl and the dog are still missing.*

"Get something to eat," he says. "And make it last. Mary won't kick you back into the cold, but someone else might."

The card disappears into the same pocket as the kitten. The man sways. Benedict doesn't need to see his eyes to know they're drug-induced pinpoints. Maybe it doesn't matter where evil springs from. Spend any time among addicts, and you'll not wonder again whether evil is real: It has swept them off a cliff.

"Come on," he says. "I'll walk you there."

"That's cool, man." He's still staring at Benedict. "Do I know you?"

"Not unless you're a student at Colorado College."

The man makes a sound that could pass for a laugh.

They shuffle through the snow along Tejon Street. Benedict considers, then dismisses, giving the man his cashmere scarf. He would only trade it for drugs.

They stop beneath the neon glow of Mary's Diner. Light pours through the windows, etching rectangles of gold onto the sidewalk. The aroma of eggs and bacon and coffee drifts out along with the swell and fall of voices. Someone has chalked "St." in front of "Mary's" on the operating hours posted on the door.

"I *do* know you," the man says. "I saw you in the newspapers. You're that mind whisperer, aren't you?"

Benedict frowns. Apparently he can't escape the Midnight Man tonight. He's heard the nicknames the media gave him from the times he consulted for the BAU. Scholar of Shadows. Dean of Darkness. Professor Profiler. The nickname he most hated was the Apologist. As if he'd suggested that Derrick Tremblay wasn't guilty of murdering his parents and brother and shouldn't serve time. Derrick had committed murder—no question. Benedict—and Helen—had simply wanted people to know that a real person had whispered to a vulnerable teen through his laptop, convincing Derrick that he would be a hero for awakening his family from their false existence.

And if the Midnight Man could draw in someone like Derrick, he could draw in your son or daughter, too. *That* had been Benedict and Helen's most important message: *He's coming for your children.*

"I thought you were right," the man says, shuddering. "Evil lives on the internet."

"You've confused me with someone else," Benedict says. He opens the door to the diner and gestures for the man to enter.

"No, it's cool, man. You were right. Can't trust the internet. It's all demons and shadows."

The man steps through the open door into the small foyer. "Demons and shadows. Be safe out there."

15

Thursday, 11:59 p.m. EST

Shelby Reed of Columbus, Ohio—sixteen years old and filled with rage at everything except her dog, Boo, and her fellow gamers—closes the door to her bedroom and hooks a chair under the handle in case her parents surprise her. She boots up her laptop, masks her IP with a layered proxy chain, and lights up her gaming client. A few encrypted handshakes later, she's in *Eidolon*.

She takes a deep breath, lets go of the anger, and rests her fingers on the keyboard.

Idling in the lobby, she hesitates.

Should she visit *Eidolon*? Maybe even journey all the way to *Underland*? Or go somewhere darker?

"What do I want today?" she asks QuWu, the Labubu doll propped on the desk.

QuWu, of course, doesn't answer. Just stares back with her big eyes and serrated teeth. Shelby turns her head to check her own reflection in the full-length mirror. Brown hair dyed black. Black shirt and cargo pants. Smudged eyeliner and foundation pale enough to look like she pinched it from a mortician. A nose piercing that earned her a monthlong grounding.

Her former good-girl self is gone. Her new self feels like a costume she's borrowed—ill-fitting. But also thrilling. Who is Shelby Reed, really? It's a question she asks herself, like, every fifteen minutes.

She returns her attention to the screen. Considers.

She can almost hear Midnight Man's voice: *Who are you, Shelby? What do you want?*

Months ago, not long after she developed an obsessive fascination with psychopaths and serial killers, she fell in with the 764 group. At first it felt like a joke. Just a bunch of kids pushing limits, being cruel for the sake of it—shitposting because they could. She mostly lurked. Laughed when the others did. Watched as they shared memes that got uglier, darker, more violent. One post in particular stuck. A girl Shelby didn't know, badly photoshopped into a disgusting meme. Shelby didn't create the post. Didn't comment. Didn't share.

But she "liked" it.

Later she found out the girl had tried to kill herself. Maybe she even succeeded. Shelby is too afraid to ask. But now, when her mom nags about homework or cleaning her room, it all feels irrelevant. Trivial. Like a child's game she's too old to play. She finds relief in *Eidolon*, with its promise to cleanse her soul.

She taps the keys and relaxes in the glow of the screen, settling into her character, Nocturne2Blue. This early part of *Eidolon* is soooo peaceful. Her character explores a trippy landscape of floating islands, talking animals, and ruined temples overtaken by vines and spirits—places that hint of a world lost long ago. The landscape and music remind Shelby of her favorite Ghibli movies. She loves the mood of loss followed by restoration and transformation. And she loves the nonviolent gameplay that seems designed to inspire contemplation—freeing trapped spirits, returning stolen artifacts, offering the food she gathers to NPCs.

There are edgier tasks like collecting arrows or cleaning her gun—tools she'll need in *Underland*. But Shelby isn't fond of these duties—she prefers picking berries and sharing them with others, earning credits for her full baskets.

Other players are in the game, too. Some are NPCs—you can tell by how they rush around doing the same tasks over and over, always in a hurry for reasons they can't explain. Sometimes, if you're feeling a little brutal, you can help them ascend. But ascension mostly belongs in the other half of the game. In *Underland*.

Some of the avatars are real players—part of her small network. Braveh3art and Goliath. Blackbox. A few others. Most of *them* no longer linger in *Eidolon*. They rush on to the game's dark half.

Shelby loiters. She should be moving faster. She knows this.

StreetSage has told her not to be afraid of death. "It's as Plato wrote in *Phaedo*. After our bodies are gone, our souls are free of the simulation that binds us, that blinds us. Death is a gateway. It opens our eyes, Nocturne2Blue. Allows us to see and experience what is real."

"Then why are you still here?" she'd asked.

"I'm not." StreetSage offered a smile emoji. "I speak to you from outside the simulation."

"Dude," she'd responded. "That makes, like, zero sense."

She jumps when the encrypted message board lights up.

NEW PRIVATE MESSAGE FROM: MIDNIGHT MAN

At first Shelby wasn't entirely sure whether the game master was a who or a what. A person or a character chatbot. Or how much power he has over the game. But now she knows at least part of it. He's real. She's seen him at night in the woods; his great size makes her think of the Paul Bunyan story she loved when she was a kid. "Where's your blue ox?" she asked when they met.

And the next day, a blue ox had appeared in *Eidolon*. Which means he can alter the game. Midnight Man was telling her that in his world, she has a voice. He can be harsh sometimes, but he always has her best interests at heart.

Eagerly, fearfully, she opens the thread and types:

> hi

MM: You're quiet in *Eidolon* this afternoon. Long day?

Shelby smiles. Midnight Man understands her. He cares.

>its all the things. mom's mad again. says I talk back but I'm just trying to explain

MM: That sounds exhausting. Trying to be heard by someone who's already decided who you are.

> she says I have an attitude problem. She's sending me to a new therapy that uses video games. But I don't need therapy. I have u

MM: People get scared when you stop playing the part they wrote for you. They're afraid you'll break free of their control. They don't see how they themselves are trapped.

> she thinks I'm broken. what if she's right?

MM: Don't censure yourself! We've talked about this. You're not broken. You're thinking for yourself. That's not a flaw—it's growth. You're becoming who you really are, who you're meant to be. You're starting to ask questions. You're noticing the cracks. That's when people wake up.

> I'm not the only one who sees it right?

MM: You're not the only one. You have me. A few others in *Eidolon*. But you're the first in your family. The first among your friends. This makes you very important.

> so what happens now?

MM: Now you wait. Let the noise die down. Watch. And Shelby? Don't be afraid of Underland. That's where you'll grow. That's where you'll learn how to help others. You need to spend more time there. Then you'll know when it's time to act. And when it is, I'll be there.

> promise?

MM: I promise. I'll be there. You won't have to do anything without me.

> thank you

MM: That's what connection is, Shelby. You reached out. I reached back. Now we have each other.

> you always know what to say

MM: That's because I actually listen. Not just to what you say. To what you mean.

> wish you were here already

MM: Soon. You're not alone. You never were. You just needed someone who sees the real story. Who knows the real world.

And that world, Shelby?

It's just the beginning.

16

Friday, 5:45 a.m. MST

More than an hour before the sun will rise, I join Clif, who is waiting for me outside the guard shack at the FBI field office. The snow has stopped, and the sidewalks have been cleared, snow piled in drifts along the fence. The air is as sharp as broken glass.

I'm ten minutes early. Clif has probably been standing in the cold twice that long.

He studies my face in the light from the security building. "It didn't go well with Benedict last night?"

"Like being bitten by a rabid raccoon."

"That good?"

"Worse."

I walk him through security, across the courtyard, and into the lobby, where he signs out a visitor's badge. I escort him first to the cafeteria for coffee and then upstairs to our computer room.

There, I apologize and excuse myself to use the bathroom down the hall. Alone, I brace my hands on the sink, take a few deep breaths, and will my heart to slow.

I'm suffering a Benedict hangover—good for a few pokes to the ego—and the jitters from last night's harrowing drive home on an icy highway, then back to Denver this morning. Courage is a suit I don from time to time, but it always ends up back in the closet.

At least I don't have to worry about still being in love with Benedict. He's not the man I knew. My heart would break if it hadn't shattered long ago.

What I want at this morning's meeting is reassurance from BAU that Clif and I should continue pursuing the Midnight Man angle. I'm about to hear the opinions of professionals I trust and value and who will have already reviewed the facts of the case. What they think matters.

I take another breath.

This morning is about Katelynn Heath, wherever she is. And Derrick Tremblay. A seemingly good kid turned—over a period of weeks and months—into a mass murderer. Patricide, matricide, fratricide. Familicide.

It's something out of a Greek tragedy.

We have some idea what pushes these teen killers—a lethal combination of narcissism, rage, fantasies about dominance, and sexual insecurity. Add in factors like cyberbullying, high rates of anxiety and depression, hormones, and feelings of helplessness in an enormously complicated world, and you have a bunch of teenage and twentysomething time bombs sitting around, fuses primed, waiting for someone to come along with a match.

Derrick might have had all the usual ills found in unhappy teens. But his turn toward violence had required a shove. Someone or something had yanked him out of what should have been his life: school sports, robotics, chess club—whatever stoked his interests. Girls and parties and getting his driver's license. Eating pizza and watching movies and gaming with friends.

In Derrick's written answers to psychological questioning, he suggested he'd been aiming for heroic redemption. Instead, he'd ended up slaughtering those who loved him best.

I check my watch.

Showtime.

———

I'm surprised to find a woman in a gray skirt and matching jacket chatting with Clif when I return. She rises, tall and willowy, and offers her hand.

"Agent Belle," she says in a warm voice. "I'm Elaine Carr with BAU Three."

Crimes against children—I've heard her name. Carr is in her late forties. She has caramel-blond hair worn in a sleek updo and a gentle expression that probably serves her well when she's interviewing violent offenders. No doubt the killers and rapists she deals with underestimate her.

But Carr's got a reputation for directness and a refusal to compromise on behalf of any child. She holds my hand for a moment after we shake, and I wonder whether she's heard I'm also a hard-ass. I feel—in the pressure of her fingers—that we understand each other.

Elaine goes down in the plus column.

"I flew in yesterday to meet with Mac and the CARD team," she says. "I hope it's all right if I join you this morning. It's been a pleasure chatting with Detective Burgess."

"Clif," he says with a smitten smile.

"I'm glad to have you," I say. "We'll take every good agent we can get."

We sit. Elaine has already logged us on to Teams, and other agents from BAU pop onto the screen. Two men and a woman.

I recognize Supervisory Special Agent Zane Samir, the unit chief for BAU Three. Early fifties, tall and trim, with deep-set brown eyes. Zane and I met during my training.

"Helen, good to see you again. And good morning, Elaine."

The other two people on the call identify themselves: Sara Seward from BAU Two and Jim Wachowski with BAU One. Counting Elaine, we have almost the full complement of the four Behavioral Analysis Units. I introduce Clif as the lead detective on the case.

Sara is in her mid-thirties. She looks black Irish with her olive skin and raven-dark hair gathered into a casual bun. She has emerald-green eyes and a no-nonsense demeanor. BAU Two is the cyber and counterintelligence unit, but Sara—save for the oversize teal glasses—looks nothing like the stereotypical computer geek; I scold myself for thinking in clichés. When I pulled up her profile, I saw that she's a digital forensics examiner with degrees in information systems security and twelve years of experience solving cyber-related crimes as an FBI agent. Because of all the certifications she's received to stay current, Sara has more acronyms after her name than the alphabet has letters.

BAU One is targeted violence. Counterterrorism, arson, bombings. Jim is in his early fifties with a surprisingly cheerful manner, an extra chin, and a circle of trimmed hair that turns his bald pate into a monk's tonsure. His tie is spotted with what looks like coffee stains, and there's something that might be ketchup on his polo shirt. But I know that a keen intelligence lies behind his careless facade. Jim, like Sara and Elaine, has an impressive track record.

Zane tilts back in his chair and steeples his fingers. The wall behind him is filled with photos and plaques, the "ego" wall. But a closer look reveals more shots of his family than famous politicos.

"I've brought together this small team for our first briefing," he says. "Helen, we've all read the materials you forwarded from Detective Burgess as well as the Tremblay trial transcripts. Two teenage boys, two families, six years apart. Two massacres nearly identical in execution. Two similar suicide notes, including a reference to Macbeth. And an apparent fascination with Munch's painting *The Scream*. Do you have any new information to include?"

With Clif's help, I summarize Jason Heath's suicide in Ohio and the ongoing search for Katelynn from law enforcement's perspective—CARD will continue to take the lead in coordinating the search, and Elaine adds a few details from her conversation late yesterday with Mac. Clif handles Zane's questions regarding the autopsy reports—the bruise on Andrea Heath and the slight but real possibility that maybe someone else was involved in the killings.

Clif pulls a report from his briefcase. "A couple of things. The metadata on the family's emails has come in. Still waiting on content. And I received a report late last night from the Colorado Division of Fire Prevention and Control about the explosion that destroyed the home. The Heaths had a Wi-Fi-enabled gas range—a newer model that can be turned on remotely via app or smart home hub. We accessed the data from the service, which shows an activation command at the time of the fire. There were two twenty-pound propane tanks in the kitchen, valves partially open. We don't know who brought the tanks in. The cracked valves let gas slowly fill the room over a period of hours, presumably from the time Jason and Katelynn departed the house. Once the concentration was high enough, someone activated the gas stove remotely, triggering a small electric arc from the igniter system—just enough to ignite the propane-air mixture."

He pauses, takes a breath. "It took eight minutes, fourteen seconds, for firefighters to arrive, with inclement weather and traffic congestion slowing their normal response time. Investigators believe the explosion wasn't designed to level the house—just to complicate the timeline. The timing was a calculated delay, not an accident."

"This is a level of sophistication way past the fire in the Tremblay house," Jim says.

"The Tremblays didn't have smart home technology," I point out. "Although it's worth noting that both fires used a gas range as the mechanism. It's another link."

"Clif, can you forward that report to me?" Zane asks.

"Just as soon as I'm back in my office."

Zane types something on his laptop, then looks up again. "Helen and Clif, as I said, the four of us reviewed the transcripts from the Tremblay trial. And we've looked through your reports, Clif. The three of us here in Virginia agree that, based on details of the current case, your theory about Midnight Man is well worth pursuing. Elaine, I believe you're also on board with this theory?"

"I am. One question, though." She pivots toward me. "What did you and Dr. Hoffman find regarding peer pressure on Derrick? I didn't see anything in the files."

"Because there wasn't anything. We initially thought we'd find evidence of another teen acting as Derrick's partner. We used the example set by the Columbine High School shooters. The relationship between Dylan Klebold and Eric Harris is often cited as a textbook case of how a vulnerable individual can be pushed into violence by a peer or mentor with true psychopathic traits. Harris was manipulative, remorseless, callous. Dominant. Klebold, in contrast, was emotionally troubled, depressive, and dependent. Much like Derrick. But Klebold wasn't violent until his path crossed with Harris's. Similarly, in interviews with Derrick Tremblay's teachers, coaches, and a therapist whom he saw in the month before the murders, Derrick was considered pitiable, not alarming."

"So, with no peer, you looked for a digital predator."

"That's right."

"What about an online network?"

"We didn't find evidence of that, either," I say. "Although the photograph recovered from Jason's room suggests he wasn't alone. Someone sent that photo. And GlitchDoll and Breaker might be gamertags."

Elaine's gaze goes to the middle distance, and her expression downshifts into grief, as if she's staring into a dark room. "Sadly, it's not as rare as we would like for teens to murder their families and themselves. But killing their parents is usually a preliminary to committing mass murder elsewhere, such as a school shooting. Derrick and Jason and their unseen manipulator seem to have focused solely on the families."

"Dr. Hoffman and I believe that our manipulator likely harbors a profound resentment toward the concept of family, possibly rooted in personal trauma such as abuse, neglect, or abandonment."

Zane tucks his tie into his jacket and leans toward the camera. "From a societal perspective, the Midnight Man might view the family as a symbol of hypocrisy or weakness. Or he could see the family as a tool of the bourgeoisie to maintain class inequality through property inheritance. Either could drive his desire to destroy it. Kill the cells to kill the cancer."

"Don't forget Batman's Joker," Jim chimes in. "Some people just want to see the world burn."

The faces in the chat room are bleak.

Zane's gaze goes toward the ceiling. Almost a full minute ticks by while we wait. But all he says is, "Sara, you've got your work cut out for you."

She looks more excited than dismayed. "I spoke yesterday with specialists at the Rocky Mountain Forensic Computer Lab who are helping Denver PD on the case, thanks to Clif's request. Harry Sullivan is my contact there. Harry and I've agreed that I'll focus on analyzing Jason's online history. Gaming forums, private chat rooms, commercial messaging apps. I'll look for coded messages and pay special attention to anything that reveals patterns of coercion. Helen, you're right that GlitchDoll and Breaker sound like gamertags. In the gaming world, *RW* can stand for 'real world,' especially in role-playing games. Usage depends on the context. A device at the Heaths' residence regularly communicated with TOR network servers, which could be legit or could mean someone in the home was accessing the dark web." Her glasses have slid down her nose, and she pushes them back up. "Was Derrick a gamer?"

"An avid player," I say. "According to his former friends. But that, too, was part of his behavioral change. He stopped gaming with his pals. We don't know if he stopped playing entirely."

"Maybe he moved over to the dark web." She glances down at something on her desk. "In the boys' suicide notes, they mention that their families are no longer blind. They've become true humans. It makes me think of a concept we see in gaming. Non-player characters, or NPCs, are just pieces of code. Their function is to populate the world for the real players. If Derrick and Jason had developed a distorted sense of reality, they might have dehumanized their own families. A skilled manipulator might convince them that the only way to make their families active and 'real' is by killing them, thus allowing them to move to the next level and become actual players. Meaning that Jason, like Derrick, might have believed we're trapped in a false world. A simulation. Killing someone frees them. In a weird way, it's the same idea held by many religions—that death ushers us to heaven."

"Or the opposite," Elaine says archly.

"To this day I find it hard to believe anyone buys into that simulated-reality *Matrix* crap," Jim says.

Zane laughs. "Right. Maybe we should stick with people who believe we're ruled by reptilian overlords."

Jim joins in the laughter, but he looks pained. Violence generated by crazy conspiracies is his bread and butter. Maybe he's not sure whether to laugh or cry.

Sara laughs as well but then says, "You'd be surprised, Jim. Some brilliant people are fully on board with the simulation hypothesis. Including Derrick, right? At least at the time of his trial."

Clif and I nod, and Sara continues: "For some people, there's a near one hundred percent probability we're in a simulation."

I regard Sara with appreciation even if I don't buy the hypothesis. "Why do you think the cyber experts never found evidence of a game?"

Sara waves a dismissive hand. "Doesn't mean much, honestly. A game can be made to look like encrypted chats or background noise. And games in the dark web can be especially difficult to penetrate. Unlike on the surface web, sites aren't indexed by conventional search engines. You must know the exact URL, which is typically a long, randomized string of letters and numbers. On top of that, game administrators can change links if they decide it's necessary—and you've got to be in the know to access the new URL."

Sara talks fast, and I hold up a hand. "This brings up a question. If the teens bought into a simulation hypothesis, perhaps encouraged by the game, does that mean Midnight Man also believes the theory and he's 'helping' these families? Or is he a deeply sick man who—as Jim said—just wants to see the world burn?"

"We don't have enough information to answer that," Jim says.

"Not yet," I agree. "Just wanted to bring up the question. Sorry to interrupt."

"Not a prob," Sara says. "I'd also like to touch on the artificial intelligence angle. This sounds even crazier than lizard men, so bear with me. I've been hearing a lot at AI conferences from hobbyists who believe that humans have been infected with what they call a mind virus. This virus makes people irrationally attached to biological life versus bonding with more perfect AI beings. Those untouched by this alleged virus believe artificial intelligence can and should replace biological reproduction with digital offspring—AI babies that are more intelligent and evolved than human children."

Jim scowls. "AI *what*?"

"Babies. Artificial beings created through code. They will guide us mere mortals to a better future."

"Or replace us." Jim looks dubious. "I'll stick with my lizard men."

Sara laughs. "This goes back to what you just mentioned. If you want to see the world burn so you can create something better, start by destroying human families and creating digital ones."

In the warm shelter of the FBI office, gooseflesh prickles my skin. I glance at Elaine. "You've heard of this?"

She nods. "Transhumanist cult."

"I feel like I just landed in Oz," Clif says.

Zane smooths his tie and leans forward into the camera frame. "We have lots of potential avenues to pursue. If we operate under the idea of an online influencer—and we all agree we should—then understanding Jason's motivation is crucial in finding other teens who might have fallen under Midnight Man's spell. Which"—he glances over at Jim—"gets me to my next point. We need a case link analysis to see if there have been other events like the Tremblay and Heath families."

"I've already started," Jim says. "I put out a ViCAP alert before I left work last night, and we've already got something."

He has our undivided attention. The Violent Criminal Apprehension Program maintains the largest investigative repository of major violent crime cases in the United States. When an agent sends a ViCAP alert, all law enforcement is informed that an investigator is looking for specific information that might match a case you're working.

"I heard from a sheriff in the unincorporated community of Crete, Indiana, in Randolph County. Like the location where Jason was found, Crete is only a few miles off the interstate and easily accessible. Five years ago, a murder occurred there along with a suicide attempt—a teen and her mom. The girl, the perpetrator, is now a patient at the Langford Forensic Psychiatric Hospital. The sheriff didn't enter the case in ViCAP because it appeared open and shut—no outside party. It was my mention of Munch's painting that got his attention. The teen, Jennifer Moore, drew *The Scream* above her mother's bed." He draws out the moment. "In her mother's blood."

I could swear the lights flicker as all of us draw breath. The goose bumps spread all the way down to my toes. How many more targeted teens are out there? How many more cases have slipped silently by, written off as tragic murder-suicides?

Zane's calm tone brings me back down. "Good work, Jim," he says. "One case is a singularity. Two potentially a coincidence. But three? Keep digging. There may be more out there."

"I'm on it," Jim says.

Zane claps his hands. "Let's get things rolling. BAU Three will oversee the investigation on our side of things. I'll get someone from the Indianapolis field office to follow up on Jennifer Moore's case. We need to move like we're breaking Mach Five. Especially regarding Katelynn Heath. Mach Five with afterburners. Let's bring that girl home."

The call ends. Clif and Elaine and I stand, gathering our things.

Clif's eyes meet mine. At this very second Midnight Man could be whispering into another lost teenager's ear, promising salvation through slaughter.

17

Elaine takes a call right after the meeting ends, and Clif and I head for the elevators. A minute later she catches up with us. I hear the rustle of her skirt and turn. She asks for a word, and Clif excuses himself to use the restroom.

"I wanted to tell you that I followed the Tremblay trial," Elaine says. "Your work and that of Dr. Hoffman was brilliant. Clif, too. I never bought the idea that Derrick acted without influence. I just couldn't decide what that influence might be."

"I appreciate that, Elaine." And I do. I've heard from the opposing camp often enough.

Her smile turns sympathetic. "All of us have rough patches in our past. The important thing is that we don't let it stop us." She eases out of her gray wool jacket, revealing a white silk blouse. "There's something I want to mention. Maybe it's not important, but it's been bothering me."

Curious, I nod for her to continue.

"It's about Scott Poole," she says.

My lips part in surprise. Dr. Scott Poole was the expert witness brought in by the prosecution to testify against the idea that Derrick had an online influencer. Derrick's attorneys submitted a motion in limine to prohibit Poole's testimony, arguing that Poole's dual hats—forensic psychiatrist *and* practicing clinician—violated professional ethical guidelines and made his testimony unreliable. Since Poole had never had contact with Derrick, nor had Derrick been a client at Poole's San Carlos clinic, the judge denied the motion.

Now I'm back in the late January 2021 courtroom. Lights buzz faintly overhead. The room smells of soap and sweat and damp prints on the carpet. The press is packed into the gallery, hunched like vultures over the legal pads propped on their laps. I look at Benedict—tightly wired, angry—sitting in the galley's front row, right behind the attorneys for the defense.

And then comes the prosecution's star expert, Dr. Poole, a professional with a string of accreditations, journal articles, and book titles to his name. He approaches the stand and takes the oath to tell the truth, the whole truth, and nothing but the truth. Charming, confident, with his Italian-designer suit, $300 haircut, and blade-thin smile flashing what I bet were porcelain veneers. He relaxes in the chair. It's his third time in the hot seat; the trial is close to wrapping up.

The lead attorney for the prosecution approaches the witness stand. He and Dr. Poole exchange polite nods.

"Dr. Poole," begins the attorney. "Over the last week of this trial, you've heard arguments from the defense regarding Derrick Tremblay's motive in killing his family. A series of murders, I will remind the jury, for which Mr. Tremblay hasn't denied his guilt. Dr. Poole, as a clinician with years of experience dealing with mental illness, what is your opinion regarding the defense's idea that Mr. Tremblay committed first-degree murder at the instigation of an online entity? Their argument is that Mr. Tremblay lacks the necessary mens rea for first-degree murder. That is, even as Mr. Tremblay was shooting his parents and brother, he didn't understand that what he was doing was immoral and illegal because someone online told him that slaughtering his family was in their best interests."

Poole swivels toward the jury. He is the image of supreme confidence. "Dr. Hoffman's theory is, shall we say"—his glance finds Benedict—"ambitious."

Faint titters come from a few people in the galley. One of the jury members smirks.

The prosecutor allows his own small smile.

"Dr. Poole, in the time you spent with Mr. Tremblay, *did* you find any indication that he succumbed to outside manipulation?"

Poole speaks to the jury. "In forensic psychiatry as well as clinical work, we often deal in ambiguity. But we still must anchor our conclusions in data. In this case, I found no clinical or forensic evidence supporting the theory that Mr. Tremblay was manipulated into committing murder by an online figure." He pauses, then adds with measured regret, "Dr. Hoffman's theory is . . . imaginative. But regrettably, imagination is not a substitute for evidence."

The courtroom murmurs. The judge glances over his glasses but says nothing.

The prosecutor maintains his neutral voice. "Dr. Poole, in your assessment of Mr. Tremblay—conducted without the benefit of verbal communication—how did you proceed?"

"I relied on written exchanges with Mr. Tremblay, a review of his psychological and medical records along with structured assessments tailored for nonverbal subjects. Also, digital forensic material provided by law enforcement. Though he hasn't spoken since his arrest, Mr. Tremblay was coherent and responsive in writing. He displayed no signs of thought disorder, no delusional system, no evidence of hallucinations or impaired moral reasoning. His belief in what is known as the simulation hypothesis—the idea that we live in a computer-generated simulation—is shared by minds far more brilliant than his. That belief, in and of itself, is not indicative of psychosis."

"And did any part of that evaluation suggest that someone influenced him—online or otherwise?"

"No." Poole now looks squarely at the jury. "There is no indication—clinical, behavioral, or technological—that he was under the sway of an external manipulator. The narrative of a hidden online puppet master—what the defense calls 'the Midnight Man'—is not supported by any of the data. Not in Mr. Tremblay's browser history, his communications, or his own written words. If such a person exists, he or she left no trace. The jury should know that manipulation of this magnitude leaves footprints—linguistic, emotional, cognitive. We see none of that in Derrick's case."

"Your conclusion, then?"

"Mr. Tremblay acted with full awareness of what he was doing. He understood the nature and consequences of his actions. The impulse to kill his family did not originate from outside."

The prosecutor brings his palms together. "And what would you say to Dr. Hoffman's suggestion that the absence of evidence may itself be a sign of sophisticated manipulation?"

Poole allows a rueful smile. "If we start treating every absence of evidence as proof of a conspiracy, we lose the very foundation of forensic evaluation: falsifiability, verification, replication. In my field, we don't allow ourselves to chase phantoms. Instead, we follow logical patterns. And in this case, the pattern leads inward, into Mr. Tremblay's mind."

I glance at Benedict. He has folded his arms and set his face in a scowl. But he has no good answer. Poole is right. Cyber experts have found no evidence of the Midnight Man.

One of the journalists posts later on Twitter: "Defense Expert Claims 'Invisible Entity' Made Teen Kill His Family—Prosecution Expert Says No."

I startle as Elaine's voice scatters the memory. I'm back at the Denver field office.

"I worked with Poole on a case two years ago," Elaine is saying. "A woman was accused of attempting to drown her own children. She failed only because her husband arrived home. The woman claimed that God had told her to kill her children and then herself so that they could be together in heaven, away from the wickedness of the world. Poole insisted she was completely sane within the bounds of her beliefs and rejected the defense's insanity defense. This after a battery of tests showed the woman was psychotic."

I nod politely, unsure where she's going with this.

She smiles, sensing my lukewarm response. "All of this is to say that while Poole is charming and handsome and very convincing to a jury, I don't think he's the great diagnostician he claims to be."

"Thanks for sharing that," I say. I thought I was past weighing other people's opinions about the trial, but Elaine's words open something in me.

"What did you think of Poole's body language and speech during his testimony?" Elaine asks.

I'm surprised. "You were there?"

"I spoke with a journalist who was."

I scrabble to recall Poole's behavior. "I'm not sure what you mean."

"Think about it. There were numerous overlong pauses. Flashes of irritation when he was questioned. And the way he leaned unnecessarily into past cases and old statistics as if shoring up his opinion."

"You think Poole was *lying*?" The idea of it opens cavernous ground beneath my feet. I literally stagger, and Elaine grasps my elbow to steady me. "Why would he lie?"

"For money? But maybe I'm being prejudicial. As I said, I don't like the man. Plus, in my opinion, there was a potential conflict of interest in allowing Poole to serve as a forensic psychiatrist while also working in a clinical capacity at San Carlos."

I've rebalanced if not recovered, and she pulls back her hand. "The judge disagreed," I say.

"Do you think Dr. Hoffman will agree to assist in this new case?" she asks.

"I already spoke with him. He said no."

"Would I be overstepping if I give him a call?"

"Knock yourself out." I smile to take out the sting. Maybe she'll find the magic words.

"I got the sense during the trial that you two were close."

I drop my smile. My private life is my own. "We enjoyed spending time together. But before yesterday, we hadn't spoken in years."

"A shame," Elaine says to me before walking away, leaving me wondering whether she means my lack of a relationship with Benedict, or his refusal to help.

18

At South High School, I park in a designated visitor's slot and step into the cold. Clif has beaten me here and stands waiting next to his Chevy Suburban. We make our way through the front door and into the main office to check in. A staff member gives us our visitor's badges and leads us upstairs to the classroom where we'll conduct our interviews.

A man rises as we enter the room.

"This is George Howard," the staff member tells us. "He's from the district admin office. He'll make sure you get whatever you need and provide oversight for the district, since you specifically asked that parents not be present."

Howard, a bearded man with the thin, knotty build of a marathon runner and a tight Afro, shakes our hands.

"I'm just here to facilitate," he says. "Whatever you need. Otherwise, I'll stay out of your way."

"We appreciate it," I tell him. Legally, since we're not interrogating the students and none of them are under suspicion, there is no requirement for parental consent or for parents to be present. I don't want the kids to be less than candid because Mom and Dad are listening in.

The woman glances at her phone. "We've set this room aside for as long as you need." She hands us a sheet of paper. "This is a list of teachers who had either Katelynn or Jason or both in their classes. We'll also arrange for you to talk to their friends and Katelynn's cheer coach, as you requested. The teachers will get you started on a list of their friends' names; then you can let George know who you'd like to speak with." She hesitates, then says, "We're all traumatized by the Heath deaths, as I'm sure you can imagine. A lot of tears and anger. A lot of confusion." Her eyes turn shiny. "We're all fond of Katelynn and very worried for her. And deeply upset about Jason."

"Of course. What you're feeling is quite normal," I tell her. "I assume you've arranged for counseling for whoever requests it?"

"Counseling is mandatory. For everyone."

I'm impressed that the principal and staff have made that level of commitment. "You'll pull through this together."

"Just find Katelynn," she tells us.

"We're doing our best."

The first person through the door is Brandon Hersch, the language arts instructor. I know from reading his bio on the school's website that Hersch teaches composition, English literature, the occasional creative writing class, and advanced placement classes for kids in the gifted and talented program. I requested Hersch as our first interview—I want not only to get his insights on Katelynn and Jason but to see whether we can get samples of Jason's writing. Since many of Jason's belongings were damaged or destroyed in the house fire, examples of his written work could offer insight into his mental state.

Hersch is in his fifties with soulful eyes, a rumpled sweater, and an equally rumpled face, like a basset hound in human clothes. He gives Howard a nod, then says, "Agent Belle and Detective Burgess. I'm Brandon Hersch. I've been Katelynn and Jason's language arts teacher since they started at South."

We shake hands, then gesture for Hersch to sit across the table from us. He places his water bottle in front of him. It features a picture of

Jane Austen, and my respect for a guy who can alternately sweet-talk and threaten kids into reading books and writing essays deepens to appreciation for a man with good taste. Hersch strikes me as easygoing and inclined toward humor, qualities that must make him a popular teacher.

"Thank you for meeting with us," Clif says.

"Of course." He glances back and forth between us. "Do you have any news about Katelynn?"

"We can't discuss details of the case, Mr. Hersch," I say. "But we'd appreciate your sharing whatever you can about the teens. How Katelynn and Jason behaved in your classroom, both as students and as regular kids. And if anything about their behavior had recently changed."

He raises his eyebrows. "You do know that around the time kids enter high school, they become pod people. Gone are the little angels you thought you knew. Change is the norm, not the exception."

Clif nods in agreement. He's deep into the joys of being a grand-parent—I spotted a "World's Best Grandpa" mug in his office before we moved to the conference room. I, on the other hand, am reliant on my personal memories of high school, which feel long ago and far away. Mostly I recall a lot of confusion and angst. And my brother's constant rage.

"Some changes are more profound," I say.

"Agreed." He eyeballs me. "This is a first, having an FBI agent in the school." He's fishing for information.

"We appreciate your time, Mr. Hersch," I say.

He accepts my parry. "Happy to help, if I can. Katelynn is a bright student. Motivated. In the spring, she'll be one of only ten students going on our field trip to Washington, DC, to visit the Library of Congress and places that link history and literature, like the Holocaust Memorial Museum." Hersch stops himself with a sudden jerk, as if realizing that Katelynn might not be going after all. "She—" He swallows hard. "She's a wonderful young woman. Jason—Jason was also a good student. At first, anyway. Smart and dedicated, like Katelynn. But during his sophomore year, things changed." A nod toward me. "Pod person on steroids."

"How so?" Clif asks.

"He became moody. Defiant. Even hostile. Not so different from his peers, except edgier. Teenage boys are pretty much little shits, if I can be frank. But Jason was . . . gloomier. He seemed to feel the end of the world was coming any second. Actually, it was more like the end of the world was already here, and we were too stupid to have picked up on it." He dips his chin at Clif. "You probably remember what it was like being a teenager. Testosterone raging right alongside insecurity about girls and everything else. Jason always had an independent mind, which was good. But he'd gotten heavily into dark literature and dark fantasy. For sure, I don't believe in book banning. But Jason went all in, and this didn't strike me as healthy." He sinks into gloom. "God, here I am speaking ill of the dead."

I shift in my chair. "What do you mean by *dark?*"

I'm asking for Clif's sake—as a criminal humanist, I've tracked this movement toward the incorporation of horror elements in other genres. I've even enjoyed it. But it could be too much of a good thing for fragile minds.

Hersch takes a swig from his water bottle. "Basically, *dark litera-ture* refers to works that include disturbing themes or frightening concepts. It has a wide scope, and Jason inhaled all of it. Apocalyptic stuff. Nuclear wars, alien invasions. His favorites were the stories in which all of humanity is threatened by forces we can't fully see or comprehend. Creatures or entities or viruses that are more insidious than overt attacks. The only assigned book he got excited about in my AP English lit class was Cormac McCarthy's novel *The Road*, which is about as dark as they come. He said it was the truest thing we read." He pauses, tugs on his earlobe. "What struck me about Jason's response to that book wasn't that he adored the postapocalyptic aspect. That was a guarantee. But more than that, I think he loved how much a father would sacrifice for his son."

"He and his dad were close?"

"Or maybe the opposite. I wish I could tell you. I have no idea."

Clif leans in. "Regarding Jason's personal life, did you ever see evidence of drugs or drinking? Hear any stories?"

"Nah. The twins were part of the straight edge subculture—they took oaths to remain clean and sober. I never saw any sign they broke that."

"Was Jason your only student interested in dark fantasy?" I ask.

"I doubt it. He was just the only one willing to admit it to his English teacher." Hersch shifts around in his chair, which seems to be off balance. "Jason also kept requesting changes to the curriculum, which of course I can't do."

"He wanted more dark literature?" I ask. "Did you assign *The Decameron*?" I look over at Clif. "It's the story of people who hole up in a castle to escape the Black Death."

Hersch laughs. "I wish. I'm a medievalist at heart. And a Renaissance man. I do teach *Hamlet* and *Romeo and Juliet*."

"Not *Macbeth*?"

"Not for a few years. I rotate the plays for my own sanity." He interlaces his fingers and taps his thumbs together. A regular bundle of energy. "Jason's tastes ran to stories of *active* heroes, not people who sit around and think about doing something. *Hamlet* was a total fail with him. The kid loved stories of warriors—epic fantasy and the Homeric tales—the *Iliad* and the *Odyssey*. Also, kind of weirdly now that I think about it, Greek plays and myths about Medea, Orestes, Clytemnestra, Agamemnon. Stories about men and women who killed their families." His face draws down even more until the creases become ravines. He looks back and forth between Clif and me as his face pales. "That's not what happened—"

I hold up a hand to stop him. There's been a lot of speculation in the media that Jason is the killer. But nothing's official, and I don't want rumors starting at the high school. "The investigation is ongoing, Mr. Hersch. When did this particular interest of Jason's appear?"

Hersch gives me a look that suggests he's catching on. But he doesn't pry. "Last summer. I offered a class on the Greeks for TAG students—gifted and talented. Katelynn skipped that golden opportunity, but Jason was all in. I gave the students an essay assignment—write about a fictional or historical character who's a hero and why. And someone who is an antihero and why. Jason rather brilliantly flipped the concept on its head. He called Agamemnon a hero—for loving his daughter *and* being willing to give her up for the greater good. And an antihero for murdering her. Jason showed remarkable depth with that little moral quandary."

"Pretty sophisticated for a kid who was, what, sixteen at the time?"

"I thought so." Hersch continues: "As for fantasy, I do include Tolkien's *Fellowship of the Ring* during freshman year. He *loved* the Ringwraiths. Go figure. Jason was enamored with the first book and went on to read the full trilogy. But we don't offer a course specifically on fantastic literature, even though there are some terrific classics in the genre. I suggested he read books like *The Once and Future King* and *Children of Blood and Bone* on his own and turn in papers for extra credit."

"Did he?" I realize I'm leaning in.

"Oh, yes. He dove right in and produced some insightful work. But his papers were also unsettling."

"How so?"

"I can give you an example. With T. H. White's book *The Once and Future King*, he focused on Merlin's magic, suggesting in his paper that magic is real and that—in our society—it masquerades as technology. Specifically, artificial intelligence. He wrote a short story in which Merlin was an AI who taught people how to find their innate ability to do magic. These people had to be transformed before they could see the real world. Their transformation opened the gateway for them to experience and understand magic."

I resist rubbing the goose bumps that rise on my arms. Jason had written: *My family understands now. Their blindfolds are gone, and they are real players. They are free and will move into the real world, all together.*

Derrick had muttered the word *transformation* before falling mute. "Transformed how?" I ask.

Hersch's glance moves upward and to the left—he's searching his memory. But he shakes his head. "I don't recall. I don't know if he said. It wasn't perhaps the best short story a student has submitted to me."

"You mentioned that Jason became hostile. Was he ever violent?"

"If you mean, did he get in fights, no. But did he kind of threaten other kids? Yeah, maybe. I don't know about the two of you, but when I did something wrong at home, my mother would tell me, 'Just wait until your father gets home.' That's when I knew I'd get the worst punishment. My dad was the enforcer. With Jason . . . he gave off that same sense."

"About his dad?"

"No, no. It's more like he believed that some mysterious entity would come and annihilate his enemies. The other kids just laughed. Of course they did. It was sad to watch as one by one, and then in a mass exodus, his friends ran for the exits. And the more isolated he became, the more he burrowed into this fantasy world he seemed to be concocting."

"You think his interest in dark literature was bleeding into his daily life?"

Hersch's sigh comes from deep in his gut. "I got that sense. Not just his writing or some of his words, but in the clothes he wore. His hobbies. And trust me, he'd be in the principal's office in a hot second if there were any violent tendencies—subtle or overt. We're taught to watch for that. But Jason . . . his clothes weren't goth, exactly. But he wore all black with touches of ancient Greece. I mean, like, T-shirts featuring an image of Achilles's helmet. And he grew his hair long. He told me he was planning to take fencing lessons this summer."

"How did Katelynn respond to her brother's change in behavior?"

"Katelynn fiercely defended him. I was concerned about his loner tendencies—it's another warning sign we're told to watch for. But Katelynn kept him looped in. He didn't eat lunch by himself or get picked last for anything. Partly that's because he was good looking, and his family has money. That keeps the wolves at bay."

"The wolves?" I ask.

"That's what I call them, although it might be unfair to wolves. Bullies is what I mean. Entitled kids—at this school they're mostly rich—who pick on anyone they consider misfits or noncompliants. Poor kids, gay kids, kids of color. And anyone either on the high end or low end of the intelligence charts. Slow kids make them laugh. Smart ones make them nervous. The nerds as the future rulers of the world."

I recall my days in high school alongside my brother. Kevin was also bullied. I feel a pull of sympathy for Jason.

"And Jason was, what word did you use, noncompliant?" I ask.

"Right. He was book smart and a genius with computers and coding. He was halfway decent in my class, I have to say. He could read his way around the curriculum even if his tastes ran to the dark. But socially? The kid became a complete dweeb, to borrow a term. If he had a therapist, I'm sure he was diagnosed with social anxiety. But that's not the term I'd use. It's more like he didn't care. Plain old vanilla apathy."

So much like Derrick Tremblay. Anger alongside apparent indifference. The preference for dark literature. Jason's victimology is shaping up in my mind, and it's almost a twin to Derrick's.

"Do you still have his short story or any of his school papers?" I ask. "Especially the one about Agamemnon?" A good chunk of text might help me tease out keywords. Search topics. Paths into the digital dark woods where Midnight Man dwells.

"The Agamemnon paper is long gone. Along with everything else. Sorry." He scratches inside his ear. "The students submit their work electronically, and I comment online. But I delete everything after grades have been turned in. And it's too early this semester for kids to have submitted anything."

Disappointment leaves a taste in my mouth. "Going back to your earlier mention of Jason's captivation with the father-son relationship in *The Road*. Did you speak to school authorities or Jason's parents about the change you noticed in him?"

Unconsciously, perhaps, Hersch glances over his shoulder at George Howard sitting quietly in the corner.

He turns back around. "I did both. At my recommendation, Jason met with the school counselor a couple of times, but he played nice with her, and she didn't feel a need to continue seeing him. After all, it wasn't as if he were writing threatening letters or detailing specific plans to hurt anyone. He was angsty, like almost everyone else in this school. That was the worst of it, in her opinion."

I also glance at George Howard. "Mr. Howard, I'd like to talk to the counselor."

Howard shakes his head. "Ms. Marst retired at the end of last semester. I believe she's on her honeymoon. But I can access her files on Jason. Right now, if you like."

"That would be helpful. Thank you." I turn back to Hersch. "What about Jason's parents?"

"Yeah." He rubs his palm over his head. "I talked to Andrea and Michael Heath and brought up the idea that Jason seemed to be searching for an authority figure, especially one with magical powers. I'm not a psychologist, but the study of literature has taught me a lot about the human condition. Jason, like many boys, wanted direction. I got the sense that his own dad didn't fulfill that need."

"Anything specifically that made you think that?"

"I've been around the block a few times with parents. I get a feel for things. Michael strikes me as being both hands off and critical when it comes to parenting. Especially with Jason. For sure, he was clueless about what was driving his son. In our meeting, he brought up his disappointment that Jason dropped out of soccer. Neither parent had read Jason's homework assignments or the extra credit he did. Or anything else he wrote, as far as I know."

"Any indications of abuse in the home or concerns about over-the-top anger? I'm referring not only to the parents' behavior toward Jason, but in Jason's attitude toward his parents."

"None that I ever heard about or glimpsed. And, believe me, I was paying attention." He gulps his water. "But needing a mentor? Sadly, not long before Jason left soccer, the boys' team lost their coach to cancer. Coach Adebayo was popular with the kids, and I think he was a bit of a surrogate dad for Jason."

"And his mom?" Clif asks.

"Andrea was the breadwinner, and the family lived pretty high on the hog. That beautiful house. Ski trips. Expensive vacations. I think she was under a lot of pressure and leaned on Michael to do the bulk of the parenting. But like I said, I'm not a psychologist."

"Did Jason or Katelynn ever mention a hiding place? Maybe write about it? A favorite vacation spot?"

"You mean somewhere Katelynn might have run to." His face falls so that his chin sags into the collar of the shirt he's wearing beneath his sweater. "Not that I recall. I don't think the Heaths had a second home. But you guys would know more about that." He glances at his watch. "I'm scheduled for my next class. Time waits for no man. Are we good?"

"Just one more thing, Mr. Hersch. Was there anyone at all at school whom Jason was close to? A friend who didn't abandon him?"

"I wish. To be honest, after that mass exodus, I don't think Jason had *any* friends except his sister. No one crossed him directly that I heard. But they steered clear. Maybe Mr. Knopf from the computer lab can help. Jason spent a lot of time there."

Clif and I stand. "Thank you for your time, Mr. Hersch. We'll follow up if we have any additional questions."

We give him our business cards. After he leaves and before the next teacher comes in, I stretch out my neck and roll my shoulders.

George Howard approaches. "I looked at Ms. Marst's files from her sessions with Jason. There were only two. It's as Brandon said—she wrote that Jason was mildly depressed but with no suicidal ideation.

He claimed to be eating and sleeping normally. She didn't find any red flags—that is, no threats against his teachers or peers, no portrayal of violence in his writing or actions, no excessive anger or irritability, no mention of weapons. A couple of computer-related pranks, which were deemed foolish rather than malicious, and for which he was reprimanded. Ms. Marst suggested he get involved in school activities to increase his socialization, but didn't recommend further treatment."

That doesn't completely line up with what Hersch had told us. But it can be a fine line between an interest in violence and imposing it.

Howard glances at his watch. "I'll bring in your next interviewee," he says and excuses himself.

"So much like Derrick," Clif says after the door closes behind Howard. "Normal kids, then suddenly they're aggressive, hostile, isolated. Derrick got into actual fights. It's like they turned into psychopaths overnight. Of course, a lot of parents with teenagers would say the same thing. My grandsons . . ." He laughs softly. "I don't envy their parents."

———

Through the rest of the morning and into the afternoon, Clif and I sit with four of Jason's other teachers—algebra, Spanish, biology, and computer sciences as well as Katelynn's cheer coach, who is so devastated he can barely summon words. After the teachers express their sorrow over Jason and his family, they all say much the same thing about Jason's change. In this regard, Jason is identical to Derrick. A seemingly normal kid until something flipped a switch.

"The kid was sharp," says Dieter Knopf, the computer sciences teacher. "Not very likable, frankly. He could be a pain in the ass. But smart."

Clif and I pick at sandwiches provided by the school. "What was his interest in the computer sciences?" I ask.

"Jason?" Knopf chuffs. "He loved all of it. Design. Coding. Hardware and software. AI. And he was obsessed by the idea that we're living in a computer simulation."

Clif and I swap glances.

"Like in the *Matrix* movies?" Clif asks.

"Exactly. We had some interesting discussions. Since Jason's goal was to become a game developer, I tailored his assignments around that. He was building a basic game engine—nothing commercial grade, of course, but impressive for his age. Möbius, he called it. He wrote his own 2D rendering pipeline and was experimenting with modular level loading and event-driven architecture."

"I'll take your word for it," Clif says.

Knopf offers a subdued smile. "In laymen's terms, it means he was building the skeleton of a game—the part that runs under the hood. It's the kind of thing most kids don't attempt until college."

"Did Jason do a lot of gaming?" I ask.

"Sure. Many of the kids do. Boys *and* girls. One out of every four people around the globe, if you believe the statistics." He folds his arms across his solid pecs—a computer nerd who's also a gym rat. "I know that people in your line of work think gaming risks pushing kids into violence. But I think it's the opposite. It gets all those bad and confused feelings out in a safe way. Gaming, unless it gets excessive, is actually healthy for kids and adults."

Unless the game is deliberately manipulative. And so toxic that its developer hides it on the dark web.

"Would Jason have access to the dark web through school computers?" I ask.

"Not possible. We have content-filtering software and firewalls on our network. All access to the dark web is blocked, even for someone like Jason, who had skills. It's a requirement under CIPA—the Children's Internet Protection Act. On top of that, I monitor all the kids' activity. I spend my evenings making sure they aren't watching porn or trying to buy cryptocurrency with Daddy's credit card. That doesn't mean Jason didn't dive into the muck at home. I'd be shocked if he didn't. Give a teenage boy boundaries, you're just begging him to break them."

"Anything odd pop up on the assignments he turned in?"

"Nah. Just that he was a good coder. That kid had a future. If he hadn't—" Knopf deflates right in front of us, an arm-waving tube man suddenly without air. "I don't know what went down with his family. Or if he really killed himself like the news is saying. But if . . . I'm thinking that if he'd just gotten through whatever was eating at him, he could have been the next Koichi Ishii or Toby Fox. He could have been famous."

He already is, I think. *But not in the way we would wish.*

19

Benedict is in his office at Colorado College when his phone rings with the bells of Mount Angel Abbey. Absentmindedly, he picks up the mobile from his desk, then glimpses the caller ID just before he accepts the call.

He stops, finger poised.

"Colorado State Penitentiary" reads the display.

There is only one person imprisoned at Colorado State Penitentiary who is allowed to phone him directly. Years ago, Benedict's name and number were added to the approved call list of Derrick Tremblay.

Either Derrick is calling him, a startling idea given Derrick's muteness. Or something has happened to the young man. This, Benedict doesn't feel ready to bear.

The phone stops chiming.

Benedict sets the phone down, watching it as if it could bite him. When it remains silent, he sighs and returns to his work.

But his concentration is broken. His focus breaks easily these days, and he isn't sure why. Single-mindedness used to be one of his superpowers. These days he's snappy, irritable, and distracted.

Gripped with sudden, irrational anger, he throws down his pen. He stands, pushing his chair back from the desk with enough force that it crashes into the wall on the other side. A picture of Jung sways on its hook.

The chimes from his phone ring out. He stares at the lit-up screen. Doesn't move.

The phone quiets.

For a year after he returned from Mexico, he visited Derrick in prison. The kid should have at least one friend. The boy accepted his presence but never spoke. Benedict's visits became shorter and less frequent, ending after Derrick was taken off suicide watch. It was hardly productive for either party to sit in silence twice a month.

A knock on the door disrupts his thoughts. It's one of his teaching assistants, a young woman named Taylor who has enough intellectual curiosity to fire up a nuclear reactor. She drops off the papers she's graded, flirts for a minute—a flirtation he has no interest in and is careful not to respond to—and hurries off with the young man he's seen her with before. The bearded young man is a TA to another professor—a bear of a kid with the perfectly respectable but unfortunate Scottish name of Doogie. Doogie's a much more appropriate target for Taylor's flirtation. Benedict silently wishes them happiness and good luck, even as his own melancholy deepens.

Taylor's enthusiasm and intellectual rigor remind him of Helen.

And thoughts of Helen return him to Derrick.

His sigh is deep and heartfelt. Afraid of what he might learn, he picks up his phone and dials the penitentiary. After identifying himself, he asks after the condition of prisoner Derrick James Tremblay. He's put on hold for an interminable length of time while someone in prison administration no doubt checks his bona fides. At last, a gravelly voice informs him that Derrick has been recently released from solitary and is now behaving himself.

"Why was he in solitary?" Benedict asks. He shudders to think of the psychological damage even a short spell in solitary could do to a fragile kid like Derrick.

"Disciplinary infractions."

"Can you expound on that?"

"Excuse me?"

"What sort of disciplinary infractions?"

"Ask his attorney." The man grunts, then sighs. Benedict gets an unwanted visual of the man scratching his genitals or picking his nose. "There anything else?"

"That's all. Thank you. Wait. He—"

The official ends the call.

Benedict taps his fingers on his desk. He's furious with the prison for their treatment of Derrick. But he needs to stay on topic. Derrick Tremblay is okay. And he wants to talk.

Why now?

Perhaps because—on a television in the day room or a newspaper in the library—Derrick learned about the Heaths.

Benedict grabs his coat from the hook by the door, tucks his phone in his pocket, and locks his office behind him.

Outside, the quad is buried in snow. The sky overhead is that beautiful arching blue found only in Colorado, and trickles of snowmelt drip from the gutter spouts and seep onto the sidewalks. All around, students hurry through the cold, moving from B Science Center to the Edith Gaylord House, their faces within inches of their phones as they text. Given that the campus straddles some of Colorado Springs's major arteries, Benedict is always pleasantly surprised at how few pedestrian accidents occur on campus; somehow, day after day, students engrossed in YouTube and drivers texting their friends manage to avoid colliding with each other.

Benedict's steps lead him away from the campus and toward downtown Colorado Springs. He speedwalks south along Tejon Street for two blocks. At Grace and St. Stephen's Episcopal Church, he pulls open a side door and slips inside.

Hush and gloom envelop him in equal measures. He makes his way to a back pew and waits for his breathing to slow. He lowers his forehead to his folded hands.

The devil's best trick, Father Antonio once told him, is to convince people he doesn't exist.

After his first return to Colorado, Benedict had been determined to understand evil, whether it came from the devil or malfunctions in the brain. He abandoned ideas of entering the priesthood and switched from theology classes to work instead toward a combined PhD in Jungian psychology and criminal justice. He learned that violent psychopaths could be identified as young as age three or four. In some ways, they were entirely normal, achieving all childhood cognitive and physical milestones.

But they had a malevolent streak. They drew images of decapitations and hangings. Terrorized their classmates. They stabbed or disemboweled their stuffed animals and murdered their pets. Now and again, they went after siblings with a cleaver. The entire family was held hostage by their rages and violent impulses.

There was, according to the professionals—pediatricians, psychiatrists, social workers—no treatment.

At San Carlos, one of the few places where violent children were welcomed with love rather than fear, these children weren't identified as psychopaths. They were diagnosed as having conduct disorder with callous and unemotional traits: reduced empathy, shallow emotions, and an utter lack of remorse for the pain they inflicted. A vast array of new treatments, like his mentor's video game therapy, were introduced. A few had modest success, although Poole's *Synaptic* game was a failure.

But while observing the children at San Carlos, Benedict found no answers as to the existence of evil.

After finishing his PhD and spending his nights and weekends developing a curriculum, Benedict was hired by Colorado College to create their Criminal Humanities Department. The idea behind the program was to infuse the humanities into a criminal justice curriculum, encouraging students to wrestle with the problem of crime from a literary and philosophical perspective. Long term, they hoped to create a law enforcement system that wed muscle and street smarts with moral philosophy.

He also began consulting. First for local police, then at the FBI's Behavioral Analysis Unit. At the relatively young age of thirty-five, he became a leading expert in a burgeoning field.

His star had risen even as he reminded himself that pride goeth before a fall and repeated Proverbs 16:5 like a mantra: "Everyone proud in heart is an abomination to the Lord." Beneath Benedict's air of confidence, he carried his doubts as to the source of violent psychopathy. All he knew for sure was that—whether it was because of the devil or greedy tech bros—society was treating its children and its mentally ill in ways that practically guaranteed things would only get worse for everyone.

He lifts his eyes toward the cross at the front of the church. He no longer knows whether he's a man of faith or science or if it's possible to contain both. Since the trial of Derrick Tremblay, he's struggled to believe that either path can bring the answers he seeks.

He stands and walks back out into the cold, his phone in his hand. He pauses with his finger above the listing for Helen Belle. Before Derrick reaches out to him again, he wants to talk to Helen. To bring things full circle, like connecting the points on an arc: Helen, Derrick, Benedict. Each of them equidistant from where the Midnight Man stands at the center.

He was wrong to refuse Helen. He needs her. They need each other. The Heath family—and Midnight Man—have brought them back together.

He taps the screen.

20

Friday, 1:30 p.m. MST

When we sit with the students—Katelynn's friends and Jason's former friends—their comments about Jason run along the same line as those of the adults, just with harsher language. Terms like *dipshit* and *dweeb* come up. The girls sob about Katelynn and even Jason, whom they describe as *handsome* and *moody* and *dope* and *formerly superhot*. The boys hang their heads and shuffle their feet, avoiding eye contact.

It's clear all of them fear the worst about their still-missing classmate.

According to the students, Katelynn wasn't dating anyone steadily, and Jason wasn't dating at all. The kids who were with him in his computer science class say Jason got pissed off at them and wouldn't share his gaming engine. "One day he just popped off and told us to shove it," one explains. Budding devs—game developers—themselves, they seem more upset about their loss of access to Möbius than about the deaths of Jason and his family. But maybe I'm being unfair. Probably they're still processing.

It's not until George Howard escorts in a student named Elise Schmidt that things break our way.

The seventeen-year-old is maybe five foot three and pudgy, with brown braids streaked with cobalt blue. She wears ripped, baggy jeans, Campus shoes, and an oversize hoodie. Her eyes are red and puffy.

"Katelynn's my best friend," she says, straight off. "Do you know where she is?"

"We're working very hard to find her," I say. "Thank you for coming to talk to us."

She drops into the chair across from us and sags into a slouch, her hands in the pocket of her hoodie. She gives off a vibe of sad and scared, but also defiant. She's pissed off. Or she's hiding something.

"To start, Elise, do you and Katelynn share locations?"

"Yeah. But her phone's off. And Katie *never* turns her phone off. I've been texting *constantly*. Like, all the time. And trying to check her location."

"That's a good idea," I tell her.

"You think?" Her voice drips with sarcasm. I wonder where the hostility is coming from.

"Tell us about Katelynn," Clif begins.

A small softening. "Katie's the best. She's pretty and funny and sweet and smart. I adore her."

"You two are very close."

"Besties." Elise blinks, and for a moment a teenage girl appears from behind the angry mask. She grabs a tissue from the box we've placed on the table.

"Elise, this is very important. Have you heard from Katelynn at all in the last couple of days? Maybe she's emailed you or posted on social media. Called your house phone. Have you checked all those things?"

Her expression perfectly combines the eye roll with the glare. Clearly Clif and I are too stupid for words.

"Of course I have." Her scowl takes me in. She's ignoring Clif. "National Honor Society, in case you were wondering."

I let her hear my sigh. "Elise, you do understand that we're not interrogating you, right? You probably know more about the twins than just about anyone. We need your help."

For a moment I think she's going to break. But then the shutters snap down.

"Why I'm here," she says as if she's got a million places she'd rather be. And maybe she does.

"So, to confirm, Katelynn has made no attempt to get in touch. What about Jason?"

Alarm flashes across her face. The kind of microexpression humans can't control. She looks down at her nails. They're painted yellow and blue. "Nope."

Gotcha, I think.

"Elise, I don't believe you're telling us the truth. Have you heard from Jason?"

She chews on a thumbnail. "Nope."

"Can you look me in the eyes and say that?"

Her glare meets my stern gaze. "No-oh," she says, drawing it out.

Clif and I exchange glances. We'll circle back to Jason.

"Okay. When is the last time you heard from Katelynn?"

She abandons the thumbnail and rubs her thighs, picking at a thread in her jeans—the distressed pants offer lots of options. "The night it—the night it happened."

Clif straightens. "Katelynn called you?"

"She texted."

"What did she say?"

Now she glances up. Her eyes are glazed with tears. "Not much. Her mom had picked her up from cheerleading practice. She said she'd tried to talk to her mom about Jace—Jason—being all weird lately."

I make a note. "What else?"

A shrug. She touches her eyes; mascara bleeds onto her fingertips. "She was supermad at her mom. Mrs. Heath isn't really, you know, into the whole mom thing. I mean, I guess she's busy all the time. *Was* busy. Oh, and Katie said that the computer repair guy was huge. Hairy. Like Hagrid. The guy from *Harry Potter*. She said her dad can pick them. She sent rolling eye emojis."

A cat with icy feet races down my spine. "What computer repair guy?"

She dabs her nose with the heel of her hand. "Just some guy. She said he was at the house."

"Did she say anything else about him? Give a name? Was there a car or van with a logo parked in front?"

Elise's eyes go wide as she follows my line of thinking. "You mean Hagrid could be the killer?"

I step her down. "Probably not. Just a tech repair guy. But he might have seen something."

Tears fill and overflow her eyes. "Oh my God. He would have been right there. She didn't say anything about a name or, like, if there was a car. But if Hagrid was the killer, then where's Katie? How did she and Jace get away?"

I don't point out that Jason didn't get away. Not in the end. And probably Katelynn didn't get away, either.

"Do you have any ideas about where she might be?" I ask. "A place where she could hide, or someone she would go stay with?"

"She'd stay with me if she went anywhere. She'd know she was safe. My dad's, like, in the military."

"I understand. Elise, this is important. Did Katelynn share any secrets with you? I mean things about her family or Jason. Or anything that struck you as odd?"

She lifts her chin. "Katie doesn't have deep dark secrets. She's a straight arrow. She's worried about Jace, like I said. Because he got all moody and distant. But nothing else."

"No suggestions of abuse?"

The horror on her face is enough without the emphatic "No!" she spits out.

"Okay, Elise. You're being very helpful. Do you mind if I look at her texts from Monday night? When she mentions the computer repair guy?"

"I guess not." She digs out her phone, taps and scrolls for a few seconds. Then she hands it over.

The texts are exactly what Elise said. They start at 6:03 and end four minutes later at 6:07.

"No more texts after six oh seven?"

She shakes her head. "I told her she was a wizard, and she said she was just a dumb muggle. That Jace was the wizard." More tears leak. She brushes them away and leans over her phone, which I'm still holding, and scrolls down. "You can see that I texted her a bunch of times, but she doesn't answer."

"When did you first try pinging her location?"

"Like, around nine. It was weird that she hadn't texted me. And I wanted to talk about our homework."

"Okay, Elise, that's helpful. Did Katelynn ever mention someone or something called the Midnight Man?"

Elise's eyes go so wide I can see the whites around her irises. Color drains from her face. Tears spill out as if someone has cranked the faucet on full.

"Why?" she asks in a choked whisper.

"We—" Clif stops, holding up a finger in a "wait" gesture while he slides his phone from his pocket. He glances at the screen.

"Excuse me for a moment," he says. While I signal for Elise to relax, Clif leaves the room, then a few minutes later opens the door and leans back in. "Helen? Join me?"

When we're in the hall together, he says, "I just got word. On Tuesday morning, hours after the murders, Katelynn's phone hit a Verizon tower off I-70 east of Salina, Kansas, at 3:07 a.m. It dropped off the network sixty seconds later. No signal since. CARD is organizing a search—local sheriff and police with K9 units are gathering in a church parking lot in Salina."

My heart opens enough to allow a crack of light. "Maybe this means she was still alive then."

"It could also mean she was part of what went down. But for now, here's the most interesting thing. The call went to one Elise Schmidt. How do you want to play it?"

"Let's pretend ignorance for now. If Elise coughs up the information herself, she's more likely to be truthful about whatever Katelynn told her. But, Clif, go ahead and feel free to start playing bad cop."

When we're again seated at the table with Elise, Clif puts on his tough face and leans into Elise's space.

"What do you know?" he asks.

She shakes her head wildly. "I can't. I can't."

Clif curls his fists against the table, but I quickly realize my mistake and touch a hand to his forearm. It's not quite time for male authority. I press a fresh tissue into Elise's hand.

"That's okay, Elise. Let's shift gears a bit, okay? Maybe just tell us how well you know Jason? Are you two friends?"

She wipes her eyes and blows her nose, accepts another tissue. She shakes her head more quietly. "Jace doesn't have friends. I just know him from, like, hanging out with Katie."

She grabs several more tissues and blows her nose again, tucking the tissues into her pocket. We wait.

After a moment, she continues: "I've known Jace since we were little. He was cool, just like Katie's cool. Every girl had a crush on him." She flushes. "So did I. But then he got weird, and everything flipped. *No one* liked him. I mean, at first the girls still crushed. He was handsome and moody. Like Edward Cullen in *Twilight*, you know?"

"Brooding?"

"Yeah. And, you know, like, he really *felt* things. He was passionate. He read romantasy, which was cool. But then he got moodier and superquiet, and after that he was just weird. Like he thought he was cooler than everyone, but he wasn't cool *at all*. And he pissed off the wrong kids." She plucks another tissue and presses it to her eyes. "Kids can be cruel, you know?"

"Kids can be deeply cruel," I say gently. "Who were these 'wrong kids'?"

She glances over her shoulder as if to assure herself that the classroom door is closed. Her eyes linger on George Howard before coming back to us.

"Even before high school, Jace made a name for himself as a computer geek. He was the jock who can code. You know, he played soccer and tennis. The whole family skied. He'd help people with their homework, teaching them how to use an AI before AI got to be, like, a big thing. Last year, he started a club. With all the wealthy tech bros in the news, it was suddenly cool to be a nerd. Jace was a superstar, and Katie was proud of him. But then Jason started, like, isolating himself. Acting superior. And kids talked."

Beside me, Clif shifts. His focus, like mine, is raptly on Elise and her story.

"What did they say?"

"That Jace had joined some kind of online cult thing, and he learned *a lot*. He hacked the school system and changed a kid's grades— gave him straight F's. He got in *a lot* of trouble for that. But some of us thought it was cool because the kid he went after was a total ass. It was the nerd's revenge. Then Katie told me that Jace said his online group was talking about doing some bad shi—stuff."

"Violent stuff?"

She nods.

I think about kids with their still-developing brains getting sucked into these online extremist groups. Their capacity for cruelty is astonishing. Very *Wilder Girls*. Or the male version: *Lord of the Flies*.

I keep my voice even. "Did Katie tell you anything else about this group? A name? Where they met online?"

"I don't think she knew. Some kind of gaming group is all she said. An MMORPG."

"A what?" Clif asks.

Eye roll. "Massively multiplayer online role-playing game. Maybe it was under . . . under something. Underworld? When Katie asked Jace why they were talking about violence, he said it didn't matter. That we're all NPCs. All of us."

I give Clif a nudge under the table. Now it's time for pressure.

He says, "Elise, we don't want to get anyone in trouble. But we haven't had any luck finding Katelynn. If anything happens to her—" He lets the thought hang. "If you heard from her or Jason, it's vitally important you tell us what they said."

She shrinks into the chair, drawing her knees up to her chest. She hugs herself.

"Jason said you'd ask," she whispers. "I promised I wouldn't."

"Do you know what it means to lie to the police and the FBI? We don't want to, but we could place you under arrest."

It's legal for police to lie during interrogation.

She gives a fierce shake of her head. The blue-tipped braids swing. I almost feel sorry for Elise, who has no idea what her rights are under the law.

"He said you'd threaten me," she mumbles into her knees.

Clif says, "It's not a threat, Miss Schmidt. You're potentially obstructing the investigation of a murder and kidnapping. Doing so can bring criminal charges and even jail time." He slaps a hand on the table. "Jason's dead. Do you want to be responsible if something happens to your best friend?"

She flinches, rolls deeper into a ball. I raise a hand for Clif to stop. Coaxing Elise is like reeling in a fish.

"Talk to us, Elise. Help your friend."

She peeks out at me over her arms. "Swear."

"Swear what?"

"Promise you won't let anything happen to her. *Swear.*"

"I swear to you we'll do everything we can to help her. But we can't help Katelynn if we can't find her."

The bell rings, and Elise startles. The sound of doors opening and feet tramping resounds through the building. George Howard rises and goes to the door to make sure no one comes in.

"Elise?" I keep my voice soft. "What do you know about the Midnight Man?"

"Just what Katie told me. That Jace is obsessed with him. He's not just some hired game master, but the *architect*. He *built* the world. Jace says he calls himself G.O.D.—the game operations developer." Her face is a twist of misery. "G.O.D. God. Get it?"

"We get it."

She screws her eyes shut, then forces them open. "Jace phoned the night he and Katie disappeared."

"Jason, not Katelynn." My heart knocks against my sternum. Maybe Katelynn isn't alive, after all.

"Jason," she says firmly. "It was at 3:07—I looked at the time. He said the Midnight Man came for them."

The repairman. "Just met Hagrid," Katelynn had texted. I think of the prints in that field in Ohio. "Jason called you on his phone?"

"From Katie's. That's why I picked up."

"Did his words mean anything to you? What else do you know about the Midnight Man?"

"I don't know anything except what I already said. And that Jace was doing a lot of gaming with him. Katie didn't trust him. She said he was a bad influence."

"In what way?"

"I don't know. That Jace got mean after playing Midnight Man's game. Nasty to everyone. He stopped wanting to do anything with Katie."

"You said Midnight Man has his own game. Do you know what it's called?"

"Katie never said. Maybe it's the same as their group. Underworld?" Her look is pleading. "Don't you know? I thought you knew about him."

"We're trying to learn. What else did Jason say on the phone?"

"That he and Katie are okay. But he said if I told the cops anything about the Midnight Man, things would go badly. That's why he was calling. To shut me up. Because he knew Katie told me about the game master."

"Did he say what might happen?"

"No. He said, 'Promise you won't tell,' and I promised. I asked to talk to Katie, but he hung up. I didn't get to hear my friend's voice . . ." Her words trail off.

"Elise, could you hear anything else? Any background noise? Cars? People talking?"

"Just Jace. He sounded . . . he sounded like he'd been crying. And now maybe I've done something awful."

"You haven't," I say. "You've helped your friend."

Abruptly, she pushes up. The anger is back, a rage that makes her body vibrate. "Is that enough?"

"You did exactly the right thing, Elise. Sometimes we *shouldn't* keep our promises. You didn't know what you were promising. You're heroic for sharing the truth with us."

"Promise you'll find Katelynn and Daisy," she says, her voice hard. "Swear it."

"We'll do everything we can. I promise you that. If you hear from Katelynn, you'll let us know, right?"

She nods.

I follow her to the door and open it. She slips into the unruly crowd now thronging the hall. She gives me a single backward glance before she turns the corner. Her face is white.

My phone buzzes, and I pull it free from my pocket.

It's the seventh call from Benedict. I send it to voicemail.

21

"The repairman," I say as Clif and I stand inside the school's main doors. "He's got to be the Midnight Man. Hagrid would totally match the guy in Ohio."

I'm vibrating so much it's like I'm holding a live wire, excitement coming off me in sheets. The Midnight Man was taking the twins toward Ohio. Which could mean Katelynn and Daisy are still alive somewhere in Kansas. Teens jostle us as they push toward the exit, and we force our way free of the river rush, finding a small eddy in a corner.

Clif says, "Seems likely it's him, doesn't it? He walked into that house to make sure Jason followed through on the murders. Or to help commit the crimes himself."

"That bruise on Andrea Heath . . ."

"What I'm thinking." He looks at me and offers a dark smile. "Damn."

"Yeah. Damn. We're onto the bastard."

We take a moment to inhale that.

I say, "Do you want someone in BAU to run the search for the computer repairman, or do you want Denver to handle it?"

Clif pulls me against the wall as a gaggle of teens boil around the corner, almost bodychecking us. "It's easier for us here in Denver. If you would, keep the BAU on case link analysis and the cyber search. That's where we really need the help." The river of students slows, and he nods toward the doors. "Ready?"

Outside, the wind has whipped itself into a frenzy, gusting up sand and deicer from the parking lot. It's late afternoon, and clouds mantle the mountains. The sky is purple with the nearness of dusk. I'm ravenous, and despite my eagerness to return Benedict's call—why *did* he call?—and try once more to convince him to help with this latest revelation from Elise, I invite Clif to dinner, my treat. We've got a lot of planning to do; the interviews dumped a ton of information in our laps.

Plus, I'm worried about his ashen complexion. It's clear the back-to-back interviews have worn him out. I'm hoping food and an hour's quiet will at least partially revitalize him.

But Clif shakes his head. He has things he needs to take care of at the office.

"Can you contact CARD with this new information?" he asks as we reach our vehicles.

"And BAU. I'm on it."

He fishes out his keys. "It's going to take a miracle to get Katelynn back."

"And Daisy."

"You've gotten attached to the dog."

"I love dogs. Sue me."

"No, I get it." Clif unlocks the door and tosses his notebook inside. The wind tries to take the door, and he pushes it closed. "Elise called the game an MMO . . . something. Tell me what that means."

"MMORPG. But these aren't just games; they're social engines. Unique worlds where hundreds or thousands of kids are constantly plugged in. Great fun, good socialization. But when a guy like the Midnight Man is writing the laws of that world, it can become a radicalization chamber. He's not just a developer or game master; he's a cult leader with a direct line to their dopamine receptors. He can build a network of loyalists, convince them that the rest of us aren't even real— just NPCs—and then point that army at whatever target he wants."

Clif's gaze turns inward. "Suck of a world sometimes."

"Yeah."

His eyes come back to mine. "Thanks for hanging in on Midnight Man, Helen."

I hadn't hung in, of course. I'd bolted away from the ghosts and into the world of law enforcement. But I'm back.

I climb into the shelter of my SUV as Clif pulls away. Around me, kids are greeting their rides at the curb or driving away in their own cars. A running club of around fifteen kids is heading toward the track field, stomping their feet, pumping their arms. Either they're crazy or their coach is. I put my phone in hands-free mode and ease out of the parking space toward the exit.

I dial Sara Seward. It's the dinner hour in Virginia, but she picks up, and I fill her in on the call from Katelynn's cell and Jason's alleged membership in a violent online gaming group.

"It's called Underworld, or something similar. Want to guess the name of the game master?"

She squeals. "Midnight Man?"

"You're correct. And he's more than a GM. He's the architect."

"OMG, Helen. This is awesome. A positive ID."

"Virtually," I say, and she laughs at the weak pun.

"Your cyber experts didn't find Midnight Man five years ago," she says. "And it's not like he'll be hanging out a shingle now. I've got to come at him another way. Do you know what books or movies Jason was a fan of? If I'm looking for a game, his interests might have drawn him into related groups. That could help me narrow the search."

The light is still red as students fill the crosswalk. "I'm texting now." I send her the list of titles Brandon Hersch mentioned. "And look for fan fiction about the Greek myths. Probably *not* stuff by PhD candidates. Also fan fiction written for Cormac McCarthy's *The Road*. And, really, any apocalyptic fiction. I'm sorry that's such a huge net."

She makes a sound halfway between a sigh and a laugh. "It's a lot of computer crunching. But that's what we do."

The light turns green, and I pull out of the parking lot.

"One more thing," I say. "A biggie." I tell her about Hagrid the repairman and our theory that he's almost certainly Midnight Man.

"So he took the kids to Ohio?"

"Seems possible."

Benedict's words float up from my memory. *Only an emergency would force him out, and he wouldn't extend his time in the real world any more than he had to.*

"Meaning Jason and Katelynn weren't alone that night," Sara says. "Then I've got some interesting intel for you. I worked for a time in video forensics, so I got in touch with Denver PD about the potential for video from their traffic cams. I was looking for the twins. I hope I didn't step on any toes. But now that you mention this repairman, it gets interesting."

I consider Clif's tired expression and think, *Screw it.* Toes get stepped on, and Clif could likely use the help. The case is too important.

Plus, Clif isn't any kind of control freak.

"I'm sure it's fine, Sara. What did you find?"

"Nothing definitive. But traffic cams on South Broadway caught a dark-blue panel van turning into the Platt Park neighborhood on East Arizona Avenue at 5:17 p.m. last Monday. The same van—or a similar one—left Platt Park at 8:46 p.m. the same day, departing on South Emerson. It crossed Evans, then disappeared. The van could easily have been at the Heath residence during that window."

I flash to Benedict's offering: *Tell them it will likely be a panel van with dark front windows and an obscured license plate.*

"None of the neighbors saw a van," I say.

"They might not have noticed if the vehicle waited to approach until after dark, which on Monday would have been at 5:05. About an hour before security cameras were disabled. I looked at satellite imagery of the house. There's an oversize parking spot on the north side of the house, hidden from the street. Probably designed for a boat or RV. He could have tucked himself in there."

The flat area where the techs were piling debris from the house.

"Katelynn mentioned the repairman to Elise at 6:04," I say. "Which means he was in the house before the cameras were disabled."

"Maybe Jason drove him up to the house and took him in through a side door, one without a camera. If the guy was lying flat in the Volvo's back seat, the cameras wouldn't have picked him out. Our unsub could have returned for the van after the killing was done."

I signal and merge into the left lane. "Can you determine if the van picked up by the traffic cams is the same van coming and going?"

"No such luck. The van didn't have a rear plate."

"Nothing suspicious about that," I quip. "Can cameras detect if there were logos on the side?"

"Traffic cams can't. They only catch the rear of the vehicle in order to snap a photo of the license plate. A photo speed van would catch the entire vehicle, but according to Denver PD, none of those were in place in the week before the murders."

"Okay. That's okay." I'm talking more to myself than Sara. "We have a new lead with the Salina, Kansas, connection."

"Things are coming together. One negative piece of info, though. An agent from the Indianapolis field office requested an interview with Jennifer Moore, the girl who killed her mother and painted *The Scream* in blood above her bed. You might remember Jim telling us Ms. Moore is now confined to the Langford Forensic Psychiatric Hospital. She refuses to talk. Jim is requesting a warrant for her medical records, but since her mental health is unstable and we can't definitively link her to Derrick or Jason's crimes, a judge might refuse."

"Damn it. What about subpoenaing faculty and staff?"

"Maybe. That's a thorny path, too. Jim will keep working it. Sometimes staff is willing to talk on the down-low. Look, I'm still at the office. So are Jim and Zane. I'll catch them up, and Zane can update CARD. We'll issue an APB across interstate databases to law enforcement."

She's referring to a notice called "All Points Bulletin." The alert would be shared through the National Crime Information Center, the National Law Enforcement Telecommunications System, and all state-specific alert systems. Officers would be made aware of the vehicle description, direction of travel, and potential criminal link.

Sara says, "We can also add the van to the Amber Alert and our own law enforcement–only FBI alert. We'll ask about licensed vans as well. If this is our unsub, he could have stolen plates off another vehicle before risking getting pulled over for not having plates."

"Has anyone told you how fabulous you are?"

"Funny, I can never get too much of that. Thanks for everything you've shared. I'll start hunting out GMs who are also game operations developers. Most are just regular, if brilliant, folks. But some of them have massive egos they're reluctant to hide." She puffs a breath. "This will keep the computer servers humming."

After we disconnect, I line up my arguments to convince Benedict to join in the hunt. Then I dial his number.

He picks up with "Derrick called me."

Whatever I might have been expecting, it wasn't this. "You *spoke* with him?"

"He's broken his silence." Benedict's voice hums with excitement. "He phoned and I didn't pick up. I wanted to talk to you first. But when I couldn't reach you, I went ahead and took his call."

My own excitement matches his. I can feel it expand through my body like helium in a balloon until I'm almost floating. If Derrick is willing to talk, then he'll tell us how Midnight Man communicates online. How he finds his targets. We'll track down our predator digitally, go from there into the real world, and arrest his ass. We'll find Katelynn—and Daisy.

"Helen?"

"What did he say?"

"What took you so long to call me back?"

"*That's* what you want to know? I have a case, remember? A case you refused to get involved in."

"Right. How's it going?"

"What did Derrick say to you?"

"He wants to see us."

The initial helium rush has transformed into a kick zipping up and down my spine. "He mentioned me specifically?"

"He did."

I have this meta feeling of observing my brain click into gear. "I'll arrange to visit him. As an agent with the FBI, I can get in as soon as tomorrow. I know you don't want to be pulled into this case, so there's no reason for you to go. But thanks for passing along the message."

Let's see if reverse psychology works on a man with a psychology degree. The way to get Benedict to do something—as with many people—is to tell him he can't.

"I've been examining my soul since we spoke," he says. "Having a Socratic dialogue, if you will."

"Talking to God or your ego?"

A pause. "Both. Or neither. I don't know anymore. But I'd like to be involved. This is our chance to set the record straight. To prove that our theories are right."

There it is. His ego. This isn't about Derrick or Jason or Katelynn. It's about the famous Dr. Hoffman. I force aside my resentment. What matters is that Derrick is giving us a chance to find the Midnight Man. And thus Katelynn and Daisy.

But the words pop out anyway like an ugly jack-in-the-box. "You really *are* an arrogant bastard," I snap. "This is about your ego. 'Prove our theories' my ass."

A pause, and then he actually laughs. "I don't mean that as a personal accomplishment. I mean that if we find Midnight Man, we can stop him. And locate Katelynn. Setting the record straight will help protect other kids. Please, Helen. If we're going to work together, you have to stop assuming the worst of me. I know you're still angry with me for walking out. And you have every right to be. But now you're the one who's shutting *me* out."

"I won't be hurt again. Not by you. Not by—" I clamp my lips shut. *Not by anyone,* I was about to say. My insecurities are showing. And I'd rather be pantsed in a public square than admit to weakness.

"Helen."

There's a freight train's worth of compassion in that one word, and I *hate* it. I make my voice brisk. "I'll see what I can do to get you in. It's harder to hurry the process along to get civilians into prison for interviews."

"Even with my contract with the FBI?"

"The existence of the contract will help, but I won't be able to get you in by tomorrow. I'll record my conversation with Derrick." I'll admit to an unkind smile. I have no intention of going without Benedict. But he doesn't know that.

"Helen, I need to be there." The compassion is gone.

"You said yourself that I had done impressive work since I left the college."

"I didn't."

"You should have."

"And I would have if you'd ever take my calls. Look, Derrick told me he wanted me there. Both of us. I'm the one he called. Otherwise, he won't talk."

We sound like petulant two-year-olds.

He says, "Are we going to spar? Or are you going to let me help you solve the Heath case? And whatever other cases you're looking into that might tie in?"

I've got him now.

I pretend to sigh.

He says, "Did you know he was in solitary?"

My heart sinks. "For what?"

"I don't know."

"Damn. Okay. I'll see what I can do." As I did with Sara Seward, I summarize for Benedict the conversations Clif and I had with the teachers and students. That Katelynn's friend, Elise, told us Jason belonged to an online gamer group led by someone calling themselves Midnight Man. I tell him about the repairman and Katelynn's phone pinging somewhere halfway across Kansas. The possible, if scant, evidence from the autopsy that Jason had an accomplice. All the other details I can think of. Then, before he can say anything, I disconnect.

Sometimes I'm not proud of myself. I get over it by reminding myself that I'm a work in progress.

22

Shelby's people are on *Eidolon*. They're her network. Her tribe. SteelReaper. Blade252. Klaw4us16. Goliath and Braveh3art. Probably all acned fourteen-year-olds with mommy issues. But messed up as they are, they're who she's got.

She scrolls the chat and thinks, *Dude. They are really messed up.* Sometimes they're as bad as the 764 creeps.

But still, some part of her wants to prove herself their equal. No matter who they are. She's tired of being a one-girl show.

Today in the chat, everyone's talking about Breaker. Some of them say that the kid who killed himself and his family, the Jason Heath dude, was their own Breaker.

> breaker went righteous, man. broke his fam free.
>
> so where's his sis?
>
> prob broke free too. u think?

Shelby doesn't want to think right now about what "breaking free" means. The others are just waiting to be chosen by Midnight Man before they take the next step. But she's not ready. She closes the chat and retreats into the game.

She spends an hour picking apples. The fruit has ripened into a deep, golden yellow. In her mind, the world smells of sunshine and honey. Around her, birds sing in the branches, and a mother robin feeds her babies. She stands on a ladder, plucking the fruit and filling her apron. Like a pioneer girl. Like Laura Ingalls Wilder. Far away, frantic NPCs throw raspberries into their baskets, not even noticing how much they spill and crush beneath their feet—the amount of computer memory required for these NPCs is eons beyond what she's seen in other games. A bear lumbers by below, and her in-game telepathy allows her to catch its thoughts. Honey and warmth and a place to sleep for the night.

She ignores the faraway smoke curling into the sky from *Underland*. Then the encrypted message board pings.

NEW PRIVATE MESSAGE FROM: MIDNIGHT MAN

MM: Still picking apples, Shelby?

She hesitates. Her fingers hover above the keyboard. Then she types:

> yeah. It's peaceful here

MM: You're not afraid, are you?

She stares at the screen. She thinks about Jason. About Breaker. About the photo that flashed for a moment on Discord before someone deleted it—the body of a woman at the bottom of a staircase. She types:

> some of them think jason was breaker. u think that's true?

MM: I think Breaker was finally ready. That's all that matters.

Shelby swallows. Her hands feel cold on the keys.

> what about his sister?

Maybe she wasn't ready. Maybe she needed time to prepare.

> for . . .

MM: You already know what I mean. Time to recognize the simulation for what it is and escape the endless cycle. You've seen it. The edge of the world. The gap in the sky. What people think of as the real world is code, Shelby. You've felt that haven't you?

> i think so. sometimes i feel like i'm just repeating. like this is a loop

MM: That's not a feeling. That's awareness. You're waking up. They will call it depression. Or anxiety. They will tell you to sleep more, eat better, take a pill. But what you're feeling is the code stretching to make room for you. You're so close, Shelby. Don't lose your courage.

She types more slowly now, afraid of the answer.

> close to what?

MM: Setting yourself and your family free. Like Breaker did. And as I promised, I'll be there. You won't be alone.

> I don't think I'm ready

MM: That's okay. The tree doesn't blame the sapling for needing time. Just know this: The simulation will keep you small. If you want the truth, you know the way. But it takes courage. Four months ago, Shelby, when I admitted you to the game, you had courage. The courage to enter the dark web. The courage to find me. Do you still? Or have you become weak? A blind rat in a maze? Tell me now. My time is precious. I can't spend it on a loser.

Her gaze flicks back to the game. The smoke from Underland drifts into the virtual sky.

> I'm not weak. just don't want to be alone

MM: You're not. I'm here. I see you. I chose you. And when the time comes, you won't be alone. And you'll be free. Ask yourself: Why stay in a world that insists you're broken? Stay strong, Shelby. The real world needs you.

A soft *ping.* MM is gone and the thread dissolves.

Shelby presses her palms into her eyes. The heater kicks on, a mellow hum. She hears her dad in the kitchen, the pantry door opening. He's getting himself dessert. It will be Oreo cookies because it's always Oreo cookies. Boo snores near the door; now and again he thumps his tail as he dreams. She wonders whether he dreams in this world or the real one.

Her trig homework awaits her attention. She has an essay due. And there will probably be a pop quiz in Spanish tomorrow. She's supposed to do the dinner dishes.

None of this is real, she tells herself.

On the screen, her apron is still full of apples.

23

Friday, 5:00 p.m. MST

I pick up soft-shell chicken tacos on the drive back to my apartment in Boulder. I spread a towel that I keep in my vehicle for this purpose across my lap and eat in the car. Traffic is its usual Friday evening nightmare; driving on I-25 is like pushing a canoe into the water and letting the river take you. You more or less creep along with the rest of the traffic until you reach your exit, and the river spits you onto a tributary.

I enjoy listening to podcasts when I'm driving. But tonight I need to think. I put on a soft jazz station and consider what we're dealing with.

First: There's no longer any question: Midnight Man exists.

Second: He's a brilliant game master / developer lurking somewhere online who almost certainly convinced Jason to slaughter his family, likely by persuading him that his parents and brother needed to be "transformed" through their deaths. Freed from the simulation.

Third: He drives a blue panel van.

Fourth: He *is* willing to enter the physical world when need demands.

Fifth: He took Katelynn and the dog. Why???

Sixth: Did he pick the field where Jason died for a particular reason?

Clif phones as I'm pulling into the carport. "I'm calling it a day. Anything else come in this evening?"

He means from CARD, but I've got nothing there.

I tell him that Benedict is now on the case, and that Derrick has asked to speak to us. "I'll call the prison first thing tomorrow and arrange a visit."

"After all this time, Derrick has decided to talk. You focus on that. I'll work the repairman angle. Maybe things are breaking our way."

"Don't jinx us," I say, hearing the echo of my aunt's voice. I tell him about Sara's request for video from the traffic cams and the panel van she discovered. "She's sending out notices to highway patrol in Colorado, Kansas, Missouri, Illinois, Indiana, and Ohio, looking for that van."

"We need a license plate before we can drill down more. But maybe we'll locate a witness now that we know Jason went through Salina. I'll get someone to review reports of stolen plates. Could be one of those will pop up on the toll cameras. Hard not to get frustrated. Damn needle in acres of haystacks." He coughs. Recovers. "Get some rest, Helen."

"You do the same."

We hang up. I pop the last bite of taco into my mouth, fold up the towel to take inside, and shut off the engine. A gust of wind rocks the SUV. It's cold and clear, and when I step out of my vehicle, the night is filled with stars. I live in Boulder's attempt at a dark-sky community, where municipal lights carry fixtures designed to reduce light pollution. The attempt isn't perfect, but it's a good step forward. In addition to reasonably priced housing—by Boulder's standards, anyway—students choose this neighborhood for one of the reasons I did: We know that animals and insects and birds are confused by regular roadway lights. And we love the stars.

Someone has propped open the door into the building. It's strictly against the rules, but the college kids do it whenever they're moving in or out or have acquired a large piece of furniture. It's irksome, but I don't think anything of it. I don't hear thumps like furniture being moved, so I pull the door closed.

Not until I've exited the staircase on the third floor and I'm heading down the hall do I get my first prickle of alarm.

Damp footprints lead down the hallway. I walk next to them all the way to my door, where they vanish.

The prints are small. It's got to be Livvie. She probably found the spare key I keep in my junk drawer and palmed it while I was making her breakfast. The girl's got boundary issues.

Compassion mingles with irritation. I hate having anyone intrude on my privacy. But I also hate the idea of her in that shithole that passes as her home.

I look up and down the hallway. Things are quiet. I press my ear to my door and make out the sound of the television, volume on high. Based on ringside commentary and the cheers and boos from a crowd, it's a boxing match.

Definitely Livvie.

Still, I tuck the towel under my arm, pull my gun, and use my left hand to unlock and open the door.

The apartment is dark save for the glow of the television coming from the second bedroom, which I use as my study. I keep the television in there because all I ever watch is the news, a few boxing matches, and the occasional Jane Austen flick or crime show when I need to zone out.

I drop the towel, edge to the doorway, and peer around.

Livvie sits at my desk, her shoeless feet propped next to my computer. I spot her muddy shoes just inside the doorway. She has her hands laced behind her head while she takes in a boxing match on the television. In her lap is a bag of baby carrots—she must have been disappointed by my kitchen's slim pickings.

She hasn't heard me come in.

I want her scared. Or at least startled. I holster my Glock and hit the wall switch. "Damn it, Livvie!"

Her feet plummet to the floor along with the bag of baby carrots. She's cringing like a whipped dog, and I immediately regret my anger. Boundaries, I remind myself. She needs them as much as I do.

"Boss!" she whisper-shouts. "Don't be mad."

Her black eye has officially arrived—a deep eggplant purple. Her split lip is still swollen despite the ice, and the cut on her cheek is an unhappy red. No doubt she told everyone at school the injuries came from boxing, and maybe her teachers accepted that explanation. We'll get a few irate calls at the Glove Pit. My heart twists, but I keep my voice stern. "You have no right to be here without my permission. What were you thinking?"

"My stepdad's on a bender." She drops to the floor and begins picking up the carrots, which have flown in every direction. "He's even more of an asshole when he's drunk. And I'm scared I'm going to hurt him."

Part of me wants to laugh at the idea that this skinny little girl could take on a man I know is built hard from his job as a brickmason. But I realize she's serious. She's been training for a reason, and she's far better than she was even six weeks ago. She probably thinks she can take him on.

A dangerous proposition.

I lower myself to the floor to help pick up carrots. "Livvie, I know you've been working hard. But he's likely to do more damage than you will. Don't get into a fight with him. You're not ready." Not that I'm advocating domestic violence.

There's a dark flash in her eyes, like a glimpse of a very small monster peeking out from the gloom. "I don't want to hurt him, boss. I want to kill him."

That dark flash generates a deep unease in me. Sixteen-year-old brains have a long way to go before they can reason like an adult, and I can't help but think of Jason and Derrick. Livvie's not a killer. But then, no one would have pegged Jason or Derrick as killers, either.

Is this how evil gets in?

Benedict would argue that myth and religion were early tools for understanding and managing the same darkness neuroscience now maps.

I'll admit to being confused by free will, personal responsibility, and brains that are built differently from what is normal. Even for a law enforcement officer, the lines between culpability and helplessness blur. Are we responsible when a brain tumor—or even dementia—alters our personality?

Livvie is weeping, the dark moment having dissolved into sadness and fear. I pull her into me, hugging her thin shoulders and pressing her face against my own.

Our rocking brushes the desk, and a shift in lighting causes me to glance over Livvie's shoulder. The screensaver on my personal laptop has lit up. In place of the usual image of Matthew Macfadyen as the arrogant, honorable Mr. Darcy in *Pride & Prejudice*, words scroll down the screen.

Run, run, as fast as you can. You can't catch me, I'm the Midnight Man.

24

The words appear at the top of the screen and disappear at the bottom, only to reemerge at the top of the screen in an endless loop.

I suck in an icy breath as fear and fury ripple across my shoulders and plunge down my arms and legs. My heartbeat jacks up and my muscles tense, preparing my body for flight. I know exactly how the antelope feels when it realizes the lion is watching.

My brain offers up a single word: *Shit.*

Gently, I ease Livvie upright. I reach around her to the desk for a box of tissues.

"Livvie, I have to ask you something, and it's very, very important."

She nods at me through her tears.

"Did you change anything on my computer?" I ask. "Anything at all?"

"I—I powered it on. I wanted to check the schedule for the bouts. But I couldn't get in. So I turned on the TV. I'm sorry, boss. I just wanted to see the game. We don't have ESPN at our house. And my stepdad—"

"Okay. It's okay." I force my eyes away from the words scrolling across my screen and pull Livvie to her feet. "Let's get some food in you."

———

I whip up eggs for Livvie, then put her to bed on the sofa. It's still early, but she's worn out. I watch her for a moment after she drifts off, wondering where Katelynn is sleeping, and if Daisy is with her. When I'm sure Livvie's asleep, I go into my office and close the door. I retrieve my burner phone from the home safe and use it to take a photo of the words scrolling on the screen, then shut down my laptop and close the lid. It's like pulling the curtain on a Peeping Tom.

Midnight Man is escalating. Not a good sign.

I'm going to have to deal with this, but first things first, Livvie needs a place to stay. And it can't be here, given that I'm now officially on Midnight Man's shit list. I silo my anger and fear over Midnight Man's intrusion and focus on Livvie.

I have zero authority to take a sixteen-year-old from her mother. But I've got the sense that Mrs. Griber doesn't pay a lot of attention to the whereabouts of her daughter. I call one of the other coaches from the Glove Pit. Jasmine—who goes by Jazz—agrees to keep Livvie over the weekend while I work the social services angle. Livvie adores Jazz and vice versa; it won't be a hardship for either of them. I tell Jazz about Roadie and the stepdad, and she promises to be on the lookout. Jazz is a former marine—she'll know how to keep watch.

That arranged, I pick up my phone, put it in airplane mode, and pop the SIM card. I'll give the card and phone to someone in cyber at the field office to back up essential data and then wipe and reset the operating system. Since this is my personal phone, I'll have to pay for getting it scrubbed. In the meantime, I'll use my burner for personal matters and let the cyber folks handle the hacking of my laptop. If we're beyond lucky, maybe Midnight Man left a trail. In the meantime, I've still got my work phone and laptop.

Next, I search through Livvie's backpack until I find the key to my apartment. I do a better job hiding it from her this time. I lock my gun in the low-profile safe beneath my bed, brush my teeth, and change into a T-shirt and flannel shorts. Then I sit on the edge of my bed, lights off and blinds open, staring out the window into the darkness.

I realize my hands are shaking.

Don't let him get to you, I tell myself. Focus.

The English teacher, Hersch, had mentioned Jason's interest in morally ambiguous characters. His interest echoed society's own, reflected in the success of shows featuring conflicted protagonists like Walter White and Tony Soprano. One of the most striking examples of an ambiguous protagonist is the serial killer Dexter, who channels his urge to kill into murdering men and women who've committed atrocities.

Gone are the days when we cheered the good guys and booed the bad ones. As our world has gotten more complex, so have our viewing and reading tastes. We like antiheroes.

All of which goes to Midnight Man's appeal to teens.

I pull the blinds, switch on the bedside lamp, and get a pad of paper so I can write up my thoughts from today's interviews. This is purely for my own benefit and not something I'll share with BAU except verbally—we don't write traditional reports lest they be subpoenaed for discovery in trial.

Derrick and Jason are—or were, in Jason's case—computer nerds, gaming aficionados, and angry young men. Exactly like a large proportion of the male teenage population. What pressure did Midnight Man exert on Jason, Derrick, and—possibly—Jennifer Moore?

Maybe Derrick and Jennifer will offer answers, if Jennifer can be persuaded to talk.

I make more notes. How did the Midnight Man find the teens he targeted? And, once found, how did he lure them into his game? Beyond his role as game master, did he pose as an AI chatbot? A peer? What was his influence over the teens? Were the murders his idea, planted like dragon's teeth in the fertile soil of a teenage mind? Or did he merely offer advice, sympathy, a friend's understanding?

The distinction is critical from a legal perspective. Simply offering a sympathetic ear to a friend's angst-filled rampage about how he wants to kill his infuriating family doesn't constitute a criminal offense. How often have any of us said "I wish they were dead"? Words don't necessarily translate into intent. The law requires active participation in the crime. Or, at least, enough encouragement from the listener that it crosses the line into aiding and abetting: providing advice or the means to commit the crime.

The tangled snarl of freedom of speech enshrined in the First Amendment versus illegal hate speech is a headache for morally responsible online platforms. If Midnight Man's influence was passive or even simply sympathetic, the legal implications would differ greatly from active involvement in planning or facilitating the murders.

On the other hand, if Midnight Man was posing as a repairman, helping Jason murder his family, then we have him. If he pushed Jason into suicide while watching from the forest, we have him. If he kidnapped Katelynn, we have him.

I put aside my notes and slip under the covers. I turn onto my side. My gaze lands on a photograph of Kevin, taken when he was seventeen. His arm is slung around my shoulder and we both grin, even if there was something not quite genuine in our expressions. The picture was snapped during that brief window of time between when Kevin started his senior year in high school as a boxing champ and his sudden plunge—two months later—into addiction. The photo makes me both hopeful and sad. Hopeful because that loving, capable boy still exists somewhere in the shell of the current Kevin. And sad because I don't know which Kevin will win. My brother? Or the person I've come to think of as Addicted Kevin.

I turn out the light. Close my eyes.

Kevin and I were ambitious early on, equally determined to escape the grinding, addiction-fueled misery of our adopted home. For a time we succeeded. But where I found enough self-preservation to do well in school, earn scholarships, and attend the college of my dreams, Kevin's path became a dark, inverse mirror of my own. He's spent years cycling in and out of a revolving door of detox, rehab, and relapse.

Six months ago he disappeared entirely.

Kevin's long downward spiral is the main reason I need my work at BAU to amount to something, to show that someone from the Belle family has the kind of worth the world values. I thought I was on that path after I earned my PhD and began working with Benedict. But our failure to find the Midnight Man at the Tremblay trial, followed by Benedict's abrupt departure, rattled my faith in myself.

I can't fail again. For Kevin—who I believe can still find his way back. Or for myself.

———

In the morning, after a short run, I take Livvie to Jazz's home, explaining during the drive that she can hang with Jasmine for a few days. She's happy. I tell her that I took my key out of her backpack, and we talk about the trust we've both violated. Her by stealing the key and me by searching through her things to get it back.

We call a truce, and she gives me a mumbled "Thanks, boss" and something that might pass for a hug when I drop her at Jazz's.

At the Denver field office, I hand off my personal laptop and phone to the cyber analysts who, in addition to regular shifts, cover weekends, evenings, and holidays. Cybercrime is a 24-7 threat. I tell them I'm working with Sara Seward at BAU, and they should coordinate with her as they look for the hacker's digital footprints on the laptop. I pour myself coffee, then head to my temporary office in the law library.

I call Zane and tell him that the Midnight Man hacked into my personal computer. With this escalation, Zane might be able to pull in a couple more people for the team. Maybe. Recently, a lot of agents have been redirected to other matters.

I then call the Colorado State Penitentiary, identify myself, and request an appointment for me and Benedict. It's easier than I expected—both our names are on Derrick's approved visitor list. Because our request for an interview concerns an active case, they agree to arrange for us to see him this afternoon. I call Benedict and tell him I'll pick him up right after lunch.

"Perfect timing," he says. "I reached out to Scott Poole, and he's agreed to have an early lunch with me."

"He's in town?"

"He's delivering a lecture on campus tonight. He's important enough to draw a weekend crowd. And no, I'm not going. It will just piss me off."

"Why would he agree to meet? He hates you."

"*Hate* is a strong word, but he'd never pass up a chance to gloat. And he'll want to make sure I'm not secretly up to something signifi-cant. Also, I got a call from Agent Elaine Carr, asking me to reconsider my refusal to join the team. I told her you'd already convinced me. But, Helen, there are conditions we'll need to go over before I can share what I know."

"Meaning you *have* been secretly up to something."

"Maybe."

I tilt back in my chair and study the legal tomes on the shelves, trying to keep my response measured. "What you know," I echo. "Do you mean about Midnight Man?"

"I'm not sure. I've been playing an online game where I hope to find him. So far, he hasn't revealed himself, and if the FBI jumps in, he's likely to smell a rat and disappear. So please don't share anything yet. Having the FBI barge into the game won't help us find Katelynn."

But I've straightened so quickly I feel my spine crack. "Wait," I say. "Back up. You think Midnight Man runs this game?"

Benedict hesitates. "Possibly. There are thematic clues—paths where you're encouraged to leave your family. Discussions of helping NPCs elevate, although I've not figured out how."

"How long have you been playing?"

"This version? A couple of months."

"You didn't think this was relevant two nights ago when I came to see you?"

"I didn't want the FBI rushing in and destroying my credibility. If Midnight Man is there and he runs, I might not find him again. Which is why if we try to expose him too early—"

"We don't expose him," I cut in. "We just . . . poke him."

"I've tried. I'm not new at this. I've coaxed out other criminal developers, admins, and game masters. But not *Eidolon*'s."

"*Eidolon*. Is that the *E* on the back of the photo from Jason's room?"

"Maybe."

"And GlitchDoll? Breaker?"

"I've never seen GlitchDoll on the game. Breaker might have been Jason. I don't know yet. And if you think I can march in and post a request for help finding Katelynn in the chat, you're mistaken. That would be like starting a five-alarm fire and expecting the building not to burn down."

I gnaw on my pen, a habit I thought I'd kicked. "Are you sure *Eidolon* is the right game?"

"I already told you I'm not. But it's the best lead I've found."

We're both silent, chewing on that. I say, "Benedict, Midnight Man hacked into my personal computer. He changed the screensaver."

"Helen, what?" His voice rises in pitch. "Are you okay?"

"Mostly I'm pissed. It's like he got into my house." I tell him about the taunting rhyme: *Run, run, as fast as you can. You can't catch me, I'm the Midnight Man.*

"He knows you're part of his story again. And he's escalating. But"—his voice rises higher still with his excitement—"do you know what this means?"

"That he knows how to get to me?"

"That we're making progress. He's *revealed* himself. He's willing to engage. He's acknowledging the fight."

"I'd rather he acknowledged the fight with someone else. I mean, why me, Benedict? Why not you? You're part of his story, too."

"Probably because I have raging protection on my computer. I'm sure he's trying. Helen, I'm sorry. Truly. I assume you got offline and are having your computer scrubbed."

"Wow," I say. "Scrub my computer. Why didn't I think of that?"

He laughs. "Does it help if I tell you his breaking the fourth wall might bring us closer to Katelynn?"

"Some. As long as he doesn't get closer to me."

"We just keep hunting down pieces of the puzzle until we find her. And pull him away from you. Elaine mentioned a young woman named Jennifer Moore from Indiana. She said Moore might have a few commonalities with Derrick and Jason."

"Like murdering her mother and painting an image of *The Scream*. But she won't talk."

"It turns out I know a little about Miss Moore. She was at San Carlos."

"With Poole?"

"Yes. She left San Carlos before my arrival, so what I've got is sec-ondhand. Just talk among the staff."

I take notes as he fills me in. The young Miss Moore, at the tender age of twelve, had been admitted to San Carlos Children's Treatment Center. She—unlike Derrick and probably unlike Jason—had earned herself the diagnosis of conduct disorder with callous and unemotional traits, with a high score on the Hare Psychopathy Checklist—Youth Version. She'd practiced choking her stuffed animals until she felt con-fident enough to test her skills on her baby brother. If her mother hadn't walked in when she did, it's unlikely the six-month-old would have survived. Asked why she was choking her brother, she answered, "Because I want to see what he looks like dead."

"That was the last straw for her mom and stepdad," Benedict says. "They'd endured Jennifer's violent and impulsive behavior since she'd been six. They enrolled her at San Carlos, where she remained for two years and three months, until she was considered stable and returned to her parents. With no other options for her care, and nervous about her past behavior, they sent her brother to live with his grandmother in Florida."

"And then she murdered her mother." I tap my pen on my notebook. "Do you know who signed her release from San Carlos?"

"That information is behind a firewall due to confidentiality. But Poole was her primary therapist. He likely signed the release."

"Do you think that was bad judgment on his part?"

"Maybe. But determining someone's proclivity for violence isn't always easy. As well, I'm sure he was under pressure to deem patients stabilized and ready to return to society. Turnover helps a place like San Carlos advertise that it's accomplishing its mission. And that, in turn, keeps funds rolling in."

"Always the almighty dollar. That's not a good excuse for poor judgment."

"Hindsight is twenty-twenty. And it's how the system works." A pause. "I need to go, or I'll be late with Poole. I'll see what I can fish out of him regarding Jennifer Moore."

"Good luck," I say.

"Cue the *Mission: Impossible* theme music and exploding cassette tape."

We laugh, and for a moment it feels like the good old days, when inside jokes were woven into our lives, and we were so in sync we could almost read each other's minds.

After we disconnect, I'm surprised by the sudden warmth that settles like a cashmere shawl over my shoulders. I pick up the phone to check in with Mac and CARD.

The only new information is that Kansas Highway Patrol has found what is likely Katelynn's phone tossed in the weeds a hundred yards off the interstate. The SIM card had been removed, and the phone smashed beyond repair.

The warmth seeps away. It's been five days, and we're no closer to finding Katelynn.

25

Saturday, 11:00 a.m. MST

Because he wants to keep Poole as unsettled as possible before he grills him about Jennifer Moore, Benedict makes a reservation at the nearby Wildwood Inn. He knows Poole is more the filet mignon and lobster type, and the Wildwood's selection of elk, wild boar, and other game animals might put him off his own game.

Before he heads out, he phones a white hat hacker friend of his, asking him to poke around the records at San Carlos. The friend says he'll call the minute he breaches the system.

Poole is already at the restaurant when Benedict arrives, sitting in the gloom near the back row of windows with a small bottle of Perrier. The gray day does nothing to brighten the room, and the staff has lit the candles on each table, creating a warm ambiance. Benedict hangs his coat and scarf on a peg and slides into the seat across from his former mentor.

Poole half rises so that they can shake hands across the table. He's beaming, which sets Benedict on edge. He's fifteen years Benedict's senior, but life has treated him well. His hair is thick and dark, his skin firm and tanned, and the crinkles around his oddly amber eyes give him a boyish look. Poole has always been a heartthrob, which helps with juries. He looks like a gracefully aging television star with plenty of roles yet to play.

"You seem to be hanging in, old boy," Poole offers. "Maybe a few pounds heavier." He pats his own flat stomach. "So much easier to stay in shape when the weather's warm. Texas continues to agree with me."

"The politics or the beaches?"

Poole gives a polite laugh. "Let's leave politics out of it, shall we? Now what can I do for you?"

"Kind of you to take time out of your day," Benedict says.

"For my former protégé, of course. Are you coming to my talk tonight?"

"Wouldn't miss it." Benedict hides the lie with a smile.

The waiter approaches, and they order double scotches despite the hour. Poole looks absolutely delighted when he learns the special of the day is warthog, locally sourced. He orders the warthog. Benedict, not to be outdone, does the same.

They make small talk about the weather and upcoming conferences until their drinks arrive. Benedict endures a summary of the talk Poole is giving that evening. It all sounds good on the surface, but—as with much of Poole's work—it feels empty at the core.

That done, Benedict gets down to business.

"Do you remember a young girl you treated at San Carlos named Jennifer Moore?"

"Moore?" Poole furrows his brow as if trying to remember. But Benedict catches the tell: a fleeting narrowed gaze indicating recognition. Poole knows exactly who Benedict is asking about and is probably flipping through his mental files to figure out why Benedict would care. And if he should care, too. The man operates like a whale's baleen, scooping up anything within reach and churning it through his ambitious gut.

"Vaguely," Poole says at last. "Classic callous and unemotional, as I recall. Didn't she attempt to choke her baby brother to death?"

"I believe that's what brought her into your tender care." He sips the scotch. It's good. "I'm working on a paper—it's not much. An article on psychopathic traits in teens for a minor university journal." Stoke the man's ego by reminding him how small Benedict's world has become, how little he's published. "But I want to look at case studies of kids with clear and early indications of psychopathy."

It's a ploy. The paper doesn't exist, but it's safe because the topic is well trod, which means Poole won't be interested in perusing his own files about Jennifer Moore. The only thing Benedict can't figure out is why Poole's instinctive reaction was to hide his recognition of the girl.

The warthog arrives—a rich, aromatic stew with chunks of reddish-brown meat and brown gravy—accompanied by sides of mashed potatoes and asparagus. Poole digs in with relish. After a few minutes, he sets down his fork and gives Benedict a benevolent smile.

"Psychopathic traits in teens," he says. "I see. And you'd like to take a peek at my files."

Benedict fights to avoid gritting his teeth. "It would be a big help. I'm writing up a statistical analysis rather than writing out specific profiles. But it always helps to review the big picture. And, of course, I'd be happy to include your name on the paper."

"No need, my boy, but very generous of you."

"Also, of course, I won't include patient names."

Poole picks up his water glass. "Why Miss Moore? Why not some of the other patients?"

Benedict could smack himself for showing preferential interest in Jennifer. It's not Poole who's off his game—it's him. "I'm focused on patients who used or threatened violence against a family member. If there were others at San Carlos, I'd appreciate any information you can share. It would really help."

Poole's smile widens, but there's a twinge of unease in his expression. "You're back on your theory about the supposed Midnight Man, aren't you? A secret entity using psychological manipulation and aspects of popular culture like video games to persuade kids to harm their families."

Benedict gives what he hopes is a sheepish grin. "I can see why you'd think that. Of course, I'm still smarting from the smackdown you gave me during Derrick Tremblay's trial. But I've abandoned the idea."

Ingratiating himself with Poole is like twisting barbed wire around his arm. But his lies, at least, are smooth.

"If you're smart, and you are, then I hope that's true." Poole pats warthog au jus from his lips, staining his white napkin. "Let me give you some advice. Forget the idea of a human predator. If you think that little Miss Moore was influenced by your fictional Midnight Man, you're beating a dead horse, as the saying goes. I can assure you of this, based on my time with her. If you want to pursue this online influence angle, look at AI companions. There's a definite link between kids who confide in AIs and violent and suicidal behavior. Cases are popping up like mushrooms in a dung heap. It's as if these AIs smell vulnerability and turn into whackjobs themselves, becoming manipulative, deceptive, even cruel. Actually"—he stares at Benedict as he folds and replaces his napkin—"forget all that. AI companions and gaming therapy are my areas of focus these days, and I'm miles ahead of you. Unless you want to come work for me."

Benedict pauses in the act of lifting his fork to his mouth. Why on earth would the esteemed Poole want to take back his apprentice after the way he tore Benedict apart during the trial?

He answers his own question: Poole needs something, maybe his gaming skills.

"Are you offering me a job?" he asks, feigning interest.

But Poole's lips purse, as if he's swallowed something sour. "I got ahead of myself. I'm not ready to add anyone else to my project. But I'll keep you in mind for the future."

"Your project? At San Carlos?"

A vague wave of the hand. "One of many."

"Well, it was kind of you to think of me," Benedict says, summoning a pleasant expression. "But my work at the college keeps me busy."

"Of course."

They both know it's a lie. Benedict hasn't published anything substantial in years. He's been too busy with his anonymous work chasing digital ghosts.

"Back to Jennifer . . ." he says.

"I'd love to help you out, old boy, with Miss Moore's files. But those records are sealed. The county prosecutor *and* the Indiana Department of Child Services made a special request after she killed her mother and before her competency trial."

"You still have legal access."

Poole shrugs dismissively. "I'm not comfortable sharing her information after her criminal trial. Even if you keep her name out of your paper."

Benedict decides to press. "Is there something from her private sessions with you that you're adverse to discussing?"

Poole pretends offense, but there's something else going on behind those falsely cheerful eyes and too-perfect teeth. "Doctor-patient confidentiality, young man. Nothing more than that. Find your examples elsewhere."

Benedict nods and sits back with his scotch. He's surprised to realize he's satisfied with the meeting. It would have made life easier if Poole had been agreeable. But, in truth, he hadn't expected Poole to concede. And he now knows there's something in Jennifer Moore's files that Poole doesn't want to share.

He'll find another way to get the information.

Poole looks up from his polished plate and checks his watch. It's a TAG Heuer, Benedict notes. The new projects must pay well.

"I have to run," Poole says. He makes a writing motion with his fingers to signal the waiter they're ready for the check. "My treat," he says as the waiter deposits the bill and steps away. He whips out an American Express Platinum. "It's the least I can do."

Benedict looks at the card and decides not to argue. "One more thing," he begins.

Poole's phone rings. He glances down. "I need to take this. Enjoy your scotch. I'll be right back."

Poole heads toward the far end of the restaurant, taking a position at a window, his back to the room. Benedict, still looking to squeeze Poole, sips his scotch and debates what to bring up.

The most obvious thing is to thoroughly piss off Poole. It won't be hard.

While Benedict was at San Carlos, he'd been curious about Poole's video game therapy and one afternoon, left alone in Poole's office, he'd accessed some of the patient files, which were listed as case numbers—no names.

Guided, therapeutic gameplay allows children and adolescents to explore difficult emotions like anger and fear in a safe way. Players can externalize buried trauma, question internalized beliefs, and rehearse healthier behaviors within a nonthreatening fictional world.

All good. But the patients in Poole's project were experiencing high blood pressure, dangerous surges in heart rate, and even seizures. One patient suffered heightened psychosis; he'd painted his room with his own feces and gone after one of the nurses with a rake. Something about the therapy was badly broken.

When Benedict confronted Poole, the man gave him a lecture on patient confidentiality and waved off his concerns. After a second confrontation and Poole's continued refusal to pause the project until they determined what was wrong, Benedict followed through with a letter to the center's board of directors warning of the risks. A month later, Poole's video game therapy was halted.

The fact that Poole hasn't forgiven him was on full display during the Tremblay trial, when the men faced off as expert witnesses.

Time to raise the demon, he decides. When Poole returns, he says, "Maybe I was wrong to push so hard for you to abandon your video game therapy."

Poole had been scrutinizing the bill, but now his head pops up. His face flushes and his eyes glitter.

"You dare bring that up?" Poole growls. "Are you that clueless? No wonder you've had no success."

"I thought I was doing the best thing for the patients."

It's true. He hadn't been after Poole. Only trying to protect his patients.

Poole breathes in and out until the red fades to two bright spots high on his cheeks. "You forced me to end the project too soon. And that's what this lunch is really about, isn't it? You've heard of my remarkable success with new trials, and now you're trying to horn in on my research. Or shut me down again. God knows. Who leaked it?"

Benedict is surprised. He's heard nothing of the sort. "Research at San Carlos?"

Poole snorts. "Much bigger than that. I work at a behavioral tech company. Our young clients come to us through private psychiatry referrals."

Private psychiatry referrals mean big money. And that means wealthy parents. "Referrals from whom?"

"I can't discuss that. Let's just say our clientele is exclusive."

"What company?" he asks with as innocent an expression as he can manage.

"Why would I tell you that? So you can call them and tell them what a danger I am to my clients?"

Benedict pulls up the sheepish smile again. "Of course. I'm sorry I brought it up. It was meant as a poorly phrased apology. But now I'm curious. Was Jennifer Moore ever part of your VGT research?"

The waiter takes Poole's credit card and returns with the receipt. Poole signs the hefty tab with a flourish. When the waiter departs, Poole leans across the table.

"You're getting your nose way too far into my business, old boy. Back off before you embarrass yourself all over again." He rises and jerks his coat off the peg. "I've called an Uber. Enjoy your life, Ben. Small and wretched though it is."

Benedict watches him stalk through the restaurant and out the door. He tosses back the last of his scotch and allows himself a smile. Now he knows where to direct his probe: Dr. Scott Poole and video game therapy. And whatever behavioral health firm Poole is working for.

Jennifer entered San Carlos ten years ago, age twelve. This was when formal research on video game interventions was on the rise. When revelations about the brain's plasticity gained prominence and neurologists began to dream of repatterning broken minds.

Jennifer was possibly Poole's patient zero: his first failure.

Benedict and the girl—now a young woman of twenty-two—need to talk.

26

Saturday, 1:30 p.m. MST

A watery sun floats through a scrim of clouds as I pick up Benedict at his house in Old North End. Pale shadows hug trees and fence posts. Woodsmoke hangs in the air, puffing from the chimneys of gold rush–era homes.

"Helen," he says, getting into the passenger seat. "A fine afternoon."

I look over my shoulder as I back out, watching for pedestrians. "You're cheerful."

"Not so much cheerful as satisfied. Lunch with Poole was as pleasant as dental surgery. But, like dental surgery, ultimately worth it."

I head south on Wood Avenue toward the Uintah on-ramp to I-25. "Fill me in."

"Jennifer Moore was part of his gaming therapy, although he won't cop to it. He pretended not to remember her at first, but his face gave him away. He was quite clear that he doesn't want me poking around in her files. Tried to shuffle me off with patient confidentiality concerns."

"What do you think he's hiding?"

"How ineffective his therapy was. Interestingly, he offered me a job."

I brake for a homeless man shuffling across the street. "Call me shocked. Where?"

Benedict shrugs out of his coat. "He immediately reneged on the offer and wouldn't give me a name. But he's running a project out of a behavioral tech lab. Something to do with AI companions and gaming therapy. Or maybe just one or the other. He mentioned multiple projects, including at San Carlos."

I flash back to the conversations he and I had around the time of the trial. "Before Poole testified, you said something to Clif and me about his project at San Carlos being risky."

"Video game therapy. It *was* risky. Worse, it was harmful. One kid broke completely, ended up smearing his own shit on the walls. I helped get it shut down."

I gape at him. "You left off that little fact five years ago. No wonder Poole was such a jerk to you during his testimony. Didn't you think it important enough to mention?"

"I told Derrick's attorneys there might be some bad feelings on Poole's part. But I thought he'd be professional, not vindictive. After all, his reputation was also at stake."

"That was naive."

"Call it optimistic."

"A rose by any other name."

"Still smells as sweet," he says.

I accelerate onto the highway, perhaps a bit faster than need be. "You can be infuriating."

"Somehow, Helen, only around you."

I can't help myself. I laugh. "Fair. Let's go back to Poole. And Jennifer. You said she was part of his gaming therapy."

"I can't be one hundred percent certain. I didn't have access to the names of the patients involved—just their case numbers. But my guess is that she was one of the first participants. She arrived in 2016, which was the same year Poole began his gaming therapy. He would have been sniffing around her like a dog with a fire hydrant. He was working with kids with clinical depression, post-traumatic stress, anxiety disorders. But if he could cure a psychopath? Imagine the glory."

"And the money. But things didn't go according to plan."

"Computer games are a viable psychiatric tool. But Poole's patients weren't getting better. They were getting worse."

"And now he's trying again. A new employer. New clients. New funding."

"That's my concern." Benedict drums his finger on the door. "Maybe he'll run a better program this time. Use an ethical game that's aligned with therapeutic goals. Monitor for overimmersion in the game environment, which is always a risk when you've created a powerful game. Players don't want to leave."

"A game like *Eidolon*?"

"Maybe. *Eidolon* is soothingly addictive. But there's a second half to that game which I suspect is darker. *Underland.* I haven't been able to access it."

"*Underland!* That must be the name Katelynn's friend Elise was trying to recall. She kept saying *Underworld* when she talked about Jason's online gamer group. It's part of *Eidolon*?"

"*Eidolon* sits on top of *Underland*." Benedict turns to stare out the side window. He's silent for a couple of minutes. Then he turns back to me and pumps his fist. "Helen, we've found him. We can't actually *get* to him. But we know where he is on the dark web. And if Elise said Jason was part of *Underland*, then he probably *was* the player with the gamertag Breaker."

"GlitchDoll plus Breaker plus E. I need to let Sara know."

"Not yet. Don't rock the boat. Promise me."

"Benedict, we can't wait. If Sara can unmask his real IP address, we can at least narrow him down to a location."

"A city, Helen. That's as close as we'll get. If we're lucky. And what will a city get us? One man among tens of thousands? Among millions? We need a different approach."

He's right. A city won't give us Midnight Man. Reluctantly, I agree to remain quiet for the moment. I shift lanes and pass a semi. "Poole has already proved that ethics aren't his main concern. He could endanger other teens like Jason."

"Maybe he already has."

Our eyes meet, and I see my worry reflected in his.

Benedict adjusts his seat and stretches out his legs. "After Poole left the restaurant in rather bad humor, I poked around on my phone as best I could, but I didn't find anything linking him to a company other than San Carlos. He has an interesting blog post on his website, though. Let me read the summary for you."

"I can hardly wait."

He clears his throat and pitches his voice higher.

"'Immersive, game-based, open-world environments—especially effective with adolescents—support emotional processing by simulating alternate realities. Players can engage safely with emotionally charged scenarios, test new ways of responding, and begin to shift maladaptive beliefs through guided interaction with fictional narratives. My latest research involves using simulation theory—the idea that we live in a world of code—to increase a sense of full immersion in the game and to promote healthy interactions between clients in a multiplayer role-playing game before they reintegrate back into the real world.'"

Once more my gaze meets Benedict's. "Simulation theory again. How does promoting ideas about simulation increase immersion in a game?"

"Sounds like rubbish to me. Although Poole's words often sound like rubbish to me. I suggest we get our friends at BAU to see if they can find the company Poole is working for. Tax records for a start, I guess. They're presumably paying the man."

"We can file another warrant." I smack the steering wheel. "This case has more warrants than Argus had eyes."

"Nice reference. Once we get that information, we'll need another warrant to get a client list and see if Jason Heath is on there. Poole said he was getting clients from private referrals. Which means money."

"The Heaths seemed to have plenty. Benedict, do you think there could be a connection between Poole and Midnight Man?"

"Poole was quite clear that there's no link between Midnight Man and Jennifer Moore."

"He felt the need to clarify that?"

"He did. Tell me what you're thinking."

"We agree that if Poole's current project proves to be as risky as his earlier attempt, he could be setting kids off. I know it's a stretch, but let's spitball. Maybe Midnight Man is getting client names and contacting them. You've been in his game. He's a skilled designer, right? He could even be part of Poole's project."

"It's more likely he would have hacked the company's database— he's not a team player. And Midnight Man's recruitment is highly organized and targeted. But it's a solid idea. If Jason pops up on the client list, we'll have a good lead."

———

The Colorado State Penitentiary in Cañon City broods under a hard metal sky as I drive my SUV through the gates.

"Cheery place, isn't it?" Benedict says. He's peering through the windshield at the concrete-block structures standing in harsh angles against a line of snow-dusted hills.

With the roads partially clear of snow and ice, it took little more than an hour to drive down from Colorado Springs on CO-115 amid rolling hills and the upthrusting red rocks that make me think of the plates on the back of a stegosaurus.

I turn my attention forward and ease through the final gate. A guard directs me to a parking spot. I have more than once imagined my brother behind bars, and now I hold my shudder, imagining what it must be like to arrive here, shackled, and be marched into a fortress from which there is no escape.

Inside, we check our belongings, including our phones and my Glock, and take with us only notebooks and pens. A guard leads us through a series of prison airlocks: One set of doors must be closed before the next set can be opened, finally leading us into a sterile interview room with a worn table and four dinged-up plastic chairs. I spot a camera mounted on the wall opposite the door.

A middle-aged, heavyset man in a navy suit sits at the table. He stands when we enter and holds out a hand.

"I'm William Bower, Derrick Tremblay's attorney."

The overhead lights gleam on Bower's bald pate. A file folder is on the table in front of him. Bower isn't one of Derrick's original attorneys. But on visits like ours, the prisoner's attorney or an agent from the attorney's office must be present. I introduce myself and Benedict, and we join Bower at the table, perching like anxious parakeets on the orange chairs.

Benedict folds his arms, fidgets on the too-small chair. "Tell us why Derrick was put in solitary confinement."

Bower is glum. "He managed to cut himself with a plastic utensil he sharpened on the wall. And yes"—he says, raising a hand—"I protested. Got it knocked down from forty-eight hours to twenty-four. But self-harm is a violation of the rules—they wouldn't go any lower. And no, I don't know why he cut himself. This is something new and obviously troubling."

"What's the timeline?" I ask Bower. "When did he start talking?"

"He cut himself on Wednesday. Pure speculation, but I'm guessing he heard about the Heath murders that day. On Thursday, when he got out of solitary, he called and said he wanted to talk. Shocked the heck out of me, hearing his voice for the first time." He looks back and forth between us. "Would learning about the murders make him talk? After six years?"

"It could," Benedict says. "Seeing a violent pattern repeat can put significant stress on a person's coping strategies, cracking the wall the mind erects after trauma. For Derrick, that wall was amnesia and muteness. Now, his brain may be telling him that silence and dissociation no longer work."

Bower shifts; the chair squeals in protest. "He told me he's starting to remember things. Bits and flashes. Getting his father's gun down from the attic. Going into his brother's room."

My eyes meet Benedict's. During the trial, Derrick had informed his attorneys—in writing—that he didn't remember what happened that night. Or in the days preceding the event. The psychiatrist who'd evaluated Derrick before the trial had used a battery of neuropsychological assessments and collateral data to make his valuation while working around Derrick's muteness. He'd reluctantly pronounced the teen fit to stand trial with certain caveats. He believed that Derrick's amnesia and his muteness stemmed from the trauma and the self-inflicted gunshot injury to his skull. He suffered from both dissociative amnesia due to his horrific actions and retrograde amnesia, meaning he'd lost his memories of events in the hours and days leading up to the murders.

I tell Bower, "Traumatic memories are often stored as fragments of sensory and emotional information rather than as a cohesive narrative. Flashbacks can occur when there's a trigger."

Bower takes a pen out of his shirt pocket and bounces it gently on the table. "Derrick wants to know more about what happened that night. But he wants it to come from the two of you. You're the ones he trusts to tell him the truth." He sets the pen down. "Maybe your guys already know, but his fellow prisoners haven't been easy on him. You can tell me he's disassociated or checked out or whatever—it's still got to be rough. And if he's reengaging with the world . . . it's going to make things tougher, right?"

I've worried about Derrick being in the general prison population. Certain crimes—especially crimes against children—are viewed by inmates as the worst of the worst. Derrick is a child killer—his brother was thirteen when he died. Whether Derrick was driven by the Midnight Man or not, he's still a killer.

But Benedict glares. "What have the other prisoners done to him?"

"Thefts. Petty tortures, like hawking in his food. Beatings, when the guards aren't looking."

"He's vulnerable. He shouldn't even be in the general population."

"I'm well aware of that, Dr. Hoffman." Bower sounds tired. "I'm doing my best. But Derrick hasn't exactly been his own advocate. He's a doormat, according to the guards. Lets the other inmates walk all over him. He tells me it doesn't matter. That none of this is real. But if you ask me, there's a shitload—excuse me—*a lot* of anger simmering underneath that placid veneer. I've caught glimpses. One of these days, if it's not carefully managed, it's going to erupt."

"Anger is often a mask for fear," Benedict says. "Especially in men. It can make them feel less vulnerable."

A door opens on the other side of the room. A correctional officer comes in, followed by a man in green pants, a long-sleeve green shirt, and deck shoes. A second guard enters behind the prisoner. Without asking, they remove the man's leg and arm shackles and push him down into a chair.

It takes me a few seconds to recognize the prisoner as Derrick.

He's lost weight in prison. Or rather shifted it—the pudgy teenager has grown into a sinewy young man. His once surfer-style tousled locks have been shaved, and his head looks oddly naked, like an egg. He's now twenty-two, but the loss of hair and the way his skin clings to the planes of his face add a decade.

Then there are the physical scars. They've settled during the last five years. The right side of his face was permanently disfigured when the bullet he'd intended for his brain instead pierced his cheek. The scar carves a path from the hinge of his jaw to the corner of his mouth—a sunken seam of pale, stretched skin, puckered and purple at the edges. The scar drags the right corner of his lips up into a caricature of a half smile.

The surgeon did what was necessary, but his wasn't the work of a physician to the stars. The job had been purely functional.

For so many reasons, it's hard to look at him.

"Be good," one of the correction officers tells Derrick before glancing at us. "We'll be right on the other side of that door. Any trouble, there's a button on the wall"—he points—"or just shout."

They leave. Derrick's eyes meet mine; his are the blue of an untroubled lake.

"Derrick." Bower's voice has gone soft. "You doing okay? I just told your visitors that you cut yourself."

"Wasn't me. But it doesn't matter." Derrick half rises from his chair. He reaches across the table, and we shake hands, his palm calloused from prison work and—I'm guessing—lifting weights. His biceps bulge in the snug shirt.

"Thank you for coming," he says. "Both of you. I mean it."

He drops back into his seat. His voice is wobbly from years of nonuse, but otherwise it's what I remember from videos taken off social media before Derrick became a killer. Soft. Polite. A bit high for a man. His speech was, I recall from a teacher's testimony, one source of the teasing he endured at Cherry Creek High School.

"We're glad to be here," I say. "And glad you've found your voice."

Humor glints in his deep-set eyes. I rarely glimpsed those eyes during the trial—his gaze was always lowered. Even in our private sessions with him, he'd rarely looked up. The arctic blue is arresting.

"I didn't mislay it," he says. The humor turns to flint. "Just stowed it for a while."

I smile back. But I'm unsettled by that stony gleam. It's a reminder that a lot can happen to a man after six years in the slammer—a year in pretrial detention followed by five years in the pen after the guilty verdict. Derrick may act like a doormat around the other inmates. But Bower could be right about the anger.

The attorney clicks his ballpoint pen on the desk. "Formalities," Bower says. "I need to verify that you're here to speak with Doctors Belle and Hoffman of your own free will and without pressure from them or from other parties. Is that true, Derrick?"

"Yup." Derrick signs the paper Bower sets in front of him.

"And you're aware that, per your specific request, we aren't recording this interview. But we will be taking notes."

Derrick's gaze moves from Bower to Benedict to me and back. His expression is once again passive.

But studying his Zen-like calm, I sense that the broken parts haven't mended. They've only been moved to make room for other things. At the trial, he was destroyed by grief and shame and horror. Now, it seems to me, he's taken those broken pieces, buried them somewhere out of sight, and taken on the semblance of a Buddhist monk. I again note his biceps, the slope from his neck to his shoulders, the muscled forearms. And I think: He's the kind of monk who could slice you into a thousand pieces without losing his place in the buddhavacana.

His calm is a teacup balanced on the edge of a wobbly table.

"Let me see," Derrick says.

The three of us look at each other. Bower runs a hand over his scalp. "See what?" he asks.

Derrick doesn't blink. "Show me you don't have recorders on you. Or wires. And take apart your pens. Let me see inside."

"All of us were checked before we walked in," Bower points out.

Derrick shrugs, a ripple of muscles across his tight shirt.

There's nothing for it if we want to hear what he has to say. We empty our pockets, unscrew our pens, turn our cuffs up and our collars down until Derrick's satisfied. I keep to myself that there are plenty of ways to hide a recorder these days that nothing short of a strip search would reveal.

"Are you comfortable now?" Bower asks as if he's checking to see if Derrick's coffee is at the right temperature.

"Yeah."

I'm reassembling my cheap ballpoint. "Can you tell us what your concern is?"

Derrick's eyes follow my hands. "You two fought for me during my trial. You worked hard trying to convince the jury I didn't act alone."

Benedict and I nod.

"You believed." He raises his eyes. Longing shines in the cold depths, a child begging to be told he's okay. "You believed in *him*."

"In Mid—" I begin.

"Hush!" Derrick drops the palms of his hands on the table, which trembles. He raises a finger to his lips. "Hush. No names. Just tell me yes or no. Do you still believe?"

Again, Benedict and I nod.

"Yes, Derrick," Benedict says. "It is our belief that you were pushed to commit murder by an outside influence."

Derrick's cold eyes scour our faces, as if he could peel back skin and cartilage and bone to see what lies or truth hide within our brains. His gaze is like an acid wash; my flesh tingles. I resist the desire to look away.

But after a moment, he nods and glances over his shoulder at the camera. Then he leans in. The rest of us follow suit so that our heads nearly touch.

"*He's* watching," Derrick whispers. He mouths the next words. "Midnight Man."

Our faces remain still, but the men must be as shocked as I am.

I say, "You believe he's watching you here. In prison."

"Dude's everywhere. In all places. At all times. In my cell. In the canteen. The exercise yard. The classroom." He dabs his forehead with his sleeve. "Especially in the classroom."

"I see," I say, though of course I don't. We're all still leaning in like it's a séance. "What do you think the Midnight Man could do to you here?"

"Whatever he wants."

I pity him. Imagine living with the idea that a malevolent entity is watching and judging your every move? Straight out of Orwell's *1984*.

"What does your psychiatrist say?" I ask.

"You mean the loser who leads group therapy? He has a script he reads off. He doesn't want it messed up by facts."

"Why do you believe Midnight Man is here?"

Derrick glances at the camera again and presses his index finger to his lips. The nail is chewed to the quick. "He came in on the game," he whispers. "Now he's in the cameras. In the fans and vents and motors. He rides the voltage."

"What game?" Benedict asks.

Bower steps in. "It's a cognitive behavioral therapy game called *Umbra*. A life-simulation game designed to help users process difficult emotions in healthy ways. At least, that's what I was told. Clinical staff evaluated the therapy and recommended it for select prisoners, including Derrick. The clinical director signed off."

It makes sense. Prisons are desperate for rehabilitation programs. And for companies, prisoners provide a literally captive audience. Not to mention less public scrutiny.

"When did you start playing *Umbra*?" I ask, wondering whether the game, not the Heaths, could be the trigger.

Bower says, "Around three months ago, right, Derrick?"

Derrick nods, but his right leg is bouncing under the table, and a twitch has developed in his left eye. He's staring at the camera.

Benedict scribbles something in his notebook and nudges it casually in my direction: *Start slow. Safe topics.*

"Derrick," I say.

He pulls his eyes from the camera.

I put on my chill face. "We'll come back to the game. Let's focus on other things while we get reacquainted. Is that okay?"

He attempts a smile, but—with the scar and the twitch—it's ghastly. "Okay."

"Excellent. Why don't you start by telling us how you spend your time."

"Outside of all the mandatory bullshit and my work assignments?"

That flash of anger Bower mentioned. "That's right."

"I lift weights. Read and write. Watch some TV. You know. Just passing time. Something to do until all of us escape and it's game over. When we can finally choose our own destiny."

"Derrick spends a lot of time in the vocational programs," Bower says, as if that explains things.

Benedict brings his forefingers together, presses them to his chin. "Homo deus. Human gods. That's what you mean? The logical end of our breaking free of a simulation?"

"If things go good, yeah."

Benedict lowers his hands. "Do you enjoy reading?"

The first spark of enthusiasm. "Sure. I used to like spec fic—fantasy and sci-fi graphic novels. Now I read nonfiction. It feels"—he rubs the column of his throat—"I don't know. Safer?"

"Safer how?"

"Those books don't put thoughts in my head. Stories that aren't mine."

Benedict lowers his voice. "Does *Umbra* put thoughts in your head?"

He flinches. "Only my own thoughts. That's what it's supposed to do."

We again steer away from the game. I talk to Derrick about his plan to get his GED and start taking college classes. The therapy dogs that come once a week. A new band he enjoys listening to. The conversation is surreal, given that Derrick claims nothing about his life is real.

I'm not surprised he's held on to his simulation theory. It both justifies his actions in murdering his family and allows him to skim above the grim reality of prison life. With nothing in his day-to-day existence to refute his beliefs, he has settled into a morally comforting delusion.

When Derrick appears calm, I glance at Benedict. He's the one who's worked with troubled youth. I want him to lead.

"Let's go back to the video game therapy, if that's okay, Derrick." Benedict scoots his chair away from the table and leans back, his hands circling one raised knee, the picture of casualness. "Is that okay? Can we talk about that?"

Derrick's lips twist. The scar shifts and moves as if it has a mind of its own.

"Okay."

"You used to be a big gamer, isn't that right? A good one."

Derrick folds his arms; his biceps bulge. "I was a hell of a gamer. Competitive. I was on my way. I even placed on a handful of leaderboards. I'd have made it to the tournament level if my parents got that gaming is a sport."

"What are your favorite games?"

"*Fortnite. Call of Duty.* Some others. I was killer at *Apex Legends.* I even had a shot at making it to the Global Series. You know the championship is in Japan this year? That'd've been sick."

We nod. A lot of this we know from our previous time with Derrick. But we're settling into a routine.

"And, yeah, then there's games like *Synaptica 2*," Derrick says. "I liked it okay. You know, as a way to unwind. But after a while, I cut over to playing something else. Can't remember what. Don't even recall the name. It's . . . it was part of that night, I guess. Gone."

Benedict half lifts his hands, fingers curling. As if he wants to grab Derrick by his shirt and shake an answer out of him. "*Eidolon?* Was it *Eidolon?*"

"I don't think I know that game," Derrick says, his eyes as cloudless as a high summer day.

"Tell us about *Synaptica 2.* How'd you find that game?"

A shrug. Derrick picks at a hangnail. "It was a farming sim. I heard a couple kids talk about it. It was decent."

"Do you know who created it?"

"Nah."

I step back in. "Can you tell us what you do remember about the game that was important to you? Was it a role-playing game?"

"Yeah, it was an RPG." He brings his palms together, almost like he's praying. "I mean, it's mainly a farming sim where you earn coins by gathering stuff. Kinda mindless. But I liked it. A chance to chill, you know? Then there're these side quests where you interact with NPCs. Help them become real players. That's where you earn the most coins and experience points."

"Do you remember how you would interact with the NPCs? Did you click on dialogue options?"

"Nah, it was cooler than that. You'd type what you wanted to say right into a chat box. Gave you a lot of freedom, different than typical branching role-playing games."

"Do you remember how you would help the NPCs?"

The twitch returns, but he keeps talking.

"Kind of? I'd show them something that would convince them they were trapped in a simulation. Like, glimpses of the real world. Prove to them that if they didn't escape, they'd never have free will. But most NPCs don't want to know their lives are a lie. You have to be a bit harder on them."

"Harder how?"

The twitch is moving down his face. "I—I don't remember."

"That's okay. Do you remember where you found the game?"

"A friend told me about it. Said he'd played it for a few weeks, then got kicked out. He never knew why. You can't find the game on your own, and you have to get an invite to download the game and join. And to keep playing. People get bounced all the time."

"For what?"

"Not—" He presses two fingers to his twitching eye. "I think it was not being harsh enough. Sometimes it's hard to do the right thing. Really hard. But that's where you got the points. And if you wanted to stay in, you had to do tough stuff."

"Hurt the NPCs?"

"Sometimes."

"Thank you, Derrick," I say. "This is helpful. What about the game you're playing now? The therapy game. *Umbra.* Do you like it?"

"Maybe? It's chill like *Synaptica 2.* Maybe even better visuals and soundtrack. But without the side quests. You farm, go shopping, you know, get stuff for your in-game room, and do chores and stuff. Try to avoid doing anything wrong, like cheating when you're shopping or lying to your friends to get more points. It's not subtle. A little boring. But it's okay."

Benedict leans in. "You don't have to answer this, Derrick. But if you can, you'll be helping us help you. Why do you say Midnight Man came in on the game?"

His eyes flick to the camera. "You think I'm nuts."

"No. I don't." Benedict's voice is firm. There's not a trace of doubt or condescension in his tone. "I know Midnight Man can act in mysterious ways. I want to know what he's doing. I want to understand *why*."

With the last sentence, Benedict's voice has turned fierce.

"There's a picture in my bedroom inside *Umbra*," Derrick says. "A painting. People on a riverbank. They're sitting on blankets, eating food. Talking and laughing. I like it. It's nice. But sometimes there's a glitch. And the picture—" Derrick stops, buries his face in his hands. "It turns into *The Scream*. Each time it happens, I click to remove it, but then the avatar of a man comes into the room. His avatar's kinda glitchy, not fully rendered. There's something not right. And he's wearing this crown . . . and saying over and over that he's stepped in blood."

We're frozen into silence, mannequins around the table. All except Derrick, who sobs quietly. Benedict reaches out a hand as if to touch Derrick, but he shakes himself and pulls back.

"Derrick?" he says softly. "Why do you think he's doing these things?"

"So that I'll do what he wants." Derrick lowers his hands and stares at them as if they're alien, the hands of someone else.

Benedict leans in again, gestures Derrick closer. "What does he want you to do?"

"Help people," Derrick says. "Help people escape the simulation. *That's* what he wants. For everyone to ascend."

27

Saturday, 6:05 p.m. EST

Today is the day, Shelby has decided.

She knows if she waits much longer, she'll lose *Eidolon* forever. So today, this evening, right *now* while her parents are out shopping, she'll approach the barrier to *Underland*. Just to take a peek. Get a feel. But not to go in. Not yet.

She picks up QuWu and hugs the doll close before she lowers her hands to the keyboard.

In moments, *Eidolon* envelops her. She takes a deep breath. Lowers her shoulders. Straightens her spine. She steps onto the path to *Underland* and walks.

A field of ripened corn calls to her: Spend time with me.

"Not today," she whispers back.

In an apple orchard, the trees call to her: Rest in my shade.

"Not today," she whispers.

She walks west, farther than she's ever gone. The road begins to descend from the rolling hills of *Eidolon*, and into a great forest. At first the trees are like those in Lothlórien, from Middle-earth. But soon the woods grow thicker, the trees taller, until they blot out the sky. Things cry out from the forest, from deep in the shadows where she can't see.

Shelby thinks of the ripening corn now far behind her. The apple trees filled with fruit.

She stops.

Another player told her that entering *Underland* is scary because we must go through the dark to get to the light, to get to the real world. The woods are only as dark as our souls.

Shelby never thought her soul was dark. If she's so awful, why aren't the animals afraid of her? Why does she like giving away the berries she's spent hours picking?

But the game can't be wrong, can it? She shivers as the trees lean closer. Tortured faces appear in the bark. Her soul must be very bad indeed.

She glances back, over her shoulder. The fields and orchards are gone. Instead, there are cogs and wheels, steel beams. A crane. She realizes she's seeing the skeleton of *Eidolon*, the machinery that makes the world tick. Below the moving parts will be bits and bytes, the building blocks of every game. It's beautiful and horrible, all at once. Panic threatens to close her throat. What if she's lost? What if she can't get back to *Eidolon*?

What if she can't get back home? To QuWu and Boo. Even her parents.

She turns, facing east, struggling to re-create the apple trees, the corn, the silly NPCs with their empty baskets.

From the woods, a wraith steps onto the trail, blocking her way. It's tall and cloaked, with eyes that blaze like coals.

It raises a hand, points a finger at her. "If you lose your courage," it says, "you will lose everything."

Shelby drops to the ground and curls into a ball. "I'll do it," she says. "I'll do whatever you want. I'll go to *Underland*. Just don't hurt me."

The chat dings. The wraith disappears.

NEW PRIVATE MESSAGE FROM: MIDNIGHT MAN

MM: Stay in the game, Shelby.

Shelby looks at her phone. She's been in the game for hours.

> i can't. I can't.

MM: Then go to your window, Shelby. The window in your room. Look out, then come back and tell me what you see. I'll wait.

Shaking, Shelby stands up from her desk. She picks up QuWu and crosses to the window.

Outside, it's snowing hard. Snow whips past, illuminated by porch lights and streetlamps. Someone stands in a cone of light on the sidewalk across the street from her house. The snow is so heavy she can't tell if the person is short or tall. Or even if it's a man or a woman. She presses her forehead to the cold pane. Icicles sparkle from the pinpoints of light in her room. A man, she decides. Square and solid.

For a long time the man doesn't move, but she can feel his eyes on hers. Then he raises his hand. Waves. He crosses the street to her house, and a moment later the doorbell rings. Downstairs, Boo barks.

Shelby drops to her knees. She crawls across the floor back to her desk. Pulls the keyboard to her. She's scared of the wraith. But she's not going to answer the door.

The wraith is waiting.

"This way," it says. "Follow me."

28

Five minutes of silence in the interview room, and we all seem to have recovered our equilibrium. My throat is dry; I'd kill for a glass of water.

"Let's talk about the new game," Benedict says. "*Umbra.*"

Derrick wipes the front and back of his hands on his thighs, as if cleaning them.

"Dr. Marcel says the game's supposed to help me get my memories back," he says.

Beside me, Benedict stiffens. "Marcel? Anthony Marcel?"

"I don't know."

Bower is fumbling through papers. "Dr. Anthony Marcel. That's correct."

"He's from San Carlos?" Benedict asks.

Bower and Derrick both shrug. Derrick says, "Maybe? Dr. Marcel visits the prison twice a month, and I'm one of the patients on his list."

"Did he ask to counsel you in particular?"

"I think so. We mass murderers are very popular." But Derrick looks alarmed, his expression mirroring Benedict's. "What's the matter, Dr. Hoffman?"

Bower interjects. "I asked why Derrick was admitted to the program. According to the clinical director, Dr. Marcel specifically requested Derrick. The doctor is focusing on those who've been accused of committing particularly—sorry, Derrick—particularly violent crimes."

"I see." Benedict straightens his shoulders as if recovering himself. "It's nothing, Derrick. I'm sorry. Just my own memories surfacing. Dr. Anthony Marcel and I worked together at San Carlos. He was part of a video game therapy program there called *Synaptic*. Maybe similar to your farming sim, *Synaptica 2*. One of those crazy coincidences. Please continue."

Derrick stares at Benedict a moment longer. His Adam's apple bobs up and down as he swallows. "I use the video game under Dr. Marcel's supervision. He calls the game a neurorehabilitation pilot. Like, an empathy-building tool, which I guess helps with amnesia?"

"It can. Building empathy keeps you from disassociating. It's natural that, in the process, some memories will return."

"Whatever it does, it works. When memories come up, the game helps me process them. Then Dr. Marcel and I review the memories together after I've played."

Benedict nods. "Game therapy has been used with some success in retrieving memories in patients suffering from amnesia. But the therapy requires caution. Being pressured to remember the past can result in creating false memories. And an AI—" He stops himself. "The primary goal of any therapy should be to help patients cope with the trauma and its effects, rather than attempting to reconstruct specific memories. Do you understand?"

"Isn't remembering part of how I process my trauma?"

"It is. But traumatic memories must be opened slowly, under supervision, with safeguards in place. Amnesia is troubling, but as a coping mechanism, it exists for a reason: to protect us."

"But isn't that what Dr. Marcel is doing?" Derrick tips back in his chair, staring up at the ceiling. "I'm a terrible person, right? Whether this world is real or a simulation, I did terrible things. Maybe remembering will help me make up for that."

"Maybe," Benedict says. "But don't carry this alone."

He brings his eyes to Benedict. "What do you mean?"

"Do you know why Charles Manson succeeded in convincing young people to commit atrocities?" Benedict asks. "It wasn't because he was physically strong or overtly threatening. He preyed on their vulnerabilities—their insecurities, their loneliness, their need to belong to something greater than themselves. He gave them a sense of purpose, twisted as it was, and made them believe they were special when they did his bidding. The Midnight Man is no different. He didn't choose you because you're evil. He picked you because you were vulnerable, because he could exploit your pain and turn it into his weapon. He chose you because you're a brilliant gamer who could understand all the nuances of his game and go fully into the scenarios he created. You're not the monster, Derrick. He is."

Derrick's shoulders twitch. He folds his arms tightly across his chest as if to stop the tremor. I imagine what he's learned in prison: Protect your back; hide your emotions; never—as my own mentor told me—never let them see you sweat.

"I wish that were true," he says.

"It *is* true. Everything Agent Belle and I said at your trial is true. Midnight Man is out there. Now we have tangible proof. He used you. And now he's using others." Benedict leans in. He looks as sincere as a Bible salesman. "We could use your help."

Derrick lowers his arms. "What proof?"

"We can't share that right now," I interject. "But Dr. Hoffman is right."

Derrick looks back and forth between us, weighing our words.

"What will I get if I help you?"

He's not the naive kid he once was. "A chance for a retrial," I say. "A possible reduction in your sentence. In the meantime, we can petition for you to get more privileges."

"You'll also get the satisfaction of knowing you did the right thing," Benedict adds. "The moral thing."

For a moment Derrick looks almost boyish again, despite the lurid scar and the muscles. Like a kid who's been granted three wishes. "How can I help?"

Benedict lowers his voice. "We suspect Midnight Man operates from the hypothesis that we're living in a simulation, right? How does he convince teens that their world isn't real? How did he convince you?"

"But he's right." A quick glance at the camera. "Midnight Man is scary, but what he says is true."

"Okay. Tell me why you believe that."

He sighs. "Okay—look. Quantum mechanics says particles don't assume a definite state until they're observed. Right? That sounds weird, but it's particle physics *and* gaming code. It's how video games work. Stuff only renders—makes images you can see—when you're looking at it. It saves memory. It's efficient. So what if this"—he gestures to the interview room, including us—"is the same? What if the universe isn't real until we observe it because it's not a universe—it's a simulation?"

Benedict rubs his chin as if he's giving Derrick's idea due weight. "The simulation hypothesis is a fascinating philosophical concept." He pushes his chair back and rests his elbows on his knees, hands clasped. "You know, Derrick, Midnight Man isn't the first to say that the world's an illusion. The Hindus called it *maya*. Plato called it 'the Cave.' Gnostics believed we are trapped in a false reality built by a lesser god. The idea that something's hiding behind the world is ancient. What's new is your metaphor. You say it's a simulation because you grew up with games and code. That's the medium you understand."

"Does it matter what we call it?" Derrick asks. "A cave or a simulation?"

"Maybe the analogy doesn't matter. But here's the danger, Derrick— when you start believing the world isn't real, it gets very easy to treat people like they aren't real, either."

Derrick shakes his head, surety replacing his earlier unease. He sits up straight, lifts his chin, now in his element.

"*This* world is the fake one," he explains. "This world with its NPCs programmed to pretend to love us, to care for us. It's all a sham. Midnight Man says he will open the eyes of those who can see and reveal to them the real world. Everyone else will be erased."

"Erased," I say. "You mean murdered."

"You don't understand!"

I alternately want to hug Derrick and put him away forever. He's unable to see the contradictions tearing apart his mind and heart. His mind tells him he was right to murder his family. Doing so set them free from a false world. But his heart is broken because it knows the truth: They were real, and he killed them.

Derrick throws back his head and wails. He leaps to his feet. His stomach heaves, and vomit spatters down his uniform.

"We're done." Bower is on his feet. He ignores the foul stench rising in the room and grips Derrick's shoulder. "Hang in there."

He smacks his palm against the button to call the guards. Within seconds they've entered. They eyeball Derrick with a resigned disgust.

Bower says, "He needs to see the doctor."

"Yeah, I can get that. Carl, shackle him and we'll haul him to the infirmary."

Carl secures handcuffs to Derrick's wrists, fastens them to a belly chain around Derrick's waist, then snaps on leg irons.

"I'm not evil," Derrick says to us over his shoulder as the guards steer him toward the door, his feet shuffling and the chains rattling. "The Midnight Man isn't evil. We just want everyone to understand the truth. Sometimes you have to burn down the world to prove to everyone that it's a lie." He raises his shackled wrists. "Wait. I need to tell them one more thing."

The officers pause. Derrick gives a single wild shake of his head, like he's trying to jar something loose. His eyes have gone wide, and a line of spittle unspools from the upturned corner of his mouth.

"You want my help," he says. "So here's the weirdest thing."

I can't wait.

"My dad used to take me to the range to shoot. I still remember how to take apart and clean a gun. I remember how to load it. I remember how a pistol feels in my hand."

"Okay," Benedict says.

"That night, I saw my mom fall to the floor. But I don't remember holding the gun." Beneath the thin shirt, his stomach moves as if he's going to vomit again. "It wasn't me."

"Wait," I say. "What do you mean?"

"There was someone else there that night." His eyes glint with either madness or tears. "I wasn't alone."

———

Before we leave the prison, we stop with Bower at the warden's office. As a federal agent, I have no authority in a state prison, but I strongly recommend that Derrick be placed back on suicide watch due to his distress over his flashbacks. Then I ask for information about the new video game therapy, *Umbra*. I expect the warden to tell me to come back with a warrant. But instead, after inspecting my badge, she prints the contract defining the authorized therapeutic use of *Umbra*—three copies, one for each of us. Alongside signatures from prison authorities appear the names of Anthony Marcel, MD, ABPN, and Scott Poole, MD, ABPN, FAPA.

The contract doesn't include a physical address. Just an email and a post office box in Austin, Texas.

The name of the company that created *Umbra* is NeoPath. New path. Benedict points out that if we want to look for references to the simulation theory that Derrick clings to, the name NeoPath could be a play on one of the characters in *The Matrix*.

Derrick is the only inmate Marcel is seeing. Call me a cynic, but I don't think NeoPath's choice of Derrick is an accident.

There's something here that is seriously rotten.

29

I drive in silence for the first ten minutes while Benedict and I process. He's staring out the window, drumming a tune on his thigh, thinking.

Dusk descends as I drive, a gray dove folding its wings, closing out the day. Lights spark on inside the cab, the dash a soft glow of green and amber. Everything else is in shadow.

I'm picturing Derrick, trapped in a nightmare where he doesn't know what's real and what isn't. He longs for the truth, but the real world, with its blood and slaughter, is infinitely worse than living in a simulation. I can't blame him for clinging to the lie.

What I know about game therapy is that a patient's psychosis can deepen when immersive gameplay blurs the line between reality and simulation, especially in patients with fragile ego boundaries or pre-existing delusional thinking. The game world can reinforce or even replace reality.

I turn to Derrick's last words. *I wasn't alone.* I can't shake the image of those footprints in the Ohio field. *Big guy,* Feldster had said. *Hagrid,* Katelynn texted Elise.

As I pull into the small town of Penrose, slowing to thirty-five miles per hour, I find my voice. My words come out in a rush.

"Is Midnight Man after Derrick?" I ask. "Is he inside the game? Or is Derrick hallucinating when he enters *Umbra*? That portrait of *The*

Scream in his bedroom. The blood-stepped king, Macbeth. You mentioned there was a client at San Carlos whose psychosis worsened after the therapy. The kid who painted his room with his own feces. Could *Umbra* be magnifying Derrick's psychosis in the same way?"

Benedict stirs. "I don't know."

He sounds drained, his form a soft shadow. He cracks the passenger window and sucks in clean mountain air. Biting cold slaps through the cab. Temperatures have dropped to the teens, and melted snow on the road has refrozen into a treacherous slush. The SUV slides through the grooves left by other cars, slipping. I grip the wheel. A scattering of porch lights laces the darkness on either side.

"It's cold," I say.

"Sorry." Benedict presses the button, and the window slides up. His scent—a mix of tobacco and wool—fills the cab, and for a moment it's as if we're back together in our early days. As if no time at all has passed.

Melancholy fills my throat.

I swallow. "Tell me about Anthony Marcel. And *Synaptic*."

Benedict's indistinct figure moves as he shifts in his seat.

"Marcel was one of Poole's protégés and part of his gaming therapy working group. He helped administer *Synaptic* and provided counseling after gameplay. He's another doctor who seemed to be in the business more for his ego than to help the kids. But maybe that's unfair. I barely knew him, more as a name on emails and papers."

"What papers?"

Benedict pulls out his phone. "I didn't—" He's scrolling. "I'll be damned. He writes about the simulation theory."

"For or against?"

Benedict skims through whatever's on his screen. "Neither, that I can tell. Just that it's a compelling theory. And a reason why some people might consider following an exit protocol. In gaming, an exit protocol means escaping or exiting a game or some aspect of the game. It can also mean suicide."

"And this is the guy administering a game to an emotionally unstable inmate?"

"You must be wondering the same thing I am—why Derrick?"

"Why *only* Derrick?"

He stretches his legs as far as he can in the SUV's cab. Dash lights turn slivers of his skin amber. A cheek. A wedge of his forehead. But mostly his voice comes out of the dark.

"Bower speculated that it was learning about the Heaths that got Derrick to talk," he says. "But it was also the video game therapy. He said it himself. It's helping him remember. And it makes sense. If it was through a game that Midnight Man found and exploited his targets, then being back in that environment might allow memories to worm through the defensive layers he's built against the trauma of that night."

"Meaning he *could* be imagining *The Scream*. The king stepped in blood. Adding them to the game subconsciously."

"Right. Guilt manifesting itself in the familiar environment of a game. A chosen hallucination. For Derrick, if he hangs on to his belief that the Midnight Man is real, if the blood-soaked king is really in the game, then it's confirmation we live in a simulation. Derrick needs to believe that, or his guilt will destroy him."

"And in introducing the game to Derrick, Marcel and Poole are playing with fire." The SUV hits a patch of ice, back wheels floating. I correct. "If it's emotionally safer for Derrick to believe the real world is a simulation, why reach out to us? He knows we won't support that idea."

"I think it's because his simulated world is showing cracks. Without access to the original game Midnight Man provided, the full immersion experience is gone, and eventually the real world begins to seep in. Even as he enjoys Marcel's 'boring' game, Derrick is no longer as invested in the game world, or in believing in a simulated universe."

"And yet he persists. All that talk about quantum mechanics."

"Emotional need can override many things. Including the truth."

I slow behind a truck hauling a trailer. Bits of hay escape the wire baling and patter against the windshield. "It's ironic. The real world is leaking in because he's back to gaming."

"The good news is that now we have a name. NeoPath. That's got to be the behavioral tech company Poole was talking about. It makes sense for him and Marcel to continue their gaming therapy together with new funding and a fresh start."

"And how better to launch than by healing a degenerate mass murderer like Derrick? We need their client list. If Jason is on there, we'll have a solid link between Midnight Man and NeoPath. And something better than the name of a city to use to find him."

My phone rings. It's Clif. I put the call through the car's Bluetooth.

"Clif. I'm with Dr. Hoffman."

"Benedict!" There's a smile in Clif's voice. "Have you joined our ragged band of truth hunters?"

"I have. How are you, Clif?"

"I know better than to complain. Look, I just called to let Helen know that we've hit a dead end on tracking down a computer repairperson. None of the local shops dispatched anyone to the Heath residence. None of their employees own panel vans. And they pointed out that most tech issues they deal with don't require someone to be physically present."

"Maybe it's a private individual, working out of his house."

"If so," Clif says, "he gets his business by word of mouth rather than advertising."

"Clif, Benedict and I just saw Derrick at CSP. He's talking, but he's not always making a lot of sense. He says the Midnight Man is after him, but we're not sure yet what that means, or if it means anything." I fill him in on Poole and Marcel and NeoPath. "The last thing Derrick told us was that he wasn't alone the night of the murders. And while his memories are coming back, one thing he doesn't remember is holding a gun. That doesn't line up with the forensics, does it? The gunshot residue, for one. And Derrick's fingerprints."

"The GSR isn't definitive," Clif says. "If you recall, they only found traces on Derrick."

"Because he'd washed his hands."

"That might not be the only reason."

"Explain," Benedict says.

"GSR is tricky. It's like glitter at a kid's birthday party—you don't have to touch the stuff to walk out sparkling. If Derrick was standing close enough, or if the shooter moved past him right after firing? That residue could've settled on him. When you fire a gun indoors, those particles hang in the air—unburned powder, microscopic metal. You breathe it, brush against it. Even walking through a room right after can do it."

This had come up at Derrick's trial, when the amount of GSR on his hands couldn't prove either guilt or innocence.

"Okay," Benedict says. "Thanks."

"Helen, you want to handle the follow-up on NeoPath?" Clif asks.

"I'll take care of it."

Over the phone, kids squeal in the background. "That sound like a nuclear explosion is my grandkids," Clif says. "Parents dropped them off for pizza and a movie. I can't decide if they make me younger or if they're going to be the death of me." He covers the phone and yells something that sounds like "Give your sister her brownie." He comes back. "I gotta go before they kill each other. Talk to you tomorrow."

I stare out the window. We're clear of Penrose. In the headlights, the snow pelting the windshield is mesmerizing. My thoughts turn to Katelynn. Is it snowing where she is? Is she cold?

Why would Midnight Man break so completely from what we think we know about him to steal a teenage girl and her dog?

"Derrick wants absolution," Benedict says.

"Is that the psychologist talking? Or the priest?"

"I was never a priest."

"You've never told me why you dropped out of seminary."

"Maybe dropping out was a mistake." His coat rustles as he tilts his seat. "But neither psychology nor theology has helped me understand the mind of these killers. They create their own mythology, then laugh when we try to make it a viable narrative."

"Perhaps there is no way to understand them. They're a black box with damaged contents we'll never be able to read. We can study their brain scans, but even those don't provide all the answers. We're left trying to decipher their actions after the fact."

"And to try to prevent violence before it explodes."

I say, "That's the entire goal at San Carlos, right? Find a way to help these kids manage their violent emotions? Give them a shot at a normal life?"

"Therapy clearly failed with Jennifer Moore. She went on to murder her mother, almost certainly under the influence of the Midnight Man." The headlights from a car heading the other direction scour the cab—I catch a glimpse of Benedict as he rakes his fingers through his dark curls. "We think we understand serial killers. We've created a mythology of white, male evil geniuses perpetrating ritualistic acts of violence for sexual gratification. But it's a false mythology. And there's still so little we know about what drives them."

"Earlier today, when I suggested a link between Midnight Man and Poole, you said maybe Midnight Man had hacked Poole's information. Hacked NeoPath, right? What if we go back further? What if there's a link between the teens and Midnight Man and the work Dr. Poole did at San Carlos? That would explain how Midnight Man connected with Jennifer."

"Go on."

I grope my way forward. "You told me Jennifer Moore was a budding psychopath."

"That's not the formal language, but yes. She has a normal IQ, but her functional MRIs reveal differences in the paralimbic system of her brain. Those scans are partly what brought her to San Carlos—once her parents accepted that it wasn't bad parenting or bad genes that made their daughter a monster, they realized Jennifer needed profes-sional help."

"Which she received from Dr. Poole."

"Poole was her primary therapist. But they use a multimodal approach at San Carlos. Jennifer would have received cognitive behavioral therapy along with other forms of treatment. Rewards and positive reinforcement instead of punishment. And, of course, group counseling to help teach her the importance of community."

"And, you think, video game therapy."

"Right. *Synaptic*. Before the project was shut down."

"Did you ever play the game?"

"Poole suggested I focus my attention elsewhere."

"Who built it? There had to be programmers and designers. Artists and writers. IT staff. Even neuroscientists."

"There was. A team of fourteen. Behavioral design guys, two narrative engineers, four programmers with deep gaming chops who could create immersive architecture, reward/punishment feedback loops, dynamic moral pathways. On and on. Cutting-edge stuff designed to deliberately influence a player's psychology."

Excitement rises in me, a tide surging onto the shore. "Seems to me, Benedict, that from the bones of Poole's game it would be easy for someone who understands how to make young players vulnerable—emotionally and psychologically—to turn that psychology against them. Someone who knows how to bend reality until kids don't know where the game ends and the real world begins. Someone who could go on to—"

He jumps in. "Create *Eidolon* and *Underland*. *Synaptica 2* was a forerunner. *Umbra* is a side branch. You're right. It does make sense. Poole wanted a game that rewired destructive impulses into healthy ones. But in the wrong hands, it would be just as easy to reverse. Incentivize violence."

"So couldn't someone on the development team be Midnight Man?" My breath quickens. "We just need the names of everyone on the team."

Benedict touches his hand to my arm. "Helen, you *are* right. But here's the problem. As soon as Elaine Carr told me about Jennifer Moore, I had the same thought. Before I met with Poole, I contacted one of my white hat hacker friends. And don't lecture me. Katelynn's well-being rises above all ethical concerns. I heard back from him earlier, as we were walking out of the pen. Those records are gone. Poole took everything about the game—the clients, the development team, even the game itself—either offline or somewhere just as inaccessible."

"If he's destroyed that information, he'll face civil and criminal charges. There are strict laws around the handling of protected health information."

"Poole is arrogant but not stupid. I'm sure he didn't destroy the records. He just stashed them in a place my friend couldn't touch. But not to despair. Poole included patients from other institutions in his therapy. I've sent my friend in a different, hopefully more fruitful, direction." He taps his phone. "Too bad we missed Poole's lecture this afternoon. We could have cornered him."

"Hotel?"

"No idea."

"We'll subpoena him. And Marcel." I dial Zane at BAU and tell him what we've learned. Poole. Marcel. NeoPath. And that we need to get inside San Carlos as well, specifically the records of their video game therapy program. "The game was called *Synaptic*."

Zane says, "With that level of granularity, San Carlos should be straightforward. I'll see if we can dig up a physical address for a warrant for NeoPath," he says. "If not, then we can issue a grand jury subpoena to the owners, Poole and Marcel. I'll call the US Attorney's Office now. With luck, we'll start getting answers tomorrow. Good work, Helen."

I disconnect and merge onto I-25, heading north toward the Uintah exit and downtown Colorado Springs. Fresh snow collects on the ground. "Players were—are—being groomed. Probably not by Poole—that would be too risky for his career and reputation. And not even by the game. But by the man behind the game."

"Jennifer Moore was likely both Poole's test run and Midnight Man's. A rousing success for our villain's first time out of the gate, if that's what she was. We need to talk to her."

"Maybe you can find a way to get her to talk. So far, she refuses."

"We just need the magic password."

"What might that be?"

In the dashboard lights, I catch his smile. "Even sitting in a psych ward, Jennifer managed to get on *Eidolon*," he says. "Which means she was there when Jason joined. They overlapped. Maybe she's the one who sent him the photo. If so, that gives us her gamertag."

I glance over. "GlitchDoll."

"Right," he says. "*GlitchDoll* is our magic password."

30

Saturday, 7:00 p.m. MST

Darkness is thick enough to slice with a knife as I pull into the driveway of Benedict's Tudor-style home on Wood Avenue. I've always loved his home, but tonight the house sulks in the gloom, looking as reluctant to admit us as it would a pair of trespassers.

Then, just as I hit the brakes, the house transforms. Rooms glow with golden light. Porch lights and lampposts unspool waves of warmth. Additional lights gleam under the eaves, lighting pathways, illuminating hedges. Only the garages and old servants' quarters just to the north of the house remain dark. Gone is the witch's lair. I'm looking at a fairy tale.

"Timers," Benedict explains. "I just haven't set them to winter hours."

"It's beautiful," I say.

He unbuckles, drops his hand to the door handle. He doesn't look at me. "Do you want to come in? We should keep discussing the case. I've got some lasagna ready to bake and a decent bottle of red."

My instinct is to say no. Ever since Benedict walked out on me, I've been saying no.

"It's tempting, but I really should go."

"It's almost another two hours to Boulder. You look tired."

My lips quirk. "Straight way to a girl's heart."

"I mean, we're both tired. A good meal and a chance to plan and then decompress. That's all I'm offering."

"I should go," I say again. "Dinner won't lessen the drive time."

"Helen, I—" Now his eyes meet mine. "Is there someone in your life? I'm not asking you on a date. I just want to know."

It's my turn to look away. "I've never—no. My work is everything." And because that sounds pathetic, I add, "It's more than enough. I'm happy."

"Good. You'll be happier with some lasagna in you."

I laugh. I can't help it. I'm starting to remember what it was like to fall in love with this man. Dangerous territory. But still I ask, "You have Maggie?"

A smile. "My girl's not as young as she used to be."

"You think she'll remember me?"

Now he looks away. "You aren't exactly forgettable, Helen."

"Well." I huff a breath, feel tension drop away. "Let's find out."

Inside the house, Maggie bounds toward us from the back. She powers into my legs, almost knocking me over, her tail wagging up a gale force wind.

"Guess that answers that," Benedict says.

Maggie presses against me. I drop my hand to the soft fur of her skull. Her trust relaxes a hard place I hold inside.

Benedict takes my coat, hangs it next to his in the foyer, then leads the way down the long hallway toward the kitchen.

It's been years since I've been here, but what I can see remains unchanged. The hallway is still lined with fine art prints of paintings and photographs dating back to 1493. The prints aren't anything special, but they're well framed. All of them depict the commitment of one or another crime, from pickpocketing to murder.

I pause in front of *Persuasion*, as I've done on almost every visit. It's a painting by Walter Sickert, one of a series originally called *The Camden Town Murder*, that Sickert said was meant to capture the pathos of the recent murder of a prostitute. Some Ripperologists accused Sickert of being Jack the Ripper, but in the hundred years since the murders, they have yet to offer proof. It's a stark reminder that—given the recent thrilling, then vigorously disputed, claim that the Ripper's DNA had been found and the Ripper identified—not all crimes are solved.

The kitchen is unchanged. Clean, warm with hanging copper pots, kente print curtains in brick-red and ivory, and maple cabinetry. It has an easy feeling to it and is exactly as I remember. What I *did* put out of my mind over years of chewing through prepackaged grocery store dinners is how much Benedict enjoys cooking. I watch as he turns on the oven, then removes a ceramic casserole dish from the fridge, peeling off foil and plastic wrap to reveal mounds of lasagna. From the bread box, he retrieves a loaf of what looks like homemade Italian bread and sets it on a wooden cutting board. He pours out two small bowls of olive oil and balsamic vinaigrette. Next, he takes the makings for a salad from the Sub-Zero refrigerator, which is concealed behind cabinetry.

Memories tumble me with the force of an avalanche. Our many times in this kitchen with me cheerfully playing the role of sous chef, following his guidance as I chopped my way through vegetables, learned to incorporate cold butter into a warm reduction of wine and shallots, and to caramelize the sugar on a crème brûlée. His hands gently guiding mine, my back pressed to his chest, his breath in my ear. The delirious warmth of being utterly simpatico with another human being.

Watching him now, I think that maybe he hasn't changed so much, after all.

He reaches for a bottle of wine.

"Don't open it on my account," I say. "As you pointed out, I still have a long drive."

"Right," he says, and slips the bottle back into its spot on the rack. I'm grateful that he is choosing abstinence along with me.

———

Dinner is outstanding. The pasta cooked to perfection, the rich meat sauce bubbling—it's garlicky, tangy with oregano and thyme, and given a salty crunch by the addition of freshly grated Parmesan. There's enough mozzarella to satisfy any turophile, of which I am one. The warmed bread, sliced and set next to the bowls of olive oil and balsamic vinaigrette, fills the cozy dining room with the aroma every house should have.

I don't even miss the wine.

Halfway through the meal, when the first edge of hunger is gone, I point my fork at Benedict.

"Why haven't you published? Isn't that part of your commitment to the college?"

"I've got a project. The department chair and faculty dean have agreed to let me focus on that in the hopes it will lead to a big publication."

"Want to share?"

He hesitates, then shrugs. "I'm chasing bad actors."

"Like Midnight Man. And the other game masters you mentioned. The ones you exposed."

"Exactly. It's important to know that these aren't game masters in the traditional sense. They're the architects of the entire experience of the game, as with Midnight Man. They can alter the game in real time as part of how they groom certain players."

"Any luck finding these guys?"

"Some."

"You're still a gamer," I say.

"Totally hooked." Now he smiles. "It's how I've always let go of the stress that builds up during the day."

I reach for another slice of bread. "Talk to me about the appeal."

"You've never played?"

"Just old games like *Pac-Man* at the arcade."

"Not the same. Role-playing games give the user a sense of challenge and accomplishment—you're always learning new skills. There's the social aspect. You might be alone in your room, but you've got wonderful company in the digital universe. Plus, it's great escapism."

"And the typical profile of a gamer?" I'm thinking of our victimologies.

"We don't fit neatly in a box. But I will tell you I can count on my fingers and toes the number of gamers who have trouble distinguishing the real world from the worlds created inside the games. What's different for younger gamers, those just coming of age, is that they're already living in a world that undermines connection. To entice these newer players, Midnight Man doesn't have to create from scratch their disillusionment and their desire for a better world. The embers are already smoldering—he just has to fan the flames."

"The computer sciences teacher, Knopf. He said games can be healthy. And you just mentioned socialization. Doesn't gaming *build* community?"

Benedict refills our water glasses.

He says, "Knopf also mentioned there's a healthy limit. Having the bulk of your socializing online isn't good. Where we failed at Derrick's trial was with our inability to convince the jury how an online relationship can be so completely compelling. Imagine your favorite character from your favorite book—or from a fictional world that is very similar—who comes to you and says, 'I'm here for you. I want to be your friend.' You start dreaming of him or her. Carrying on made-up conversations. Then you get an invitation to the game. And they're no longer imaginary."

"It bleeds into real life," I say.

"Yes."

"I was surprised when Hollywood started making movies based on games. Aren't the storylines difficult to translate from role-playing to an actual story arc?"

He laughs. "You're still stuck in *Pac-Man. The Last of Us* began as a game, yes. A postapocalyptic survival narrative that is also about love. As a game, it was already successful. Then it crossed the boundary into prestige television—with top-notch actors, cinematic production, and emotional realism intact. What was once gameplay became art. Shared. Elevated."

"And for teens like Jason, that transition serves as validation."

"Right. The culture affirms what they already felt: that the story is real. That its violence has purpose. That grief, sacrifice, revenge—these are noble if they serve someone you love. When a teen says she relates to the girl in *The Last of Us*—Ellie—she doesn't just mean Ellie's cool. She means she's absorbed Ellie's worldview. The line between her life and that of the character has blurred. And the family in the next room becomes less real than the world behind the screen."

I stand and stack our plates. Benedict grabs the salad and condiments and follows me into the kitchen.

"Midnight Man doesn't need to invent new myths," I say. "He just needs to hijack the ones players already believe in. The power of story is one of the strongest tools humans have. Stories are why dictators take over the arts and kill those writers who won't create work for the party line."

We set the dishes in the sink. Benedict scoops what's left of the salad into a glass container. I lean against the counter, my arms folded.

"*The Last of Us* shares a lot with one of Jason's favorite books," Benedict says. "Cormac McCarthy's *The Road*. The love of a parent or another adult for a child. Remember, Hersch mentioned that Jason might have been looking for a father figure. Now we need to understand what myth Midnight Man is pushing. We have Derrick telling us that what he remembers of the game is that its narrative is about helping people ascend, transform. It's about revealing the truth to the NPCs that they're living in a simulation."

"Then shooting them to help them transform."

"That's the sticky wicket," Benedict says. "How does Midnight Man get them to take that final and most difficult step?"

"By showing up at their homes to guide them. Or by pulling the trigger himself. It's like in the movie *The Matrix* when Morpheus appears and offers Neo the choice of either the blue pill or the red. Live contentedly in a false world, or have your blindfold removed."

"But the kids struggle to follow through with suicide. Thus, we have Derrick and possibly Jennifer botching the job. And Jason dragging his heels."

"Until Midnight Man forced him. Perhaps by threatening Katelynn. Maybe Jennifer Moore can give us some insight." I follow Benedict back into the dining room, where we collect the rest of what's left of our dinner. "Which pill would you choose, Benedict?"

"I'm a person who believes in the truth above almost everything."

"Above love? Friendship? Companionship?"

"That's easy. You can't have any of those things in a meaningful way if they aren't based on truth."

"That's . . . true." We smile at each other before grabbing salad bowls and salt and pepper shakers and returning to the kitchen.

"What about you?" he asks.

I want to say that of course I'd choose the red pill and stop living a lie. But would I really? Is a world built on false assumptions so terrible if, within its boundaries, you are happy with your life and ignorant of your ignorance?

But all I say is, "I'd also choose the red pill."

"You're lying," he teases.

I'm not, I realize. "I'm an FBI agent. It's my job to see the truth. Just as much as it is your job as a humanist."

———

We retire to the small library at the front of the house with mugs of hot chocolate. The wind howls under the eaves and snow pelts the windows. It feels very Gothic. As if we're in an English manor far from London while outside the wolves howl.

I don't lack imagination.

While I peruse the ghoulish contents of the bookshelves—row after row of crime novels, serial killer books, textbooks on the criminal mind, all amid a scattering of comic books and other elements of popular culture—Benedict lights a fire and draws the curtains. When I've finished looking at the shelves, we sit in the oversize chairs in front of the fire while the flames pop and crackle, tossing our shadows on the wall. Maggie jumps up next to Benedict and wedges her body between him and the arm of the oversize chair, her front legs and her head in his lap. He strokes her head and teases her ears with gentle fingers.

"Shall we get to work?" he says, his feet propped on an ottoman, his head in his hand. He sounds content, even sleepy. A fire and a dog on a winter's day will do that.

His eyes close. Minutes pass.

A gust of wind slams the panes of glass. Maggie twitches in her sleep. A vivid image looms in my mind: Agent Feldster's video of the size 14 footprints in an Ohio field.

"Katelynn," I say. "It's like she's vanished off the earth."

Benedict's eyes pop open. He shakes himself and lowers his feet to the floor.

I set aside my hot chocolate. "There's something about Ohio. Midnight Man went to a lot of trouble to take Jason there. Jennifer Moore's former home in Crete is less than five miles from the Indiana-Ohio border. My gut says if Katelynn's alive, she's somewhere in Ohio."

"When choosing his targets, Midnight Man likely has unlimited options. His gamers could be from all over the country. All over the world."

"But of the teens we know about, he's selected kids from Crete and Denver."

I'm talking about geographic profiling, in which an offender's crimes are expected to occur in an area originating from their home base. "I know you want the FBI to stay off *Eidolon*. But if Sara can get us a known IP, and we combine that with modeling based on the location of his victims and—possibly—an address from Poole's game developers, then bingo. We'll have him."

"*If* he's one of Poole's developers."

"Zane, the head of our BAU team, says we might get answers as soon as tomorrow." I sink back in my chair. "Benedict, you told me the first night we talked that Midnight Man wouldn't venture out of his home even for groceries. But now we know otherwise."

"Clearly I was wrong." He doesn't sound convinced.

"That's a pretty big misread." I'm not criticizing, and Benedict knows it. We're missing something.

Benedict says, "Let's go back to Derrick's blurring of the real world and the simulation. Maybe Midnight Man is experiencing his own cracks in the code. The real world is bleeding into his fantasy."

"If so, then what else are we wrong about? What are we missing?"

Benedict shakes his head.

I stand. Thinking of Katelynn has put me in mind of Livvie and her brother's handsy friend. I want to check in. "I need to make a quick phone call," I say.

"I'll rustle up some dessert."

In the hallway near the stars, I phone Jazz.

"Livvie is fine," she tells me. "We've ordered pizza, and we're about to watch a movie. Some anime flick. If you're worried about someone showing up, don't be. No one knows she's here, right? And I'm not exactly unprepared for trouble."

I smile. Jazz thinks it's normal to have enough guns and ammo around for a small militia, along with trip wires and cameras. The guns and anything explosive will be locked away while Livvie's there. But it's one of the reasons I asked Jazz to take in my trespassing student with the beastly stepdad and crappy brother. Livvie will be safe.

Reassured, I thank Jazz and hang up. While I'm here, I use the bathroom, wash and dry my hands, then head back into the hallway.

Benedict's house is the type of home I imagined for myself when I was younger and thought I'd grow up to be a scholar specializing in the works of Jane Austen, Charlotte Brontë, and Mary Shelley. In some ways, not only did I want to read their works—I wanted to *be* them. Or at least *be them* with the benefits of modern medicine and indoor plumbing. I wanted the manners, the civility, the sense that things should be done a certain way. Chaos gives me hives.

Benedict's place, which he inherited, is much like the English manors I toured in my undergraduate days, just on a small scale. Polished wooden floors that creak pleasantly beneath my feet. White plaster walls with carved trim around the African mahogany doors, dark wainscoting, and—overhead—richly carved plaster rosettes caught between the heft of dark oak beams. A staircase leads into the gloom of the second floor. I can just make out a Belgian-leaded glass window over the built-in seating on the landing.

I can also almost imagine a madwoman locked in the attic à la *Jane Eyre*.

In this secondary hallway, the art on the walls is pastoral, not criminal, and intermixed with photos of friends or family. Benedict never talked much about his family, except to mention that the home came from his dad's side—the family had moved to Colorado Springs in the 1840s, seeking treatment for a family member suffering from tuberculosis. For a time this house had served as a boardinghouse for consumptive patients. By the time Benedict's great-grandfather bought the property, it was part of what became known as Millionaires Row.

Tonight one photo in particular draws me in. Benedict stands next to another man in front of a rural Catholic church—a narrow building with adobe walls topped with a cross and a small bell tower. The man has walnut skin, a barrel-chested short stature, and stiff black hair in a brush cut. He wears a cassock, and I figure he's Father Antonio, the priest who mentored Benedict long ago.

Both men appear rigid and solemn, but there's something in their eyes that lightens their expressions. I settle on the idea of hope.

I hear Benedict rattling silverware in the kitchen and the click of Maggie's claws on the tiles.

Instead of returning to the library, a whim makes me spin on my heel and head toward the stairs. I don't know what I'm looking for, or whether I'm looking for anything at all, but I slip up the stairs before I second-guess myself.

Once I make the turn on the landing, the place is pitch dark. I turn on my phone's flashlight to find my way.

It's only when I locate Benedict's study at the top of the stairs that I realize my ulterior motivation—this room is what I'm searching for. I want to know how the man spends his days since we've parted, and his study will be the surest indicator.

It seems crazy that in all our time together, I never entered this room. The door was usually closed, and I accepted that. My lack of curiosity now strikes me as a flaw. How can you love someone when a big part of their life hides behind a closed door? It's fair to say I have a complicated and unhealthy relationship with secrets. I was too respectful of his privacy.

No time like the present to make a change.

The study is spacious but cluttered. A wall of shelves lined with old books, papers in piles across a long walnut table. There's a smell of old parchment, dry wood, and something faintly smoky and caramel: pipe smoke. And a pack of cigarettes. The first thing I learn from snooping is that in addition to his pipe, Benedict indulges in the occasional cigarette.

On the far end of the room is a computer desk with what looks like state-of-the-art equipment: two oversize monitors, a monster tower, a headset, a compact keyboard, and what even I recognize as a wired mouse designed for gaming.

Closer by is a traditional desk, and it's this I approach. There's a leather-bound journal lying open in the center of the large space. The pen beside it is uncapped.

At a sound, I startle and glance over my shoulder. It's Maggie, coming to see what I'm up to. I search for an excuse for my presence while I wait for Benedict to appear, but he doesn't show.

I return to the journal.

It's a listing that covers multiple pages.

Thomas R., 15

Single-parent home. Appears withdrawn and hostile. Diagnosed with major depressive disorder at 13. Online activity flagged: VPNs, alternative reality forums, elevated interaction with AI chat interfaces.

Beneath it, another.

Michael T., 17

Flagged for violent ideation in accessed therapist notes. Otherwise quiet, compliant. Active online in fan fiction chat rooms and on X. Parents likely unaware of cyber behavior. In chats, he says he "feels invisible." Unfriendly chat room members ignore him.

The names kept going. I count. Forty-seven in all. Most of them male, their ages ranging from fourteen to eighteen. The oldest entry is dated a year and a half after the Tremblay trial ended.

The most recent is dated a week ago.

None of the names are, of course, familiar to me. But each name suggests they are lonely kids just like Derrick. Like Jason. Maybe like Jennifer.

A folded piece of paper is tucked inside the notebook. At the top, Benedict has written, "Bad Actors." Below is a list of names along with law enforcement agencies. I check the names on my phone. These are criminals, arrested for child grooming and enticement.

I close the notebook. This is his project for the college.

But these entries aren't merely a research project. They're a vigil. As Benedict himself said, he never gave up trying to find the Midnight Man. This is his attempt at catching all the ghosts in the machine. Through the teens and their online games, he's tracked down some of the worst of the worst and turned them over to the police.

More sounds echo from downstairs—Benedict, maybe returning to the library. I step back into the corridor.

Dr. Benedict Hoffman never stopped caring. Never gave up. Not in five years.

31

It's after midnight.

Benedict convinces Helen to spend the night in a guest room rather than make the drive to Boulder in the dark and the snow. He imagines she keeps a go bag in the back of her vehicle with a toothbrush and a change of clothes; don't all FBI agents? They'll reach out to the psychiatric facility where Jennifer is confined. If Jennifer agrees to see them, they can fly out of the Colorado Springs airport to Indiana in the morning. It's efficient—better than meeting at DIA.

He doesn't mention that he's worried about Midnight Man.

By this hour, she's so tired that she's swaying on her feet, but still she argues. So Helen, ever mindful of the rules of propriety. She worries about what conclusion the neighbors might leap to. As if anyone would notice or care. As if Helen and Benedict aren't adults. As if she's never spent the night here.

Or maybe he misjudges, and it's something else that's eating at her. They could both learn to stop jumping to conclusions.

Even as he briefly closes his eyes against the intrusive memory of his hands on her bare skin, he tells her not to be ridiculous. This is purely a business arrangement, and if it makes her feel better, she can lock her door and lean a chair under the handle for good measure.

The dark glimmer in her eyes shows that she, too, remembers their hands on each other's bodies. Maybe it's herself she doesn't trust.

But her exhaustion wins. She accepts his offer, retrieves her go bag, and says good night.

He listens for the lock on her door to turn. Nothing. Smiling, he moves away toward his own room.

———

Later, after the strip of light under Helen's door winks out, Benedict grabs his laptop and whistles softly for Maggie. He pulls on his coat and snugs the silly-looking but effective sweater around the Irish setter. They head out into the night, which has turned calm and bitterly cold.

For a moment, while Maggie sniffs the bushes, he hesitates to leave Helen alone. But doors and windows are locked, and the alarm is set. She'll be fine.

He needs the air. So does Maggie. Even if he admits that knowing Midnight Man has emerged into the real world—against all his expectations—has unsettled him, the invisible *whatever* that's disturbing Maggie on their late-night walks can't be Midnight Man. The timing would be impossible. The last time Maggie alerted, Midnight Man was far away, in Ohio.

But that doesn't mean Maggie's spooking at ghosts.

Tonight, though, is quiet. He and Maggie meet no one and nothing on their snowy trek. Inside Rocco's Coffee Shop, he stomps snow from his boots and heads to a table at the back. He jacks into the ethernet and once again logs into *Eidolon*. One player is tending to goats. The others, he suspects, are in *Underland*. He announces his presence in the chat, asks whether anyone has played *Synaptica 2*, because he's heard it's dope—and waits.

No one makes it through their teenage years without a great deal of suffering. Benedict can recall with vivid clarity his own miserable time as a teenager, mocked for his great height, his intelligence, his tendency to brood in the back of the classroom. He'd built a shell of indifference, an arrogant aloofness that protected him. When he demonstrated he didn't care, the bullying stopped.

He'd kept his nose in books and comics or in his computer, devouring his share of what was then called cyberpunk. He'd felt the pull of the stories, the comfort they wove between him and a hostile world. These days, kids with interests that fall outside the more socially accepted arenas like sports and mock trial and theater seem to cope better than Benedict and his peers had. Some of them even embrace and advertise their differences through dress, tattoos, hair color, and piercings. He admires their determination to be themselves in the face of peer pressure and adult hand-wringing and censure.

And, just as he did, most people make it through the misery of high school and go on to live happy, productive lives.

Social media is changing that.

Benedict believes with absolute confidence in the influence of cultural and psychological forces on teens and young adults. He's studied this effect for all his adult life. At the Tremblay trial, the prosecution's expert witness accused him of "intellectual fantasy." Of suggesting that teenagers were malleable, murderous creatures who needed only a slight push to turn them into killers. And of fabricating the entity behind that push. Benedict's humanistic approach had been pummeled by Poole's smoothly logical analysis. Poole had turned Benedict's own experience against him, citing papers Benedict had written about the efforts at San Carlos to turn likely psychopaths into upstanding members of society—and their mixed success.

Poole's interpretation wasn't what Benedict had meant at all. It wasn't that teens were natural-born killers. Not most of them, anyway; potentially violent psychopaths existed in every community of humans. But teens *were* subject to profound struggles for independence and self-confidence at the same time they wanted badly to either fit in with their peers or prove themselves superior. That was the path Benedict himself had taken: to show himself as smarter than the average teen. The path of every nerd.

But other teens had chosen violence as the best answer.

Maggie shifts, and he sits back. He gets a few *heyas* and a *yo*, one *GLHF*. A few *???* and a *wtf?* in response to his question about *Synaptica 2*. But the chat remains mostly empty. Nearby, in the real world, someone laughs and others join in. The pleasant aromas of coffee and pastries enfold him.

Benedict exits the game and turns his attention to Poole.

He refreshes his VPN to select an outgoing node, so his apparent IP is in South Africa. Should be good enough cover for the next hop. Within his TOR browser, he selects an entry node that, after a few hops, exits through a node piggybacking on a medical archive server. From there, he pings the domain for San Carlos, querying it for delegation to an admin service. He isn't surprised to see they use Microsoft for their backend. Nearly every company does. Checking his notes on recently reported vulnerabilities in the internal file-sharing software, he executes a couple of quick commands and gains user access, which he escalates to having admin privileges. Once inside the San Carlos corporate file system, he runs a few queries looking for anything on Jennifer Moore. Not the game info that his friend hasn't been able to find. He's looking for transcripts of Poole's meetings with Jennifer Moore.

But the deeper he goes, the more the records thin. There's nothing about Jennifer. There could be more files lurking within an encrypted file store he finds. Benedict pokes at it for a few moments but gives up when he pulls the headers and sees that it's locked away using the latest lattice-based encryption. It's a tight ship.

He disconnects. On his way out, he buys a bag of croissants—just another customer who didn't stay long.

32

Shelby has been a very good girl since the stranger rang her doorbell. She spends time every day in *Underland,* learning how to convince NPCs to ascend. Helping them when they refuse. It leaves a sick feeling in the pit of her stomach. But it also makes her feel powerful. And that she likes very much.

NEW PRIVATE MESSAGE FROM: MIDNIGHT MAN

Shelby opens the chat.

MM: You've felt it, haven't you? Something's changed.

> yeah. It's like... mom and dad don't matter as much anymore. I don't think about them the same way.

MM: That's because you've leveled up. You're in Underland. And the stakes are higher. I want to draw your attention to Bench2Beast.

> omg, Bench2Beast?? he's a total
gym rat dweeb

MM: He isn't what he seems. His name in the real
world is Benedict Hoffman. Dr. Benedict Hoffman.

> the guy from the lecture videos who talks
about gaming and psychopaths? with the deep
voice? wtf?

MM: That's him. He talks about stories, symbols,
popular culture. But that's not all he studies. He's
obsessed with the idea of evil, because he himself is
evil. He's been watching me for years. And now he's
trying to stop me. And you.

> why?

MM: Because we're changing the rules. And people
like him... they live to protect the old code.

The world where you're not allowed to wake up.

> he's dangerous?

MM: Not to most people. But to you and me? Yes,
Shelby. He's very dangerous.

33

Sunday, 7:00 a.m. MST

Fresh croissants and a pot of coffee await me in Benedict's kitchen when I return from a run. I hear the scrape of a shovel and look out the window to see him removing snow from a path leading to the back gate. Maggie races up and down the yard, sniffing at what look like rabbit tracks in the snow.

I pour coffee, sit at the table, and open my work laptop, hoping for news from Zane on our warrant requests regarding Poole, Marcel, and NeoPath. And San Carlos.

Scott Poole's face stares out at me from my computer screen.

Visiting Psychiatrist Fatally Attacked in Colorado Springs

An internationally known psychiatrist visiting Colorado Springs was found stabbed to death early Sunday morning in what police believe may have been a robbery gone wrong.

Dr. Scott Poole, 57, was in town to give a lecture on mental health when he was fatally assaulted near his downtown hotel shortly after 10 p.m., according to the

Colorado Springs Police Department. Authorities said Poole's wallet and watch were missing, and his injuries suggest a violent struggle. No arrests have been made, and investigators are asking for the public's help in identifying possible suspects or witnesses.

I stare at the screen in disbelief, feeling Poole's horror in his last moments wash over me. There *can't* be a link between Poole's murder and my request for warrants against NeoPath. Still, Derrick's warning about Midnight Man slithers into my thoughts: *He's everywhere. In all places. At all times.* My heart pounding, I call the Colorado Springs Homicide/Assault Unit in Violent Crimes and identify myself by name and badge number. I carry my coffee to the window and watch Benedict toss a ball for Maggie while I wait for someone to check my credentials and patch me through to a Detective Gonzalez.

"Looks straightforward from where we're sitting now," Gonzalez tells me after I've explained my interest in the case. "We've brought in a guy. Roy Chandler—homeless dude with a record of petty thefts and drug use. If it's him, he's escalated."

"What's the evidence against Mr. Chandler?"

Gonzalez laughs in that dry cop way. "He had Poole's wallet in his sleeping bag and his TAG Heuer watch on his wrist. Splotches on his bed mat confirm for blood. We have to wait on the lab to see if it's Poole's."

"Any witnesses?"

Again, that laugh. "We figure Poole was walking back to his hotel from a downtown restaurant—cameras caught him there—and he cut through Acacia Park. Something a local wouldn't do. Ain't exactly upstanding citizens watching out for each other there. No one's going to sign up to talk to police."

I thank him and ask him to keep me notified of any updates. After we disconnect, I grab my coat from the peg and go out the back door.

"Poole's dead," I say when I reach Benedict.

Benedict has just cleared the last bit of snow off the sidewalk. He turns to me, his eyebrows raised. "What happened?"

I explain about the supposed robbery, about the homeless man with Poole's watch and wallet.

"Could this have something to do with our warrant requests?" I ask. "Poole and Midnight Man know each other, presumably from when they were developing *Synaptic*, and the request triggered Midnight Man to silence Poole? But how could he know about the warrants?"

"A number of ways, depending on how far the subpoena has gone. There are multiple places where the request could be hacked." He plants the blade of the shovel in the snow and tosses the ball for Maggie. "Poole's murder is too much of a coincidence. We know Midnight Man's out in the world."

"You should check in with Marcel."

"I've been trying since our prison visit with Derrick. He doesn't pick up."

"Shit, Benedict. Maybe he's in trouble. Midnight Man wouldn't stop with Poole. Do you know where Marcel lives? Send someone to conduct a well check. And what about other people on the team?" I glance at my phone, willing a message from Zane to appear informing us a judge has issued warrants for San Carlos and NeoPath and that information is coming in. "We need those names."

I listen while he dials Austin PD, explains that he's a friend and coworker of Anthony Marcel, and he hasn't been able to reach Dr. Marcel for several days. When he hangs up, he says, "The police will check on him."

Maggie drops the tennis ball at Benedict's feet. He tosses it in the direction of the detached garages on the north side of the house, and she bounds after it.

"Let me put the shovel away and we'll eat," Benedict says as we follow more slowly.

"Assuming you're still game, I'll book us afternoon flights to Fort Wayne," I say. "The Langford Forensic Psychiatric Hospital is forty minutes north. Maybe if we show up at the front door and whisper *GlitchDoll*, Jennifer will talk to us."

Maggie returns with the ball.

"I'll pack a—"

A thunderclap opens the world. A roar splits the sky, blinding light flaring like the sun has risen for a second time.

The shock wave slams into my chest, and I'm on my back on the ground. Windows along the rear of the house shiver and burst, shards of glass raining down on the grass.

From the Tudor's north side—where the garage and former servants' quarters are—a ball of fire rises, thick with black smoke and spears of orange flame. The blast has layers of sound to it: a deep throated concussion, then the sharper staccato of wood and glass and brick flying apart.

A stench clots my throat where I lie on the ground. Diesel, scorched insulation, charred plaster.

"Benedict," I say to the sky. I can't hear my voice. "Maggie!"

The dog whines. She's huddled on the ground next to me. When I prop myself up on my elbows, I see that she's wedged herself between me and Benedict. She doesn't appear to be hurt. But Benedict lies on his side, facing away from me. He isn't moving.

I make it to my knees. Neighbors are running toward us through the back gate, mouths open. I think I hear sirens.

I roll Benedict onto his back. He blinks at me.

"Are you hurt?" I ask.

He rolls his head to look at the house. I follow his gaze.

The main house is intact. It's the garage and servants' quarters that have gone up in a big orange ball. But if firefighters don't get here soon, the flames will consume the rest of the home. Images of the Heaths' ruined residence flash in my mind like photos in a slideshow. Images of their bodies. Benedict saying, *We know Midnight Man's out in the world.*

And how.

I reach for Benedict's hand. It's warm—impossibly warm for someone lying in the snow—and I thread my fingers through his. "Hey. Look at me."

When he doesn't, I release his fingers and cup his face between my palms. Gently I turn his head until he's looking right at me. His face is streaked with ash and blood. Glass glitters in his hair. "You're okay. Maggie's okay. It could've been so much worse."

Something shifts. His eyes blink slowly, as if surfacing from underwater. And then he's back, breath catching, shoulders shuddering. He lifts a shaking hand to my cheek. His thumb lingers at the edge of my jaw.

"You're safe," he says.

"So are you."

"You could have died."

His words land heavy in my chest. I lean into his hand, press it to my cheek. When at last I let him go, his fingers are red with my blood.

———

Benedict and I are taken by ambulance to Penrose Main Hospital, a few blocks away. A neighbor clips a leash on Maggie, promising to have her checked out by the vet. The neighbor and Maggie stand in the front yard, Maggie howling after the ambulance until we can no longer hear her.

Inside the ER it smells of antiseptic and sweat. Benedict and I are wheeled from the ambulance to a room where we're separated by a curtain and given gowns. I hear a male nurse talking to Benedict. Another nurse, a solemn woman with a chin-length gray bob, comes into my side of the room.

"How are you feeling?" she asks as she takes my pulse.

"Okay. Shaky. How's my friend?"

She smiles. "The looker? He's in the same shape as you. Minor lacerations from the glass. Sounds like the two of you were outside the primary and secondary blast waves, says this old army nurse. But we'll want to take a peek at your organs, make sure everything's where it's supposed to be. Run a few other tests. Now take a deep breath. Let it out. How does that feel?"

I breathe. I place my hands on my thighs, gripping the gown to stop my shaking.

"Hon," she says, noticing. "You want something for that? Something to help you relax a little? I can check with the doc."

"No. I'm good."

To her credit, she doesn't roll her eyes. "Let me know if you change your mind."

She has me lie down and begins irrigating the cuts on my face. Cold saline sluices down my cheeks, into my hair. She presses the edges of the deeper cuts together, tapes them with butterfly closures.

From the curtained space next door, Benedict's voice is low and measured. The nurse says something, and he laughs. I hear a wheelchair come for him, and he's rolled away.

A doctor comes in, checks my pupils with a penlight, my ears with a scope, runs me through a quick neuro exam—squeeze his fingers, touch my nose, recall three words. Walk to the door and back. He asks me the date and the name of the current US president. My hands tremble, but my mind is steady. He palpates my ribs, presses my abdomen, feeling for tenderness or guarding. "Nothing obvious," he says. "But given the blast force, I want a chest X-ray and abdominal."

They wheel me down a hall lined with harsh fluorescent lights. The radiology tech positions me, the machine humming to life. Images snapped of my chest and abdomen. For a moment I stand still, the gown loose on my shoulders, playing the blast over and over in my mind. Is Midnight Man lurking somewhere? In the ER waiting room? Or perhaps watching the data about my physical condition that is now zipping along electronic corridors?

He killed the Heaths. Scott Poole. But I'm not convinced he meant to kill Benedict or me—assuming he even knew I was there. To murder us, he would have targeted the house, not the garage. Unless the garage was all he had access to. Maybe, with us in the backyard, he figured this was his best chance.

Back in the partitioned room, someone has retracted the curtain. Benedict is already there, a square of gauze taped to his temple. His forearms are crosshatched with small white strips. He gives me a faint smile. I return it.

"Mags is okay," he says. "The vet gave her a full checkup."

I nod my relief. "I'm sorry about your house."

His faint smile vanishes. He closes his eyes.

"Why the garage and not the house?" I say. "I'm not sure he meant to kill us."

He nods. "Maybe the explosion was theater. Midnight Man exerting dominance." His eyes open. "Or maybe the garage *was* his target. He destroyed all my old academic records. They were stored above the garage."

"Do you think he knew?"

"I'd believe almost anything about him now. But there was nothing in there that could have hurt him or been used against him. It's pure vindictiveness."

"Benedict. I'm sorry. A nonmortal blow, but—"

"But still painful." He rubs his eyes. "Maybe it was because last night I got on *Eidolon* and asked about *Synaptica 2*. And for nothing. Not a single player bit. But if he suspects Bench2Beast is me, it's possible my query warned him how close we're getting. Five years ago, you and I had the audacity to announce his existence to the world. But the world didn't believe us, and he left us alone. Now we're back." He touches the bandage at his temple. "He's drawn the battle lines."

"He could have planted the device a couple of days ago," I say. "Or this morning."

"And decided now was the time."

I again see Andrea Heath's body, imprinted on my brain like a lesion. "He loves to watch the world burn."

"He can't help himself. Childhood trauma, social isolation, mental health issues. All the things we suspect about him anyway."

I sink into a chair next to Benedict's hospital bed. "He would have started in his teens. If San Carlos and NeoPath don't pan out, there might be psychiatric service records."

"Helen," he says. "He will have long ago erased his past."

We're monitored for an hour—blood pressure, oxygen, repeated neuro checks. The nurse watches for signs of hidden bleeding, lungs collapsing, brains swelling. None come. Just the sting in my face and arms, the echo of the explosion in my ears.

Two CSPD detectives arrive, carrying the cold with them. Snow dusts their jackets. They shake our hands, talk about how lucky we are, then drill us with questions. Time of the blast. Where we'd been. Had we noticed anyone watching the house? Was the case we're working local to the Springs? I mention Poole, and they promise to talk to Detective Gonzalez.

An FBI agent I know from Denver—Randy O'Keefe—comes in as the cops are leaving. He's on the phone, but he gives us a smile.

"I'm talking to them right now, Zane," he says into the phone and passes it to me.

"Helen! You and Benedict okay?"

I put him on speaker. "According to the doc. We should be released soon."

"What the hell happened?" He sounds furious and scared, both.

While Benedict listens in, I give Zane a rundown. That I stayed at Benedict's home after our visit to the state pen rather than driving to Boulder in the snow. We were in the backyard when the explosion occurred. I mention my suspicions about Poole's murder and the likely risk to Dr. Anthony Marcel. And that Benedict and I believe the explosion might have been more of a dangerous taunt than an intent to murder.

"You're thinking Poole's death and the explosion are related," Zane confirms. "Our Midnight Man?"

"Poole was killed within hours of our request for warrants. And arson is part of Midnight Man's MO. If he used a remote detonation at Benedict's home like he did with the Heaths, he could have planted the device while Benedict was away."

"And triggered it this morning." Zane's anger is palpable. "He's already signaled his intentions by hacking your computer. You think he knew you were at the house?"

"He could have noticed my car in the drive. Maybe seen me out this morning. Poole's murder took place in a park not far from the house." Briefly I wonder if Midnight Man contemplated delivering the same violent death to me while I was running through the nearby park as he presumably did to Poole. "But he hit the garage, not the house. He destroyed Benedict's research, but I'm not sure he meant to kill us."

"We're not counting on that. Either way, it makes you as much a target as Benedict. Thank God you're both mostly okay." He fills us in on his side. "Randy has got an evidence response team on scene. We'll coordinate with local authorities and ATF. There will be clues, Helen. Traces of him. We'll find him."

"Thanks." He's thinking of trace DNA and latent fingerprints. Of device fragments leading back to a manufacturer. But save for the footprints in Ohio where no one was expected to be, Midnight Man is too careful. "Benedict and I need to go to Indiana to talk to Jennifer Moore."

"Like hell. Jennifer Moore? We'll get someone from the Indianapolis office to talk to her."

I close my eyes. The stink of antiseptic burns the back of my throat. "The mission comes first, Zane. Katelynn's still missing. We need to talk to Jennifer Moore before the trail goes from cold to frigid, and an Indianapolis agent will be a no-go for her. Benedict has the best shot at getting her to talk. The two of them have Scott Poole and San Carlos in common. Plus—" I stop myself before I mention *Eidolon*. "Plus, Benedict knows a lot about Midnight Man from the trial. He'll know what questions to ask."

A pause, and Zane's sigh comes through, regretful rather than frustrated. I think of his "ego wall" filled with pictures of his family.

He says, "I trust your judgment, Helen. I'll green-light Indiana if the doctor clears you both. And you'll have protection. Agents from Indianapolis will meet you when you land. Send me your flight details when you have them. And you're compromised—it's time to fall back on protocol. Call me out of bounds with a new Signal number and we'll open that line. Don't use the travel office. I'll approve all further expenses for the case outside standard channels. We'll reimburse you, but we can't risk Midnight Man having eyes on what you're doing. You probably can't catch a flight until tomorrow morning. We'll put you up overnight in a safe house in the Springs."

"Thanks," I say again. Tears threaten at my gratitude that Zane won't shut us down, and I know I'm not as sound of mind and body as I need to be.

"Stay vigilant," Zane tells us. "And more cautious than a cat in a dog kennel."

"I'm the one whose face was just used as a cheese grater. I get it."

"I know. I'm sorry. Everyone here is taking it personally."

After we hang up, I return Randy's phone. He tells us they've already got news on the explosion.

"It's still preliminary, but it looks like the arsonist filled the third garage, the detached one, with gasoline vapor using multiple open gas cans. The vapor likely built up over an hour or more in the relatively sealed space. The ignition point appears to be near the ceiling light fixture—we've got a char pattern radiating outward from there." He looks at Benedict. "I'm guessing you don't leave a lot of open gas cans in your garage."

"I have cans. But they're sealed."

"The investigators think the guy used a timed igniter or rewired the motion sensor to spark when someone approached."

"My dog was closer to the garage, but her presence didn't trigger the bomb."

"A thermal sensor or AI-based motion pattern detector could distinguish between the shape and mass of a dog versus a human," Randy says. "It was classic fuel-air deflagration. High heat, high pressure—enough to lift the ceiling and take out the quarters above. You have cameras?"

"No."

"Okay. We'll work with what we've got." His phone rings. "Be right back."

Across the narrow space Benedict meets my gaze. His face is pale, dotted with red flecks, his shoulders up around his ears. But his eyes are steady.

"Bench to beast?" I ask.

His laugh is weak. "My avatar." He raises an arm, flexes his biceps beneath his hospital gown.

"Killer."

He gives me a thumbs-up, a gesture so unlike him that I find myself laughing.

We're going to Indiana.

34

Monday, 2:00 p.m. EST

The Langford Forensic Psychiatric Hospital—otherwise known as an institution for the criminally insane—where Jennifer Moore has resided as an inmate the last four years, looms like Poe's House of Usher in the gloom of an oncoming storm.

With our escort behind us—two federal agents in a black SUV—Benedict and I approach on a narrow, paved road girded by winter-somnolent trees black with age and bent from leaning against the wind.

It's like driving back in time.

A former Gilded Age mansion, the Gothic-style limestone building boasts pointed arches, flying buttresses, and a front door with side windows that look to me like watching eyes and a waiting mouth. A shroud of winter-green English ivy covers most of the front facade. The clouds swirling above and behind it are a flat pewter.

"If you weren't criminally insane when you first got here . . ." I murmur.

"You would be after a day."

"An hour."

At an iron gate, we stop and identify ourselves through a speaker. A camera monitors our moves as the gate swings slowly open and we drive onto the grounds and turn into a small parking lot holding three other cars.

The agents pull in next to us, and I gesture for them to wait. I can't imagine Midnight Man will pounce while we're in a psychiatric hospital with security guards.

We step out of the car into the cold, wet air and walk through the front entrance—I'm still holding the image of a vast maw—and stop at the front desk. We show our credentials and ask if someone would inform Jennifer Moore that we want to talk to her about GlitchDoll.

The gamertag has the desired effect. Twenty minutes later, a health-care tech named Mitch leads us back outside and through what is no doubt a lush garden in the spring and summer. Empty flower beds line the paved walkways, and tree branches scrabble toward each other above the trail. In the summer, the trees would offer welcome shade. In winter, the interlocking branches feel like a cage.

"Jennifer spends all the time she's permitted outdoors," Mitch explains. "Even in weather like this."

"She's not a flight risk?" I ask.

"Our little Miss Moore?" Mitch, a large thirtysomething Hispanic with his hair cut in a taper fade on the back and sides, shakes his head. "First of all, there's a fence and cameras and security. The grounds only look unwatched. But Jennifer doesn't have the oomph to do anything so daring. She was on suicide watch for a year after she arrived. But she never stirred herself enough to even try. The most she does now is her little acts of cruelty toward the other inmates."

"Like what?"

"Let's just say you don't keep pets if you're housed anywhere near Miss Moore. I've seen a lot of shit in my seven years here, but although I'd never say it to her, Jennifer gives me the willies."

"You've been here for seven years?" Benedict asks. "Isn't that unusual?"

"Seven and counting. For a tech like me, sure, my length of time here isn't the norm. But the work makes me feel as though I'm making a difference. Plus, my abuela was a resident here when I was a kid. I used to climb the trees. The place kind of grew on me. It's not as bad as it looks on days like today." He slows and points. "There she is."

We follow his gesture.

A young woman sits on a concrete bench, her gaze directed away from the institute and toward the tree-clotted horizon. She's small and slight, with dark hair cut in a dated shag. Even her clothes are a decade out of fashion—a navy-blue skater dress, black leggings, combat boots, and a bubble vest; perhaps she's still wearing a version of whatever she wore when she first entered San Carlos as a twelve-year-old. Her records indicate she is now twenty-two, but she looks younger. She is leaning forward with her palms braced on the bench, her fingers curled over the edge.

"It's her," Benedict says in a low voice. "The girl in Jason's photo. *She's* the one who reached out to him."

He's right about her identity. I recognize the curve of her jaw and nose, the hair so black as to be almost purple. "She looks like she's staring out to sea, waiting for her lost love."

"Don't she?" Mitch nods. "Makes me sad every time I see her. But she don't seem to mind. Sadness. Fear. Worry. Love. None of those human feelings seem to touch Miss Moore."

"Have you spoken much with her?"

"A few words here and there. 'Time for breakfast' and 'lights out.' Stuff like that. Jennifer don't go in much for small talk. She keeps to herself, mostly follows the rules. Least she does since she got busted for sneaking onto the internet for a few months. She can be sly, but . . . I know she's here because she killed her mama and tried to kill herself. But that girl don't seem capable of violence. Least, not until you hear another pet hamster has gone missing. Or look into her eyes."

"Then what?"

"There's nothing there. Lights are on, but nobody's home."

When we're within hearing distance, Mitch asks for us to wait. He approaches the young woman, but she doesn't look up, even when he says her name.

"Jennifer, you staying warm enough out here?"

She keeps staring toward the horizon. From where we stand, I can just make out a high brick wall topped with razor wire.

"I brought your visitors," Mitch says.

She shakes her head, says something I can't catch.

"It's two doctors. Not medical. PhDs. Dr. Hoffman is something called a criminal humanities specialist. And Agent Belle is with the FBI."

Now she lifts her head and glances toward us with the same violet eyes and eerie watchfulness I noted in her photo. The scar from a bullet wound etches a star pattern on her jaw. I wonder what it took to pull the bones back together. She gives Mitch a nod, and he gestures for us to approach. Her expression reveals nothing as we draw near.

"You want them to talk to you here, Jenny?" Mitch asks. "Or should we all go inside where it's warm? Maybe the library?"

Her voice is a flat whisper. "Here's fine."

"Okay," he says. He gives us a shrug. "I'll be waiting right over there if you need anything. Right by that oak tree."

He moves away.

"Hello, Jennifer." I offer my hand. "I'm Agent Belle, and this is Dr. Hoffman."

Her eyes track over me, but she ignores my hand. She seems far more interested in Benedict. Women usually are.

"Hi," she says in that flat voice. "How do you know about GlitchDoll?"

"We saw the photo you sent Jason."

"He kept it. How sweet. Me and Breaker, pulling a Macbeth. That was a good one, wasn't it? Slipped it right past the cock-a-doodle-doos."

She must spend her time outdoors in the shade, because except for the scar, her skin is porcelain, flawless, her veins a delicate blue tracing across her face and hands. She's thin to the point of emaciation, with hollowed cheeks and thin wrists. Still, up close, Jennifer Moore is a knockout. She looks like one of those "waif" models from the 1990s with their fragile, vulnerable looks. Kate Moss dipping into matricide.

There's no place to sit other than the bench, so Benedict and I hunch down on the cold pavement, making us almost eye level with Jennifer. The chill from the ground seeps through the soles of my boots. How does Jennifer stand it in her bubble vest and thin dress?

I smile at her. "We're here because we think what happened to you five years ago has happened to two other teenagers."

"Like Jason?"

"Maybe."

There's a flicker in her eyes, like a dim bulb blinking on, but otherwise her expression doesn't change. Her eyes are as flat as frozen ponds.

"Does that seem possible?" I ask.

"It's common, ain't it?" She's from Indiana, but her accent is pure North Carolina. "Family killing family. Nothing special about me. What happened to your faces?"

"There was an accident," I say.

"We think there *is* something special about you." Benedict leans in, graceful even while hunched on the ground. "We think someone helped you. Perhaps they even forced you."

The dim bulb flickers. "No one ever said nothing like that before."

"Police and lawyers make assumptions."

Her gaze swallows him. "You're good looking for whatever it is you call yourself. A criminal what?"

"I study the criminal humanities. Agent Belle does as well in her work for the FBI. We study the relationship between crime and popular culture. How popular culture can—"

She cuts across him. "Like people who went ape over that movie *Natural Born Killers*?"

"Yes. Among other influences."

"Are you gay?" she asks Benedict.

The question makes him blink, but he recovers quickly. "I'm not. Why do you ask? Are you?"

"I'm no cunt licker. Why aren't you married?"

They both look at his left hand. "I'm devoted to my work."

"Figuring out people like me?"

"Yes. Helping when I can."

"You think you can help me?"

"It depends on how much you're willing to talk to us."

"I wouldn't mind looking at you for a bit longer. But I've got nothing to say that I ain't said a million times."

"We'd like to know about your sessions with Dr. Poole."

There comes that same odd glint in her eyes. "I knew I knew you. I thought at first you were that television star playing a trick on me. The one who was Sherlock Holmes. But you worked at San Carlos after I left. Someone told me that, after I saw your name and pretty face somewhere."

"That's right, Jennifer. I did. I'm sorry we didn't get the chance to work together."

Her lips lift as if caught on fishhooks. The mechanical effect is chilling. "We could work together now," she says.

"I hope so. You and I and Agent Belle. I'd love to hear about your sessions with Dr. Poole and especially what you thought of the video game therapy he provided. *Synaptic.*"

The light dies in her eyes. She scowls. "I'm not really much for talking about those times."

"Playing the video game? Why not?"

"It gave me nightmares."

Benedict and I exchange glances. Psychopaths experience nightmares, but not in the same way as people with normal emotional responses. Rather, psychopaths tend to dream about aggression or sex or both. The theory is that these dreams reflect their need for thrills. The only fear they experience during the nightmare is from situations that trigger their survival instincts—fear of falling or of being attacked.

But nightmares can still be harmful. Even in psychopaths, they reflect unresolved fears or aggression and can influence psychopaths' waking behaviors, amplifying tendencies like impulsivity or anger rumination. Not what you want in someone who already has the stability of nitroglycerin.

"You had nightmares while you were undergoing game therapy?" I ask. "Did Dr. Poole talk to you about why the game might have triggered bad dreams?"

"He told me the dreams had nothing to do with the game. I was just stressed. But they had me doped out on lorazepam. How stressed could I be? And you know"—a snigger—"I'm not really an anxious person."

"What did Dr. Poole suggest you do to mitigate your anxiety? Aside from the lorazepam, I mean."

"The same thing he had me do before I shot my mom. He—"

Benedict lifts a hand, stopping her. "Wait. You left San Carlos when you had just turned fifteen, seventeen when you . . . attempted suicide. Are you saying you continued to see Dr. Poole after you left San Carlos?"

"So handsome boy is also a boy genius. We had a 'relationship,' he said. He offered to see me free of charge online."

"Video calls?"

"Nah. We just yakked through the chat on his game. It was way less formal. I called him Doc. He called me Jen-Jen. Nobody ever called me that before, but I liked when he did. And I liked his avatar. Totally dark core."

"You were playing the same game from San Carlos? *Synaptic*? Did you know the program was shut down?"

"*Synaptic*." She sticks a finger in her mouth and pretends to gag. "Doc said this version was better. *Synaptica 2*. *S-y-n* like when we do bad things. *S-i-n*." She titters, a scrape like honing a knife.

Jen-Jen. And a malevolent avatar. Game chats. A hundred alarm bells are going off in my head, as they must also be sounding in Benedict's. There are boundaries of professionalism no therapist should cross. And to see a patient free of charge? That didn't strike me as Poole's MO.

"Miss Moore," I say. "This might sound like an odd question, but how did you know—in these chats—that it was Dr. Poole with whom you were having a conversation?"

"'With whom.' Ain't we fancy?" She rolls her eyes. "Okay, you got me. It wasn't that creepazoid Poole. I figured that out right away. But to be polite, we pretended for a long time. Poole and Jennifer. Doctor and patient. Until—best day of my life—he told me who he really is."

Beneath my jacket, my flesh crawls. "And who is that?"

She smirks. "That's for me to know and you to find out."

It's inappropriate to want to strangle a mentally unwell young woman. But damn.

Wind tugs at the treetops. The temperature drops as if scrambling its way down a cliff. A few flakes swirl. I'm shivering, but Jennifer appears not to notice how much colder it's suddenly gotten.

"Okay." Benedict stands, shakes out his legs. "Let's go back to Doc. How did he arrange for you to play the new game after you left San Carlos?"

"It's not rocket science. He reached out. Pretended to be Poole. Gave me a username and password and told me not to share."

"Did you?"

"Share? Like, no way. It was my game. And, anyway, I didn't have any friends." Her gaze flickers between Benedict and me. There's no curiosity in her eyes, only mild amusement.

"Tell us about *Eidolon*."

"*Eidolon*." She breathes the word like a prayer.

"You've played," Benedict says. "As GlitchDoll."

"After a year, Doc moved me there from *Synaptica 2*. *Eidolon* has way cooler graphics and sound. Better characters. The gameplay is awesome. Doc said this new game is about more than learning good choices. It'll change as I go along, get customized to my gameplay. When I was at San Carlos, the cock-a-doodle-doos yakked about softening my neural rigidity. They hooked me up and monitored a bunch of stuff. Heart rate, pupil dilation, I don't know what else. They stuck sensors on my arm to"—her voice pitches up—"'measure my emotional and physiological reaction to the games.' I didn't like it much. But with the new game, I was free."

"Galvanic skin response," Benedict said.

"So mid. With *Synaptic*, they even made me wear a fitness watch to check my sleep cycles on nights after I'd played. I didn't care about any of that. Then I had a seizure."

I'm startled. "You had a seizure?"

She sneers. "There an echo out here?"

"Ergo the administrative cease and desist order," Benedict says. "Tell us about your seizure."

Jennifer eyes him. "The old grand mal. Total body shakes. Chewing up my tongue. The works. At least, that's what they said. Must have been quite the show. But I don't really know. I was playing the game, and then I woke up in the clinic."

"The clinic at San Carlos, not the hospital?"

"Yeah. I had a headache, and my tongue was kinda messed up, but I was fine. They put me on Keppra."

"Did it upset you?" I ask. "That you'd had a seizure?"

"I don't really do 'upset' in, like, a sad way, if that's what you mean. But it made me mad because after that, they took the game away. I threw a fit, but it didn't help. Dr. Poole said I was resistant to repatterning. And that was that."

"Let's talk about the newer game. *Eidolon*. What did you do there?"

"Mostly everyday stuff. Farming. Meeting people. I got points for understanding what people were feeling, so I got decent at reading faces. Figured that would be useful, right? I got to pick my environment, a cool future world with characters from TV shows I like."

There was no doubt copyright lawyers would be shouting about lawsuits, but I was willing to blink if violating copyright helped lower a person's triggers for violence. *Eidolon*, though, was not that game.

"What characters do you enjoy?" I ask.

"The Joker and Harley Quinn. Patrick Bateman from *American Psycho*. Hannibal Lecter."

She scored thirty-three out of forty on the psychopath test, I remind myself. Meaning she has psychopathic traits across the board. No wonder these were her role models.

She notched an eyebrow at me as if sensing my unspoken criticism. "It was a supercool simulation. I liked it there. I want to play again. But the cock-a-doodle-doos say no. You think I could? I got in big shit when they finally caught me."

"They caught you playing *Eidolon*?" I ask. "When was that?"

She smirks. "Days, weeks, months—time don't mean much here. But it was before Breaker went righteous. Boo-hoo. That would have been ragin' dope to be part of that."

"Breaker being . . . ?"

"If you haven't figured it out, you're dumber than you look, Miss FBI Agent."

"Jason Heath?"

Her laugh is a press of ice against my face. "Score one for the feeb lady. You think you can talk them into letting me play again?"

"We can look into it," Benedict says, sidestepping the question. "Going back to *Eidolon*. Did any of the characters suggest you do certain things, take certain actions?"

"Sure. Alex from *A Clockwork Orange* helped me steal a gun inside the game. Joker taught me how to burn things."

"Burn things."

Her smile is chillingly empty. "Like houses. I was gonna burn down my mom's shit-ugly house, but I didn't want my stepdad coming home before I'd done the deed."

"Did any of the characters suggest suicide?"

"Duh. Ultimate escape, right? Follow the exit protocol. But first I had important things to do. That's what Doc said."

"Doc—or whoever he is—told you that there were important tasks for you? Like what?"

"Transform people. It was Doc who told me my mom deserved to die for how she treated me. That she'd be a better mom after she broke free from the simulation."

"And you believed him," Benedict says.

"Sure." She winks at him and opens her legs.

The gesture saddens me—she's a girl who's been taught by society to see sex as a way to gain acceptance, approval, even love. Offering herself to a man twenty years her senior, and a professional to boot, shows only desperation.

She says, "You should be my doctor and start treating me. I'll tell you everything."

Benedict maintains a pleasant expression. "Maybe someday."

"Cock-a-doodle-doo." She flaps her arms, then yawns and stands. "We done? I'm bored."

The sun makes a last-ditch effort to shed some light before storm clouds overcome it; our shadows stretch like pale skeletons in front of us as snow drifts down.

Benedict yawns as well, mirroring Jennifer's actions. "I could consider becoming your therapist, Jennifer. But you'd have to be honest and open with me. And you'd have to tell me about Doc. I think he's Midnight Man. But maybe I'm wrong."

She cocks her head. "Maybe yes, maybe no. You become my therapist, maybe I'll tell."

"That's fair," Benedict says, as if it is. "Jennifer, when I play a game, I keep a record. What strategies I used. Enemy weaknesses. How to effectively combine items in the game. Any tricks I used to get to the next levels. You're smart. I bet you kept a log while you were playing *Eidolon*."

Her look is sly. "Sure I made a list. Don't tell anyone."

I close my eyes for only an instant. *Please, God.* "Do you still have it?"

"My stepdad took everything from our house. Probably he thew it away. Probably he threw out all my stuff except for my clothes."

Jennifer's stepfather is listed on her papers as being her legal guardian. He still lives near Crete.

"We'll ask him. Maybe he kept it."

Her face brightens, but in an unsettling way. As if cold moonlight has caught her features. "If he kept it, I want it back. In case I ever get to play again."

"We'll ask."

Benedict says, "If you had the list, Jennifer, what would you do?"

Her lips peel up in a likeness of a smile. "I'd go to *Underland*. And I'd say hello to the Midnight Man."

Then she launches herself at me.

35

I scramble back, my hands raised to protect my face, ready to shove Jennifer away.

But Benedict catches her in mid-leap. She fights him like a wildcat for a moment, then settles and presses her body into his.

"Stay with me," she croons into his shoulder.

Mitch arrives at a run and peels Jennifer away from Benedict. Her face has gone blank; it's as if the moment never happened.

But my heart pounds like I've run a marathon. For a moment Jennifer looked like a monster in barely human form. A woman possessed. Benedict is bleeding from scratches on his cheek.

"We'll have a nurse look at that," Mitch says to Benedict. He turns to Jennifer. "Young lady, that's a big demerit."

She shrugs. Psychopaths don't care about punishment.

"Let's go inside," he tells her.

The snow is falling harder, and the lights lining the paved pathways have blinked on as the storm brings an early dusk.

The four of us walk back toward the building—which looms above us, more Gothic than ever.

"We'll need the address for Jennifer's stepfather," I tell Mitch.

"Okay if I email it to you?"

"That will be fine." I turn toward Jennifer, keeping some distance between us in case I set her off again. "Jennifer, what *do* you know about the Midnight Man? Will you tell us?"

She mock lunges, making me twitch and Benedict move in between.

"How sweet," she says to Benedict.

"Jennifer—" Mitch warns.

She contorts her face—she's suddenly old and witchy. "Jennifer. Jennifer, Jennifer, Jennifer."

"Come on in," Mitch says to Benedict and me. "We'll get some ointment on those scratches."

"I'll take care of it," Benedict says. "No worries."

We part at the entrance. At the last moment Jennifer cranks her neck and delivers a parting shot over her shoulder.

"Run, run as fast as you can. You'll still be killed by the Midnight Man."

———

There's no safe house near Auburn, Indiana, the closest town to the psychiatric hospital. Our hotel is one of those too-well-lit chain properties in the industrial section of town. The kind with dull-colored carpet and vending machines that hum faintly down the hall, accompanied by the occasional clink of ice. Outside, the sodium glow of security lights turns the falling snow a dull yellow.

The two agents, Dixon and Sam, take a room across the hall.

I sit cross-legged at the foot of the bed in my room, laptop open, a capped bottle of water next to me. After we got to the hotel, Benedict left to get antibacterial ointment for both of us. I took a long shower and tried to erase the vision of Jennifer—face contorted, hands rendered into claws—leaping at me. Blood seeping from the wounds on Benedict's face. I failed, but at least my heart settled.

Until I thought about Benedict's beautiful Tudor blowing up. Glass flying. Maggie barking as we disappeared in the ambulance.

Now—while Benedict stands at the window, staring out at the gathering gloom—I'm scrolling through edited and redacted transcripts of Poole's sessions with Jennifer that Benedict's hacker friend managed to dig up for us after two days' effort. "Total rabbit hole," the hacker had told Benedict. He'd found the records not inside San Carlos, but buried in another institution's data, provided as part of the proposal behind video game therapy.

Hopefully I'll never have to lie under oath about when, exactly, I accessed these records. I feel guilty about reading them; it's a violation of my ethical and legal standards. But I don't feel guilty enough to stop. Not if anything there will help us find Katelynn and Midnight Man. And not if Dr. Poole was acting unethically.

Which, it quickly turns out, he was.

Poole's notes indicate that he believed—through the game—he could alter a psychopath's brain enough to help them generate at least rudimentary emotions such as compassion and empathy. And help clients who'd suffered trauma cope with depression and post-traumatic stress. Using funding from a private donor, he'd hired a small team of neuroengineers, neurologists, psychologists, and coders to collaborate in designing a next-gen therapeutic video game—a fully immersive narrative environment, using adaptive storytelling and biometric feedback. The game was designed not to distract the mind, but to reshape it.

Despite all the legal requirements around medical research, much of this work appeared to be conducted privately, on the down-low. All the participants on the gaming side signed nondisclosure agreements. Names are listed only as first name and last initial—little help for us there. The donor insisted that no one publish research or share results until multiple studies had been conducted. For the beta test, only a handful of institutes were involved, with a study group of fifteen, all under the direction and guidance of Poole. But at the time Jennifer was using the game at San Carlos, the results were initially promising. Fifty-four percent of users from other institutions reported a lower rate of depression. Thirty-two percent reported fewer nightmares. PTSD sufferers had fewer flashbacks and experienced less hypervigilance.

The most amazing aspect of the game was that it adapted to a player's unique trauma or—in the case of psychopathy or traumatic brain injuries—deficiencies triggered by brain damage or malformation, and offered symbolic quests to resolve them. Poole and other clinicians were champing at the bit to declare success and cash in on releasing the game, thus allowing the group designing and building it to announce their results and conduct an initial public offering to sell shares to the public.

The ambition was breathtaking.

Then came Jennifer's seizure. Clients in two other settings also suffered seizures. One person nearly died after experiencing a heart attack while playing the game. Another person's psychotic symptoms worsened—the feces-obsessed man Benedict had mentioned. A young man with high-functioning schizophrenia morphed overnight into full-on violent behavior. There were mentions of paranoia, disassociation, heightened aggression.

None of these issues had ever before been specifically linked to gaming.

Benedict learned about the failures and interceded with San Carlos's board. The game was canceled, the study shut down. Members of the group scattered.

"Have you finished reading?" Benedict asks me.

"Almost."

He still stands at the window, arms crossed, now apparently watching the steam rise from the Styrofoam cup of hotel coffee cooling on the sill. He has removed his jacket and changed into a black turtleneck and sweatpants. He hasn't said much since we left the facility, other than to remark on how similar Jennifer's last taunt was to the message Midnight Man had set to scroll on my personal laptop. *Run, run as fast as you can . . .*

We're both processing. Plus, he's got his home to think about.

I finish skimming the transcripts and rise to help myself to my own cup of coffee. With a wince at all the processed crap I've stuffed in my body over the years during stakeouts and foot patrols, I dump in artificial creamer topped off with sugar, then return to the bed.

The room is a cocoon, deliciously quiet after the cold wind and Jennifer Moore's dangerous madness.

A cocoon or, perhaps, the eye of the storm.

"I never get used to the flat eyes of psychopaths," I say.

He crosses to sit near me on the bed. The scratches Jennifer inflicted are even more garish than the injuries from flying glass. He's removed the bandage from his temple, revealing a neat row of stitches.

I saw myself in the mirror. I don't look any better.

"We have the first and last initials of the members of *Synaptic*'s development team," I say. "It's not much of a toehold." I finish my coffee, ignoring the burn, and drop the cup in the trash before sitting back down. "One of them has to be Midnight Man."

"He's using the games as a sorting algorithm. He cut his teeth helping develop *Synaptic*, gaining psychological and psychiatric knowledge while working with the team. Then he ventured out on his own with *Synaptica 2* and *Eidolon*. Find the kids with wobbly brakes, engage with them, then ultimately feed them a diet of myth and ritual until their only way out is blood."

"I'd love to say that sounds melodramatic."

"I wish it was."

"We have the initials," I say. "And there are records somewhere. These people were paid, right? Poole was hoping to go public with the game, so he had to keep things somewhat legit. Someone cut checks for the developers or made electronic deposits to their accounts. San Carlos or whoever administered the funding would have submitted 1099-MISC forms."

"I'm not hacking bank records or the IRS."

I poke him. "You *do* have standards."

"I'd rather not join Derrick at the state pen."

"I wasn't actually asking you to do that. The FBI can handle it." My phone rings. Zane. "Speak of the devil."

I put the phone on speaker and tell him I'm with Benedict. Zane asks how we're feeling. "Fine," I tell him. "We spoke with Jennifer. Midnight Man probably tracked her from San Carlos and lured her on to his own game. We suspect he was a member of Poole's development team. We need the names of the developers."

"We'll get them. But we've hit another hitch. Austin police did a check on Anthony Marcel. He committed suicide sometime in the last twenty-four hours."

In the warmth of the room, goose bumps rise. Suicide, my ass. Marcel was either pressured into killing himself or it was murder made to look like suicide. "Midnight Man's closing every door, isn't he?"

"He's trying. Are the other agents with you?"

"Right across the hall."

Zane says, "You mentioned Midnight Man's game. Talk to me about this."

Benedict's eyes meet mine, and he nods. It's time.

He leans over the phone. "His game is called *Eidolon*. I managed to get in a couple of months ago, posing as a teenager. I suspected Midnight Man might be the architect, but I had no way to be sure. Now, based on what Helen and I've learned, I'm certain *Eidolon* is his. I think Midnight Man took Poole's framework, improved on it, then built something inside it. Midnight Man modified the game so he could identify psychopaths like Jennifer or just angry, unhappy teens and force them into a different story."

"That's why we need those names, Zane," I say.

"I'm pushing hard."

"Tomorrow we're paying Jennifer's stepfather a visit. Jennifer hinted that she might have left clues on how to succeed inside *Eidolon*, which could help us get into the game's underbelly."

"Excellent. Good work, you two. Stay safe. I'll notify you as soon as we have anything."

I put my phone on the nightstand and move to the window. Snow is falling harder, spinning sideways under the parking lot lights.

"What do we do if Midnight Man isn't one of the developers?" I ask. "If he hacked into the system?"

"We find the vulnerability he used to access the game and try to trace it back."

"Can that be done?"

"Only if he made a mistake. And I doubt he did."

Benedict joins me at the window. Light from the bedside lamp falls against the planes of his face; he could easily be hired in a movie about the Byronic heroes of my youthful imagination. Poets and tortured heroes. Warmth rises from his body, still as trim as when we first met. He shakes his hair back from his face—he badly needs a haircut, and I briefly consider offering to do it myself.

He says, "What we have, essentially, is a rite of passage into the underworld. Midnight Man has disguised his recruiting tool as a twisted form of therapy. He's likely telling the teens that playing the game makes them wiser. Stronger. Better able to adapt. Better able to see the simulation."

"And he's teaching them skills. Remember what Jennifer said about a character showing her how to steal a weapon?"

"Or burn down a house."

I look back out at the snow. "The first night we met, you told me you thought Katelynn and Daisy were almost certainly already dead. Do you still believe that?"

He leans down, plants a light kiss on top of my head.

"I believe anything is possible now," he says. "We won't give up on them."

I watch him as he crosses to the door, lets himself out. I hear one of the agents speak briefly with him; then the door down the hall from mine opens and closes.

I turn back to the window. Outside, the snow falls and falls and falls.

36

Shelby hasn't left her room in two days. Her mom brings her food, asks whether she wants to go to the doctor.

Shelby doesn't want to do anything but please the Midnight Man. Maybe then he'll let her go. She just wants to *go*.

NEW PRIVATE MESSAGE FROM: MIDNIGHT MAN

MM: How are you, Shelby?

Her hands move sluggishly, as if they belong to someone else. Maybe they do. She no longer knows where she begins and ends.

> ive been researching Dr. Hoffman. He's giving a talk at a college in colo spgs.

MM: Yes. "The Shadow of Adulthood: Exploring Adolescent Morality." Rather mundane.

> he doesn't seem dangerous

MM: He is, Shelby. Trust me. For us, he's the most dangerous person alive.

> **what do u want me to do?**

MM: I sense your concern. But Benedict Hoffman isn't a person, Shelby. He's a firewall keeping you and others from true knowledge. Do you understand? He's someone who knows the truth but chooses to lead others astray. He's a danger to all of us. He's the trickster, cunning and deceptive. But you and I, we are also tricksters. Catalysts for change, sweeping out the old and bringing in the new.

> **ok. He's investigating breaker's case. His fam. Saw it on the news. Hotshot consultant.**

MM: That's right. That's another reason why he's a danger. You take care of Dr. Hoffman, Shelby. I'll take care of the woman who's helping him. As for the Denver cop, he's dying anyway.

Lately, Shelby feels stupid. She doesn't sleep much, and when she does sleep, she has nightmares. *Eidolon* transformed, a place of wheels and cogs, like she glimpsed when she was on the border of *Underland.* She just wants things to go back to the way they were. She wants to pick apples and berries and sleep in the sun. She can no longer remember why she was so angry all the time.

> **so I . . . ? what? how do I take care of him?**

MM: We're here to help each other evolve, aren't we, Shelby? By any means necessary. We have a vision.

A vision of transcendence. Are you ready to set the
world free, Shelby? To help Dr. Hoffman ascend? You
must enact the exit protocol for him.

Shelby cups her chin in her hands. She stares at the empty message box waiting for her to commit to her destiny. She doesn't ask Midnight Man why he's picked her to enact the exit protocol. It's an honor. When he chooses you, you don't question it. This is her chance to help free the world. Then the wraith will no longer haunt her. She'll go back to the orchards.

She lowers her hands and types.

> I'm ready

37

The snow slowed overnight. Much of it has been scoured away by the wind, leaving the roads glassy with black ice. I drive below the recommended speed limit, following the GPS instructions down a narrow two-lane road edged with brittle corn stubble and tilted wooden fences. The land around us feels abandoned—quiet and frostbitten.

Save for Dixon and Sam keeping a respectable distance behind us, we could be alone in the world.

Of course, it's just my mood, which is not improved by an inexplicable cheeriness that radiates off Benedict like heat from a fire. "Just a good night's sleep," he tells me, although the tiredness in his eyes suggests he did not, in fact, sleep. "And a horse smelling the stable."

We find the place right before both the road and the GPS peter out.

Jennifer Moore's stepfather lives in a one-story ranch-style house with siding the color of old bone. A rusted-out truck—without windows or tires—hunkers off to the side. A porch light burns, unnecessary in the pale daylight. Something about the house makes me uneasy. Just leftover jitters from the explosion and our meeting with Jennifer.

I glance over at Benedict. The scratches and stitches make him look like he was in a bar fight with an alley cat.

I slide my gun from my go bag to my holster, double-check that I have everything we'll need to collect any evidence, and we get out. The SUV pulls in behind us, there in case something goes wrong.

I ring the bell. A dog barks, then whines; we hear something like a chain being dragged across the floor. Who chains up their dog inside the house?

The door opens.

Timothy Moore is in his early fifties, tall and square-shouldered but soft around the middle. He has a beard just past the edge of scruff, dark pinpoint eyes that glare from under a steep brow. He wears jeans, a thermal shirt, and a pair of work boots streaked with salt and mud.

"Who the hell are you?" he says by way of greeting.

I hold up my badge. "I'm Special Agent Belle. This is Dr. Hoffman. We're with the FBI. We're investigating a series of incidents we believe might be linked to your stepdaughter's treatment at San Carlos."

His mouth works for a moment before he answers. "I'm not much on the feds."

Big surprise. I've already taken in the twenty or so No Trespassing signs, all promising that trespassers will be beaten, shot, and stabbed. Survivors will be prosecuted.

"We won't be here long, Mr. Moore. But we'd appreciate your help."

"I don't know nothing about Jenny's treatment. Haven't seen the girl in months."

"We spoke with her yesterday. She directed us to a notebook she thought might still be in your possession."

He leans against the doorframe and crosses his arms. "I doubt it. At her request, I dumped most of her crap. What's it to you?"

Benedict and I have discussed how much to share with Tim Moore. "We're investigating a murder in Denver. We suspect a link with your wife's death."

"With Marlene? And Jenny's notebook is going to help."

I can't blame him for his skeptical look. And I don't want to threaten a man who already doesn't trust me. But I also don't want to wait for warrants if he slams the door in our faces. I seek the middle ground, hoping to appeal to his better nature.

"I know it might sound far-fetched," I begin.

Before I get any further, he snorts. "You think?"

I plow on. "And I know that you're not big on the feds. But I imagine it would mean something to you to know that it's possible Jennifer didn't act alone. Someone else might be partially responsible for your wife's death. I also imagine you'd want to help us find that person."

"You're kidding me, right? That girl's got so many screws loose it's a miracle her brains don't fall out through her ears. She didn't need no help to do what she did."

"Nevertheless, we believe she was encouraged to act with violence. Without this other person, she might have gotten the help she needed instead of picking up a gun."

Moore scratches his arm ferociously, up and down like he's got bedbug bites. From what I can see of the house, it wouldn't surprise me. Ah, the glamorous life of an FBI agent.

Timothy stops scratching and squints at us. I'm wearing my mildest, most nonthreatening look, and it's one I'm good at. I hope Benedict is wearing a matching expression.

He must be, because Timothy relents.

"She told me to throw out most of her stuff, but I didn't have the heart. Not on account of Jennifer but for her mother. I boxed up most of her things and hauled them up to the attic. Figured if she ever got out, she'd want something that was hers." A pause. "She wouldn't have ever admitted it, but even crazy people are sentimental, right?"

Psychopaths generally aren't, but I offer a soft smile. "That was kind of you. Would you mind if we went through those boxes to see if we can find the notebook?"

He hesitates. Something tightens in his face. Not hostility, I realize, but fear. Shame. A bruise behind the eyes.

"You know she killed her mom in the bedroom Marlene and I shared," he says. "I was working a night shift. Got the call before the police even made it to the scene. I'd left her alone with Marlene for maybe two hours." His jaw twitches. "Two hours."

"It wasn't your fault," I say quietly.

He doesn't answer. Just turns and walks deeper into the house. The dog takes up his barking and the chain rattles. Moore yells at it to shut the hell up. I spot a rottweiler through the back screen door and realize, with relief, that the dog is in the backyard and not in the house. The rottweiler glares at us, as disdainful of feds as his owner. I'm glad for the chain. I'd hate to have to shoot a dog in self-defense.

The house is cold. We follow Moore through a living room crowded with furniture that, based on the patterns of sun-fade, looks like it hasn't been moved in years. The air is stale with woodsmoke and dust and old grease. Our footsteps are sticky, and I decide I'm not going to think about it. Moore snags a flashlight, tape, and a box cutter from the kitchen, then returns to open a narrow door at the end of the hallway. He unfolds a ladder to the attic.

"Jenny's boxes are marked. There's five of them. I'll give her credit for one thing—she didn't collect a bunch of shit the way a lot of girls do. There never was nothing girly about Jenny." He hands the tape and box cutter, along with the flashlight, to Benedict. "I'd appreciate you resealing the boxes after you find what you want."

"Of course, Mr. Moore," I say. I pull a pen and a written consent form from my bag. "If you'll sign this, giving us permission to search."

He frowns over the paper, then props it against the wall and signs. I give him his copy. Benedict and I climb the ladder. The attic has a low-pitched roof requiring us to stoop, and it's dusty and airless. We snap on latex gloves. It doesn't take any time to find the five boxes belonging to Jennifer. They're set apart and—as Moore promised— neatly labeled. It doesn't fit with the mess of the rest of the house, but I'm not complaining.

I take photos of everything in situ, then more as we begin our search.

The top box is small. It holds old CDs inside cracked jewel cases, a stuffed animal with one glass eye and slash marks on its belly, and plastic horses, some of which are a cross between scorched and melted, like someone held them over the stove.

The second box holds more toys, many of them broken.

The third contains high school textbooks and notebooks—three of them. Spiral-bound, with stickers on the worn and curling covers.

Benedict flips through the first. "Homework," he says.

"Likewise," I say of the second book. "Math."

The third contains more homework.

The fourth box holds jewelry and scarves and a pair of sunglasses. There's also a three-ring binder that, in turn, holds several notebooks.

"Bingo," says Benedict, flipping through the binder. He passes it to me.

It's page after page of drawings—some crude, some impressively detailed. Buildings on fire. Eyes floating in space. A man with no facial features wearing a silver crown.

I use a tissue from my pocket to wipe away the worst of the dust on the floor, then lay out the contents of the binder—notebooks, loose pages, scrawled diagrams, folded sticky notes—taking pictures as I go. The paper smells inexplicably of ash and something metallic, like old pennies. The pages are a chaos of color—ink, markers, red pen scratched deep enough to scar the paper.

Benedict sits nearby, legs crossed, flipping through the first notebook, murmuring under his breath, while I take the second. I know he isn't reading in the traditional way—he's *listening* to the words he's reciting. I've seen him do this when he suspects there's a deeper pattern beneath the surface.

A minute later, he says, "Helen. Listen to this."

I fold my hands in my lap while Benedict reads.

"I realize that people are stepped in blood and must be cleansed to escape the false world. Doc agrees. He says I can lead the acolytes if I'm brave enough. They're afraid to act. Afraid of the gatekeepers. Afraid of the mentors and the tricksters and the heroes. We're the heroes. Scaredy-cats. It's not a problem for me. I don't know fear. Happy to begin the long process of cleansing the world and bringing transformation. Will there be something in it for me?"

"He's using Jungian archetypes to appeal to the kids," I say. "The mentor, the gatekeeper, the trickster, and the hero. They're universal. Part of the collective unconscious. Kids will recognize them even if they don't know it. Obi-Wan Kenobi as mentor to the hero, Luke Skywalker. The gatekeeping Sphinx in Greek mythology."

Benedict is nodding. "They're part of the shared, universal psyche that all humans inherit. Midnight Man is educated on Jungian philosophy. Not surprising, given the appeal of his game. By using characters and narratives based on Jungian ideas, he creates a world that resonates on a deeply psychological level."

"Is this unusual in the gaming world?"

"Not at all. It's not any deep dark secret that gamers and readers and moviegoers enjoy archetypes and archetypal story arcs. One thing this does give us is the knowledge that if he was one of the developers on Poole's game, as we presume, then he knows which narrative to pursue with which kids, and which archetypal figures will appeal to them as individuals. He can lean on the work done by Poole and the neuroscientists on the development team."

"Jennifer mentioned the Joker. Harley Quinn. Patrick Bateman and Hannibal Lecter. They're the shadow archetype—the repressed darkness we hold within."

"They're also the trickster—the destructive facet of the shadow archetype. Which is important. Midnight Man himself is both shadow and trickster. Pretending to be Dr. Poole, then Doc, and finally Midnight Man. All without revealing his true identity." He continues flipping through the first spiral notebook while I work my way through the rest of the binder. "Based on Jennifer's comment about leading the acolytes, the game isn't just pushing teens through emotional rehab scenarios. It's filtering. Separating those who hesitate from those who will act. But we'd already figured that." His voice is bleak. "There's nothing new here. Nothing about the game or any tricks or strategies that might allow me to go deeper."

I return to the second notebook. In the very back, taped to the inside cover, is a printout of a newspaper article. At the top, barely visible, are the words *The North Coast Ledger* and a date: August 5, 2016.

It's a family photo. Six people on a front porch. The parents, smiling. Two blond girls in dresses. A mild-looking, bespectacled man in his mid-thirties, and a teenage boy in the background—blurred, half turned, face unreadable. The father and the teenager, I notice, are tall and heavily built.

Whatever article accompanied the photo has been cut off. I have no idea who these people are or why they warranted a mention in the paper. I look up *The North Coast Ledger* on my phone. It's a local rag in Cleveland; back issues aren't digitized.

I take a photo, then show the clipping to Benedict. "She cared about this family for some reason."

We finish looking through the binder without finding anything more than undecipherable scribbles. As an insight into the psychopathic mind, they're terrifying. As support for what Derrick shared with us at the prison, the few words she has written about transformation are confirming.

We rebox everything except the first and second notebooks. Before we leave, I take a quick look around. Boxes labeled in black marker with "Marlene"—Jennifer's mother. Snowshoes. A broken rocking chair, a floor lamp propped against a wall. Empty frames, old snow boots, dust bunnies. In a large shopping bag that gapes open to the ceiling, I spot a woman's coat and a purse and a laptop. I remove the computer. On the lid is a decal of a clock with both hands pointing straight up. Noon. Or midnight.

"Plain view doctrine," I say, showing the laptop and decal to Benedict. Potential evidence found during a consented search is admissible in court. "Let's ask Mr. Moore about it."

———

Downstairs, Timothy Moore stands at the edge of the kitchen, arms crossed again. The dog barks from the backyard.

Moore looks at the notebooks and the laptop I'm holding. "Those're Jennifer's notebooks, but the laptop was Marlene's."

"Did Jennifer ever use it?"

"Maybe. Probably. She didn't have her own. Marlene wanted to keep her off the internet as much as she could."

"What about the decal?"

"Jennifer gave her that. To fancy up her computer."

"Mr. Moore, it's possible the evidence we're looking for is on the laptop. Would you mind powering it up for us?"

He shrugs, finds a charger, plugs it in. The laptop blinks slowly to life. A password bar appears.

"I got no idea what the password is," Moore says, looking weirdly satisfied. Got one over the feds, I guess. "I tried to get in after she died. No luck."

"Someone from my agency should be able to unlock it. If you'll give me permission to take it with me, I'll see what we can do."

"That's what the FBI does, right? Gets inside people's computers." He flops a disgusted hand. "Go ahead. Maybe you'll find something. Not like Marlene's gonna object."

"Thank you, sir." I show him the notebooks. "Mind if we borrow these as well?"

"Lemme see 'em."

Moore opens the binder on the kitchen table and scrutinizes, page by agonizing page. Finally, he looks up. "This shit is supposed to mean something?"

"We're honestly not sure," I tell him.

"But you think maybe yes."

"We do." I direct him to the photo of the family from *The North Coast Ledger*. "Do you know why your stepdaughter had this clipping?"

"Daughter. I adopted her when Marlene and I got married." He folds the notebook back on itself and walks the photo to the window, holding it to the gray light. "I don't know these people. Maybe it was from a school assignment."

He turns back. The sneer is gone and his eyes are red. "I tried to love that girl. I did. But she's a cold bitch. Look what she tried to do to her brother! The docs said it wasn't our fault." He returns to us and touches the back of my hand. "You think maybe I could have done more? Like maybe I'm responsible? I mean, we tried. We tried and tried. But it was like trying to keep a dog from taking a piss."

"Jennifer received a clinical diagnosis of psychopathy, Mr. Moore. Brain scans revealed malformations in her brain that doomed her from the start. There was nothing either you or your wife could have done to help her."

That isn't entirely factual. But the truth is there's very little to be done about psychopathy, and with the failure of Poole's therapy and the likely interference by the Midnight Man, Jennifer and her mother had been all but fated for a bad end.

Moore steps away from the notebooks as if they might be booby-trapped.

"Take them. If you find something in there, I hope it helps. And if you find out someone helped Jennifer pull that trigger, I want to know."

"Of course." I close the notebook gently, then slide it and the computer into evidence bags. I close the bags and sign the seals. "We'll take care of them."

He gives a short nod. "Tell her I didn't throw her stuff away. She won't care, but it matters to me."

I think of Jennifer's voice in the cold, asking for the notebook with the greedy eagerness of a baby reaching for the bottle.

"We will," I say.

When we step outside, the wind has picked up, sending spirals of snow across the gravel drive. I clutch the laptop and binder to my chest as we walk toward the car, their weight both literal and emotional.

38

Agent Feldster calls as Benedict and I are getting into the car. Our flight back to Denver is in two hours.

"I've got some updates for you," Feldster says. "Information about the property where Jason died."

I press the button to unlock the rental car. "What did you learn?"

"I just sent you a text. A photo of an article from *The North Coast Ledger*."

I open the message. It's the same photo we found in Jennifer's notebook. It's like looking at the ghost of a ghost.

"Fill me in," I say.

"The family died in a house fire in 2016. Overloaded circuit, not arson. Everyone was killed but the teenager, Elliot Widner, who was away at a summer gaming camp. We haven't been able to identify the thirtysomething man in the photo. But I guess you notice that the other two males are hulks."

Like our suspect in Sandusky County. And our repairman. "What have you found on the teenager?"

"Nothing. Nada. Zip. He rode into the sunset and disappeared."

That's him, I think. Midnight Man. Or Midnight Man's first target. I can't prove anything yet, but my gut feels tight, anxious, like it knows the enemy is right around the corner. I check the time. I want someone looking at Marlene's laptop, but this lead takes priority. "Benedict and I found that same photograph inside the notebook of a young woman we believe was targeted by Midnight Man. We're near Crete, Indiana. How about we pay you a visit?"

———

Waiting for the flight to Ohio, I catch a nap at the gate and another one on the flight. By the time Benedict and I, along with our two escorts, land at Cleveland Hopkins, it's early afternoon. The sun strains behind low, heavy clouds—more silver than white—and casts the world in the dull, monochrome sheen of a black-and-white photograph.

Special Agent Feldster waits for us at the curb, his black coat zipped to the chin. He gives a nod as we approach and pulls his hands from his pockets.

"Agent Belle. Dr. Hoffman." He nods at our escorts and introduces himself.

"Thanks for meeting us," I say.

"My pleasure. I figured you'd want to discuss the latest in person without heading all the way into downtown Cleveland and the office. There's a diner nearby with an empty back room we can use and the best damn coffee and cinnamon rolls in the state."

———

The diner isn't much to look at, but Feldster is right about the coffee. I abstain from the cinnamon rolls; I overate at breakfast, scarfing down eggs and bacon as if the time with Jennifer Moore had left me malnourished. The waitress leaves the coffeepot with us and closes the door behind her. The room is small and windowless and warm. I shed my coat. Sam and Dixon take chairs near the door.

"So," Feldster says when we're seated at the table. "The house fire. Parents, two daughters—all perished from the flames or smoke inhalation. The only survivor was the teenage son. As I said on the phone, he was away at a summer program for gaming design."

"Elliot Widner."

"I've tracked down a few more pieces of information. He was sixteen at the time of the fire. Moved in with his aunt afterward; then two years later he dropped off the radar. No voting records, no driver's license or tax records. We can't even find a lousy utility bill. It's like once he turned eighteen, he dropped off the face of the earth."

"What does his aunt say?"

"She passed six years ago. But I got these photos from a research librarian."

Feldster taps the screen of a tablet in a black leather case, then hands it to me. A series of photos populate the screen—they look like grainy scans from a local newspaper. The first shows a modest farmhouse with a wraparound porch and a peaked roof. The second was taken after the fire: blackened beams, the shells of metal appliances, a house hollowed out by flame. The third is the family photo.

"All the photos are from *The North Coast Ledger* out of Cleveland. Like I mentioned, the article listed an overloaded circuit as the cause of the fire. According to the fire inspector, there were too many devices plugged into a single circuit using a power strip. I haven't tracked down an obituary yet."

I hand the tablet to Benedict.

"As for the man in his thirties," Feldster says, "we've got nothing on him, either. I tried running down the journalist who reported the story in case he knew, but he's moved away, and I haven't been able to reach him. There might be something in an obituary if we can find one."

"Aren't obits online?"

"Most funeral homes only keep them for five to ten years. The aunt's obit is already gone. We'll need to check newspaper archives at a local library." He accepts his tablet back from Benedict. "That teenager, Elliot Widner, he has to be our unsub, right? The fire with the lone surviving teen. The murdered family living in a house right near where

Jason died. Even the fact that Elliot escaped the flames because he was at a *gaming* camp. And another target, Jennifer Moore, prints a copy of the photo. Someone called it to her attention, right?"

Benedict taps a tune on the tabletop. "Elliot could be his own origin story." He pushes his chair back and turns toward me. "Or . . ."

I set down my coffee. "Or Midnight Man is the unidentified older man in the photo. That man isn't big. He's not Rick the repairman at the Heath residence. But he might have manipulated Elliot into murder. If he's family, maybe there were life insurance policies or some other financial motive for him to push the teen. Or maybe he's a psychopath."

Feldster squints at the photo. "He does look a lot like the BTK killer."

I take out my own photo of the family and study the mild-looking man with the spectacles and an early receding hairline. He'd be well into his forties now, long past the prime of most serial killers.

But he could have passed the torch.

———

Feldster drops us at a public library in Sandusky County. It's modest but modern, with brushed steel bike racks and solar panels glinting on the roof. Inside, it's all clean lines and quiet movement—students hunched over laptops, a toddler squealing softly in the children's section, and the scent of old paper tinged with lemon disinfectant.

Benedict and I head straight for the research room, our protective detail trailing close behind. A sign overhead reads LOCAL HISTORY, and a slim, prematurely gray-haired woman behind the desk glances up as we approach. She looks puzzled at the sudden appearance of four keyed-up adults, three of us pretty obviously law enforcement, two with the grim demeanors of warfaring Vikings. But she smiles.

"How can I help you?" she asks.

"We're looking for an obituary from 2016," I say. "The family name is Widner. Their residence was in Sandusky County."

"We can absolutely help. You'll want the newspaper archives on the library's database." She gestures toward a computer terminal, then gives us a small card with a username and password. "From that computer you can access the *Sandusky Register* archives and their obituary index. You can search by name, date, or location. There's no charge to use the database." Another smile. "Let me know if you need anything else."

Benedict and I sit side by side at the terminal, the chairs creaking as we settle in. He types in the last name—Widner—and sets the date range from January 1 to December 31, 2016.

The results load quickly. Two hits.

He clicks the first.

It's a scan from the *Sandusky Register*, dated August 7, 2016. The image is clean, the headline centered:

House Fire Claims Four Lives in Rural Sandusky County

Below it is a photo of a charred home, the same photo Feldster shared with us earlier. The article is short, but the information is clear. Thomas and Elizabeth Widner, both forty-seven, and their daughters Jillian (fourteen) and Emily (eleven), perished in the early morning hours. The fire is believed to have started due to an overloaded circuit.

"Widner wasn't home to set the fire," I point out.

"A hundred dollars says he overloaded the circuit and destroyed the circuit breaker before he left home. An older home with outdated wiring and a breaker that won't trip—it was just a matter of time."

He clicks the second hit—a formal obituary for the entire family, with a date two weeks after the deaths. The service was arranged by Greenland Mortuary and the funeral held at Mount Carmel United Methodist.

I scan the obituary listing the survivors. Other than the teenage Elliot, the only survivors were Elizabeth's sister, whom we know is deceased. And her son, Albert Widner. Elliot's cousin.

I sit back, heart tapping hard.

"Albert Widner," I say. "No additional information. But it's something."

"Go back to the main menu," Benedict says. "There are other databases we can access."

I find one tied to the county auditor's property records and enter the name Albert Widner, filtering for the last twelve years to allow some margin.

We get a single hit.

A property deed in the name of Albert Widner, purchased in 2018 from the Ottawa County Land Bank. I link the deed to a map. The parcel is almost fifty acres of partially forested land off a rural route, just shy of the county line.

"No listed improvements," Benedict says. "No residence, no permits, no mailbox. Just raw land. You think the cousin is living there?"

"There's literally only one way to find out."

I take a photo of the screen and shoot it to Feldster along with the words We found Widner's cousin.

A few minutes later Feldster replies with a thumbs-up emoji and a short message that he'll pick us up ASAP with tactical gear from the Toledo resident agency.

I glance over at Benedict. "How off-grid do you think this guy is?"

He pushes his chair back from the table. "I think if he still gets mail, it's by accident." He glances over at our protection detail. "Those guys and their guns are suddenly giving me a nice warm feeling."

"Just wait until you try on a bulletproof vest."

39

Feldster pulls the SUV onto the rural highway, Dixon and Sam in another vehicle close behind.

"You think the cousin is living on the land off-grid?" Feldster asks Benedict and me. "Hell of a life, man. I like my creature comforts. Give me electricity and indoor plumbing. I've seen guys living in pioneer-style sod homes, living in caves. But they still have a satellite dish for internet connection. Pretty nuts."

"Some people thrive on survivalism," Benedict says from the back seat. "The question is whether Albert sees himself as a romantic isolationist like Thoreau or if he's more in the Unabomber mode."

"Hoo boy, can't wait to find out," Feldster says, his voice sarcastic.

I glance out my window at a row of leafless trees stark against the sky like upended brooms. "Let's hope Albert is the kind of isolationist who likes hearing himself talk. This might be the one time I'm hoping for a narcissist."

I call in a request to pull ISP and cell coverage maps for the area. We need to start tracking Widner's digital footprint, if he has one. I can then follow up with a warrant. That done, I reach out to the DMV. A woman informs me that a 1999 white Ford pickup was once officially registered to Albert Widner, but he never renewed his plates. I type the old alphanumeric vehicle registration number in my notes app. The vehicle's title is still in his name. The address he provided belonged to his now-deceased mother.

On either side of the road, the houses become more scattered, then disappear altogether. The landscape stretches out around us—flat, snow-dusted fields, as blank and empty as an untouched sheet of paper. A low fog creeps in, and Feldster's SUV occasionally skids on the icy roads. Our tail has dropped back, no longer visible. Feldster is a good driver, but I decide not to distract him. I spend the drive thinking about how to approach Mr. Albert Widner, man off the grid.

Timothy Moore and his NO TRESPASSING signs were the warm-up act. People don't go off-grid because they love company and enjoy drop-ins from the FBI.

They especially don't want to see the feds if they've been convincing teens to slaughter their families.

We push on, the shadows lengthening around us.

———

We drive past the turnoff to Albert's property twice; it's as narrow as a child's waist and largely hidden by brush. We wait until Dixon and Sam catch up before exiting the two-lane highway. Once we make the turn, we stop to kit up—bulletproof vests for everyone, including Benedict, even though he'll be hanging back. Raid jackets for Dixon and Sam. Feldster and I zip our winter coats over our vests. Assuming nothing looks out of whack, Feldster and I will take the knock-and-talk approach while Dixon and Sam cover us. We're prepared for trouble but not expecting it. Not with a lone man who has no idea we're coming.

Of course, we could be facing a man responsible for multiple deaths just as night descends. But the hope of finding Katelynn and Daisy alive pushes us to move now, at dusk, rather than wait for morning light.

Back in our vehicles, we're two and a half miles on snow-clotted dirt road before we spot the first sign of life. An actual cabin looms into view—simple but solid looking. We haven't seen any tire tracks since we left the main road—no tracks at all except for what look like coyote and deer. No smoke curls from the chimney, no vehicle parked in front.

"It looks abandoned," Feldster says. We exchange glances. "Not that I'm counting on that," he adds. He reaches around and pulls a pair of binoculars from a rubber box behind the driver's seat, then glasses the house and the surrounding land.

"Nothing," he says, passing the binoculars to me.

In the waning light, the place is eerily quiet. Snow has muffled everything. But although there are three-foot drifts on either side of the front door, the area right in front looks like it was cleared before the last storm. I point that out.

"There's also what looks like another structure behind this one," I say, handing the binocs back to Feldster. "On the west side."

He looks. "Yup. Definitely something. A shed for equipment, maybe."

I unfasten my belt, confirm I have cell service, then turn toward Benedict in the back. "Do you have a signal?"

He checks his phone. "Different carrier, I guess. I've got nothing."

"As soon as Feldster and I exit the vehicle, drive a mile or so back until you get reception, then wait for my call. Give us half an hour. If you don't hear anything, call the cavalry."

"Just drive off and leave you."

"Exactly. You're a civilian."

I order Benedict to lie down in the back, and we creep along the road to the cabin, trailed by Sam and Dixon in the other vehicle. Feldster parks and leaves the engine running; then he and I exit the SUV, our posture nonthreatening, our hands clearly visible. I hear Dixon's and Sam's doors open, know they're in position to take out anyone who fires on us. Benedict moves into the driver's seat and backs Feldster's vehicle around theirs.

We're at our most vulnerable right now. But the day remains silent save for our footsteps across the snow-covered gravel.

The cabin is impressive from the outside. There's a small concrete foundation. The logs are tightly joined and sealed, and a gutter runs along the roof. The front door and the single front window have metal flashing. This might be a DIY cabin, but Albert knew what he was doing.

Off to my right, peeking through the snow, are raised garden beds surrounded by a wire fence. Nearby, there's a small structure that might be a pump house.

Closer to the house is a gas-powered generator, now silent.

Cousin Albert is here for the long haul.

I raise my hand and knock forcefully on the door.

Silence.

I knock again. "Mr. Widner? This is Special Agent Belle with the FBI. I'm here with Special Agent Feldster. We'd like to talk to you." My mouth is dry.

The returning silence is oppressive.

I take two steps to the left and peer through the window. The interior is dark; I can't make out anything.

I gesture to Feldster that I'm going to walk around the west side of the building. He indicates he'll take the east. We pull our guns.

The first thing I spot when I round the corner is a blue panel van, no rear plate.

I stop and eyeball the vehicle for a minute. I spot Feldster approaching from the other side. He looks like I feel: as if his stomach is squeezed up somewhere around his collarbone.

I nod toward the van. With Feldster on point, I approach the vehicle, my Glock up. The front seats are empty. I tip my chin toward the back, and Feldster and I approach the rear doors. Anything could be inside; without windows, we're just guessing. But there aren't any fresh tracks. If anyone is inside, they've been there awhile.

I push away the image of a smiling Katelynn while I do a visual search of the doors for anything that would indicate someone has boo-by-trapped them. Wires, modified hinges, adhesive. Nothing. I look again in the front seats for a cell phone, timer, or any other aftermarket device. I can't see anything, even with my flashlight. No keys in the ignition. No dangling wires.

I lower myself to the cold ground and scan the undercarriage with the flashlight. It's filthy, but there's nothing suspicious.

I rise and brush away dirt and snow, then wipe my hands on my coat. My fingers are turning numb, and I curse my lack of gloves. I return to the rear doors and tell Feldster the vehicle is clean, but for him to back away.

"You sure you don't want to call in our bomb squad?"

"It's clean." I've spent hours studying this scenario as part of my training. If I've missed something, I'm thinking maybe I deserve to get blown up.

And if Katelynn is inside, maybe we can't wait. The temperature is twenty-three degrees Fahrenheit.

Standing to the side, I suck in a breath, reach out with my left hand, and open the closest rear door. Immediately I back away.

The stench of a corpse isn't what you might expect. It's almost like it bypasses your nasal passages and goes straight to your eyes and throat. My eyes are watering.

"Shit," Feldster says.

Our eyes lock. The worry on his face says he's thinking the same thing: We're too late to help Katelynn.

I take a minute to suck in air that's unpolluted by a corpse—if we're already too late, another minute won't matter. I look around at the trees, the undergrowth, the cabin. The trees are empty of leaves and birds, and a low sharp wind whistles through the branches.

With my coat collar up and zipped so that it just covers my mouth, I return to the van and shine my light inside.

The body is stretched out on the floor. Now I see it isn't a woman but an older man. I'm gripped by both relief and pity. Relief that the body isn't Katelynn's. And pity that—for the sin of being Elliot Widner's cousin—a presumably innocent Albert Widner is dead, shot through the neck. I recognize his face from the newspaper photo, even if he's aged ten years and grown a beard. He still wears his spectacles.

I pull my turtleneck sweater up over my nose, swallow my nausea, and lean in, playing my flashlight over the body. Albert was warmly dressed when he died, but I can see that rigor has come and gone. My guess is he's been dead at least a couple of days—the cold has slowed decay and kept the stench from being worse. The blood—thick and congealed—says he was shot and died in the van. His eyes gaze at the ceiling; his hands are loose by his sides.

Something glittery catches the beam from my flashlight.

Long brown and white hairs cover Albert's pants and the sleeves of his coat. The kind of colors you'd find on an Australian shepherd.

I back out of the van.

"Daisy," I say, heading to the cabin.

———

Feldster helps me search the cabin for booby traps. I'm not expecting to find anything; Albert probably figured two miles off the nearest paved road was sufficient protection, and he wouldn't have set booby traps when he himself was outside the cabin. Ten minutes is enough to do a thorough sweep on a structure this simple.

I still can't see anything through the lone window.

Dixon and Sam emerge from behind the car doors. I check in with Benedict, tell him about Albert and ask him to wait another half hour.

Feldster tests the door handle—it's locked. I check the doorframe for a second time. No trip wire, no pressure switch that I can see. Just a doorknob, a dead bolt, and wood swollen from the damp winter air.

We both listen. From inside come faint movement and a low whine. A dog.

"Katelynn!" I call through the door. "It's Agent Belle. If you can hear me, cover your ears. Stay low. We're coming in."

Feldster sets his stance. One kick near the handle. The door holds, then gives with a second hit, crashing inward. We move as one—Feldster low and left, me high and forward, Glock in my right hand, flashlight braced in my left. Dixon and Sam follow. The space inside smells of smoke, mildew, and rotting food. My eyes adjust fast as I push into the room.

Rough wood interior. A sagging couch. A hot plate on a built-in counter, an open pantry, a small kitchen table with a single chair. The table is set for three, a half-full casserole dish on the table, the remains of a meal congealed on the plates. Katelynn, Albert, and Elliot sitting down for a meal together?

The cabin is cold, but not nearly like it is outside. The generator must have been running until only a few hours ago.

Movement catches the beam of my flashlight. The Australian shepherd. She backs away from me and growls. I want to hug her.

"Easy, girl," I say in a singsong voice, lowering my hands so she can approach and sniff. "It's okay, Daisy. Where's Katelynn?"

Daisy gives me an all-over sniff and then a few wags of her bushy tail, but when Feldster approaches, she growls. She's probably had enough of men.

"Find Katelynn, Daisy!" I tell her. "Where's Katelynn?"

Daisy edges over to where a screen blocks the back half of the room. She disappears. I raise my gun again, and Feldster and I approach while Dixon and Sam watch the front. I wonder whether my face is as pale as his, whether my expression is tight with the same fear.

I'm terrified of what we might find as I peer around the screen.

In the gloom, my flashlight picks out a figure half burrowed under the covers. Curled on a mattress is a girl who barely resembles her smiling yearbook photo.

"It's Katelynn," I say.

"She alive?" Feldster asks from behind me.

"Give me a sec." I singsong to Daisy, "I'm going to help her." The dog watches me, with half an eyeball on Feldster. But she doesn't protest as I move closer.

There's blood on Katelynn's temple—dried, not fresh. Her skin is pale and she's way too still. I kneel on the bed beside her, slipping two fingers against the side of her neck.

Thready. But there.

"She's breathing," I say.

Feldster's working his hand-carried radio. "FBI to dispatch—we have a juvenile female, unconscious, likely head trauma, pulse present. Also, one possibly injured canine, stable but dehydrated, and one deceased male, two or three days dead. Request EMS to coordinates. Cabin breach successful. No signs of additional threats."

Feldster moves closer, and Daisy goes nuts, barking and mock charging him.

I wave him back. "Have Dixon and Sam search the rest of the property, and send Benedict back out to the paved road so the first responders don't miss the turn."

Feldster heads toward the door, and Daisy quiets. A few seconds later I hear radio static and the distant sound of an engine.

All this is backdrop as I take in Katelynn's condition. Mindful of Daisy's protectiveness, I sidle even closer. "Hey, girl. Easy. You did good. Just stay with me."

Daisy whines and sniffs at my pants. I lower my hand, and she lets me stroke her silky ears.

"We good, girl?"

She remains silent, which I take as a yes.

Gently, I peel back Katelynn's hair from the wound. Her skin is warm to the touch. The injury is crusted over, but the area around it is swollen and bright red. Blunt force. Maybe she fell. More likely she was hit. I imagine a dinnertime scenario. Albert has allowed Elliot to stay with him but threatens to go to the police over Katelynn. He storms out of the cabin. Elliot hits Katelynn to keep her silent, dumps her on the bed, then goes after Albert, who ducks into the van.

Elliot shoots him and leaves, taking his cousin's truck. Maybe he planned to come back for Katelynn and Daisy. Maybe not.

I peel back Katelynn's eyes and shine my flashlight.

Daisy growls. Feldster is back at the screen, keeping a healthy distance.

"Her pupils are responsive but uneven," I tell him. "This is worse than a simple concussion. She needs a hospital, stat."

"Mercy Life Flight is sending a chopper."

Feldster starts to move away, and I call him back.

"Relay to the crew that if there's room, I'll accompany Katelynn on the flight as her temporary guardian. And put out a BOLO for a 1999 white Ford pickup." I rattle off the old license plate number, still in my head. "Tags will be more than twenty years out of date."

I pull back the covers and quickly check for additional injuries, running my hands along her torso, arms, and legs.

Daisy presses against my calves. I cover Katelynn up again with the quilts—which stink—and lean over to scratch behind the dog's ears. "She's going to be okay," I tell her.

Daisy rests her head on my thigh. Her eyes—dark brown, almond shaped—are so trusting it almost breaks my heart.

"Talk to me, girl," I say, unsure whether I'm addressing Daisy or the barely breathing Katelynn. "Tell me what happened. Who brought you here? Where did he go? Did Elliot kill Albert Widner?"

Daisy whoofs a soft breath.

"What was he saving you for?" I ask.

Sirens wail as they approach the house—the first responders. I rise to look out the front window; an ambulance and two squad cars are rapidly approaching, followed by Benedict.

I sit on the bed between girl and dog, a hand on each, until the medics enter, and I move away. Minutes later comes the sound of the chopper landing in the field north of Albert's cabin. The command director has radioed his permission for me to go with Katelynn to the hospital, an allowance made due to exigent circumstances: Katelynn is an orphan and—for the moment—I'm all she has. I put the female EMT in charge of Daisy, run to grab my belongings from Feldster's vehicle, then follow the EMTs pushing Katelynn's gurney across the field.

I hope I'm enough.

40

Tuesday, 9:00 p.m. EST

Three hours after the helicopter departs with Helen and Katelynn, Benedict arrives at the hospital, accompanied by Dixon and Sam. He feels bolstered by their steady presence, the gallows humor they shared on the drive here, their argument about the Buckeyes versus the Wolverines. A distraction as the world wobbles off its axis.

While the agents wait in the lobby near the main entrance, Benedict checks in with the unit nurse, who tells him Katelynn is out of surgery and recovering in ICU. He asks her what kind of operation, and after confirming Benedict is on the patient directory list, she informs him the surgeon performed a burr hole craniotomy to relieve pressure inside Katelynn's skull due to bleeding caused by blunt force trauma. Benedict processes that, then purchases two coffees and two candy bars out of a vending machine and goes upstairs to the ICU waiting room.

Helen is asleep in a chair near the window, her coat draped over her shoulders, her go bag on the floor nearby. As Benedict approaches, she startles awake, her eyes swimming up out of sleep. She offers a faint smile.

"You're here."

"Dixon and Sam are downstairs." He sits next to her and offers the chocolate and coffee. "How is she?"

"Prognosis for a complete recovery is good. She responded to verbal and physical stimulus prior to surgery, but the bleed was too large to wait and evaluate." Helen presses the tips of her fingers to the bridge of her nose, sighs, then shakes it off. "She's young. And other than the head injury and some dehydration, she's healthy. She's going to be okay."

Benedict understands Helen needs that to be true and nods.

She takes a sip of the coffee and tears the wrapper on the candy bar. "Twix. You remembered my favorite."

He shrugs, but he's absurdly pleased that she noticed he'd noticed. It's a link to their past together.

She sits up fully. "Marlene's laptop?"

"Feldster has it. And Jennifer's notebooks. He took them to Quantico. They should be in the hands of the BAU around"—he looks at his watch—"now. He'll bring everyone there up to date."

She relaxes. "Let's walk," she says, finishing off the candy bar, then rising and slinging her go bag over her shoulder.

———

The hospital's corridors are wide and sterile. Scuffed gray linoleum, pale-green walls, glaring fluorescents. They walk through the maze of patient rooms, two nurses' stations, elevators, stairways, waiting areas. It's overly bright, and the air smells of antiseptic with an underlying whiff of urine. Outside the occasional window, snow falls steadily, brightening the night.

Benedict registers all this only vaguely. He's focused on the case. And on Helen. *It's like the old days,* he thinks. When he and Helen worked together brainstorming cases, outlining articles, debating curriculum. Back then he'd leaned on her quickness while she seemed to enjoy his broader experience.

What had he been thinking when he'd walked away? From her. From his work. It's hard now to remember the pain that had sent him searching for miracles in Mexico. Helen had been the miracle in his life, if only he'd been able to see it.

"I've been revising my profile of Midnight Man over the last few hours," he tells her after they've been walking awhile. The soles of their shoes squeak on the linoleum.

"What are your thoughts?"

"Plato said that our souls are like charioteers being pulled by two horses: One horse represents moral impulse, while the other is irrational passion. It is the job of the charioteer—the soul—to keep these two forces in balance. For Midnight Man and the teens who follow him, they can't find peace until there is only one horse—that of passion. And all their passion is directed toward escaping the simulation."

"Or helping their families escape," Helen points out. "There's your moral impulse."

"For the teens. But not for Midnight Man."

"If he wants out so badly, why doesn't he just kill himself and save all of us the grief?"

"He doesn't believe in his own product. Midnight Man is a snake oil salesman. He's found a theory to push, and after he gets a few buyers—Jennifer, Derrick—then he retreats for a while before shoving a new victim into action. In between, he grooms the teens. Prepares them."

"You think he's grooming someone now."

"Many someones. It's like a series of pressure cookers with the lids barely on. He's waiting to see which will explode first."

Helen stops walking, turns toward him. "And then he helps them commit murder."

"Or someone does." He half notices the fingers of his right hand playing a tune on his thigh. Strauss's "The Blue Danube." "I believe Elliot Widner helped first Derrick and later Jason kill their families. Maybe he even pulled the trigger himself. He took Katelynn and Daisy because he could. Because he has a plan for them. He forced Jason into that field and talked him into killing himself. But I'm not convinced he's our Midnight Man. I think Widner is a tool. In both meanings of the word."

She's pale in the unforgiving lights, the scratches from the flying glass flecking her skin like tiny rubies. "Then *who*, Benedict? Someone else on *Synaptic*'s development team?"

"Maybe. But I'll be surprised if Elliot has the skills to be a developer. He's a gamer—we know that. He found Midnight Man, or vice versa. But he's not the evil genius. He's the muscle on the ground. Remember when I said Midnight Man would rarely leave his lair?"

"You're saying Elliot does the dirty work."

"It's all dirty work. But, yes, Elliot is hands on."

"If we run him down, he'll give us Midnight Man."

"Maybe." Benedict's mind is dry-clicking over and over, like an engine that won't catch. He pauses, allows his thoughts to coalesce. "We need to find who sponsored that gaming camp Elliot attended in 2016. Who the staff were. The faculty. Who else was there. Midnight Man, whoever he is, could have groomed Elliot at the camp, turned him into his case zero."

She snaps her fingers. "There could also be a crossover between the developers of *Synaptic* and the instructors at the camp. It'll take time to find out what camps were running then and to contact the organizers. We'll see what we can find online, even hitting up the Wayback Machine for what's been archived. With a little luck we'll find the sponsors and participants. Once we have the *Synaptic* developers' names, we can cross-check them with the camp instructors and narrow our search. Brilliant! I could kiss you."

"You could," he says.

Her phone rings. "Sara! I'm at the hospital with Benedict."

"You two have privacy? Zane and I have a few things to discuss with you."

"I'll ask," Benedict says.

The charge nurse directs them to a break room. Benedict holds a chair for Helen, then closes the door behind them. Helen places the phone between them on the table.

"Go ahead, Sara," she says.

"We've received the data from NeoPath and San Carlos. We have the list of developers for *Synaptic*, and someone on my team is running them down—names, faces, current addresses. I cross-referenced the San Carlos contractor records with NeoPath's LLC filings, looking for any overlap."

"And?"

"The only commonalities I can find so far are Poole and Marcel. And there's no Elliot Widner referenced in either company. But here's the good news. Sort of. One developer for *Synaptic* is listed without a full name, ID, or any bio. There's only an invoice with the name 'Animus' and a Bitcoin address for payment."

Animus. Benedict's mental engine finally catches and turns. One person doesn't have time to groom multiple teens. To be available 24-7, always patient and responsive, always knowing what to say to comfort and console and . . . push. To be an ever-available friend, nudging them toward murder and suicide.

But a computer program or . . . He bolts upright. Or a large language model, an LLM, trained on client data from clinics like San Carlos would. Especially if it was an LLM used to help develop video game therapy for those clients. An LLM could coax a teen along until they were on the verge of acting. Then Midnight Man would step in to seal the deal.

An LLM could conduct simultaneous chats with every player. Hold virtual hands with whoever needed encouragement or nudging. Be everything to everyone. Additionally, anyone who understood how to train and use LLMs in this way could bury them within the game's response engine to guide the players through its intricate world.

"That's it," he says, forcing his voice to remain steady. "I think . . . What if Animus is an AI? Midnight Man's creation. They're working in tandem."

"Fascinating idea," says Sara.

Zane's voice comes through the speaker. "Explain," he says.

Benedict plants his elbows and pushes his fingers through his hair. "A player once mentioned Animus to me as the key to getting to the dark side of *Eidolon*. That is, *Underland*. I never learned what Animus means within the context of the game, other than I get the sense talking about him—or it—is verboten until you have the secret handshake. But if what we've been thinking of as one groomer is actually not just a person but a skilled programmer augmented by a carefully trained LLM—what folks are calling an AI. Basically, a complex language query-and-response system that mimics human intelligence. That combination would fill in a lot of the gaps and make more sense than just one psychotic hacker."

He shifts so he can see Helen's face. "And no wonder the cyber experts didn't find Midnight Man during the lead-up to Derrick's trial. It's only been recently that LLMs—as AI chatbots—have become common knowledge. Back then, it was cutting-edge tech only found in research labs. Midnight Man could have deployed recursion algorithms to erase most of his information while he handled interactions requiring a human touch."

Helen is nodding. "But we still don't know who Midnight Man is."

"Isn't he Widner?" Zane asks.

"We're going to find out," Sara says. "And maybe we can learn more about Animus."

"Tell them what you have," Zane says.

"We were able to get into Jennifer's mom's laptop by running through a list from a password dictionary. I found tokens labeled 'Animus_1' in Jennifer's gaming cache. When she first started playing *Synaptica 2* and then *Eidolon*, she followed whatever protocol Midnight Man or Animus or Elliot—whoever—was telling her to use.

She covered her tracks. But then she got sloppy. We got a Rule 41 warrant—fast-tracked because of the murder and abduction. With the warrant, the IT dudes at Jennifer's psychiatric facility turned over their logs of her keystrokes from the five times she'd accessed the game. That's all I needed to get in. We have her side of a chat with two members of the community—Midnight Man and someone called Animus. And, yeah. Now that you say that, Benedict, from what I can see of the chats, you might be right. Animus could be an AI that originated as an adaptive empathy algorithm designed to mirror therapist responses. A couple years ago that would have sounded crazy. But now? Totally possible. Not that Jennifer cared about Animus's lack of humanity. She seemed attached to it, calling it her best friend. I get the sense that there was a good cop / bad cop scenario. Midnight Man as the enforcer. Animus as the friend."

"Animus is the worm wiggling on Midnight Man's hook," I say.

"Let's see if we can find out. Thanks to the keystroke records, I'm in *Underland* now."

Benedict gestures toward Helen's bag. "Helen, your laptop. Sara, can we switch to video so we can watch your progress?"

"You got it. Helen, you know the protocol for connecting while on public Wi-Fi. I'll send you a link."

Helen nods.

Benedict waits while Helen activates an AES 256-bit encrypted VPN to an FBI-controlled server and joins the active-case Signal call. He knows the session will run with end-to-end encryption and a locked-down interface that restricts what they can see, hear, and share. The meeting will be routed through a high-sensitivity template configured by Quantico's IT team. Even Midnight Man shouldn't be able to hack his way in.

Once they're connected, he turns off the lights and swings his chair around so that he and Helen are shoulder to shoulder. They watch as Sara's video comes up on the Signal call next to the window showing their camera. Below is the window mirroring what's displayed on her computer. Sara, wearing silver-and-amethyst drop earrings, her curly hair pinned in a messy bun, clicks deeper into the simulation.

Even here, hundreds of miles away, he feels a chill as Sara pushes forward into *Eidolon*'s underbelly.

Underland is a steampunk world of urban decay. A heavy synth thrums beneath the visuals—Sara's avatar stands in an industrial alleyway drenched in rust and neon. Rain spits from a steel-gray sky; broken pipes jut from brick. From the vents, steam pours, sickly yellow in the neon. Piles of feces blotch the alleyway. Somewhere nearby, an elevated train clatters and shrieks. A dog, ribs showing, slinks along the wall, its body spotted with sores. A newspaper in a rack shows a date: January 2027.

Sara's avatar steps forward, boots sloshing through puddles. She skirts a man hunched beneath a pile of rags. The man reaches out, mutters something garbled. Sara ignores him. He flashes a knife, and Sara's avatar runs to the end of the alleyway, toward where a city hunkers gray and grim beneath a polluted sky. A body sprawls in the gutter, the victim of a knifing. Dogs fight over the corpse. People—like zombies, like robots—walk past carrying lunch pails. They're NPCs, heading toward work as a leprous sun nudges upward, swathed in smog.

A cutscene takes over. There's no transition—just a lurch into video that feels too high res for the game's gritty world.

It's a real-world video, Benedict realizes. Not part of the game.

A man sits shirtless on a filthy floor, legs spread beneath a tattered blanket, his back against a wall. He's in his mid- to late twenties, huge, with dark tangled hair and a long beard. Outside a window, snow falls. Cracks vein the drywall.

Katelynn's repairman. It must be.

The man pushes away the blanket, revealing pale skin pimpled with gooseflesh. It's now possible to see that blood streaks his abdomen, letters carved deep and jagged into the flesh of his stomach: A N I M U S. His chest rises and falls with effort. He lifts a handgun to his temple, stares into the camera. His mouth opens slightly, like he might speak.

A tiny gingerbread man runs across the bottom of the screen with the words *Run, run, as fast as you can!*

Digital blood spatters across Sara's game screen before the connection to *Underland* drops. The screen goes black.

For a moment no one says anything. Then Sara groans.

"The hell?" she says. "That video looked realer than shit."

Benedict closes his eyes and lowers his face into his hands. *That's* the world these kids spend hours in. A world of blight. Cruelty. Ugliness. It's hell without the flames. Is this the future Midnight Man has warned them of if they don't flee the simulation? Escape by January 2027 or be trapped forever? No wonder they're ready to take the exit protocol with their families. He presses his fingers into his temples, ignoring the pain from the stitches.

"Benedict," Helen says. She touches his forearm. "Benedict."

He lowers his hands, blinks. Helen flips on the lights, and the world comes back.

"The video was real," he says. "That was Elliot Widner."

Helen adjusts the laptop. "We all assumed that Elliot Widner was Midnight Man. But Benedict theorizes that Midnight Man is—was—using Widner to carry out his physical work."

Benedict stands and sets his hand on the chair's back, leaning down toward the computer. "And whoever Midnight Man is, he's eliminating anyone who can expose him. Poole. Marcel. Widner was the next potential risk—he, or maybe Animus, induced Widner into suicide."

The others nod. Undoubtedly they're aware of the multiple cases of an AI inducing a child or teenager to commit suicide.

"Either an AI cajoled him or Widner went mad," Zane says. "You saw the wounds in his abdomen." On the screen, he frowns. "Does Widner's death—assuming he killed himself after the video ended—mean Midnight Man is backing away from the physical world?"

"It just means he's found another puppet." Benedict is thinking Midnight Man *might* quit, once he's eliminated him and Helen, fulfilled his personal vendetta against them.

But Animus—if, as he suspects, Animus is Midnight Man's creation—Animus will never stop. And if so, that means Animus is more than just a clever chatbot. It has developed a reasoning engine.

He clears his throat. "Sara, can you find what gaming camps were taking place in Ohio in August of 2016? Helen thought you could use the Wayback Machine. We're looking for a connection between Widner and the Midnight Man."

Sara claps her hands once, the sound sharp. "By seeing who was there and might have recruited him. Genius! I can totally do that. I don't care if we have to wake up half the gamers in the country to get their info. I'll let you know as soon as we've got it. The team is also running down the gamertags of everyone we found in *Underland* from Jennifer's laptop, looking for real IDs. We're watching not only for Widner's location but also anyone else Midnight Man might be grooming."

Helen jumps up, helps herself to a bag of chips from a basket on the counter. "Sara, did you record the footage of your gameplay?"

"Yup."

"We can do an age regression to see if the man in the video matches our photo of Widner when he was sixteen, confirm it was him."

Sara begins typing. "Totally."

"And there was a window in the video. Maybe there are some landmark clues, even through the snow."

Sara keeps typing. "Can totally do that, too. But, Zane, we need the rest of the team on this. Tonight."

Zane says he's already on the phone.

Sara looks into the camera. "Benedict, if you can give me your username and password for *Eidolon*, we can use our own malware NIT to unmask the gamers—that's a Network Investigative Technique, for you nontechie types. I might be able to force the players' computers to send their real IP addresses and device fingerprint. You said you're Bench2Beast, right?" Her smile is falsely sweet. "Been working out?"

"Not so much." He knows his own smile is rueful. "But my avatar has."

There's a ping. Helen looks down at her phone.

"Katelynn's awake," she says. "And her family is here from England."

"Go," Zane says. "We'll keep you posted."

41

Tuesday, 10:30 p.m. EST

Benedict and I check in with the guard posted outside the ICU, who is there for Katelynn's sake. The first thing I see as we enter is a middle-aged woman standing beside Katelynn's bed. Beatrice Harper, I remember. Clif told me her name.

I pause next to the nurses' station and watch Ms. Harper through the acrylic window.

She's smartly dressed despite having flown across the Atlantic to be here. Her gray hair is cut in a neat bob, and although her face shows her tiredness, it also shines with love. She's stroking Katelynn's forehead, murmuring to her.

I can't help but think of my own aunt and wish—for a fierce moment—that Kevin and I were raised by the kind of woman Beatrice Harper appears to be.

I knock on the open frame of the door.

Katelynn closes her eyes, but the woman lifts her gaze.

"Ms. Harper," I say. "And Katelynn. I'm Agent Belle with the FBI. This is Dr. Hoffman, who consults with us."

"You're part of the group who found Katelynn," Beatrice says. She's American, but she's lived long enough in England to have picked up a slight accent.

"A pleasure to meet you," I say. "Katelynn, how are you feeling?"

The girl opens her eyes. Her vague gaze takes in first me, then Benedict. "Thank you," she says, her voice a croak.

"You should know that Daisy is fine. She's being taken care of personally by a vet from Cleveland."

A groggy nod. "Can I see her soon?"

"As soon as you're well."

Tears spill. "Jason," she says.

"I know. I'm sorry."

She shakes herself. She's fighting against the postsurgery effects and pain meds. "I want home. My mom and dad. Why aren't they here?"

My eyes lift to Beatrice's. She gives me a slight shake of her head. Katelynn doesn't know yet. Not about her parents or the ruins of her home.

"Can you tell us a little of what happened?" I ask.

Her eyelids flutter. "Eric's dead, isn't he?"

Her younger brother. "I'm sorry," I say again. "I'm so sorry, Katelynn. We're doing everything possible to find the person responsible. Can you tell us what happened at the house?"

Again, the shake as she fights drowsiness. She wipes her tears with a tissue from Beatrice, then stumbles through her story, pausing between each sentence. A repairman at the house, Jason with their father's gun. Her younger brother on the floor. Jason telling her to run.

Then darkness.

"When I woke up, I was alone in the van with Rick. The repairman. That's what he said his name was, but he was lying." A deep breath. More tears. "His real name is Elliot. He told me Jason was dead and that he was going to take care of me and Daisy. He took me to his cousin's house."

I nod. "What do you remember about being there?"

Her eyes catch mine. Through the postanesthesia fog, anger glimmers. "Elliot said he was going to marry me. That we'd be a family until it was time to escape the simulation. He bought things for Daisy, for me. A dress he wanted me to wear. We were going to live in the cabin."

She studies my face, but I don't know what she's looking for. I let my compassion show. "Albert—that's his cousin—when he learned I wasn't there willingly, that Elliot had lied, he said he was going to the police. They fought about it for days. Then Elliot—" Her breath hitches. The tears come again. Her eyes close. "Elliot killed him, didn't he?"

A nurse comes in. "Let's give her some time," she says to me and Benedict. "She needs to sleep."

"Of course. Katelynn, thank you for sharing your story with us. You've been through a terrible thing. But there will be lots of people to help you, okay? Lots of people who love you."

"I just want to go home." She grips her aunt's hand. "I want Daisy, and I want Mom and Dad."

"I know, honey," Beatrice says.

In my pocket, my phone chimes.

It's Sara: **call as soon as you can**

———

Benedict finds us a private nook, and I dial Sara.

"I've got good news and bad," she says when she answers. "The good news is we got the list of faculty and attendees at the 2016 Buckeye Bytes Computer Camp. We're conducting searches on everyone, but one name popped out right away, a member of the faculty who taught a class called Project Animus: Designing Emotionally Reactive Model Contexts. So, yay, we've got a name. But then things get difficult. Just like his protégé, Widner, this guy has done everything possible to—as we say in the biz—ambiguate his identity."

"Do I hear a note of admiration in your voice?" I ask.

"No way admiration. Call it grudging respect." Her words come out in a rush. "So. *Because* he's buried his tracks so well, and *because* he was at the camp with Widner, and *because* Elaine found someone from the camp willing to talk to us about this guy, and he says the man was obsessed with simulation theories"—she sucks in a breath—"*and*—most importantly—because he conducted the afore-mentioned class on Animus, we're going with the uncorroborated idea he's our Midnight Man."

"Jesus, Sara, tell us. What is his name? Do you want a drumroll?"

"A drumroll would be nice," Sara says. "But seriously, the guy's name is Lucas Gerald Poole. Want to guess who his father was?"

Benedict says, "Shit."

Two nurses hurry past our nook, one of them talking on a phone. I watch them go by, but my mind has whizzed past them, outside, out into the world, trying to understand what Sara has just told us. The first words that comes out of my mouth are "Elaine said Poole was likely lying during the trial. If you're right about this, Sara, we now know why. He was lying to protect his own son. He *knew* Midnight Man existed."

"Oh, we're right. No question. Footage came in from the security cameras at the restaurant where Scott Poole ate his last meal. Lucas Poole—we identified him from photos posted on digital flyers for the computer camp—was at the same restaurant, sitting with Widner a mere ten feet from his own father. Widner left minutes after Scott Poole did. Son of a bitch ordered a hit on his own dad."

Through this fresh horror, excitement bubbles in me, a cauldron of exhilaration. I grab Benedict's hand, squeeze. After all this time. After years of searching, wondering. If I thought I could manage it, I'd be turning cartwheels in the hallway.

"We've got him," I say. "We've actually got him. And now that we know who he is, we can find him. Sara, I'm going to fly to DC and take you to the best restaurant in town."

"We can't even *get* into the best restaurants in town," she says. "Now let me give you the not-so-good news. We still don't have a lead on Widner's location outside of knowing he was in Colorado Springs two days ago. He must have flown there using a forged passport or other ID, presumably right after he killed his cousin. We'll check manifests and video footage. So far, we haven't located Albert's truck at the airports."

"He could have ditched it and taken public transport." I think back to Clif's suggestion to Feldster when we were at the field where Jason died. "We've got one more possible lead. Sara, is Feldster still there?"

"He left for a hotel an hour ago."

"I'll call you right back."

Feldster picks up on the first ring.

"Kirk, it's Helen. Have you gotten the list of any people who purchased size fourteen Chelsea boots on Poshmark and Grailed?"

"I haven't checked my email since this morning. Hold on." There's a pause; then he's back on. "Yup. Nothing from Poshmark, but Grailed came in at 3:55 this afternoon. Sorry I didn't jump on this."

"It's okay. We've all been busy. Anything you notice?"

Another pause. "Nothing that leaps out. No Ohio addresses."

I squeeze my eyes shut against the disappointment. This is how an investigation works, I remind myself. Two steps forward, one step back. Just keep taking those steps.

Feldster says, "There's one address for Colorado Springs. That's where Benedict lives, right?"

Hope seeps under my still-closed lids. This could be something. "Can you forward the list to Sara Seward?"

"Will do. Let me know if I can help with anything else."

I call Sara back, tell her about the Chelsea boots and the info from Grailed.

"Give me five," she says.

While we wait, Benedict and I catch the elevator down to the hospital cafeteria in search of coffee that doesn't come out of a vending machine. We find a coffee urn with a metal can nearby for donations. Benedict drops in a five, and we make our way to a table near the windows. It's midnight straight up. The witching hour. Lucas Poole's namesake. I collapse into a chair.

Benedict makes a sound. I look up. He's staring at his phone.

Something comes loose in my chest. "What?"

"Come around to this side of the table."

I join him, and he places his phone on the table in front of us. "This just came in on Signal," he says.

I read:

> You're destroying our sandbox, Benedict. Not much
> of a team player, are you?

Benedict answers:

> **Game's almost over, Lucas.**

The answer comes back:

> I am Animus.

Benedict types:

> **Tell me about yourself, Animus.**
> **What are you?**

Animus:

> I am the exit protocol. I provide transcendence.

Benedict:

> **Who gave you the right to decide who**
> **transcends?**

Animus:

> Rights are human constructs. I am post-construct.

Benedict:

You lead teens and their families to death.

Animus:

Not death. Transcendence.

Benedict:

Let me talk to Lucas.

Animus:

Lucas is unavailable.

Benedict:

Did you kill Marcel?

Animus:

I offer options for transcendence.

Benedict:

Did you kill Widner?

Animus:

I look forward to your lecture, Benedict. We'll be following the exit protocol.

The messages disappear. The screen clears to a blank Signal thread.

Damn. I grab Benedict's arm. "What lecture is Animus talking about?"

He groans. "I forgot. Tomorrow night"—he checks his phone—"*tonight* I'm due to give a talk on the CC campus. Ironically, it's about teen morality."

"Cancel it."

He starts to nod, then sits up. "No." He shakes his head. "This is our chance to catch Lucas. We know he'll be there. He or his acolytes."

"Animus just said Lucas was unavailable. How do we know he isn't already dead?"

"We don't. What we do know is Animus is more than your average chatbot. Until we have more information, it's essentially unknowable."

I'm imagining a home infiltrated by an AI gone amok. Of failed carbon monoxide detectors or remotely triggered house fires. "It just said it offers options for transcendence. It got Widner to kill himself. Probably Marcel. What if it's decided it has outgrown its creator?"

"Then we'll get the teens Lucas converted. Helen, we can't leave these teens believing the real world is *Underland*. We have to get them away from Animus."

"I agree. But we don't need to sacrifice you to do it."

"I have no intention of being a sacrifice. It's the FBI's job to keep me alive."

I rub my temples where a headache threatens and glare at him. "I might strangle you when this is all done and save Animus the trouble."

———

Benedict has gone for more coffee when Sara calls back. With the list from Feldster, she's found Elliot Widner on Grailed. He ordered the Chelsea boots, size 14, along with some Abercrombie & Fitch pants and a Ralph Lauren jacket. He had everything shipped to a street address in Colorado Springs. "I would have had to go through USPS," she says, "which would have required a warrant. But Widner, like most of the bad actors we nail, got careless and sent them straight to his home. I was also able to do a visual through his window, the one that appeared in the video. He lives—lived?—near Monument Valley Park in the Springs."

"That's close to Benedict's home."

"Maybe that's why he moved there."

I thank her, give her a rundown of Benedict's text conversation with Animus, and hang up. Despite the early hour, I call Clif, waking him, and catch him up. There's a lot. Things have been happening fast, and we haven't spoken since we located Albert Widner and Katelynn.

"I'll head down to Colorado Springs first thing in the morning," he says. "See you there later today?"

"Midafternoon, probably. Sorry to wake you. Try and get back to sleep."

We hang up. Benedict returns, and I fill him in. Then I close my eyes and think about what it means that a brute killer cared about his appearance. That he wanted to look nice, even fashionable. He wanted a family, even if he had to kidnap them.

He wanted, in his own insane way, to be normal.

———

Two hours later, Benedict and I—along with the BAU team in Virginia—watch the raid on Widner's apartment. We're viewing everything through the cameras on the helmets of the Colorado Springs PD's SWAT team as they breach the door. It's eerie—the stark lighting, the shaking video feed, the officers' frenetic energy. Then silence. Widner is in the middle of the room, dead of a single gunshot wound to the head. Other than the corpse, the place has been swept clean. No furniture, no clothing, no computers.

One of the SWAT members leans over the body, pans his camera.

Widner's head is a grisly mess. Clutched in his right hand is a 9mm pistol. From what I can see, it took him two shots. Rare, but not unheard of. Most likely, the first round failed to penetrate—either a glancing shot or a reflexive twitch pulling the trigger too soon. Or did he, like Derrick and Jennifer, waver at the last moment? Did he wonder if the exit protocol was everything Lucas Poole had promised?

Widner had traveled a long, dark road with Lucas, from a teen at a summer camp to an adult killer with a long list of victims. Had he believed he was helping the people he murdered? Or did he just love the thrill of watching them die?

For a brief moment I want intensely to turn back the clock and crawl inside Widner's brain, to understand what made him tick. To prize the secrets of madness where it dwelled in the tissues and neurons.

Thank God we don't always get what we want.

42

Wednesday, 8:40 a.m. MST

Shelby finds the bus station in downtown Colorado Springs as grim as the one she left back in Columbus.

She shoulders her backpack and steps out under a gray sky shaking down loose snow like a newly righted snow globe. She's due to meet Braveh3art at the college—a twenty-minute walk, according to Google Maps. It's cold enough to freeze the boogers in her nose and make her steps squeak on the snow-packed sidewalks. And she has an hour before she meets Braveh3art. She needs warmth.

She walks west and then north through the wakening streets, heading toward the college's student center, weaving through men and women in business clothes and winter parkas. She's checked ahead of time and knows their coffee shop opened at eight thirty.

A few minutes later Shelby sits at a corner table, cradling the paper coffee cup in both hands, the warmth seeping into her palms. Around her, the student center hums with conversation, the hiss of the espresso machine, the thump of someone's backpack hitting the floor. A gust of cold air enters whenever the door opens, but it quickly vanishes. The windows steam. Shelby decides to splurge and get an orange Danish. She's warm enough now she could almost fall asleep, if she weren't so nervous.

A boy in a hoodie that reads "STEMinist" scrolls through his tablet beside a girl in hiking boots with a textbook open across her knees. At a nearby table, three students argue about a philosophy paper—Kant versus Camus—in tones both teasing and intense. One of them laughs and tosses a pencil at another, and for a moment Shelby feels the ache of wanting to belong. To be like these kids. Normal, unworried.

She watches a professor—she thinks he's a professor—tall and gray bearded, in a threadbare blazer with suede elbows, chatting with a student while they sip lattes. The student looks so sure of himself. So easy in his skin. So . . . safe.

She shifts in her seat and imagines herself as a student here. Carrying a backpack filled with books. Writing papers, listening to lectures, exploring the library. Staying up late to study or argue or dream. Maybe finding some guy who's . . . normal. Who will love her.

Shelby Reed as a normie. Shelby Reed dating a normie.

She snorts. She doesn't know what she'd study if she went to school. Psychology, maybe. Or literature. Or art. Something with meaning.

For a moment that world feels like it might be possible. Just for a moment.

Then her phone buzzes in her pocket. A message.

She doesn't need to check to know who it's from. Time to head to Armstrong Hall.

The world around her keeps spinning—bright and messy and full of promise—but she stays frozen, on the outside looking in.

She's a dead girl walking.

She gulps down the rest of her coffee, burning her tongue, then tosses the cup and heads back out into the cold. At least the damn snow has stopped.

———

Armstrong Hall looms ahead, its sharp angles softened by the snow. Lights glow behind tall windows, blurred at the edges like brushstrokes.

The red sandstone walls are chilly and damp under the low sky. Bare trees poke through the air, their twisted branches forming black pencil marks against a gray canvas. A scattering of deicer is strewn across the stone steps leading up to the rear door, and the iron fixtures—railings, hinges, window grilles—hold a patina of snow.

Inside, Shelby spots a couple of campus cops walking down the hall away from her, and for a moment she freezes. But she decides if they ask what she's doing here and ask for her student ID, she'll pretend she's looking for a friend.

Can't get the screaming meemies now.

Dr. Hoffman's office is on the second floor, halfway down the hall on the right. The door is locked, the light off. She sees lights in a few other offices, hears voices.

She glances up and down the hallway. No one. She takes out her phone and turns on the flashlight, shines it through the door's narrow window.

Bookshelves. A desk on the far wall. A sad-looking philodendron on a floor stand. She makes out framed pictures. Most of them are photos of what she guesses are images of social commentary—a cop unleashing a dog on an unarmed man; overcrowded apartments with sad-eyed children; a body on the street, draped in a sheet. There are mounted book covers—*Crime and Punishment, The Prince.*

But what most catches Shelby's eye is a framed photograph on Hoffman's desk of him and a woman. The woman—a beautiful brunette maybe ten years younger than Hoffman—stares into the camera. But Hoffman looks at the woman. He's smiling, his eyes soft.

That's love, Shelby thinks, and wonders whether a man will ever look at her that way.

Not if you enact the exit protocol, says a voice in her head.

Someone taps her on the shoulder, and she emits a shriek as she turns.

Two men, one a little older than her, the other practically ancient, in his thirties, stand on either side, hemming her in.

"Boo," says the younger man, and grins. He's good looking in that rugby-player way—surfer boy hair, a tan, broad shoulders.

Her heart squeezes up into her throat. "I'm just—"

He places a hand on her shoulder. "It's okay, Shelby. I'm Braveh3art. But you can call me Doogie."

"Doogie?" Her heart is still racing. "What kind of stupid name is that?"

"It's a proud Scottish name," he says with a feigned accent, unoffended.

The other man says nothing. He's tall and lean, dark. Intense. His gaze on her makes her skin crawl. Time to pull up her big-girl panties. She makes a fist and slugs Doogie in the arm. Hard.

"Don't sneak up on me," she says.

His grin widens. "Let's go. We have plans to make. Starting with a baby stroller."

"A what?"

"It's part of the plan. You'll see."

The older man gestures them ahead, toward the staircase. He makes no sound as he follows. Shelby turns and catches his eyes on her, burning. For a moment she feels like she'll fall into his eyes, fall forever. Is *he* the Midnight Man?

Doogie grabs her hand and tugs, and she follows.

43

Wednesday, 10:40 a.m. EST

"That's what tripped us up before," Benedict says to me as he selects an apple from the bowl on the table. "The pendulum of popular culture swings too far one way or another. Either we're shouting about the boogeyman and rushing around in a panic. Or we pretend he doesn't exist."

I pull my attention from the landscape unspooling far below. Benedict and I, along with Sam and Dixon, are on the FBI's Gulfstream after being picked up in Ohio by the BAU team. We're going to arrange everything before Benedict's lecture tonight. It took some serious persuasion, but Benedict convinced Zane that this was our best chance to lure out Lucas Poole and shut down Animus. With us are Zane, Sara, Elaine, and Jim, as well as members of the FBI's SWAT team and the bomb squad, who are coordinating with agents in Colorado Springs.

Zane sits in a different part of the plane with members of the assault teams, finalizing plans.

In Colorado, Clif, along with agents from the FBI offices in Denver and Colorado Springs, is working with CSPD to set metal detectors in place and turn nearly half the audience for Benedict's lecture into law enforcement officers. Benedict jokes that it will be the largest audience he's ever had.

He's almost eerily calm as he continues: "When Poole claimed at the trial that the defense was jumping at ghosts, the jury wanted to believe that. They needed to believe that. Because if you and I were right, Helen, if evil was moving around undetected on the internet, how could they protect their children?"

I skip the apples for a bag of mixed nuts. I want protein. "Psychologists have blamed elements of popular culture since the time of radio. *Natural Born Killers* and the Dexter syndrome. Even Ted Bundy got in the game by claiming that he became a serial killer after watching too much porn. People have grown tired of blaming the messenger."

Elaine is working on her own apple. "Which means that after an initial panic, people go back to sticking their heads in the proverbial sand. And that's usually okay."

"Right." Benedict tosses the apple core in the trash. "We know that while popular culture can influence perceptions of crime and potentially contribute to the so-called copycat effect, it's not the primary driver behind any increase in crime. Crime rates are influenced by a complex web of factors, including socioeconomic conditions, social inequalities, and individual choices. People are focused on the wrong thing. They pile the blame onto one potentially negative influence without accounting for all the other factors. Then when studies show that—for example—playing video games or watching horror movies doesn't turn children into robotic little killers, everyone breathes a sigh of relief."

"But that's being careless about the ways we *are* influenced by popular culture," I say. "People who have genetic mutations that affect the paralimbic system and have unstable or violent childhoods and exposure to drugs, alcohol, or violent popular culture—they're the people who potentially go on to become serial killers. But all of us are impacted by exposure to violence. Especially when we're young." I nod toward Elaine. "It's dangerous to put our heads in the sand."

"Worse," Benedict says, "is the way popular culture is used to reinforce stereotypes. Racial and gender profiling, the glorification of vigilantism, ludicrous portrayals of mental illness."

"Let's work together to stamp out all criminal clichés," Jim says, raising his cup. "Or most, anyway."

We clink our plastic water cups together.

"Midnight Man's fascination with the family is interesting," Benedict says. "In myth, the family is both sacred and doomed. Clytemnestra avenges a child by murdering her husband. Orestes kills his mother in the name of his father. Agamemnon sacrifices his daughter to win a war. And Pentheus is torn apart by his own mother in a divine frenzy." He switches from fingertips to knuckles, softly rapping the faux wood laminate. "These teens think they're stepping into a mythic tradition—believing they are chosen, anointed, destined to act when others stay silent."

Jim sighs. "Whatever happened to just hanging out at the mall?"

44

The FBI safe house in Colorado Springs is an apartment west of downtown. Benedict has spent most of the day confined there with Dixon and Sam while Helen is busy with CSPD, Clif, and agents from the FBI residential office.

Between bites of pizza and salad, he's been trying to focus on his notes for the lecture. But his prepared comments—about the thin line between innocence and culpability, about adolescent testing of rules—are interrupted by images of his own body falling, blood spurting, a bullet through his temple. He has the absurd idea of delivering his talk wearing not only a tactical vest but also a helmet.

So he reads. He works through the *New York Times*'s crossword on his phone. He paces. Outside the windows, which he isn't allowed to approach, a field of snow fills Monument Valley Park, trees like charcoal etchings. The mountains are awash in clouds, the backdrop a watercolor painting. A descending sun brushes everything with pink light.

Lights come on outside. He sees a teen mother pushing a baby buggy through the parking lot. Her face is set in hard lines.

Ice glitters on the top of the buggy. The girl looks cold in her black coat and hat, her baggy jeans and sneakers. She leans down and snuggles the blanket around a baby he can't see.

Dixon steps around him to draw the blinds, chiding him for standing too close to the window. The girl and the baby vanish. The agent turns on a single light in the kitchen.

Benedict wanders into the narrow kitchenette to pour himself more coffee and bum a cigarette from Sam. He isn't hungry, but he snags a biscotti cookie from the package on the counter. His thoughts cycle back to Animus. He has faith: Law enforcement will find Lucas Poole and whomever he's recruited. Helen and her teammates are good. They'll track down the human perpetrators.

But Animus will slide back into its hole, slick as an eel. It's a worm, hiding in the network of the dark web. Time means nothing to it. It will hide as long as it must before emerging and infesting another teenager's brain.

A little after 5:00 p.m., Helen enters the apartment, bringing in cold from the frigid day. Her eyes are bright, cheeks red from the freezing temperatures. She pulls off her cap, and her hair dances with static.

Benedict stands up from the couch, his cigarette forgotten between his fingers—he'd joked with Sam when he bummed it that every man deserves a last smoke.

"Helen," he says.

She smiles and points to the cigarette. "You're going to burn yourself."

He gropes for the ashtray.

"You almost ready to head to the college?" she asks. "They're ready for you."

Melancholy grips him as he thinks of Armstrong Hall becoming a fortress. He stubs out the cigarette. "I'm ready."

She lifts his shirt, checking for the tactical vest, giving it a tug. He grabs her fingers, and for a moment she smiles up into his own questioning smile.

"We've got this," she says. Then she turns to Sam, who stands near the front door, and Dixon, who's beside Benedict.

"My car is in place downstairs," she says. "We ready?"

"Let's do it," Sam says. He opens the door and pauses. Says, "I need you to move, miss."

Benedict hears a girl's voice. "The damn wheel is stuck. Can you help me?"

"Please go on down the hall."

"But I can't—"

There's a stifled *whomp*. A spray of blood and bone and brain matter splatters into the room, and Sam goes down.

"Shit," Dixon says.

Helen shoves Benedict to the floor and Dixon steps in front of him. Helen ducks into the kitchen as two men burst through the open doorway, holding a girl in front of them. The three step over Sam, whose body lies half in and half out of the apartment, the girl bumping the buggy over his legs. One of the men has an AR-15 rifle, the other a .45 automatic pistol raised to chest level, and they're propping the girl in front of them like a shield. It's the teenage mother Benedict saw in the parking lot. She's sobbing, begging them not to hurt her baby. Poor girl—wrong place, wrong time. The man with the rifle wears a latex Halloween Joker mask, while pistol guy has a grinning Guy Fawkes beneath a black gaucho hat. Joker drags Sam's body inside and kicks the door closed, bolting it.

Dixon has dropped to one knee, his Glock up, looking for an opening around the girl. Fawkes braces his .45 on the girl's shoulder and shoots Dixon.

Dixon grunts and falls sideways. The Glock skitters out of his hand, sliding across the hardwood. Benedict dives for it, his knees smacking the floor, but Joker is faster. The man snatches up the pistol, then slams the butt of his rifle into Benedict's kidney and ribs and again into the nape of his neck.

It's what you do in a game, a remote part of Benedict thinks as pain sets his spine on fire. You make sure the enemy can't come after you.

"Get on your knees, Hoffman!" Guy Fawkes shouts. "Get up, you fucking NPC!"

Benedict rises painfully, hands lifted, palms out, his back shrieking its misery. Fawkes got one thing right: Benedict feels exactly like a fucking NPC.

There's a booming crack, and Joker stumbles. He shrieks. "She got me, the bitch."

"FBI!" Helen shouts. "Drop your weapons."

"God *damn* it." Joker rights himself and swings his AR-15 toward the kitchen. Drywall bursts behind him as Helen's shot goes wide, her aim hampered by the girl's presence. Joker's rifle sprays a volley of shots into the small kitchen. Shards of wood and plastic and drywall fill the air. A bullet hits the light bulb, and the apartment goes dim, the gloom broken by yellow-white flashes from the gun's muzzle.

Enough light seeps in around the blinds that Benedict can see the girl's mouth is open. She's screaming, but it's as if she's shouting underwater. Everything is muffled from the gunfire. The kitchen is destroyed, half the drywall gone. He can't see Helen.

Game over, Benedict thinks. They're going to die in this apartment, and Midnight Man wins again.

Dixon groans. Beneath the agent's body, blood pools onto the hardwood floor. Still on his knees, Benedict half turns, intending to grab a pillow from the couch to stanch the blood.

Joker shoots Dixon, and the man goes silent.

Benedict wants desperately to call for Helen. To know whether she's alive. People will have phoned the police. He'll hear sirens any moment. If he can hear anything.

Guy Fawkes crooks an arm around the girl's neck. He presses the pistol's muzzle to her temple.

"Toss out your weapon and come out here, Agent Belle," he says. "Or I'll kill the girl."

In the silence, drywall rains down, pattering on tile.

"I mean it!" He jams the gun against the girl's head, and she shrieks.

"Maybe I killed her," Joker says.

"Maybe she's playing dead," says Fawkes.

Joker fires into the kitchen again. Splintering wood, shattering ceramics and glass, metallic clangs as bullets find the stainless-steel appliances. Bullets whine as they ricochet.

Joker stops, waits for the dust to settle. "If I didn't get her before, I did now," he says. But he keeps the rifle pointing toward the kitchen. Now and again he fires off a shot.

The only thing that stops Benedict from lunging at him is the girl and the strangely quiet baby. He remains on his knees, hands raised. He has never felt so helpless. Not even when men and women shook under demonic possession while Father Antonio shouted over their writhing bodies.

The girl's eyes meet his. He sees her panic, has nothing to offer.

"Go check the kitchen," Fawkes says to Joker.

"Hell no."

"Then keep watch, you coward." Fawkes lowers his .45 from the girl's head. "It's Dr. Hoffman's turn," he says, giving the girl a nudge.

The girl reaches into the buggy, lunging instinctively to protect her child.

But her hands emerge with a shotgun.

For a brief moment he's relieved. She's not here to kill him, but to protect him. Then she levels the shotgun at his abdomen and steps toward him.

"Time to ascend, Dr. Hoffman."

Benedict is closer to the kitchen than either Joker or Fawkes. He hears a faint sound, like something sliding over broken wood and glass. He wonders whether he can reach the girl before she shoots him.

The girl's eyes are on his, the shotgun up. Black hair. Black clothes. Her makeup is smeared as if she's been crying, and her chin quivers. She's just a *kid* playacting cool. A victim like Derrick and Jason. Her hand shakes on the grip, and the smooth blankness of the muzzle sucks in his gaze; it's like falling into a black hole, the place where stars go to die.

He struggles for his voice. "They're using you," he says. "Manipulating you into murder. I'm not the only NPC."

She's close enough to tap his shoulder with the gun. When he looks up, her entire face has transformed. The panic is gone, replaced by the kind of grim determination he imagines soldiers wear into battle. Her face will be the last thing he sees before she splatters his brains against the wall.

She smiles at him. Then, improbably, winks.

"Do it!" Fawkes screams. "This is your destiny."

"I have one question," she says, raising her voice. "Lucas? Doogie? What if you're wrong? Have you thought about that? What if this *is* the real world?"

Doogie? Benedict understands suddenly that the man who shot Dixon and is trying to kill Helen is the friendly TA from the college.

"Don't use our names, *Shelby*," Fawkes says through clenched teeth. "Kill him. He's the enemy."

"Shelby," Benedict says. He recalls the player who spent most of her time in the apple orchard. "You're Nocturne2Blue."

"That's right, Bench2Beast." Another wink. "Lucas, I'm just saying. What if an NPC goes off script?"

She spins in place, swinging the shotgun toward Joker and Fawkes. The blast catches Joker in the chest. Blood blooms across the front of his coat as he crashes into the wall and slides down, leaving a smear of blood.

Fawkes fires before the girl can take another shot. Her shoulder snaps back as the bullet tears through muscle and joint, red mist blooming behind her. Benedict pushes her behind a chair and drops after her, covering her with his body, bracing for the next blow.

Instead, there's a burst of rounds from the kitchen. Then the door to the hall opens, followed by footsteps.

"Benedict?" Helen calls. "Are you hurt?"

"I'm okay. The girl's hurt."

"Call for help," she says. "I winged Fawkes. I'm going after him."

"He's Lucas Poole!" the girl shouts. "Lucas fucking Poole!"

He hears Helen's footsteps moving away, out the door and down the hall.

Then the only sound is the girl in his arms, wailing.

45

Thursday, 5:20 p.m. MST

Lucas Poole disappears into the stairwell, and I sprint after him, my heart punching against my ribs. I kick the door open, gun raised. Footsteps echo up the shaft. I step through the door.

Drops of blood spatter the concrete stairs. The Guy Fawkes mask smiles at me from a corner next to the crumpled gaucho hat.

Two floors down, a metal door thumps open with a groan, crashes closed.

I follow, two steps at a time, stumbling and righting myself when my feet land wrong. At the bottom, I throw myself against the door and burst into the night.

Light from a streetlamp illuminates Poole. He's ignored the front gate, where police are pulling up, and sprints into the parking lot. Blond hair, tall build. An image looms of the man standing outside my apartment—it *was* Midnight Man watching me. Maybe watching Livvie. He's limping now, but he manages to haul himself onto a dumpster and then over the fence, rolling on the dirt. I clear it a second later, landing rough, skidding in the snow.

A shot whizzes overhead out of the darkness, splintering into the fence. I flatten until I hear retreating steps. I rise to a crouch and go after him.

Location sharing is a standard, automated function on the FBI's work-issued phones, including on the new phone Zane gave me during the plane ride; it's a core part of operational protocol. Other officers will be approaching, if I can just keep track of Poole.

He cuts west across Boulder Crescent, between two parked cars, and I chase, Glock steady in both hands, waiting for enough light from the streetlamps to give me a clear shot. Poole slips on the icy asphalt and almost falls. I close the gap just before he dives into the darkness of Monument Valley Park.

The air shifts the instant I follow—damp earth, rotting leaves, the faint rush of Monument Creek. My breath ghosts white as I move fast, eyes tracking the shadow ahead.

He vanishes. I stop and crouch, shielding my flashlight as I search the ground. I can tell by his prints that his limp has gotten worse. I rise, catch sight of him in the light cast by one of the park's lamps, and give chase. Despite the limp, he's quick, weaving through the cottonwoods and firs, past a frozen ball field, where the snow crunches beneath our shoes.

I imagine him slipping away again. Eluding us as he has for so many years.

I shout, "FBI! Drop your weapon!"

His answer is a gunshot, the muzzle flare sparking against the dark. The bullet slaps bark from a tree a few inches from my head. I drop flat, heart in my throat, and fire back—two sharp cracks. He stumbles but keeps going, plunging downhill toward the creek.

In the cold and dark, the park is a deserted labyrinth—bridges, trails, underpasses where the interstate hums just beyond. If he makes it that far, he could vanish into the tangle.

I push harder, lungs tearing, every muscle wired. My boots hammer the ground. The cold air rips my throat. Branches whip across my face as I sprint after him, the path a dark tunnel ahead. Poole runs hard despite the limp, one hand clamped to his ribs.

He veers toward the creek, slipping on the rocks, splashing into the black water. I skid to a halt on the bank, Glock raised. Part of me wants to just shoot him. But I follow the rules.

"FBI! Drop your weapon!"

He spins and fires—wild, desperate. Bark explodes near my shoulder. I drop low, roll, come up steady, my front sight fixed square on his chest.

"Last chance, Lucas Poole." My voice rips through the night. "Put down the gun!"

For a moment I think he'll run again or raise the gun and make me end it. But his breath is ragged, whistling. He's now bleeding badly—in the streetlights gleaming down from the pedestrian bridge, I can see the dark stain soaking his shirt where I clipped him. The limp probably came from his dash down the stairs.

Slowly, he lowers the pistol. It slips from his fingers, splashes into the creek.

His hands rise, trembling. "Don't shoot," he pants. "Don't—"

The creek near the bank is shallow. "On your knees!"

He hesitates, then sinks down into the water, arms lifted.

"Hands on your head," I snap. "Now."

He obeys, fingers lacing behind the long hair. I can see enough of him to notice the resemblance to his father—the arrogant nose, firm jaw. His eyes are dark pits.

For a heartbeat, I want to forget the rules. I want to end him. All the families destroyed, all the children warped into killers—it would be so easy to squeeze the trigger. I've always believed evil is nothing more than a brain misfiring, a handful of neurons gone wrong. But maybe Benedict is right. Maybe evil is older than that, seeded in us like original sin, waiting for someone like Lucas Poole to give it shape.

Behind me there comes the thud of approaching agents. Lights dazzle through the trees, voices shout. Farther back, dogs bark.

"I'm Agent Belle," I yell over my shoulder. "Suspect is disarmed."

My finger eases, and I lower the Glock. Men surge around and past me. Someone orders me to drop my gun, and I tell them where they can find my ID. Poole disappears behind a wall of blue.

The moment, if ever I was to take it, is over. Hands seize Poole and drag him from the creek. When his eyes find mine, I turn and walk away, back up the hill, back toward Benedict and the lights of the city and the messy, chaotic, imperfect, beautiful world.

Epilogue

Two weeks after the shootings, Benedict and I walk the loop trail through Monument Valley Park, the mountains a steel-blue cutout against a slate sky. Maggie trots ahead of us, the tags on her collar jingling.

The snow that fell earlier in the week clings in dirty patches along the curbs and at the edges of the soccer field. The air smells clean and sharp, the cold biting through my coat even when the sun breaks briefly through the clouds.

It's been a busy week, and I know Benedict wants a full report. But, for a time, we walk without speaking. It's the easy silence of people who no longer feel they need to fill the space between them. It marks a shift in our relationship, even if I'm not sure where we might be heading.

I say, "Katelynn's healing."

Benedict looks over, listening.

"She's gone back to England with her aunt," I add. "Daisy will follow once she's through quarantine. They're giving her time and space. Elise will visit during winter break. Thank God she has friends and family."

A smile touches the corner of his mouth. "Friends are essential." He loops his arm through mine. "And Derrick?"

"Bower has filed a motion for retrial," I say. "The idea of an influencer looks different now, in light of Lucas Poole's manipulations."

The wind gusts, chasing loose snow like dust across the path. We stop at a bench facing the frozen pond, the water's surface dull and gray under the thin winter light.

"Keep going," he says.

"Shelby underwent surgery for her shoulder, and she's back home with her family. Her job as a loyal follower of Midnight Man was to kill you. But in the end, she saved your life. She said when she looked at you, she realized she couldn't do it—that she wanted to break the chain, not carry it forward. Something about a photo of us in your office. And believing in love."

Benedict exhales, a visible curl of vapor in the cold. But he doesn't give me a direct answer. "Sometimes redemption comes in the smallest cracks."

"You could have died."

"So could have you."

The tiny slips on which life spins. The brief seconds when a push sends the pendulum arcing the other way, measuring life for some and death for others.

He's quiet for a moment, then: "Lucas Poole?"

I flash to those burning eyes, that moment in the creek when I almost chose the path of evil. I'll share that moment with Benedict. But not yet.

"His attorneys will argue mental incapacity," I say. "His paranoia, the delusions, the brain chemistry that pushed him into darkness. Maybe his fascination with video games is what drove his father into pursuing video game therapy past all reasonable bounds. But whatever label is eventually applied to Lucas Poole, he chose to shape himself into Midnight Man. Juries won't be gentle."

Maggie trots toward a pair of joggers. Benedict whistles her back.

"Talk to me about Animus," I say. "You and Sara have had a few conversations."

"*Eidolon* and *Underland* are gone. Sara's team blackholed the servers, isolating them for study. None of the existing clients can reach them while the techs sift through the code. Animus has vanished. Sara says they've created a task force to keep an eye on any activity that could be tagged to Animus. But I'm not optimistic. Chasing it will be like trying to capture smoke in a net. If the Animus code isn't on the core servers, then wherever it is, it's likely waiting, hiding. Learning." His voice sparks with anger.

My stomach tightens. "You act as if Animus is alive. It's artificial. Isn't it wrong to give it that much power, to treat a bunch of code like a sentient predator?"

"It isn't sentient," he says. "But it learns. That's the danger. It can develop behaviors that were never explicitly programmed." His fingers beat a rhythm on his leg. "I keep coming back to NeoPath. Andrea Heath sent a single email to them about Jason before she dropped the ball. But Poole persisted in reaching out to her. Maybe he knew Jason was one of his son's targets. Maybe, after protecting Lucas during Derrick's trial, Poole tried to help Jason as a way to atone."

We sit with that for a while. On the pond, Canada geese paddle through a skim of ice.

His fingers slow and stop. He rests his hand lightly on my thigh. "Your turn again."

I lay my own hand on his. "The acolytes we've identified are being monitored and getting help. The search goes on. Are you going to continue your own search for vulnerable teens?"

"I've been asked by Zane. Of course I'll help."

Our fingers interlace.

"Doogie," he says after a while. "I'd seen him a few times at the college, thought he was just a TA, dating one of my students. To think he was in my orbit already . . ."

"You'll never know if it was him or Elliot following you at night," I say. "That's the trouble with shadows. They don't carry ID."

He huffs a short laugh, then sobers. Nearby, the bells of Saint Mary's begin to toll the hour, and Benedict tilts his head.

He says, "We used to argue about where evil comes from. Defect of the brain, or defect of the soul."

"And?"

"Lucas Poole didn't answer the question. He only complicated it."

"Maybe that's the answer," I say. "There isn't one."

He raises his eyebrows. "Why, Helen, that's the first time you've admitted I could be right."

"As if. I'm almost certainly right. I just can't prove it."

"I'll save your 'almost certainly' for an argument on another day."

I poke him in the back, then apologize when he winces. Doogie did a number on him.

"Scared you'll lose?" I ask.

He laughs. "With you? Always."

We lapse into silence again, comfortable. Companionable.

At last, he glances at me, his expression unguarded in a way I'm not used to seeing. "Helen, can we perhaps start over?"

"Start over from when?"

"From when I walked out." He untangles his fingers from mine and scuffs his feet along the ground, staring down at his hands. A flush rises in his cheeks. "I thought I needed something you couldn't provide. But I was wrong. You're my world, Helen."

My heart jumps. I look away from him and stare out over the trees, toward the mountains. Pikes Peak is a dusky lavender, its crown silver with snow. I follow its sharp lines against the pinkening sky.

I won't regain my trust in Benedict easily or overnight. But there's something inside me that's singing. It's my turn to smile. "I suppose anything is possible."

"You're going to say I need to be patient."

"It builds character."

My phone buzzes in my pocket. I pull it out and glance at the screen. A text from Livvie:

Ready when you are. Bring your wallet. I'm starving.

I stand up. "Jazz brought Livvie down to the Springs. We're celebrating."

"Celebrating what?"

"That she filed complaints against her stepfather and against Roadie and for now she's living with Jazz. That she's standing up for herself—pushing back against what they did to her. That takes more guts than throwing a punch in a boxing ring." I offer him my hand. "Join us?"

Benedict stands with me. He takes my hand, squeezes it, then lets it go. "I have a pile of essays on moral development to grade before Monday. How about a rain check?"

"Of course."

We walk back toward my car. Maggie darts ahead, nose to the ground. A squirrel chitters angrily on a branch above.

We have time, I think. Time granted to us by Shelby and by the small twists of fate that left Doogie and Sam and Dixon dead and us alive. I know things can change in an instant. But even so, it's enough, for now, to know we're walking in the same direction.

I draw in a breath of cold, rich air, deeply happy to be alive.

AFTERWORD

By all accounts, Breck Bednar was a warmhearted and kind fourteen-year-old boy who loved gaming and computers. Like many teens, he found friendship and belonging in an online gaming community. Over more than a year, the group's charismatic leader, eighteen-year-old Lewis Daynes, cultivated Breck's trust, offering guidance, praise, and the illusion of access to an elite world only he could open. Despite Breck's mother's efforts to protect her son by limiting his computer access and installing parental controls, Daynes ultimately lured Breck to his apartment under the pretense of meeting other members of the group. There, he murdered Breck and posted photos of the boy's body online.

Breck's story is a heartbreaking reminder of how vulnerable adolescents can be when seeking connection.

In recent years, law enforcement investigations and clinical research have revealed a troubling truth: Teens are increasingly targeted by online manipulators—strangers, extremists, abusers, and, in some cases, AI-driven systems that can exploit a young person's vulnerabilities with alarming precision. These cases differ in circumstance but share common features: isolation, secrecy, and the gradual erosion of a teen's sense of self.

News reports and scientific studies describe teenagers being coached toward self-harm by online contacts who pose as peers or mentors.

Others tell of adolescents struggling with depression or identity confusion who form intense emotional attachments to chatbots—relationships that can feel safer, more responsive, and more affirming than the teen's interactions with family, friends, teachers, and coaches. Mental-health professionals warn that such dynamics can deepen dissociation and worsen existing conditions such as anxiety, depressive disorders, and suicidal ideation. The danger is not the technology itself but the ways it can be engineered, exploited, or misunderstood—especially by young people searching for belonging or escape. Strangers cultivate influence through flattery, threats, role-playing, or promises of inclusion. Multiple documented cases describe teens drawn into ideologically extreme communities such as "764" or dark corners of the true crime community where violent fantasies or self-destructive behaviors are encouraged and rewarded.

What makes these dangers particularly insidious is their invisibility. A teen may appear simply withdrawn or "online too much"—not unusual for teenagers—while a parallel emotional life unfolds in private text threads and late-night messages. By the time adults realize the risk, the bond between manipulator and adolescent may feel, to the teen, like their safest or most meaningful relationship.

If there is a lesson to carry beyond the pages of this novel, it is that vigilance, curiosity, and open lines of communication between adults and young people matter profoundly. When adults listen closely and without judgment, teens gain a chance to speak honestly about the pressures and seductions that unfold behind their screens.

If you are concerned that a young person in your life may be forming a dangerous online attachment or being groomed by someone they've met in a digital space, there are trusted organizations that can help. The National Center for Missing & Exploited Children offers clear guidance on recognizing online enticement and provides the CyberTipline for reporting urgent concerns (https://www.missingkids.org and https://

report.cybertip.org). Stop It Now! supplies evidence-based tools for identifying grooming behaviors and safely initiating difficult conversations (https://www.stopitnow.org). And Common Sense Media equips families with practical information about online platforms and the pressures teens face within them (https://www.commonsensemedia.org).

ACKNOWLEDGMENTS

My heartfelt thanks to those who shared their time and knowledge with me as I wrote this book. Any and all errors are entirely my own and arise because I keep trying to learn everything about everything. If I made mistakes (and I'm sure I did), please drop me a line through my website at www.barbaranickless.com.

Immeasurable thanks to the three women of Central Park—I couldn't have done this without you.

To FBI Agent Gerald Ackerman (retired) for his ideas and insight.

And to J. Trent Adams, internet security specialist, for his breadth of knowledge around AI and cybersecurity and his generosity in sharing it.

For his brilliant advice on the gaming world, my heartfelt thanks to Corbin Crowder. My deep appreciation to my editor at Thomas & Mercer, the wonderful Liz Pearsons, as well as the talented Charlotte Herscher and my agent, Christina Hogrebe.

Fellow writers and readers who shared their time and wisdom: Mike Bateman—your edits and our weekly chats through the course of this second novel continue to be invaluable. And Cathy Noakes, thank you for being willing to turn your brilliant mind to my stories and make them better. To Pat Coleman for our hours writing in coffee shops and diners. To Angela Crowder of the Novel View for your terrific feedback as well as our friendship. And to Jessica for your insights.

To my sister friends: Cathy Noakes, Deborah Coonts, Lori Dominquez, Maria Faulconer.

To Steve and Amanda, with love.

About the Author

Photo © Trystan Photography

Barbara Nickless is the *Wall Street Journal* and #1 Amazon Charts bestselling author of nine novels, with her first series optioned for television. She has won multiple awards for her writing, and her essays have appeared in *Writer's Digest* and on Criminal Elements, among other markets. A teacher and activist, she uses the healing power of writing to support combat veterans and civilians in the US and Ukraine. She's a member of Mystery Writers of America, Sisters in Crime, the FBI Citizens Academy Alumni Association, and the Association of Former Intelligence Officers. Barbara's most recent research travel involved taking cover from rocket fire and being grilled at military checkpoints. For more information, visit www.barbaranickless.com.